MORE TEXT THAN SEX

I0593214

Jim
SHOMOS

First published in 2022

Copyright © 2022 Jim Shomos

ISBN Paperback: 97806450458-8-8

ISBN Large Print: 97806450458-9-5

ISBN Ebook: 97806450458-7-1

Enquiries should be made through www.JimShomos.com

This is a work of fiction. Any similarities between places and characters are a coincidence.

Editor: Carolyn Depew

Cover design: HelzKat Design

Layout and typesetting: Irish Ink Publishing

Proofreader: Michelle Lovi

Screen rights: contact Jim via Screenrights@JimShomos.com

Don't miss Jim's debut novel, Up Here

When you've had two dream marriages, choosing your eternal soulmate in heaven is one hell of a dilemma.

www.JimShomos.com/up-here

The most original romantic-comedy this century. Artisan Book Reviews, 5*

Up Here touched my soul, a beautiful romantic comedy about love, hope and courage. Alli, 5*

Jim Shomos must have written this with a twinkle in his eyes, as moving, as it is funny. Ella, 5*

Kissing Scars

Leads your heart to a festival of love. A romantic comedy novella inspired by a true story.

www.JimShomos.com/kissing-scars

Intoxicating, organic, and simply breathtaking. The Never Ending Bookshelf, 5*

Three Women in November

An incredible true love story.

www.JimShomos.com/three-women-in-november

I loved this book...despite the tears streaming down my face. Michele, 5*

Get VIP release news about Jim's coming books at:

www.JimShomos.com

DEDICATED TO

Russell Zimmer, my first songwriting collaborator. You gave me the confidence to trust my instincts for words and ability to co-write songs. We haven't had that 'gold record' yet…but our friendship has remained top-10 in the charts for over 35 years. That's the real gold.

TRACK 1

SOME DAYS WERE LIKE THE SWEET SONGS OF YOUR LIFE, DOWNLOADING INTO your brain's favourite playlist, rocking your smile on high rotation.

Not today. Today was a *punk rock meets experimental jazz shit* of a day. Screaming loud. Disjointed. No purpose. ANNIE didn't want to be in this boardroom. Room? The bigger these corporate dungeons, the more claustrophobic, the more they squeezed your soul into a sausage-like version of yourself.

Her buddy and colleague Cat prowled around the room, marking her territory. Being a cool record label meant having a cool boardroom, but all the creative effort achieved was forging a huge man-cave, sprinkled with iconic rock photos and gold and platinum album tributes for the label's stars. The only character came from the bluestone walls and original timber frames in the high ceiling.

"Delaney wouldn't have chosen the dungeon if he wasn't interested," Annie said. Their boss hated meetings, but loved the dungeon.

Cat stopped prowling and tapped the posters on the dark mahogany table. "If 'Delooney' slashes through these ideas with his patriarchal wand, I'm out of here. Done. Gone."

If it wasn't for Cat's spunk, Annie would have been *done, gone* from Merger Music eons ago. Cat, and the eighteen-month anchor

1

remaining around her creative neck from a ten-year contract of cata-strophe. *Five hundred and forty-seven days and I might not have to depend on any day job again.*

Cat waved an arm at the eleven empty black leather chairs around the table. "Look at these. They're like giant Darth Vader helmets." Cat covered her mouth with both hands and breathed the words through her fingers, *"We're your father, Cat... all of us."*

She laughed hard, gripping the thick table to stop from sliding under. Straightening, she somehow filled the whole chair. Bless Cat, she needed that hit.

Cat plonked into the Darth Vader helmet next to her, grinning. "Girl, if you thought that was hilarious, you need an eighty-twenty weekend."

"Huh?"

"Eighty percent sex, twenty percent booze and sleep."

She liked everything about Cat except how the damn woman saw right through her.

"Unless you pick up another two boys from Barcelona like at the Purple Daze festival last summer, then you have permission to go one hundred percent raunchy. Those dudes were so ripped, don't know how you didn't end up in ICU."

More laughter crashed through her deserted body. Until she saw Cat stiffen and switch back to her war face.

"Chirpy meeting's a good meeting," said Delaney, striding through the doors to the opposite side of the table.

She almost choked trying to anchor her laughter, straightened and breathed deeply to release the pressure on her pharynx, larynx, and trachea, the precious triangle protecting her deserted gift. Delaney wasn't the devil; he was as passionate about music as her. While she chose flight when a giant boulder shattered her singing path, he chose to fight the mountain of corporate bullshit to keep Melbourne's--and one of the world's--leading indie labels relevant.

"Please share. I could do with a laugh." He slid into the chair like it was custom made, waving his iPad between them.

Annie hesitated. Maybe a joke or two would help their mission, get Delaney into softer space before stating their project demands.

2

"When you laugh, it's the closest your face gets to your old performance magic," said Delaney. "Your spotlight cheekbones and sparkly brown eyes. Not as mesmerising as when you used to sing, but—"

"We're all under the pump, so let's get straight into this." She patted the posters on the table; Delaney had done enough self-softening. "Why don't you start, Cat?" Her sweet tone a one-eighty contrast to the tension coiling in her tummy, Annie thanked the stars she could control her voice because her face was a WikiLeaks on skin.

Cat leant on the table, shoulders hunched forward, a jungle lion poised to pounce.

"You built this label on discovering awesome performers."

Delaney nodded.

"But seventy-three percent of the company's profits come from our publishing division, even though we only represent nineteen percent of expenses and thirteen percent of staff."

Staff, huh. For publishing staff read: her, Cat, and a couple of admin supports, plus an endless procession of starry-eyed interns. Delaney stared at his iPad. Boys and their tech toys. His elusive attention span was why they'd prepared the rock-style posters. She tapped Cat's calf.

Cat lifted the top poster. '*Publi$hing = Profit$*'

Annie pitched her tone a touch higher, a little louder. "But publishing revenue has stagnated and is diving."

Delaney's wild salt and pepper eyebrows nearly reached his wilder hair, focused on the poster now.

"Strangled by the contemporary focus on singer-songwriters and DJ-producers with catchy names but limited creativity." She pointed at the next poster Cat picked up.

'*Industry Choking $ongwriter$.*'

"Pure songwriters don't have a chance to break through. Performers can always busk, do free pub gigs, YouTube, a ton of social media," said Cat. Delaney glanced at his iPad, so Cat sped up her spiel. "Plus, glamour shows like *The Voice* and *Every Pimple's Got Talent*."

Delaney tapped his iPad. "There's SoundCloud and other—"

"Not enough," said Annie.

"*Eurovision Song Contest*. Never miss that show." Delaney tilted his chair back, fingers interlaced, hands around the back of his silver hair.

"*Eurovision* has become a circus for performers," said Cat. "May as well call it '*Cirque du Sold out the Songwriter*'. I bet you don't remember the writers of last year's winning song but you remember what that woman from Poland was almost wearing."

No reaction. Worse, he typed on his iPad. Loud voices from staff heading home drifted under the heavy wooden doors.

She tapped Cat's calf again, maybe more than a tap. Cat glared, but there was nothing to gain by challenging Delaney.

"A & R used to stand for 'Artists and Repertoire'. Lately it's become 'Angles and Revenue'," said Cat.

Delaney stopped typing and smiled.

"This contest will help us flush out real talent and rebuild some street cred for the label." Huh, credibility with a name like Merger Music? The investment bankers probably patted the back of each other's charcoal grey suits at their amazing creativity with the alliteration of 'M'.

Cat held up the final poster. '*Merger Music Annual Songwriting Contest = Street cred + more profit$.*'

"Love it," said Delaney.

His words bubbled around Annie's veins in a cocktail of adrenalin and endorphins.

"Does that mean you'll back it?" Cat's suspicion dripped from deep corporate scars.

"Yes." He tapped the iPad. "The weekly voting format by the punters is a cool idea." He'd actually read the one-pager.

Cat morphed from war lion to a grinning Cheshire.

"Just one thing I'd like to add to your plan."

She whipped her head at Delaney.

"Increase the budget by twenty percent."

Of all the Delaney responses they'd prepared for, that wasn't on their list.

"You'll confirm all that for us in an email?" she asked.

"Just did, and CC'd JP, our finance maestro. Fucking love this idea." He grabbed the table with arms wide. "It's going to be a bigger success than you imagined."

Ella Fitzgerald's 'Summertime' trickled out of Annie's memory bank and tickled every nerve and muscle to her core.

"That's why Robbie from marketing has to lead the project."

Horror Punk. Grindcore. Crack Rock.

Anger thrashed around her head, couldn't find a way out. Delaney *was* the devil. After all the mergers, all the fiscal battles, he'd diluted into a musical midget, and couldn't read the room if it was written on the wall. She was delusional or too loyal, believing he was still bona fide rock 'n' roll.

Delaney glanced at his iPad on the table then leant back, hands behind his head. Grinning.

Annie wanted to smash that head into the table and leave a mould of his smug face with shades of blood on the shiny mahogany. But she'd never stand a chance; Cat would get there first.

Crash!

Cat had jumped up, her Darth Vader chair smashing against the bluestone wall, Sia T-shirt barely containing her heaving chest. "Don't need help. Not that cocky little gherkin from—"

Robbie strutted through the doors in a rock t-shirt from the same online store as Delaney's. Jeans cut in the trendy places but tighter than his boss. Boots instead of sneakers. He settled into the chair on Delaney's right, opposite Cat, placing his identical iPad on the table parallel with Delaney's in sickening digital sycophancy. His aftershave drifted in a few seconds behind him, like an entourage, obtrusive, suffocating.

"Sorry, I'm five minutes late," Robbie said to Delaney with the innocent and huggable tone of Ed Sheeran.

Five minutes late? The bastards planned this. The syrupy tone and his entourage were all show. Surface stuff.

Acid gurgled from her tummy, up her oesophagus.

Breathe... breathe.

Delaney focused on Cat, his survival instincts kicking in, sitting straighter, hands gripping his chair. He still didn't stand a chance. Death Metal swirled in Cat's green eyes under super-short, parted hair, a nod to Audrey Hepburn aside from being bright blue. A few fools had underestimated the passion within Cat's one hundred and fifty-two-centimetre frame, but never more than once.

She was tempted to let Cat loose. Despite the callous mismanagement of their supposed CEO, she had to drag herself out of her inner acid bath and save the project. Save Cat from a murder trial. She stood, blocking Cat.

"Hey, Robbie, glad you could join us." Her voice threw a calming blanket over her inner turmoil and boardroom tension. Except Cat. Cat rocked back and forth like she was about to spring over and rip his throat with bared teeth.

"Hi, Annie, Cat. You don't have to stand for me." More fake Ed Sheeran.

Always assume positive intent. Her dad's mantra, which she'd ignored most of her life. Maybe Robbie went to the same room-reading school as Delaney, oblivious to the emotion bouncing off the walls, the territory he was stealing from them. Hard-earned territory. *Always assume positive intent.* She grabbed Cat with one hand and pulled in her chair with the other, forcing Cat to sit.

"Robbie's got some creative gems," said Delaney, waving his arm at Robbie to share.

His next creative gem would be his virgin creative gem, but she gripped Cat's lower arm and let her voice do its thing. "Many heads make light work."

"I'll make light work out of his head," mumbled Cat.

Robbie stared at Cat, who glared back. No contest, he turned to the safe territory of Delaney.

Delaney burst out laughing, every sound a false note. "You're gonna love working with these two, Robbie. Laugh a minute. Go on, tell them your ideas."

Always assume positive intent... until he gives me ammunition to blast him out of the building.

Robbie swiped his iPad, took a big breath, then faced her. "I thought we could produce a documentary on the craft of songwriting. It should feature Australian songwriters from all genres. We can release the interviews across our social media. With a decent production crew, we'll probably get to screen it as a feature documentary on Channel V or ABC2."

Cat's arm muscles relaxed under her grip. Annie let go and placed her elbows on the table, head resting on her hands between thumbs and fingers. One—it was a brilliant idea. Two—they'd never thought of it. Three—maybe they'd underestimated Robbie.

"I like that, Robbie. It's right on theme with what we want to achieve for Merger Music," Annie said. A few strands of hair had dropped over her right eye, making it twitch. Damned if she was going to touch her hair now with him all puppy-eyes, so she blew air up at it and flicked her face a little. With cowboys like Robbie, it was better to come across dorky-Annie than flirty.

"Of course, the contest will be dominated by many of our own artists, past and present," said Delaney.

"Can't be filled with proven performers, only unpublished song-writers," said Cat, gripping the table like a vice, the tips of her fingers white under black painted nails.

Robbie continued focusing on Annie. "That makes sense. Your one-pager is quite clear."

Silly bugger didn't have the courage to face Cat, so Annie nodded gently at the twenty-eight-year-old man-boy.

"Tell them your masterpiece." Delaney turned to her and Cat. "Pure genius." A huge grin was framed by his arms as he leant back, hands behind his head again.

Robbie swiped to another page on his iPad, pride pouring out of his cheeks, a few centimetres taller in the chair after Delaney's ego-infla-tion. "I've been researching the top ten hits over the last five years and worked out what type of songs we need to manipulate the contest for."

Cat bounced up, chair sling-shotting into the wall again, then slammed both her hands on the table. *Crash, slap-slap!*

Deep in Annie's musical conscience she noted the rhythmic percus-sion riff, but her frontal lobe screamed, *how could he make one smart step forward then slip five-thousand steps back into an abyss of stupidity?*

"Manipulate? Maaaaan-ipulate?" hissed Cat.

Delaney stared at the thick double doors, possibly admiring their strength to stay on their hinges. Probably thinking of making his escape. Robbie sat back, holding up his iPad like a shield, eyes so wide and white, his pupils must've run for cover.

"This contest is all about music lovers voting for the songs. Raw music meets raw emotions. Not some maaaan-ipulated man-marketing man-gimmick like all the other man-ure around here lately." She stood and turned to Delaney. "If you don't revise your decision about..." Cat flicked a hand in Robbie's direction. "I'm going to—"

She tapped Cat, aiming for the softer calf again, but Cat moved, and Annie's toe hit her shinbone.

"Ouch!" Cat plonked onto her chair and rubbed her shin.

Annie diva-glared at Delaney. Behind the headline posters, behind the full proposal Delaney had probably never read, Annie and Cat had poured dozens of hours into planning the mechanics. They could launch the contest tomorrow. There was reasoning for dumping someone from marketing to *help* them as neither she nor Cat had run a project like this. But putting Robbie in charge? Unforgivable. Delaney was living down to Cat's moniker, *Delooney*. Surely, he realised his mistake now he'd seen their reaction.

"Look, I'd hate to see it go that way, but if you're not comfortable with my decision, Robbie can pick his own team."

TRACK 2

ROBBIE'S GAZE STAYED GLUED ON ANNIE. SUPERGLUED. THE FIRE sparking from her eyes was like the first time he'd seen a night-time bonfire. *Focus, Robbie.* He blinked twice, then turned to his iPad. The screen had gone black, and his reflection reminded him of the main game. Delaney had thrown him more than he expected, but he was ready. This contest was the kind of opportunity that skyrocketed reputations, and he'd worked hard to reach this rock 'n' roll launching pad.

Annie turned from Delaney to him.

God, she's beautiful. Not just hot. Beautiful. He had to make this work. Work for his career, for Delaney, for any chance with Annie.

"We have to find a collaborative groove on this; it's your concept," he said, struggling to get a handle on Annie. It was difficult to not gape at her cleavage since the woman turned V-neck T-shirts into a weapon of dumb destruction. Delaney had taught him early on that if you ever want to know how someone feels about you, gauge his or her partner. Cat wasn't romantically linked with Annie, but she was a partner on this project. He consciously forced his neck muscles to include Cat, but she projected some scary, feral energy. Surely, Annie wasn't hiding that kind of anger. He turned back to her.

"We're excited to groove on the contest with you, Robbie. Ton of other little jobs to clear before we can focus on this, so we'd better get to it." Annie stood, dragging Cat up.

Robbie stood. Stared.

"You don't have to stand up for us," said Cat.

"Let's meet again in three weeks to synchronise our ideas," Annie said before ushering Cat away.

"Yeah... sure... three weeks. I'll Google Calendar you. Both of you."

"Perfect. We'll Google Calendar back." She bundled Cat through the door.

Robbie followed Annie's exit until the last strand of her brown hair fluttered out of sight. *Was that a wink? Looked like she winked. Flicked her head back and winked at me.*

He sat down and set up the calendar meeting on his iPad.

"They loved your ideas," said Delaney.

"One of them," said Robbie.

"Fifty percent in is still in. They just need time to get used to sharing. You know women and their babies. Python possessive... a biological mongrel instinct from thirty thousand years of evolution."

He nodded. "I did have some rapport with Annie. See the way she jumped up when I came in?" That had never happened to him before. It was usually him jumping up like a wimp in a music scene where gentlemen stuff was derided by women.

Oh, fuck. I jumped up like a chump when Annie stood. No wonder Cat made fun of me.

The first time he'd glimpsed Annie when he started last year sent a buzz through his core, just like the opening notes of his favourite AC/DC track, 'You Shook me all Night Long'. His curiosity hit a wall because she was an anomaly for a twenty-six-year-old, totally off the social media circus. Unbelievable. He'd seen some photos floating around the net from her early performances but that was nine years ago. She hadn't caved into the Kardashian-lips trap, her mouth a perfect organic sculpture under the cute nose and those cheekbones.

In marketing terms, her packaging was powerful. Delaney had let him listen to her demo album, which never got released back then. What a waste. The success he could have promoting Annie. Maybe this contest could be a curvy path to relaunching her career, or set up a nice vibe between them so he could ask her out. But not if he always jumped like a chump around her.

"Yep, you're in. Make it work. And don't forget those other ideas. Just don't dump all the apples into one lunch box," said Delaney.

Royal Blood, 'Figure It Out'. The positive riff pulsed through his veins, pushing his face into a grin. It buzzed to hear the validation from Delaney. This was his first major project as lead and he wasn't going to let his guru down. Surely, Cat was just having a bad day. Maybe time-of-month stuff. Once they got stuck into the contest, even she would like him. Maybe that was over-reaching. Annie, focus on Annie. Divide and conquer... and what a conquest.

CAT ripped the diet soup sachet so hard, some of the powder spilled onto the bench. The main Merger kitchen bench was surprisingly clean. Usually, between home time and the night cleaners coming through, it was a mess befitting the image of the music biz. Speaking of mess, what the hell did Annie just do with *their* contest? She loved Annie like a sister. Well, like she would love a loving sister, not like her official-according-to-her-parents sister. She still hadn't managed a DNA test. Tried a couple of times when they were teenagers, but the police always politely said they'd need to call her parents for permission, so she'd let it go and hidden the little plastic bag holding her sister's hairs.

But how could Annie let her down like that? She steadied her cup on the bench, grabbed the kettle, and dumped the boiling water in. Water splashed out, scorching her hand.

"Argh!" She dived for the sink, running cold water over the tender skin between her thumb and finger. "Today is musical death day. Worse than Bowie and Prince dying in the same year. It was Adele and Pink getting slaughtered in the same meeting." She ripped a couple of paper towel sheets. Dried her hand with one, the outside of her cup and bench with the other. She dumped the soggy paper in the bin, then picked up her soup and rested against the bench.

"Nobody died," said Annie, looking way too relaxed, sitting up with her never-ending-story legs crossed at the ankles almost reaching across the whole couch. Her own legs wouldn't reach halfway. Annie sipped on her beloved, totally untrendy cappuccino. With two sugars. *Two-sugar cappuccino with full cream milk and denim wraps around her as if she was a living goddess for jeans. Metabolism is a choosy bitch that never chose me.*

"Our project died when you agreed to let that buffoon run it." She stirred the alleged 'cream of chicken' soup, probably just white dust and a ton of artificial poisons. The MM kitchen offered heaps of healthy and trendy options—and she was usually careful with what she let into her tummy temple—but this powdered soup was comfort food from the Milky Way.

Annie raised her index finger. "We got the contest greenlit." Her middle finger joined it. "We got twenty percent more budget than we asked for." Ring finger lined up too. "And we're getting a doco produced. We've had a good day. Best day we've had here since we got little Sophie's song on *Neighbours*."

She smiled at the memory. "Never seen a more delighted thirteen-year-old, probably never will." She moved the cup close to her nose and inhaled the aroma, closing her eyes for a few seconds. Those kinds of moments were what she dreamt of every day in this gig, discovering a writing talent and placing their songs with the right show or artist. The pressure of public quarterly financial reports and developing non-performing talent didn't mix. Joni Mitchell had nailed it way back in the seventies, but nobody listened to her warning. That's why this contest—

Her eyes shot open, acid burning through her tummy at the thought of Robbie destroying their baby. "But, Annie, you happily agreed to hand over our contest."

"Delaney said Robbie was to lead. Let him *think* he's leading. We're ready to rock on this, aren't we?"

She nodded slowly, not sure where Annie was heading.

"We're not meeting him for three weeks, right? We can stall him for another two, which gives us five."

Her brow furrowed so much it hurt.

Annie tapped her iPad. "I just got confirmation from Finance that the budget has been allocated to Publishing division. We control the money, not Marketing. Starting tomorrow, we set the whole contest up. Manny in IT will build the website, Yasmin will create all the social media, and Summer will do her magic on the design stuff. The contest launches the day after our meeting with Robbie in five weeks. Let the bugger play catch-up."

Hold Me, the infectious percussion and clapping of The Teskey Brothers track, bounced through her inner world, with their soulful vocals surging joy through her pores. She could kiss Annie. The hell she could. No, their friendship was invaluable and staying platonic.

"Annie, you're a genius." She took a sip of her soup and closed her eyes as the comfy food trickled over her tongue and the hot, velvety liquid slid down her throat. Heaven.

Annie rested her coffee on the table, swung her feet onto the floor, and perched on the edge of the couch. "Credit where it's due, his doco idea is brilliant. We give him half the extra budget to run the production, and with the other ten percent we can add that interactive element of the contest we'd given up on."

"Hooking up lyricists with musos to collaborate... and we still guarantee at least one song from those collaborations gets into the ten nominated songs weekly?"

Annie nodded. "And, Cat, whenever it gets awkward with Robbie, remember—"

"We control the money."

"Yes. But, also, it's better having marketing inside the tent wanking out than outside the tent wanking in."

She stared at her cream-of-chicken soup, a volcano of vomit churning deep in her tummy. She stepped over to the sink and poured the soup out, washing it down with water as hard as the tap could flow. "Yuuuuuuck." She breathed in and out fast to fight off the nausea.

"I'm so sorry, Cat, didn't mean to be that crass. I was just letting the creamy ideas rise to the top." Annie started sniggering... giggling.

"Seriously not funny, Annie. I could have married this soup. Now I can't even fantasise about it."

Annie broke into a full-blown belly laugh.

She couldn't hold back her own laughter and scrunched down to the floor, her back to the bench with knees bent and hands covering her ears. Some laughs, some friends, were better than the best-ever songs. Rare hits. Cat hoped they'd stay in the friendship charts longer than the Stones.

Bossa Nova?

The unique drumbeats filtering out of the tiny timber cottage stilled ANNIE at her front gate. Despite the paint peeling off the window frames, the leaf-cluttered roof gutter with grass growing in the corner near the drainpipe, and the cracked loungeroom window covered by a hand length of packing tape, the rhythms tickled her musical soul.

Yes, definitely a bossa nova. She opened the low, squeaky, steel gate, skipped up the few steps to her front door, and slipped inside.

Aoham, the world's greatest babysitter, was engrossed in her homework, cross-legged on the floor with her back to the old couch, laptop and books spread on the coffee table. In the low lamplight, her huge, noise-reducing headphones made her look like a giant fly. Annie dug into her purse and found the cash she'd stashed away. It was only Monday, but she always paid Aoham a week in advance, appreciating the teenager's reliability and rapport with Lachie. The teenager greeted her with that brace-filled smile that one day would make men melt, but she made sure Aoham understood it was the commitment to her studies that would make men malleable. She put her finger to her lips. The girl indicated with her head and a cheeky eye-roll towards the closed sliding door, mouthing "thanks" as she took the money then packed up her stuff.

Annie slid open the loungeroom door that technically led to a dining room, stepped inside quickly and closed the door behind her, then fumbled through the thick curtain till she was inside their music room. Her precious gem Lachie was in the zone on his drum kit, wavy hair in a vice between his own giant headphones. She inhaled all the way to her toes. This made the circus at Merger bearable. The seasick slowing down and taking off at a thousand stops across two sardine trams from Albert Park to Northcote. Renting from a stable but stingy landlord. Eight years going on twenty-eight Lachie.

Bossa nova was difficult to master. Eight notes with his right hand on the high hat, left hand tapping a three-two pattern on the drum, while his right foot knocked out a two-four beat on the bass drum. An accomplished drummer would've added a cymbal beat with his other foot, probably a couple of creative bits, but Lachie had conquered the critical element for any drummer, a steady tempo that a singer and other band members could rely on. He continually found ways to amaze her.

Her foot tapped to Lachie's beats, triggering an ache from deep in her core to slide onto the piano stool to her right. The tips of her fingers tingled. She forced her eyes away, not ready to move the ton of dust on the old bed sheet covering the upright piano. An upright, single bed mattress covered the sliding door to the kitchen. Two mattresses stood across the corner behind the drum kit. Soundproofing good enough for her neighbours – eighty-seven years-wise Eva, strong as an ox but too proud to wear a hearing aid, and the share house on the other side whose four occupants regularly shared their musical spirit across the timber walls, blasting serious decibels of reggae, indie rock, and the occasional jazz crooner. Perfect neighbours.

Lachie spotted her and glowed without missing a beat.

Her heart skittered. She shimmied past the Maton guitar and scooped up the bongo from the floor, then joined in with Lachie's groove. They jammed like they'd rehearsed the tune a million times, not the first, just Lachie and her squeezing sweet juices from the fruits of music. Pure organic joy.

TRACK 3

CAT HADN'T BEEN THIS EXHAUSTED SINCE HER STINT IN TANZANIA building the village school nine months earlier, and she was almost as elated at what she'd achieved with Annie in the last five weeks. The songwriting contest had consumed them twenty-four-seven. Annie even bounced ideas via text after Lachie went to bed, and Annie had never before put in extra time for Merger Music. They'd also synchronised their morning commute to share the same tram from the CBD to Albert Park. She'd bonded with Annie from the first minute Delooney had introduced them, with none of the ego or posturing she'd anticipated. Turned out the job at Merger for Annie was just that, a job, and Annie was just another chick, totally oblivious to her front-cover combustible physical gifts, and buried musical gift.

Walking with Annie down to their cave office in the basement level of the old, refurbished warehouse, they were still sifting through their priority tasks. She sipped from her super-food juice – green stuff and ginger...at least she could taste the ginger—while Annie finished off her strawberry thick shake with noisy slurps through the straw. *Metabolism is a teasing bitch.* The first meeting with Robbie was at nine-thirty am, so they'd made sure they were in before nine to prepare their ambush meeting.

Except Robbie was already there, pushing a chair towards a desk. A chair and desk that weren't in their office when they'd switched off the lights the previous night.

"What the hell are you doing?" she asked, stepping in. Annie joined her shoulder to shoulder.

Robbie straightened, his beetroot face turning grey as wet concrete. "Oh, hi, Annie, Cat." His eyes on Annie, the weakling couldn't even look at her.

"Once we get rolling, this contest is going to be nuts, so I thought it would make sense if I was based in the same camp." He looked at all the designs and contest processes spread around the walls and whiteboard. "Although, you guys have already made bit of a start."

"That's not going to work." Cat threw her empty juice cup into the bin, except the bin wasn't where it had always been, and the cup splattered on the timber floor, spilling green stuff. "Shit, where's the bin?"

Robbie pointed to the other corner. "Sorry, I'll clean it up. They reckon it takes twenty-one days to break habits like that. Twenty-two days, and you'll be hitting three-pointers in the new bin location."

"I'll be hitting one head location with the bin if you don't leave in twenty-one seconds."

"Where's all our stuff?" Annie waved an arm in the area of the long table, where all their contest paperwork had been stacked.

"Yeah, that was quite a mess. I filed it in those storage bins." He pointed at plastic filing boxes on the floor next to the window wall behind them. "Most of it's in alphabetical order, but some of your files weren't labelled so they're in the miscellaneous bin."

"Whose idea was this, Robbie?" she asked.

"Mine." Eyes drifted somewhere between Annie's face and his brown Skechers.

"Whose idea, Robbie?"

"Mine." Eyes on his Skechers, high-pitched voice. Weasel.

"Robbie, look at me," Annie said in a voice that would make Julian Assange skip into CIA headquarters.

Robbie faced Annie, his right thumb rubbing hard against his left palm.

"Whose—"

"Delaney. He authorised the budget for the new furniture and computer." Robbie pointed at the flat box against the wall. "Manny will be here any minute to set it up."

She pleaded with her eyes at Annie to fix this nightmare, but Annie's eyes pleaded right back. *Roll with it, Cat, roll with it.* She dug deep for her inner Zen. She'd been to enough gurus, ashrams, and temples to make this idiot irrelevant. Closing her eyes, she breathed slowly, focusing on the air entering her nostrils and floating down her throat into her lungs... in... out... in... out... in... out. She opened her eyes.

"This isn't going to work."

"Cat," said Annie. "I'm sure—"

"You can have the new computer," Robbie said to Cat.

The unexpected gesture stalling her, she glanced at the box then glared back. "No." She pointed at where Robbie had moved her desk. "This won't work."

"I'm sure Robbie will let you have the new desk too, won't you, Robbie?"

Velvet voice and her mushy eyes, he never stood a chance, but that's not what she meant.

"I can't have my desk in that spot."

"Why?" Robbie asked, staring at her desk.

"Because the modem extender would be behind me. That's terrible feng shui."

Robbie turned to Annie.

"Yo, Mr Marketing, your target market's here." She pointed at herself with both arms wide.

Robbie looked at her. Finally. His huge brown eyes bounced nicely off his dark tan Skechers, a wasted combo on this dude.

"The modem is a gateway to the world. I can't have my back to the gateway to the world."

"Cat's right," said Manny, filling the door frame with his mainframe body. "Bad feng shui."

She nodded in quick appreciation to Manny, who had to be the sneakiest, quietest moving giant Maori on the planet.

"Okay," said Robbie. "We can turn the desk around and you can put your chair on this side." His cocky spirit began to bubble again.

Manny sucked in air loudly through his teeth, as if Robbie was complementing a boy band.

"Then her back would be to the office door," said Annie, shaking her head in a funeral whisper. "Feng shui disaster."

"Feng shui suicide," said Manny.

Cat sensed they were also having fun with her now, but Robbie was off-balance so she went with the flow. "You can't launch a huge project like this songwriting contest with horrible feng shui." Which she believed. "Delaney's spiritual, he'd be mortified." She couldn't glance at Annie because they'd explode in laughter. Delooney spiritual. Hilarious. His soul would turn in the gutter he'd left it in.

Robbie sat on his new desk, one foot on the floor, shoulders almost as low.

"Why don't you give us fifteen minutes to set up the office?" Manny requested in a tone that left no options.

"I'll have a cappuccino, two sugars, please, Robbie." *Oh, Annie, that's too easy.*

Robbie the action man bounced towards the door on a replacement mission.

"Okay, see you all in fifteen."

"Soy latte, no sugar," Cat instructed.

Robbie hesitated at the door.

"Long black for me. Thanks, mate. No sugar," said Manny, stepping inside.

Robbie pulled out his phone and mumbled the coffee orders like a mantra as he typed before shuffling down the corridor. When he was out of sight, Annie raised her hand for a five-second countdown with her fingers. Five, four, three, two, one. Annie and Manny released the laughter floodgates and she joined them a split second later. Laughter was good. In the moment stuff. Couldn't get more Zen than that.

By the time Robbie returned with coffees, Manny had done his tech-guy thing and disappeared, leaving CAT and her desk facing Annie's, angled from the corner, so they were side-on between the modem and door. Robbie's desk was squashed into the opposite corner, facing a wall and modem, back to the door. She and Annie would have to put up with the back of his left shoulder if he leant back past the plastic tubs of files they'd stacked to the left of his desk.

"Thanks for the coffees," said Annie.

Robbie placed the cardboard tray of drinks on his desk, then pulled back the basic office chair. They'd left him with the new desk and computer, but Annie had claimed the bright red, ergonomic executive chair. He rolled the older chair to the end of their desks and straddled it backwards, leaning on the chair back. Typical marketing guy, all cowboy posturing.

The caffeine fumes had stirred the natives in her head, and they were getting restless.

"I get this is an idea you have nurtured. I get you hate marketing in general." He pointed a thumb up to where marketing was roughly based on the ground level, as if he was excluded. "Probably hate all the suits."

He was in the vicinity of the hate range, but she'd promised Annie she'd behave. She glanced at the coffees, jungle drums pounding her head.

"But it's a collaboration now. We're Bradley Cooper and Lady Gaga, and together we'll make your idea a hit, bigger than the original idea."

He sees himself as Bradley Cooper?

"They were a duo and so are we." Cat waved a hand between her and Annie.

"There's a ton of successful trios—Silverchair, The Fratellis, Nirvana, Police."

"All men," Annie deadpanned.

"Dixie Chicks." Robbie's grin grated.

"You mean The Chicks?" she said. "You actually like them?"

"I love good music and I love your idea. When Delaney asked for a one-pager on why we shouldn't do it, I wrote a ten-page plan to show him why Merger had to do it."

"Delaney doesn't read documents longer than a sentence," Annie said. "And a smart man knows you never, ever stand between a Melbourne woman and her coffee."

Before he could react, Annie bounded over to the coffees, grabbed two and passed hers over.

"He read my executive summary." Robbie focused on his imaginary ally, Annie. "A one-page executive summary." He turned to her.

With coffee in her veins, the view was bearable.

"I'm not sure you understand the magnitude of the project you inspired. It's going to be massive. Together, we can smash it, create an iconic annual event."

She sipped more from her cup, peering at Annie, who was doing the same back at her.

"Fair enough. From now on we run this as a democracy. Nothing major happens unless the majority votes for it," she said.

He studied her, then looked back at his cornered desk.

"I believe in collaboration, Robbie," said Annie. "In any good collaboration, it's all about making the idea the best it can be. Surely, you can't doubt our commitment to this."

"Okay, a collaborative democracy it is."

"In fairness to you, we have a confession. We've got the contest all set to launch next week." Annie tapped the black cup lid against her lips. It was as nervous or guilty as she'd ever seen her.

She scratched at her ribbed cup, waiting for Robbie's true colours to splatter the walls with ego and anger. He straightened, rigid, focused on the floor. *Here we go...*

"I know," said Robbie. "I've had computer access to the contest site, plus all the docs and designs." He turned, picked up his coffee, and took a sip.

She glared at the shiny computer screen on Robbie's desk. Manny despised marketing. Had the bastard betrayed them?

"Finance only approved the funds on the basis of Marketing controlling—" He flicked beady eyes from her to Annie. "I mean overseeing the contest. They shared all the relevant access codes." He took a long swig of his coffee.

Annie had insisted they controlled the money but in reality, the Finance ghosts controlled everything despite never gracing any important meeting. She couldn't even recognise one of them, yet they manipulated everything from their Darth Vader chairs. She tilted her cup high, desperate for a caffeine deluge, but it was already a trickle so she launched it to the bin. Bummer. The cup bounced off the edge of Robbie's shiny desk where the bin used to be and rolled onto the floor. Robbie's twenty-one days to change a habit theory was baloney. Some things never changed.

"But everything's ready to go, so I assume you're okay?"

A spark of hope, Annie was a couple of steps ahead of her on the positivity ladder.

"Yeah, you guys have a flair for this. You could work in Marketing."

Took one step forward then dove into quicksand.

"Just kidding. You obviously are inspired about the contest, and you've got some terrific work out of all the team." He waved a hand around the designs on the walls. "Best I've seen from this place."

Mr Marketing might survive the contest alive.

"One thing I think would add to your magic." His eyes were on Annie again.

"Sure," said Annie. "This democracy is open for discussion."

Poor Mr Marketing. When he'd agreed to a democracy, no matter what Annie said, he'd basically agreed to always being out-voted two-to-one.

"In your format, we nominate the ten best songs that are open to public voting each week."

She nodded in sync with Annie.

"We need to add the photos of the writers because research proves the better looking the contestants, the more song downloads, votes, and social media activity."

Where's a guitar when you need to go all rock 'n' roll and smash it over someone's head?

Annie's phone rang and she stared at the screen, letting the ringing end without answering, then put the phone down. "You really don't get it, do you?" asked Annie, way too far on the sympathy side of the condescending spectrum.

Cat had to swing it back. "You can stuff that research through one non-musical ear and out the toneless other. This is about writers. We want voters to hear the songs... emotional craft connecting directly to their hearts. We want—" Her momentum was stalled by Annie's phone text alert.

She couldn't believe Annie picked up the phone and scrolled down the message while they were in the middle of this critical juncture with Robbie, but Annie lasered back on him, her brow creased like an Indian hill farm.

Watch out, Mr Marketing, Annie's got her mojo back.

"I agree. Just sort it out with Manny, but we still launch next Thursday." Annie rushed out, gripping the phone with both hands in front of her like it was a snake head.

Robbie turned to her with a grin she could have kicked to the top of Mt Dandenong. "Democracy is good," he said.

She jumped up, pushed his chair, rolling him backwards to his desk, then scampered after Annie.

ANNIE sensed the main door open to the toilet area because she could hear the piped-in rock music and other distant office hubbub. Silence for a second, then the distinctive squeak of Cat's Colorado boots on the polished concrete floor until they stopped outside her stall.

"You okay?" asked Cat.

Staring at the short text message didn't tame her heart rate and she was in no mood for any of Cat's meditation and mantra mumbo jumbo. She focused on a breathing exercise Tamara Ahern, her favourite singing teacher, had taught her.

Feel the air through your nostrils... down your throat... all the way into your stomach. After a few cycles, she straightened on the toilet seat and placed one hand low on her tummy, coaxing the air deeper.

"If that stalker's got your new number we need to go straight to the police," said Cat.

"Not the stalker." Annie barely recognised her own rasp, the golden triangle of muscles protecting her voice box contracting with a ton of rage and tinge of fear.

It's worse.

TRACK 4

ANNIE STARED AT HER PHONE.

Cat had triggered another red flag. This was her brand-new number. She could count on one hand how many people knew it: Lachie, his babysitter Aoham, Cat, and Lachie's principal Wilma. *So how did—*

"Let's go to a meeting room and you can talk through—"

"I'm not one of your Cat-causes." She should drop the phone in the toilet, drown the text, flush it away.

"I hear your anger projecting. I'm not leaving till you come out and let me hug you."

Cat's loyalty and patience with her contrasted to Cat's famous short fuse with most other people. Just once, it would be good if Cat lost it with her.

"One minute, then I'm climbing over."

Aghhhh! Damn woman. The internal scream came with a smile. Cat was like the Basement Jaxx track, 'Never Say Never'; the piano chords annoy and annoy and annoy until they link up with the beat and hook your heart into a sweet space in your head. She glared at the text one last time... then hit *Delete*. The phone asked if she was sure. *Yes, I'm fucking sure. Now I'm arguing with a phone.* She hit *Confirm* on the screen, stood, and shoved the phone into a jeans pocket. Cat already had her arms wide when she stepped out. Their silent hug said *I'm sorry... and I forgive you for barking at me... and I'm always here for you.*

If you could nail their hug in a melody, it would be the top downloaded track forever.

"Three days? You got more chance of a Michael Hutchence resurrection," said Manny.

"Three and a half, plus this weekend on double pay." ROBBIE hadn't got approval on the double pay, but worst case, he could sacrifice some of his doco production budget.

Manny pointed at the huge rucksack in the corner with a helmet and other climbing gear laid out on the floor. "Clock hits four and I'm doing double-time to Mount Arapiles. Nothin' gonna stop me from being first up at first light and scaling that baby monster."

Negotiating was one of his things. He loved it, so he threw down a challenge no IT dude could resist. "Okay, I'll outsource."

Manny stopped moving the mouse, sat back, and unleashed his Maori smile. Close up, he understood what all the whispers and giggles were about from female staff—and a couple of guys—when Manny lumbered through the kitchen and hallways. Charisma like that was wasted in IT. Manny should be in Marketing.

"You know Electric Mary?" asked Manny.

He nodded, unsure about the local band's relevance.

"Top band. Good musos, powerful live. Know their biggest talent?"

"Rusty? His band, really."

Manny shook his head. "They know their place. They've built a bit of a following here, a bit in Europe, but they know they're no AC/DC and they're cool with that."

"I don't see how—" He stopped as Manny raised his North Island-sized palm.

"Don't try and be Angus Young without the talent, Robbie. Otherwise, you just end up looking like an old man prancing around in a schoolboy uniform. Creepy."

What did I do well, what can I do better next time? What did I do well, what can I do better?

Robbie had trudged halfway around Albert Park Lake before he'd bounced the anger out of his system and started repeating his go-to mantra. He'd never been much of a soccer player—quitting when he turned fifteen—and his dad wasn't much for coaching or motivating, but he did teach him this simple tool because it focused on the positives, not beating your head over mistakes. It became a handy tool in many life and business situations.

What did I do well, what can I do better?

Manny had blindsided him because he'd underestimated the guy. Simple solution: more respect and preparation. A seagull swooped down to the edge of the water, beaked some bread a boy was feeding the ducks, and flew off. The kid thought it was funny. Manny wasn't his problem; he'd actually been outmanoeuvred by Annie weeks ago. She wasn't all chocolate truffle eyes and snaky-wavy hair. Snaky-wavy hair he could hide under forever.

"Eyes on the ball, always eyes on the ball." A dad threw a soccer ball to his daughter, maybe late primary school age. She controlled it on her thigh and passed the ball back smoothly along the ground.

It zapped him back to the contest ball. Focus on the song contest. Professional focus. That was his best way forward with Annie. Pro first, sex later. The vacuum decision cleared all other distractions out of his mind. He picked up his pace as two swans glided ahead, close to the edge. Walk. Breathe. A Manny strategy would land in the clear space in his head. Always did.

ANNIE didn't understand the tech behind it, but Manny's magic made the contest almost manageable. Three hundred and seventeen songs in the first week, which they had to cut down to the ten most promising before they unleashed them to the public, so they could vote in the top two. After six weeks, there'd be the final twelve, and another public vote that would establish the most popular three tracks, the winning songwriters. Manny had created a private contest app that was inspired by dating apps. Like the song, swipe right, or swipe left to dump it. When all three of them had finished their initial cull, the app listed all tracks that had been "liked" by at least two of them and those that got a unanimous right-swipe by all three.

She relaxed into a boardroom chair—once Cat had labelled them Darth Vader chairs, the discomfort of their subliminal power having evaporated—and took in the exhausted yet contented faces of Robbie on her right and Cat across the table, both staring up at the large screen on the end wall listing their final ten-track selection. Cat spread herself adjacent to the table, boots up on the next chair, picking at the wide strap of her tartan mini dress.

Cat knew her well enough to not probe around the text message the other day. If it was possible to write a checklist for the characteristics of a special friend, that had to be one of them. *Be there, don't probe.* More importantly, there hadn't been any similar follow-up texts.

"I knew we'd work well together," said Robbie, hands behind his head, legs spread wide. The dude took up a lot of space.

Cat made a soft sound that came out simultaneously from deep in her throat and through her nostrils—secret non-Robbie code—then she grabbed one of the takeaway boxes and picked around with the chopsticks. Despite the two large overhead fans, and leaving the double doors open, the air hung with a Chinese-ey sapor.

She turned back to their top ten selections. The first surprise had been the six unanimous matches. Six songs she and Cat and Robbie had swiped right for. She'd run a secret lottery with Cat and Manny, and none of them had picked higher than three. Initially, she wondered if it could have been a first week fluke, then suspected Robbie was second-guessing her and Cat's tastes just to get on side, but the longer the meeting and the more they got into sifting through the fifteen tracks with a double right swipe, the more Robbie's musical sensibility showed some actual sense.

Cat brought a solitary grain of brown rice to her mouth on the end of a chopstick and savoured it.

That made her own tummy rumble. It had been a long time since they'd started the five o'clock meeting despite only having to select the final four tracks. The hum of traffic outside had disappeared, adding to the hollow feel of the building.

"We should hit Acland Street for a snack," said Robbie, facing her. "Celebrate our first—"

"I'm already paying overtime for my babysitter, I need to get home. Maybe another time." She packed her stuff into her satchel.

"Okay, let me give you a lift." He glanced at Cat, then back. "Both of you."

"We're good, thanks," said Cat, packing her knapsack.

Annie was tempted. Two trams after ten meant she wouldn't glimpse her sleeping Lachie till nearly midnight, probably getting less than seven hours sleep. Mornings didn't work for her without at least eight hours, but give a guy like Robbie an inch and his penis would expect frequent flyer miles.

"That's sweet, but I need the walk and tram ride to wash this work out of my hair." Half a truth beat a full lie.

Cat dumped her knapsack on the floor and thudded into her seat, clunking her reusable coffee cup onto the desk. ANNIE reckoned it must have been at least half empty, because none seeped out the little hole. It was the first morning since the contest green light that they hadn't shared the tram ride from town. She could read an annoyed Cat like an annoyed cat—they let you know they were annoyed. *Five, four, three, two, one...*

"Ellen's having a mid-gay crisis," Cat said to her computer screen.

"Housemate Ellen?"

Cat nodded, slow and deliberate.

"What do you mean by mid-gay—"

"After more than twenty years in lesbian relationships, thirty-seven-year-old Ellen wants to try sex with a man."

29

"Trading in her Vespa for a Ducati?"

"*Hmph,*" escaped through Cat's throat and nostrils.

"Still voting Greens, or going Indy?"

"Not funny." Cat guzzled her soy latte.

Cheap clichés aside, it was a huge surprise. She'd known Ellen since Cat moved in with her five years ago. The woman was smart, funny, and a zealot feminist.

"She's not schizophrenic, so that leaves hypocrite and…" Cat pushed her keyboard away and pivoted towards her. "And traitor."

"Bit rich coming from a proud bi-sexual."

"I've always been bi, although if you line up ten women, I'd tingle over seven of them. Line up ten men, maybe three would spark, four max."

Cat drifted in and out of self-awareness like her slippery version of mindfulness.

"I'm all for free choice, you know me." Cat's eyes were hungry for validation.

She nodded.

"But she's already set up an RSVP account. Not Tinder, RS-bloody-VP-hetero. Going to waste a chunk of her life destroying everything she believes in. How do I save her from this toxic detour?"

Annie stopped scrolling through the endless list of emails. "Don't save her from finding a man. Help her find a typical SIP. A selfish, insensitive prick that will put her off men forever."

Cat smiled and slouched back into her chair. "You're a genius. That's so Zen. Don't fight it, go with the flow." Then she slumped forward, elbows on her desk, head in her hands. "But when? Between my voluntary work at the centre, this contest and… other stuff, where do I quickly find this typical SIP of a man?"

"Can you see that?" sang Robbie, sliding into the middle of the office, tapping his right shoulder and then his left in some kind of fly-swatting dance move. "Got so many pats on the back for the marketing success of the contest, I've got bruises. Social media activity is through to Mars, we're trending on Twitter, and contest entries have doubled this week." He wiggled a shoulder at Annie. "Chance to rub shoulders with a marketing wiz." He wiggled the other shoulder Cat's way. "Get some winner juice while it's hot."

She smiled at Cat.

Cat's mischievous grin-and-eye-roll combo spun facial gymnastics into a new elite sport.

TRACK 5

"S<small>URE, YOUR LESBIAN FRIEND, WHOSE NAME JUST HAPPENS TO BE</small> E<small>LLEN</small>, suddenly wants to explore men and you want me to be her virgin bunny," said ROBBIE.

Cat needed to lift her game if she thought he'd fall for this prank. They'd killed his high from the meeting with Delaney, but that was because, unlike him, they had no real ambition here. They were just scrolling through Merger Music like it was an Instagram page. For him it was *the* LinkedIn step that set up his future. Then again, Cat making fun of him was better than being ignored, which had to be good for team dynamics.

"I've just sent you her RSVP link, check it out," said Cat.

He studied Annie for a flicker of truth or sniggers, but she just nodded and smiled. Unfortunately, her smile wasn't on RSVP or any other dating site he'd checked out. He flicked back to his computer and clicked on the link. Okay, Ellen didn't look butch. Kind of attractive in that funky Fitzroy couldn't-be-bothered-trying way. He scrolled down her profile.

"She's thirty-seven!" *Whoops.* He glanced at Annie to see if his derogatory tone upset her, but no, her smile kept stroking his cheeks.

He focused back on Ellen's profile. "I don't know, Cat... I'm not getting a vibe here."

"I understand your reticence, Robbie," said Annie. "It would take some man to step up and be the first."

The way his name slid off her tongue, he could swirl around her syrupy voice all day and night. Any night.

"I guess you're right, Annie, it is quite a challenge. Maybe I should introduce her to Manny," said Cat.

Fuck Manny. This was actually a way he could indirectly connect sexually with Annie. If he gave Ellen an unforgettable bedroom experience, she'd tell Cat and Cat would tell Annie.

"Hells bells, Cat, set it up."

The Robbie-Ellen introduction "catch up" was flowing way too cosy. CAT fiddled with the thick cardboard coaster, started peeling it at the edges, then put it down. *Patience, Cat, patience. Robbie will slip up and reveal his inner SIP.* In the retro yet authentic vibe of Tin Pot Cafe, it was only a matter of time before his plastic-fantastic personality would jar.

"Cat tells me you've been working with Headspace for a few years," said Robbie.

"Feels like fifty years, but it's the most rewarding job I've ever had," said Ellen. "After you deduct the stress from government fools and budget fights, it's still worth it."

"There's never enough money for mental health issues. I saw those videos on disordered eating you did. Really good work."

"You watched those? Thanks, Robbie. We had a good team on that project."

Really, Robbie? Sneaky research for his sleazy goal. Annie had told her to introduce them then *"Get out of the way and let him trip himself up."* But she was enthralled by how far he could stretch this artificial rubber band before it snapped and stung. Robbie had brought a Bob Marley T-shirt to work so that he could change for the date, chocolate with black print of some lyrics for love in the world. Another calculated choice for sure, although the colours bounced off his big eyes. For a guy, he was surprisingly good with colour.

"I've been doing some voluntary work for Youthworx and one of the women there showed me the videos."

Thankfully, Ellen was just Ellen, except for the hint of shinier lipstick. At least she didn't go red.

"Oh, Youthworx is a great mob. How long have you been helping them out?"

Five minutes. Five minutes to Google an organisation relevant to Ellen's work. Five minutes of effort to impress Ellen. Transparent as the wall-to-ceiling window their table nestled up to.

"About three years now. I only go in for a half-day once a month to mentor the kids about the music biz. It's amazing how the Youthworx team guide a troubled kid towards self-esteem and a job by empowering them with real, creative work."

This guy was soooo good. Made up a whole story just to—

"Cat, don't you have to be at the community centre in fifteen?" asked Ellen, flashing her phone's clock at her.

Wow. Ellen was buying it and throwing her out.

Ellen swung back to Robbie. "Feel like grabbing some dinner? We can walk down to the Moroccan soup bar."

"Love that place. I've got their recipe book at home."

A volcano of vomit bubbled deep in Cat's tummy at the length he would go to fabricate an Ellen-focused image. "You two have a fun time. I've got to vomit... I mean vamos." She dropped enough money to cover her soy latte and scooped herself out fast. The dude would slip up sooner or later, and Annie was right--better she wasn't around when it happened.

Every time CAT stepped into the Collingwood Community Centre, the subconscious armour that helped protect her from the madness of the music biz and other survival demands on this crazy planet peeled off, each step inside becoming more of a low-gravity zone. She waved to Aunty Kyah, who managed a wave in the middle of one her animated indigenous stories to a group ranging from adolescents to elderly, some in burqas and hijabs.

Jalen, a psychologist and former monk, possibly the wisest person she'd ever met, was in a meeting room with a mother and son, maybe eleven or twelve. They'd recently escaped a violent husband and father, and Jalen was their perfect guide back into a tentative world of hope.

Hope.

The more time Cat spent around people like Kyah and Jalen, the more she believed hope was the currency that opened all the wealthy inner resources, like care, kindness, and compassion. Without hope, souls were bankrupt. Bankrupt souls made a poorer world. World of hunger and hate.

She caught the back of Santi through the double-glazed studio window, hunched over the keyboard at a right angle to the mixing desk and huge computer screen, baseball cap facing backward, same Barcelona top with "Messi" across the shoulders.

She'd helped build the little studio with generous financial support of Merger, thanks to Delooney—the one tiny spot on this planet they shared mutual respect—and other Merger staff and artists. The size of two decent bedrooms, a band could rehearse, or naturals like Santi could explore their musicality and record demos of their original material. A couple of nights a month, Cat organised group classes by experienced Melbourne musos and producers.

She slipped inside, closed the door gently, and soaked in Santi's music as he sang the lyrics in a whisper, still not confident of his raspy voice. He'd already laid down some beats and the chords, as he played the melody line over them on the keyboard. Soulful rap, not her favourite genre, but when Santi reached the chorus, the haunting, melodic hook snatched her breath, pride bursting through her, and she grabbed the round doorknob to brace herself. Incredible emotional power from the music of a fifteen-year-old.

Santi stopped playing, hit a button that killed the backing tracks, and without turning around said, "Not cool, Cat. Said to you already, ain't showin' nothin' till it's done."

Poor creative soul. Was it Scorsese who said, *"A film is never finished, it's abandoned"*? That paralysing fear of sharing their work must be the same across artists, novelists, and songwriters, from the greats to street talent.

"Hook's amazing. Dizzyfying… thought it was going to float me to the moon."

"Most corny-arsed shit I ever heard."

She couldn't tell if he meant her words or his music, but when he turned, the grin and spark in his eyes made her day. Her year.

"Only thing corny was some of the lyrics, your music deser—"

"Shit for words. You know I can't write proper. That's why this is all a time sucker. Fuck'n time sucker." He flicked the keyboard and computer off, staring at the blank screen.

She pulled up a chair close. "Santi, you're a special talent. I work in the bloody music biz and I can count on a couple of fingers how many times I can truly say that."

"You're a special talent with them bullshit words. You should done the lyrics, I'll stick with the beats."

"People don't listen to words in great songs, they feel them." It was the paradox of art—the more personal the emotion, the more universal the connection.

He flicked his round russet eyes at her, head still angled towards the screen.

If she could only get him to a level of self-esteem, just enough so he could peer over the crumbled catastrophe in which his junkie parents had abandoned him, this kid could be a star. A superstar. The ghost skin, marshmallow cheekbones and eyes created a magnetic force, even under a harsh number-one blade cut.

"You've lived extreme, raw emotions. More than most people do in a lifetime. Write what you feel, Santi. Dig deep into the darkest corners of your pain and strangle it with the words you know. Your way of saying things is what will help you stand out, what people will feel."

He searched her eyes from his fragile default position of cynicism and disillusionment. Was that a glimmer in his gaze, the briefest of inner smiles?

"We need one a them hotel signs I seen on the movies, says *no disturbing*." He flicked the equipment back on and tapped a key on the keyboard, then hovered his right hand over the record button. "Feel them words, Cat. No disturbing."

Mission accomplished. Cat put her chair away and glided out of the studio.

CAT admired the laminated sign she'd just hung on the external doorknob of the studio: 'No Disturbing'. Inside, Santi was in a hunched-over creative trance, his head almost touching his knuckles as fingers flitted across the keyboards, piano, and computer. A sharp, buzzing sound from inside her hemp knapsack flushed out all her feel-good vibe, launching a cold shiver that froze her gut. The unique vibration on her second phone always hit her that way and she could never get used to it. She scrambled for the phone in her bag as she headed out the rear door into the courtyard, quickly checking all the spaces and alcoves to make sure no one else was there before she answered the persistent buzzing.

Phone sex was the only way she could stay at a day job she enjoyed while still affording the international volunteer work as well as her commitment to the local community centre. Something had to give, so she donated a chunk of her soul to the devil. Most men called her between eleven at night and three in the morning, plus weekend and public holiday afternoons. This call was annoyingly just after eight.

"Well, hello, my toe-curling tiger." She might not have Annie's vocal magic but these men had desperate standards and she could mimic gutter-level-sultry on tap. A chilly breeze swirled around the deserted space, so she tightened her scarf and sheltered in a concrete alcove where she kept an eye on the door. As she rolled through her spiel on prices and times, her soul braced itself for the dirty side of the exchange. Part of her brain chanted the mantra *"One more credit card to clear, one more credit card to clear"* as she guided "Steve" through one of her fantasies.

By the time she'd finished with "Steve"— she doubted any man used his real name—the breeze had blown into a chilly autumn wind, and she crouched, sitting on her heels, back to the side of the alcove. Her mouth craved beer to wash away the shame and drown the self-blame. She'd hidden this part-time gig from everyone, even her house-mate Ellen.

Even Annie.

She pulled her normal phone out of her pocket, headphones out of her bag. Beer was too far away; she needed music now to cleanse her.

Santi stood outside the door, holding his roll-up tobacco kit, bull-at-a-matador-glare.

Fuck.

TRACK 6

CAT ROSE, EACH HAND DANGLING WITH A PHONE. THE LONGER SANTI stood there, still, silent, the more her soul cringed.

"How long... how long have you been there?"

"Long 'nough to hear your ho-talk."

Pass me Kurt Cobain's shotgun. "Santi, don't jump to conclusions."

"Ain't jumping to nothin. Only fuckers I seen with two phones are all gutter rat." He pointed at her with a shaking arm. "One big hypocrite. Feel them words? Gutter rat hypocrite." Santi slumped around and shuffled back inside.

Send me Michael Jackson's drug doc. Now.

The one person on the planet who relied on her for a tenuous finger-hold to the good side of this planet and she'd destroyed it. She needed to explain, to—

Her normal phone pinged with a message alert: Wings

Unbelievable. Un-shit-timing-believable.

Ellen and Cat had agreed on a code word in case she brought Robbie home. Wings. She'd never expected it to happen, let alone on a first catch-up, so she hadn't planned an alternative. Where she spent the night could wait. Her hyper-immediate problem was pacifying Santi and making sure he didn't blurt out her secret gig to anyone.

She raced inside, checking all the rooms, but there was no sign of him. She opened the door to the men's room and walked straight into Jalen.

"Whoa, you're not our cleaner as well, are you, Cat?"

She stepped back, trying to peer around him.

"You okay?"

"Me? Yeah, all good. Fine."

"You don't need my training to tell you there's a subconscious self-hanging happening here." Jalen pointed at her.

She looked at her hands, which had been pulling at either end of her scarf, let go and loosened the wool around her neck.

"Is Santi in there?"

"The cool kid with the haunting eyes and shoulder slump of a one-hundred-year-old?"

She nodded, needing to talk to him fast. Shake out whatever she'd dumped in his head. One hundred-year-old haunting eyes and shoulder slump inside a fifteen-year-old could only bear so much shock.

"He shuffled out a few minutes ago." Jalen pointed towards the street entrance.

She took off and scurried outside. No sign of his baseball cap, Barcelona top, that scruffy, baggy, hooded jacket, or slumped shoulders. A tram rocked off a few hundred metres away in the direction of his share house. Bloody trams never turned up on time when she needed one at night. The light traffic meant she'd never catch up to it on foot. If Santi was even on it. What he was definitely on was a downer, pushed over the edge by her. Her stupidity. She pulled out the good phone, scrolled his number, and hit Send.

No answer. It rang, so he had it on. No answer.

She could jump in an Uber and chase the tram.

No, she couldn't. No credit on that card. No credit is what got her in this mess. No credibility was exactly where she was with Santi.

Prince me up, Bowie.

ANNIE barely listened to the songs in one earpiece as Lachie rested against her on the couch with the other end of her phone plugs hooked into his ear. Her legs reached halfway across the coffee table and Lachie's heels now made it past the near edge. When did that happen? It was just yesterday his little legs wouldn't reach the edge of the couch. Eight. In another eight years, his heels would be dangling over the other end of the table, probably never sitting beside his embarrassing so-old mum on any couch. A shiver shuddered her core so violently she gasped and flung her hand to her chest.

"It's good but not that good," said Lachie, finger hovering over the swipe-left button on the contest app.

She forced herself to resume breathing. To channel back into this time. To cherish the choice she'd made. Wasn't difficult, immediately "in the moment" whenever she dived into the deep lagoons of Lachie's sparkling hazelnut eyes. She smiled and nodded.

Lachie swiped left, denting the dreams of another songwriter, then hit Play on the next track. His tastes and expressions were more entertaining than the songs, reeling off instant judgments on each track, often before they'd reached the hook.

"Okay for tweens... yuckers... good ballad for almost-dead people..." He'd made it quicker to plough through the growing mountain of entries and a lot more fun.

"Clever of Manny to copy the Tinder app," said Lachie.

"How do you know what Tinder is?" Eight. Eight!

His nose pointed down while his eyes shot up at her with his "Seriously, Mum?" look. "I need a break," he said, removing the earpiece, placing it on her lap and reaching for his cup of Milo.

She did the same, taking a long slurp of her four-spoon Milo. Her pancreas and processed sugar had made some sort of illicit pact and she had got over the guilt by seventeen. The sweet, warm chocolate milk melted her defences. He'd be nine in September, and if she blinked, he'd be eighteen and swiping Tinder for real, or whatever hook-up app was around. And what would she be swiping? Flies? Seagulls from her life scraps? Vultures of time?

"Mum, you know how you say I'll always be your number-one

hit?" He focused on his Milo, holding it close to his face with two hands, just like her. Cherish the moment.

"Yes, you'll always be my number-one."

He used to respond with "And you're my number-one-est." Lately he'd grown it up to "And you're mine." A warm flutter of anticipation flowed through her lungs and heart even though she knew his follow-up.

"I think you need a good number-two." He took a long sip.

Wow. Warm flutter turned icy breeze.

Her eight-year-old baby boy was telling her to get a life, one part cute, two parts mortifying. She put her cup down and pulled a cushion to her cold chest.

"A number-two with a bullet," he added, his face forward but eyes checking out her reaction.

"Between work and you and school stuff and drum lessons and—" As the fences and defences stumbled out of her mouth, she realised this guilt was exactly what worried Lachie. That he was the one stopping his mum from having a number-two. A love life. A life. "But mainly, good number-twos are rare, Lachie. Men these days—"

"Stop making excuses, you're not good at it. You're good at making things happen, like Wonder Woman."

She clutched the cushion tighter to keep her heart inside her skin, beneath the ribs pounding like an African drum.

He put his Milo down and squeezed her other hand. "Sorry, I didn't mean to upset you."

She wiped away tears with the back of her hand, then wrapped Lachie up in a hug.

"You didn't upset me, I'm proud of you. Proud of your caring heart." She held him tight for ages.

"Do you like Fernando?" he said.

She let go, grateful for the subject change. "I like ABBA, but not that song."

"No, Fernando Diaz, my drum teacher."

"Sure, that's why I took you there. He's a patient teacher and he's passionate about percussion."

As soon as "passionate" slipped out, Lachie's motive slapped her face. She pulled away slightly to get a long look beneath the sparkle in his eyes. He meant well and he was smart and worried about her but...

"Way past your bedtime. Teeth, toilet, trance." She banged her cup onto the coffee table, a few drops splashing out. Her phone clattered on the hardwood floor as she got up. Damn thing never landed on the rug or carpet, always wood or concrete.

"But I haven't finished my—"

"Now." She grabbed his cup, marched into the kitchen, and poured the Milo into the sink.

ANNIE stroked Lachie's wavy brown hair as he slept. Watching him grow, helping him every step, had given her more joy and pride than she could have dreamed. She couldn't wait for each new milestone. First smile, first Mummy—she let out a long sigh—first steps. How ironic he was now growing up too fast.

Humbling.

Scary.

His hand moved to his side, revealing two drumsticks under the pillow. She pulled them out, studying the matching contour and length of each wooden stick. Some things always needed to work in pairs. Not her. She placed the sticks on his bedside table. How could she tell Lachie she didn't need a number-two? How could she tell him his dad was a number-two thousand, so far down the charts of decency that the man wasn't worth listing? Sure, she had needs, but sex was easy. Chewing up young guys for a two or three-time fling then slipping away while they slept into the afternoon had served her well since... since Lachie turned three.

There she went again.

Her life timeline measured by Lachie milestones.

To hell with the experts, they weren't his mother. If dedicating her life to Lachie was the worst thing she ever did, it would still be the best thing she ever did. Like Kacey Musgrave sang, she was following her arrow.

Her phone pinged a new message alert from the loungeroom, an alert tone she'd allocated to one specific number, which made her sit straight as an arrow, tense as a fully drawn bow. The bastard wouldn't give up. She closed her eyes and focused on her trusty breathing exercise, sitting on the edge of Lachie's bed. Kind of meditative. Cat would be proud of her.

Ping, ping.

She would not respond, not give in to that darkness, kept her eyes closed, focused on breathing, the rhythm.

Tap, tap, tap. The front door, soft and gentle.

He's HERE. Her lungs gripped the oxygen and hung on.

Tap, tap, tap. Soft and gentle was how it always began. She tip-toed to Lachie's bedroom door, closed it softly and stood in the hall, glaring at the front door.

Ping, ping. She was so close to her phone, its volume startled her. She could call Cat to come. No, better to call the police. She tip-toed towards her phone.

Tap, tap, tap.

She pivoted a quarter turn and stormed the front door, each step pounding on his gutless spine, his fucked-up audacity after nine years, on her delusion over the last two weeks that he'd give up. She'd burn him now, once and forever, brand him so deep he'd never return. She flung the door open. "Fuck off forever or I'll—"

"Annie, what's the matter?" asked Cat.

Her lungs heaved and stung like she was chasing oxygen up a hill but couldn't catch up. Cat spun in circles in front of her, the door frame closing like a vice. She braced herself against the frame, but her arms were too short and her knees buckled. Cat caught her, squeezing her tight.

"It's okay, it's me. You're okay."

CAT sipped her vodka, savouring the fiery burn sliding down her throat. She re-adjusted her curled up legs on the armchair and studied Annie on the couch, who clutched an icy vodka in one hand, the other arm hugging a cushion to her chest, knees up close. She had an older cousin that suffered anxiety attacks but never pictured Annie in the same turbulent river, let alone same boat.

"Why are you here?" whispered Annie.

Because my lesbian housemate is going bi-stupid and she's doing it with Robbie. Because my vulnerable protégé caught me doing phone sex. Because my life's a fraud. I'm turning thirty in seven months and I don't know where the fuck I'm going.

"Turns out Ellen is more gullible than we imagined."

Annie looked up from her glass, possibly raised her eyebrows, then looked back at her glass.

"Seems like the elephant question is why did you think you should challenge the stalker shit at the door? Why didn't you just call the cops?"

"Wasn't a stalker," Annie said to her vodka. "It was Monaro."

"Monaro? Who's—" Cat uncurled her legs and perched on the edge of the armchair. "Tony Monaro?" She glanced towards Lachie's room, then swung back at Annie. "That Monaro? He's back in Australia?"

Annie nodded with the weight of the planet on her head.

"He wants joint custody of Lachie." The last syllable broke the floodgates, launching violent tears.

"Oh, Annie." Cat put her glass down on the coffee table, then moved to the couch. She took Annie's glass from her trembling hand, placed it safely on the table then wrapped her tight.

Tony Monaro, Annie's long-ago manager and lover, got her to sign a ten-year exclusive contract, got her pregnant, then got on a plane. No contact or cash for over nine years. Nothing. Annie was determined to never earn one cent for Tony's twenty percent share in her creative talent. Cat didn't know if she could ever be a mother and was in awe of Annie. Could she have given up her dreams for ten years if she had Annie's talent? Put up with Merger for almost nine? Dedicate her whole life to one little soul? That was a whole different commitment to building schools in struggling parts of the world, its every day, twenty-four-seven dependence on you. Motherhood, the most undervalued currency on the planet.

"No one's taking Lachie from you, Annie, least of all that shit. Won't happen." She stroked Annie's hair. "We won't let it."

Annie gripped her tighter but couldn't stop the tears.

She'd never felt more needed yet more useless. Annie wasn't fighting for a bit of wasteland or useless hill; her precious hold of Lachie was under attack. Guerrilla attack from the jungle of fuck-off-this-isn't-fair life. Proactive genes dominated her DNA, but what could she really do other than provide moral support, a sounding board, and a hug?

Nothing.

Or I could find the bastard and... No, this is Annie's war.

Nothing she could do. Nothing was her weakest link and this her biggest test. Sometimes you just need to be there, not leading with personal prejudices or pushing your values from behind. Just be there. In this moment of fear and angst for Annie, the magic of friendship was the magic of friendship. Just be there.

TRACK 7

ROBBIE LIKED HOW HIS *"NO PRESSURE, JUST A CASUAL INTRO"* WITH Ellen had flowed into an obvious and fun first date. Under normal circumstances, he could see the night flowing into many more dates, maybe a long-term fling. Under normal circumstances. This situation was at the extreme opposite end of the normal spectrum, but at least he couldn't fall into his usual trap of projecting.

He wasn't running, either. He took pride in trying to break one comfort zone a year and tonight was feeling more and more like a quantum leap in sexual experience. Standing outside the narrow terrace house Ellen shared with Cat in North Melbourne, their banter helped counter the town's infamous winter wind-chill.

Cat... was she home? That was a heavy-duty layer of the "Be the first man to sleep with a lesbian" comfort zone. He stared at the large bay window.

Ellen jabbed his shoulder. "Don't worry, she's not staying here tonight."

He smiled. Precautionary or cocky, it didn't matter. Ellen's fierce independence electrified him because truly independent women didn't need to proclaim it, like truly cool people never used the word *cool* to describe themselves. So many were quick to tell him, *"I'm an indepen-*

47

dent woman." Empowerment overload from a trashy online magazine. Men didn't walk around saying, *"I'm an independent man."* Despite the slippery circumstances, Ellen radiated authenticity. Not social media mangled authenticity, the real thing. Something was brewing when she'd agreed to let him drive her home and it wasn't tea or coffee.

"Why don't you come in," said Ellen. Not a question. Whether the glint in her blue eyes came from the nearby street light or powered by inner needs, her tone couldn't drip with more sultriness without getting arrested.

"Sure."

"I Feel it Coming", the Weeknd/Daft Punk version danced out of his head and bopped through his veins.

Until they stepped inside and a little dog, a terrier or something, yapped down the long hall and jumped at his legs.

"Easy, boy. Easy, boy." He tried to sound calm, but the dog wasn't buying it and nipped at his ankle. "Ouch."

"Nav!" Ellen crouched down and picked Nav up. "Naughty girl. Sorry, she hasn't had much attention today."

He rubbed the spot, but the dog's teeth hadn't torn through his jeans. He was more in shock that the little bugger had a go at him than pain. "I deserved it for calling her a boy. Nav, short for?"

"Navratilova." She grinned, not embarrassed at the obvious role model.

"In that case, I'm lucky she didn't bite my knee off."

The mention of the tennis legend and lesbian icon served him back to reality and the enormity of what he'd got into with Ellen. He should leave a little mystery for next time. No need to crash through the barrier of the comfort zone all in one night. He felt for the car keys in his jacket.

She took a couple of paces down the hall and opened a door. "My fun palace."

Fun palace... How could you not like a woman who calls her bedroom "My fun palace?"

"I only have one rule. You have to wear a condom, otherwise... anything goes. Surprise me."

Anything goes… in the fun palace. Normally he'd have bounded over, picked her up, and thrown her on the bed before you could say "Sex with Me by Rihanna", but the house was cold and Navratilova was snarling within biting range, and Ellen was effectively a virgin and he'd never deflowered a woman before. Would he hurt her? How would mini-Navratilova react to that?

"It's okay, I'll put Nav in the lounge." She'd read part of his mind.

"I'll get the condoms from the car."

"Ooh, I like the sound of multiple condoms."

A cocky lesbian. *Are they all this sexy?* Heat swirled again in his navel.

She headed down the hall with Navratilova in her arms, expectations set. He headed back to his car wondering how many condoms to get.

ROBBIE liked her room. It had an Arabian feel, with red satin fabric hanging high on the four-poster bed, round and cylindrical pillows, but not a crazy amount like some women's beds. Lamps and candles flickered against fabric and photos, creating an orangey-red haze.

"Can't find the CD I had in mind." She was searching a tallboy drawer with her back to him – or should that be a tallgirl drawer? Or person drawer. He/she, or they drawer? She'd taken off her coat, the wrap-around dress revealing a leg to mid-thigh, launching a semi-erection, a comfort zone in the process of breaking a comfort zone.

"No heater?" he asked. The high ceilings and large bay window provided little protection from the cold.

"This is a green-house, the fireplace is down the other end. I'm sure we'll sizzle the room up." Her eyes zoned in on his crotch and she flicked a grin at him, then opened a lower drawer, pulling stuff out and throwing it on the bed.

She didn't understand the shrivel-factor. How could she? Twenty years in lesbian relationships wouldn't have introduced her to the embarrassing intimacy of cold, shrivelled penis. Doonas and sheets never seemed to survive on the bed in his sexcapades and he was no wuss, but Melbourne winter wasn't a playground for slow, sensuous adventure while butt naked with no heating. A gust of wind rattled the window.

Stay in the moment, Robbie. If she can do this, I can.

Contrary to her cheeky lesbian persona earlier, her frantic search for a CD revealed obvious nerves. He needed to hold her tight and reassure her. Wrap his arms around her stomach, maybe let a hand linger low over her navel, maybe—

Look at the size of that!

Ellen had thrown a huge dildo on the bed. A strap-on dildo. You-could-play-baseball-with-it-huge dildo. It smashed him into stillness, just behind her.

"Found it," she said, waving the old-school music tech before springing up and slotting it into the CD player sitting on top of the tall-girl-person-boy. She turned and saw what he was staring at. "Oh, that's not for us. You brought your own, didn't you?"

Deep in the Eros corner of his right brain, her voice reached SWAT-level-arrest sultriness, but flight instinct dominated, his shrivel-factored penis diving deeper for cover. He pointed at the baseball-bat-thing.

"That seems like the antithesis of being a lesbian." The words sounded lame bouncing around the cold room, probably the first misstep of the night. Her frown confirmed his naivety. He'd burned any chance of sex with her, let alone turning her.

"We like pleasuring each other and exploring our bodies like any hetero couple does. The method has nothing to do with how lesbian we are." She picked the dildo up, put it in the large drawer, and closed it. "Don't judge lesbians by dildo size, Robbie. If you have to judge anyone, judge them by the size of their humanity and kindness."

"Sorry, I wasn't judging, I was just... surprised... curious." *Intimidated. For the first time ever, my pènis de résistance, the one thing nature had been so kind with, was humiliated to pygmy status compared to that thing filling all of the large bottom drawer.*

She stepped close, placing her hand on his cheek, warm, gentle, tingling. "I can't explain what has led me to this moment, and if it will ever be more than a one-off. But I like you and feel comfortable with you and... I'm curious, too." She kissed him.

Her soft, warm lips dragged him back into familiar territory. Territory his ego swelled up in. Now it was just him and her. Man and woman. Raw and erotic.

Yap, yap. Scratch, scratch.

And yappy Navratilova outside the door.

Ellen pulled out of the kiss. "Nav, enough." She kissed his neck, tongue teasing. "Ignore her and she'll go away."

Navratilova reduced her yap to a low whine but kept scratching. He tried to focus on Ellen's roving hands... unzipping him...

It was warm under the covers. That was the only positive ROBBIE could dig up from the most mortifying thirty-minute disaster in history of his time on this earth. He'd started by going down on her but she'd stopped him, which made perfect sense considering her sexual history. She wanted his penis. Pure and simple penetration. No cunnilingus.

Signature move... out.

The tantric mantra CD grated.

Navratilova yapped and scratched at the door.

Baseball-bat-dildo pounded his memory.

All his shrivel-factored penis could raise was a white flag.

"Has this happened before?" asked Ellen, the cocky lesbian replaced by a hint of fragility.

Honesty would crush her ego, creating two crushed egos in one bed. He didn't know what to say because he didn't know what happened. Or more precisely, why nothing had happened. He wet his bed once when he was seven. Worst morning in his life. In a lunchtime softball game in grade six, he tore the back of his pants down his bum seam while sliding to base. The teacher forced him to finish the afternoon with strips of white packing tape stuck across the back of his pants. Worst ever day in primary school. Wet the front of his pants at a friend's sixteenth birthday party when the hottest chick in high school,

Susie Melville, sat on his lap. Had to change schools but his parents refused to move to the suburbs, so he kept bumping into the one hundred thousand kids that seemed to be at the party. Most disastrous year of his life. But none of those catastrophes challenged the adult anti-sex party in his body and the awkward intimacy of facing that moment together in her bed.

"I'm sorry, I shouldn't have rushed us into this," she said.

"Ellen, you're beautiful and genuinely sexy."

"Bet you've never had to use the 'genuine' word with sexy before."

"Next time... at my place, or a mutual place, I'm sure it will be different."

"Do you mind finding your own way out?"

"Of course." He swung out of bed and dressed quickly.

Yap, yap, snarl, scratch, scratch, snarl.

He stared at the door, back at Ellen.

"Nav, if I come out there, you'll be sleeping outside all winter." Ellen's tone would've frozen fire-breathing dragons.

The yapping and scratching stopped, replaced by whimpering then scampering down the hall. He opened the door a little. No Navratilova.

He turned back. "Ellen, whatever else happens, can we please make one promise to each other?"

"Don't worry. I won't tell a soul, especially Cat."

Fear gripped his testicles and squeezed ice all the way up his spine. Worst fucking night in the entire world of worst fucking nights. Cat. Annie. Merger. Music career fucked because he couldn't fuck.

"Especially Cat."

Robbie slipped outside. Struck by the midnight wind-chill, he stuffed his hands deep into his jacket pockets and wrapped his right hand around the three individual condom packets, all intact. He bee-lined to his car via a neighbour's bin still out on the pavement, quietly lifted the lid, dropped the cursed condoms, and closed the lid.

Focusing on Annie last night and this morning made it easy for CAT to forget about her phone-sex drama with Santi. Helping other people *was* her DNA, buzzed her better than alcohol, drugs, or any other artificial high. By the end of their shared tram ride to work, she'd revved Annie up to her mega best, maybe stronger. It helped that she'd called Ellen and got her to spill the beans on the disaster date with Robbie. They laughed so hard, tram passengers didn't know whether to be annoyed or concerned. They had continued the fun walking through Albert Park village shops, prepping before heading to the office.

Robbie pranced in. "Good morning, my favourite music publishing people." A few branches short of a chirpy tree, forced and over the top, even for him. "All set for an amazing contest week?"

"Sure are, Mr Marketing. Annie and I thought we should all have lunch together for a change."

His eyes lit up. First time they'd included him in anything outside of the contest, apart from her intro to Ellen. Poor bugger didn't have a clue.

She held up her long bread roll. "I've got prosciutto and dried tomato. What about you, Annie?"

Annie held up a longer, thicker roll. "Got me a pizza sub, all twelve inches."

Robbie looked from roll to roll, his shoulders slumped, his bag slipped down his arm, and he dumped it on the floor then slouched at his desk, staring at the screen.

Cat didn't feel an eyebrow's hair of pity for him. Robbie had bragged to Manny that not only was he going to have sex with a lesbian, he was going to turn her. Said some typical Mr Marketing thing about the PCs taking over the world and he was going to turn one into a Mac. *Do it for us Macs,*" Manny had chided him.

"Morning, wombats," Manny said from the door, one hand behind his back.

"Manny's joining us for lunch, too," she said.

"What are you having, Manny?" asked Annie.

Manny stepped forward and held up the longest baguette she'd ever seen. "Gonna fill this baby up with a whole lotta love."

Robbie was so transfixed by the baguette protruding from the paper bag, he actually pushed his chair away from Manny.

Annie snorted.

Cat sniggered and it grew into a silent laugh.

"Then top it up with a ton of mayonnaise," said Manny.

Annie lost it, bursting with laughter.

Robbie scooted out of the office and she exploded with Manny. She'd needed the hit too. Baguette, brilliant.

TRACK 8

Typical. Bloody typical. Lachie picks today to act his age.

ANNIE slurped the leftover chocolaty milk from the bowl of Coco Pops, one eye on him, one on her phone clock. It had taken forever to drag Lachie away from the TV to the tiny kitchen bench, and now he was deliberately whirling a spoon around and around and around his half-finished bowl.

"Lachie, we're leaving in ten minutes, and we won't be late again, even if I have to take you in your pyjamas."

He pointed at the clock above the fridge with his free hand. Didn't even look at her.

Seriously? On a rainy Monday morning? Two bowls of Coco Pops down and she still craved chocolate. Not just any chocolate, chocolate ice-cream. Bad sign. She was one hundred and fifty-something songs behind on her allocated cull list for the contest. Two weeks behind on the so-called "bill smoothing" gas and electricity payments. They had a fifteen-minute walk to school and she had to sign him into the morning day care by eight so she could scuttle to her tram stop and get to work before nine. She closed her eyes to regroup. Belgian chocolate ice-cream, black packaging, body buzzing as she imagined peeling off the round lid.

"LACHIE, move!"

"But, Mum—"

"Don't but-Mum me. Move your butt-me." She was tired of his too-clever complaints about school. *"Teachers are just robots... schoolbooks are written in fossils."* All the accelerated learning stream did was make him a smarter pain in the butt. Plus, craving chocolate ice-cream only happened on the eve of her period, and she was in no mood for that.

Lachie put his spoon down and pointed at the clock again, still perched on his stool.

She needed to calm down, be the experienced parent. Draw on her almost nine years of responsible adulthood.

"You can act like a rock star, but I'm your manager and have to do whatever it takes to get you to your gig." She pounced behind him and scooped him up—*when did he get this heavy?*—then took a step towards the door.

"But there's no gig today."

She stopped, let him slide from her grip. "Of course, there's school today, it's Monday."

"It's professional development day for the robots."

Another professional development day already? Didn't they have enough holidays that made life impossible for a single mum? "When... why didn't you tell me?"

He pointed at the fridge. He'd been pointing at the fridge, not the clock above the fridge, more specifically, the notice stuck on the fridge door with two Melbourne Zoo magnets. The school notice about the three hundredth professional development day for the year.

"Schedule stuff isn't your superpower, Mum."

She stared at Professor Lachie, ran hands through her hair, finishing in a steeple over her nose, and nodded.

She'd pick up the Belgian chocolate ice-cream on the way home. Two tubs.

ROBBIE bounced down the basement hallway to the office without cringing for the first time in a couple of weeks.

He couldn't get the track out of his head. He'd spent hundreds of hours scouring bars and open mic nights and SoundCloud, and all the other online outlets for an act he might want to manage. Managing acts was his destiny, and Merger Music the perfect base to launch from. Best to find them young, then follow their work ethic and output when they did it for little if any monetary return. That's what delivered longevity—work ethic and output. John Watson did it with Silverchair, which led to Gotye and Missy Higgins, not a bad trifecta to manage. Most bands or singers didn't have the stamina. Neither did most wannabe managers. But he wasn't a wannabe; he'd hustled and stalked his way into Merger Music, worked hard, and lapped up every scrap of rock wisdom Delaney, the Godfather of the Aussie music scene in the seventies and eighties, threw his way.

Finally. Finally, this weekend he'd discovered a DJ-duo, *Dua-Luna*, that had uploaded a catchy pop-dance track, "Algorithms are Running the Asylum", onto SoundCloud. It was easy to underestimate the genre, but at just seventeen, they'd produced a polished demo layered with intangible musical magic.

After the Ellen date-disaster he'd lost a bit of his mojo – who wouldn't – but he took pride in tearing apart comfort zones, and over the days he'd taken heart from his courage to have a go at the Ellen challenge. Indirectly, it was all part of paying his dues in life. Plus he'd picked up women at bars on three different nights since then and his mechanics were working at NASA-level order again. Most importantly, Annie and Cat didn't crucify him beyond that first morning after. Respect for that. One morning of schoolyard fun at his expense, then straight back to adulthood, not even a sniff of a mention of his Ellen date.

He swung into the office and stopped mid-step. Not surprised by Annie and Cat getting there before him—their contest commitment and workload didn't give them much choice these days—it was the kid sitting on a beanbag in the corner playing on an iPad. They obviously had dragged the bean bag in from the staff room, but where did the kid come from?

"This is my son Lachie," Annie said, pointing at the kid. "Lachie, this is Robbie."

Lachie flicked a rock-salute at him like he was nineteen, not plucked out of primary school, while focused on his tablet.

Didn't feel right to rock-salute back. He must've squeezed the existence of Annie's kid out of his head, but the kid was real and a real part of Annie.

"Professional development day at school. Delaney's cool with it."

He was starting to pick Annie's tones. Most times her vocal cords wrapped around his chest, but this pitch jabbed below his ribs. Jarred him for a moment. "Whole day?"

Annie nodded. Once.

Not the right work environment for a kid. Merger wasn't filled with placid librarians from the fifties; it was a barely functional madhouse soaking with crass egos, scattered with sex maniacs, sprinkled with psychos. Not to mention the drugs.

"Come on, Robbie, you still live with your mum."

How'd she know that? My dad too, but... "If Delaney's cool with it, so am I."

"Hey, Lachie, what age are you going to leave home?" Cat asked.

"When Mum's old enough."

He and Cat burst out in laughter. For a horrible moment he tried to rein it in, worried about making fun of Annie, but she smiled at Lachie and mimicked pulling back an arrow and releasing it at him.

When they settled down, he said, "I like you, Lachie, you can come in every day."

"See that, Cat? Two boys in the room and they immediately gang up on me. I need a coffee." Annie poked her tongue at Lachie, who grinned, then she grabbed her stainless-steel cup and headed out.

He rock-saluted Lachie again... who ignored the bonding gesture. *This kid's so cool.*

When Mum's old enough. ANNIE shook her head, still smiling at Lachie's latest quip as she headed for the kitchen. Every classic Lachie moment sewed another few stitches of his heart to hers, making both hearts bigger, sweeter. She had to make the most of his first ten years because the next ten would see their souls slowly drift into separate journeys. The thought stabbed into her belly, or was it the first tummy cramp? Just a little ripple, a warning shot across the navel. Painkillers were in her handbag, but she was committed to the kitchen, almost there.

Swinging into the central foyer, her mind obsessed with the scent of salt and vinegar chips. That first rush when she ripped open the plastic bag. Or maybe she'd go for the Oreos. Pull off one of the chocolate bits and dunk it in her coffee while she licked the cream off the other side.

Loud, male laughter paralysed her.

Before she raised her eyes, before her brain registered the visual confirmation, her ears reverberated with chilling recognition.

Tony Monaro, laughing.

Tony Monaro, who'd dumped her.

Tony Monaro, who'd ditched Lachie as an embryo.

Tony Monaro, who'd dived into a sea of bullshit to escape the ship of fatherhood.

Laughing at some Delaney joke. Usually non-tactile, Delaney had an arm wrapped round Monaro like a best mate until he spotted her, then whipped his arm up and scratched his head. Monaro instantly ceased laughing, his stare turning from stunned to smiling straight off an Italian fashion magazine cover.

Her legs and brain refused to coordinate, but her heart and stomach teamed up to build a solid rock of defiance. She would not crumble with anxiety or give him the morbid pleasure of acting out her anger.

"We just signed a distribution deal for Tony's new independent label." Delaney's pitch hit a beginner's high-F with a soprano sax, eyes darting between her and Monaro. "But he was just leaving."

She'd deal with Delaney later. Her brain and body kicked in for a casual extraction. She'd ignore Monaro and glide into the kitchen like Adele on a cloud.

"I'm hungry, Mum."

Fuck.

Monaro's head whiplashed down to Lachie a fraction of a millisecond before hers. Her biological instincts pulled Lachie in tightly. *Extricate, extricate, extricate.* She couldn't lift or drag him because that would only humiliate Lachie and raise his suspicions, so she shuffled him towards the kitchen door before this potential disaster became a catastrophe.

"Hello, Lachie." Monaro's magazine smile had some soft filter on it she'd never seen.

Lachie stopped and stared at Monaro.

Fuck.

TRACK 9

ANNIE TRIED TO USHER LACHIE BACK TOWARDS THE KITCHEN DOOR— only six, maybe seven steps away—but he'd anchored himself, feet wide, transfixed on Monaro.

She glanced between Lachie, Monaro, Lachie.

Delaney's gaze darted between Monaro and Lachie.

She sensed Tracey and Pierre behind the reception desk both doing a double take.

Would Lachie notice Monaro's hair might be shorter but otherwise the same wavy mocha as his? The hazelnut eyes a touch lighter? Identical pinch-or-kiss cheeks?

Identical pinch-or-kiss cheeks. It's not fair. Nine months she carried him into this world on her own. Almost nine years she'd guided him around it, one hand holding Lachie, one arm pushing as many life obstacles out of his way as possible. Might take him nine seconds to realise he was staring at his older mirror… His…

Monaro took two steps towards them.

Annie's soul called in all the diva spirits who had ever sung, from Aretha to Adele, Streisand to Shania, Etta to Beyonce, and together they stretched her vertebrae to the ceiling, scorching Monaro with a glare.

Monaro stopped, almost cowering.

A slow, steady shake of her head made it clear this was neither the place nor the time for him to stumble into an emotional introduction to his… to Lachie.

"Come on, Lachie, let's get into the good stuff before the lunchtime scavengers. I saw Oreos this morning." Note perfect. *Bless the divas.*

Lachie flowed with her, but the poor little soul couldn't resist a peek over his shoulder before they stepped into the kitchen and disappeared behind the swinging door.

"That's him, isn't it?" asked Lachie, scrunched up on the padded retro kitchen chair, hands strung around his shins.

ANNIE emptied the salt and vinegar chips into a bowl. *Damn Monaro. Damn the weak wuss of a weasel Delaney for bringing the bastard here without any warning.*

She steadied herself, hands on the bench.

"I've seen pictures when he was your manager."

Damn the internet, libraries and memories. She grabbed a packet of Oreos, ripped it open, and dumped all the biscuits into another bowl.

"Said you were lovers."

She needed a few more seconds to regroup, get her head straight, words lined up.

"But he didn't love me, did he? He hated me."

Air blasted out of her open mouth, acid flooding her stomach, torching her heart. This wasn't about her. She turned with the bowls, placed them on the table, and sat on the other corner chair. She put a hand on top of his, but he edged away.

"Sweetie, his leaving had nothing to do with you. Absolutely nothing."

"So you threw him out."

"No, it was his decision. We were young and he was on the cusp of big things in his career and… he was selfish." Criticising his father was against every expert's advice, but *selfish* was a compliment compared to all the other spears she could throw at the bastard.

"Are you getting back together again?"

"No." The speed of the syllable coming out of her mouth created a vacuum of silence, so she stuffed a few chips in her mouth and pushed the other bowl closer to Lachie.

He peered at the Oreos over his knees. "Then why is he here?"

"Business, I guess. Honestly, Lachie, I'm as surprised to see him as you are. I'll let you know anything I find out."

"Promise?" The intensity in his glare was magnified by tears he'd been holding back.

"Promise."

Lachie wiped his eyes with a sleeve, then picked up an Oreo, split it, and licked the cream off.

A sliver of sunny pride sliced through the darkness that had almost overwhelmed her minutes ago. He'd subconsciously picked up the Oreo habit from her. *And his cute button nose.*

ANNIE stormed into Delaney's office and slammed the door, shaking the partial internal glass wall. He was on the phone and waved for her to sit on one of the plush visitor's chairs on the other side of his desk. She stood still, glaring. He turned his chair at right angles, giving her a glimpse of the laneway below and the tagged street art. Still negotiating on the phone, he opened the large bottom drawer, pulling out a huge clear bowl full of sachets of powder, pot, and pills.

Bastard.

She wrenched her gaze off the bowl, focused on the street art through the ceiling to wall window. As soon as he wound up the call, she unwound on him.

"Why did you do a sneaky deal with that sleaze? Why the fuck didn't you tell me he was coming here? Warn me?"

Delaney swung his chair around, plonking his elbows on the desk, and intertwined his fingers. Calmness radiated from his eyes. *Bastard.*

"Please sit down, Annie. I'm not the—"

"You can't trust him. You know he's just using you to get to Lachie."

"Nobody's using me." The anger surprised her. His control under pressure was as legendary as his lusting weakness for starlets. "Last time I looked, this building wasn't operating under the It's-All-About-Annie shingle. It's a fucking business. A public company business. Tony runs a cracker of an indie label in Japan and his profitability puts us to shame. Now, we get a piece of it. A piece that helps pay your wages, all of Lachie's stuff, and your contest project."

She slumped onto the visitor's chair. Delaney wasn't the enemy here. He was barely keeping the old music tanker afloat, while the Merger-Music-money-misers kept pushing him to turn faster and faster and downsize into a speedboat with tanker-sized profit. Not ready to let him off the hook, her gaze explored the room, taking in the glass-covered framed albums and old-time, framed memes with Aussie and global legends. Two huge elephants glared back at her. Monaro's one platinum album with Saint Russell, his one-hit-wonder band before he'd signed her.

And the bowl on his desk.

A surge of need pulsed through her almost as powerful as a real hit.

He picked up a card and flicked it onto the desk near her. "That's his card. As a father who's had three kids messed up because of their vindictive mother, I urge you to speak with him. I'm not getting any more involved than that."

She perched on the edge of the chair, rubbing her thighs. "I don't want the card." She stared at the bowl.

"You sure?" The manipulative bastard hadn't showcased the bowl for nothing. He knew exactly what triggers he was pulling.

But she wasn't going to beg.

He pulled out a sachet of cocaine and placed it on top of Tony's card. "You take both or nothing. That way my conscience is clear."

Calls that a conscience.

"And I had no idea you had Lachie here. Thought I'd knock over the official stuff with Monaro quick and get him out before you surfaced. If I knew about Lachie, I'd have done it down at Letters with a long black and—"

Her raised hand shut him up as she stared at the white powder in the tiny plastic bag on top of the devil's card. Heart pulsating. Fingers tingling. Nostrils flaring...

The white back of Tony Monaro's business card flashed up and down as ANNIE cut up the cocaine on the wash basin bench. One hit. She deserved one hit under fucked-up extremes.

"Annie Vuci, don't you dare." Cat's dragon fire hiss.

She hadn't heard her come in, and now Cat moved closer in the mirror.

Hunched over the bench, she ignored Cat.

"All your Maltese ancestors will haunt you forever if you fall down that black hole again."

"Fuck off, Cat." She straightened the three lines.

The toilet entrance door swung open and closed, the mirror showing Amber's head bobbing over Cat's shoulder. *Perfect. One bornagain angel and one born and bred bitch.* She was sure her parents called her Amber for short. Short for Ambitious. *Now the whole fucking office will know. Fuck them.*

Cat turned to Amber. "Spit yourself out of here and keep your mouth shut or I'll twist on that silver spoon up your arse."

Amber hesitated until Annie straightened up and matched Cat's tone with a glare. Amber backed out.

Now to get rid of angel-Cat. "You need to follow her."

Cat waved a hand at the coke. "Do this because you want to party. Do it because you want amazing sex with someone, but don't do it because of that..." She pointed at the card she was holding. "That douche."

In the mirror, the embossed ink of *Tony Monaro* seemed lit in neon, burning her fingers. She dropped the card and it landed face up next to the three lines.

"Those three lines all point in one direction. Losing Lachie."

Lachie... His name jolted her out of her desperate, needy funk. "Where is he? You were supposed to be—"

"Chill. Robbie's showing him the VR games."

She stepped back from the basin, back from the lines. Cat was right. Again.

"Let's clean up this voodoo shit and then you should take the afternoon off with Lachie. It's stopped raining. Go to the zoo, buy some ice-cream, just hang with him." Cat pulled off a couple of paper towels from the wall holder.

She needed to clean up her own mess. She snatched the paper towels off Cat and scraped the powder in with Monaro's card, crumpled them all into a ball, and dumped it in the bin.

TRACK 10

ROBBIE SHOOK THE REST OF THE JUMBO PACKET INTO THE BOWL ON Manny's desk. He'd researched Manny's Achilles' heel: chocolate bullets. He was more a snakes and jelly babies guy, but gorging on choc bullets wasn't the hardest thing he'd ever done to win someone over.

"Did you know Annie had a kid?"

Manny grabbed a handful of choc bullets and stuffed them into his mouth, nodded as his giant jaws chewed, right hand working the mouse with eyes flitting across the two screens.

Of course. Manny was the information and gossip hub of this place. He was going to be an invaluable friend and should've been on his "Key Allies" list ages ago.

"I kind of bonded with the kid. That's got to be good for me... you know... in terms of me and Annie."

Manny glanced at him, then focused back on his screens.

"I need to do something to make Annie forget that... incident with Ellen."

"Your testosterone problem."

"It's not a problem."

"Condition."

"Not a condit—" Manny's grin stalled him. The big bear was teasing, so he stopped throwing petrol on his own fire.

Manny picked up the bowl and held it between them. "You want to impress someone as sweet as Annie, stop calling Lachie a kid. No kid likes being called a kid."

"I could take him to a movie. Give Annie a break and bond more with the—with Lachie—which bonds Annie."

"Robbie, time to be frank. You're not in her league."

"I know, but with a little help she could step up."

Manny's laugh could bend mountains. Whether he was laughing at his ambition with Annie or his gag didn't matter.

Manny put down the bowl. "Okay, Annie does Latin dancing. Turn up there seven-thirty tonight, focus on having a good time, not on impressing Annie. Might take a few classes but she'll soften."

Robbie's heart sank down to his two left feet. He shook his head. "The only rhythmic achievement I've mastered is the one-three clapping at a live concert. Dancing? Dancing, I'm Jerry Lewis meets Mr Bean."

"That would only impress her more." Manny lifted the bowl and poured the rest of the choc bullets into his mouth.

ROBBIE skirted around the edge of Bachatamigos until a gap in the bench seats surrounding the dance studio allowed him to stand against the wall. The music took the edge off his nerves as soon as he'd stepped inside. Uplifting. Inviting. Teasing. The instructor—Romina, according to the A-frame outside the building—seemed to be conducting the music with floating hips, flicks of her hair, fluttering of her hands. Mesmerising. He'd seen couples burn the dance floor with amazing salsa moves, but Bachata was slower, romantic. More smoulder than sizzle. Romina finished demonstrating the next bit of choreography and her amateur male partner grinned his way back to the inner circle of seven men facing the outer circle of nine women. Most of the class hovered between mid-twenties and late thirties. A couple of older women hid their age and bodies under their urban-Melbourne layers, one guy doing the same under a cap and long scarf.

No sight of Annie anywhere in the old church hall. Maybe she was in the toilet down the back hallway? Romina counted the couples in and they danced while the two solo women mimicked their steps.

Steps.

Choreography.

Dancing.

His muscles melted into jelly, tendons into steel, a clumsy combo for the world's worst dancer. To preserve his dignity, he edged back towards the door for a quiet escape, but Romina saw him, sashayed over, and grabbed his hand.

"Nothing to fear, embrace the allegria." She dragged him into the circle and held on until she clapped. "Change." The couples disengaged and the men moved clockwise to the next woman. Romina nudged him towards one of the women. "Tina, be gentle on him. One, two, three-and-go."

Tina was tiny yet strong enough to drag him through the steps and hold him up when he nearly tripped over his own feet. He tried to be a rag doll and make it easy on her but his body was more like Lego. A couple of guys were laughing at him without missing a step, the most embarrassing moment of his life since the Ellen dysfunctionality thing. Manny had obviously set him up. Kiwi devil.

Clap-clap. "Change."

Tina spun him towards the next victim, layer-woman.

Clap-clap. "Change," was all he could remember. Not the rhythm, not the choreography. *Clap-clap, "Change."*

Manny didn't deserve chocolate bullets. He needed rubber bullets.

"One, two, three-and-go."

Two left concrete-recalcitrant feet, Bachata music, and a competent group of dancers staring. Death by mortification.

"One, two, three-and-change," sung Romina.

Tina swaggered across in leisurewear tights and crop top. He'd survived a full cycle of partners without falling, a major achievement. Fear buried enough to notice the curvy, long-stemmed red roses printed on Tina's black tights and the dangerously high-cropped red crop-top.

"You got some guts, gringo." Tina took his left hand and squeezed him in close, his right hand against the small of her non-sweaty back. Her tiny, strong body manoeuvred him within a vague region of the choreography.

Annie obviously wasn't coming that night, and something about Tina triggered his marketing brain to label her combo *Lusty Latin Leisurewear*. Fun brand, Lusty Latin.

"Nothing taps my inner dance floor like a guy with guts."

"Inner dance floors are my speciality."

"Hah," she squealed before spinning with him in a move that wasn't part of the little routine but tangled their bodies in all the wrong places for a church hall.

First thing in the morning he'd Google "Lusty Latin", and if it wasn't a brand, he'd Trademark it.

Clap-clap. "And change."

ANNIE surged into the foyer of Jovenes Musicales and a parachute of inner peace slowed her to a stop. It wasn't till her third deep breath that she'd recognised Lachie's music school had become one of her comfort spaces. The colourful Argentinian inspired, shiny coloured walls, bright chairs and sofa, and the quirky musical instruments hanging off the walls and ceiling. Latin music gurgled out of hidden speakers, clashing against the riffs of instruments seeping out of the four rooms behind the purple arch, from the potential "jovenes genios musicales", as Diaz labelled his young and loyal music students.

"Hola, madre de Lachie."

She spun around and stared, blaming her singer's instincts, but she was a sucker for a deep, magnetic tone, and Diaz's was one of the deepest and most magnetic she'd heard.

His crescent-moon smile hovered over his orange T-shirt, as he held two large African drums against each red-jeaned thigh.

"I'm sorry I'm late. An accident across the tramline took forever to clear up." True, but she'd neglected the bit about her mind had gone experimental jazz on her since the Monaro encounter and her walkabout had taken her far away from the tramline she needed, forcing her to catch a much later tram.

Diaz placed the drums beside the pastel green reception desk and waved her apology away with a flick of his wrist. "Your lateness has blessed the planet by watering the flower within you." His tanned-since-birth hands indicated towards her head.

Deep in the back of that head she sensed a line being crossed, a fault line. Her hand patted her hair. Of course, he was referring to her damp hair. "Thanks to another unpredicted Melbourne shower, which always bursts out of the sky when I'm *not* under the cover of a tram or building." And she hated wrestling with umbrellas in the wind.

"I have towels," he said, loping towards the office.

Sure he did. Probably a couch or bed too. "No, it's okay. Thanks."

He stared at her like he was searching for another poetic line.

A tremor below the fault line. She turned towards the arch.

"He's practising with the older students. Took him longer to pick up the flow today, so I thought a little peer pressure would be good for him."

Of course, Lachie was struggling with the flow. The comfortable rhythm of his life had slammed into a grindcore rock beat today, questions and uncertainty about his father drumming his heart and brain to a pulp.

"Annie."

Her name. From his mouth. First time. Purred like it had seven syllables.

He ran a hand through his wavy black hair. What was it with Argentine men and ridiculously interesting long hair?

"I need to get Lachie fed and in bed." Safer to be the mother-of-Lachie than Annie-with-seven-syllables.

"Last week he mentioned you haven't been to a gig for a long time. I've got tickets next Saturday to Paris Cat for Tamara— "

"No."

"You don't like jazz or Tama—"

"No, I do like jazz, and I've heard good things about Tamara

Kuldin." *I just don't want this peaceful piece of paradise to become a sleazy pick-up joint. I don't want to go out with my son's music teacher. As of today, I don't want any man in any way on any fucking day.*

He sat behind the desk and wrote on a piece of paper. "Please take my number in case you change your mind."

"Got your mobile, it's on your brochure."

He loped over and held out the paper. "This is different."

She took it from the tip of a corner, compared it with the number in her phone contacts. "It's the same number."

"This time is for personal reasons. In case you change your mind."

Somehow, it ended up in her little backpack. Somehow, her hand ended up in his. He raised it, lowered his face, and kissed her hand. Physically, she was stuck. Her hand in his, his eyes scanning her body. Mentally, she was clear. The fault line had fractured way too wide, and she wasn't jumping onto his side.

"I'm honoured and I'm definitely saying no." Lachie flitted into her peripheral vision. She withdrew her hand and stepped back.

Lachie walked between them without lifting his head.

Her chest tightened. He'd never greeted her with anything less than joy or humour. Ever. He must be embarrassed about finally seeing some kind of personal interaction between her and Diaz despite planting the idea in her barren heart. Who was she kidding? It was disastrous timing. Lachie surely only had one man on his mind since bumping into his father. Poor baby. She scampered after him.

CAT rarely struggled for words, but it was so much easier dragging other people out of stupid holes than scrambling up the slippery sides of your own stupidity ditch. Santi had ignored her for almost ten minutes as he mixed a tune, focusing on the busy bars of lights flickering on the computer screen, hands flitting between the mouse and keyboard. He knew she was sitting in the studio, and he hadn't thrown her out. That was something. She'd needed the time to line up her thoughts. After ignoring her calls, texts, and social media messaging for days, he'd turned up at the centre and plonked himself in the studio. She'd scooted over as soon as she got the tip-off from Kyah.

Santi loosened the headphones from his ears down around his neck, stretched his arms high, and arched his back. Didn't face her.

"Should give me ya secret-ho number. I can spread the buzz on the streets for you. Build up ya biz."

Teasing was good. Typical Santi connection.

"I'm doing okay on the biz front, thanks. And that buzz needs to stay our secret."

His eyes bored right through her. "I seen the real world, Cat. I knows there ain't no angels. But I give you everything about my life." He tapped his head and heart. "Spilled all my insides."

Cat nodded. Part of her ached for the devastating *real* world this fifteen-year-old-going-on-fifty had been dragged through.

"And ya pretend to care like… like a friend. But you hide shit, just like everyone else."

"That's the point, Santi. Nobody's perfect. It's our rough edges, the ones that don't fit the puzzle of normal life that make us special."

"Shoulda told me."

"I like you and respect you, but we aren't best buddies. I don't have to tell you everything. Even my closest friend doesn't know about—"

"'Bout the secret-ho biz?"

She shook her head.

He stared at the screen, hands on his thighs.

"Ain't no judge. And I ain't no blabbermouth."

"Still friends?"

Santi held out his arm towards her and they bumped fists.

"Can I hear your track?"

Santi swivelled back to the screen. "Not done." He placed the headphones over his ears and hunched over the keyboard.

Cat's neck and shoulders loosened, and she stopped bending the strap on her knapsack back and forth. Santi was here making music, not on the street doing deals or hiding from dealers. Maybe her biggest achievement yet. Building schools in education-starved countries was important, but she didn't get to see the end results, not for ages, anyway. With Santi, every minute he was here, every note he created, was a major step. She'd watched him blossom and her secret-ho secret would stay a secret.

ROBBIE never planned to have sex with Tina. The Bachata class mission had been all about connecting with Annie. Except elusive Annie wasn't there, Tina was. All of Tina. Slinky curves and dark, soft curls, green eyes and *slinky* curves. He'd resisted her request for a lift home until she made it clear she wasn't returning to that class. Bachata was too slow--give her some fiery Cuban salsa anytime.

Somewhere between her first lunging, plunging kiss—before he'd even started the car—and her roaming hands while he fumbled with unlocking the door of his bungalow, his moral GPS had cleared the path for Tina landing in his bed. He owed Annie nothing. Not yet, anyway. Tina pushed him through the door, wrapped him up in arms and a leg, his back to the wall, without disconnecting their lips. If Annie was half as good a kisser, he'd marry her.

Stop thinking about Annie. You need all your intensity and energy with Tina.

He wrapped Tina's other leg around his waist, picked her up, and headed for his bed.

"I knew you had a fire. Tonight, I'm going to give you—"

He tripped over something on the floor, stumbled, and just made it to the bed in time to drop Tina safely and roll next to her.

Tina giggled. "Just like your dancing."

Robbie knew exactly what he'd tripped over. "You okay, Johnny?"

"Is Johnny built like you? Is he joining the party?" asked Tina, not a hint of fear in her husky throat.

He flicked on the bed lamp. Johnny sat on the floor, back to wall, thick legs splayed in front in his usual black chinos. His trusted Walkman rested on his pudgy tummy, clutching three plastic portable CD holders to his chest with one hand and wriggling off the big head-phones with the other, making his wiry hair messier than usual.

"No way I'm three-waying with this bozo," said Tina.

"He's no bozo, he's my brother."

Johnny pointed at him. "He ain't heavy, he's my brother. Hollies 1969. Neil Diamond 1970. Zoolander 2001, Hollies and Rufus Wainright."

Robbie winked at him. Johnny's encyclopaedic music memory always amazed him.

"Whoa, Rain Man, keep that Google shit to yourself. I'm Ubering outta here." Tina bounced up, patted her crop top down, which gained maybe one millimetre, and headed out.

No point hustling after her just to yell. The rude thing didn't deserve any more of his time or energy. He shrugged off the bed and plonked next to Johnny.

"She thinks I'm stupid."

"You're not stupid, Johnny. You know more about music than me." Johnny officially was a year younger than him but was mentally a nine-year-old, except with music. He peeked at the open CD case Johnny clutched. "Eighties?"

"Nineteen eighty-four. 'Dancing in the Dark' the biggest selling single in Australia. The Boss."

"The Boss." He nodded.

"Mum at lunch." He kept nodding, but his head became heavier with each nod.

Mum at some pub. On the pokies. With no clocks. His dad worked the mines in Western Australia three weeks every month and the other one at home he slept. Or at least he kept his eyes closed. Eyes that used to dazzle Robbie with light and humour. He was determined to never let life dim his light like his dad. His power had to be self-sustainable. Johnny was the main reason Robbie stayed on his parents' block in this half-decent timber bungalow. Someone had to be around for him. It was a key reason he wanted to run his own business one day. One day soon.

"Sleep here?" asked Johnny.

"Of course. I'll fix the couch."

He dragged himself up and over to the cupboard to dig out Johnny's spare PJs and doona. Turning with arms full, he watched Johnny struggle turning the sofa-bed into a bed. Despite all the challenges loaded on Johnny from birth, his little bro had no idea how much of a saviour he'd been for Robbie. His mates thought he wasn't taking responsibility for his own life by using Johnny as an excuse, trying to be the balance of normality for his young bro. They didn't get it. Johnny was *his* anchor to normal. His touchstone. His earth.

Who knows what shit he'd be under in this crazy biz with his bloody ego if he didn't have his little brother? Even tonight, Johnny had saved him from sleeping with a woman that didn't deserve his time. A shallow, sexual experience just because Robbie could. Just because he got all the good physical and mental genes. No question, he owed Johnny. His brother's accidental intervention that night was another sign he was meant for better things.

Like Annie.

TRACK 11

"THIS IS THE MUSIC BIZ, LEAVE YOUR COMMON SENSE AT THE DOOR," SAID Delaney.

ROBBIE's fingers couldn't type the wisdom fast enough, the screen on his tablet heating up. He'd print the Delaney nuggets and stick them on his "future board" at home. Part philosophy, part warning to the world for where he was heading, including the inevitable launch of his own management business. He was lucky to have been let in the door at Merger, let alone get this kind of access to the Godfather of Oz music. He'd sweat blood for Delaney and when he was ready, when he had his first two or three acts signed up he'd—

"Nothing turns me on more than the smell of fresh ambition."

Was he that transparent?

"There's no one in this fucked up biz I can't introduce you to." Delaney tapped his own tablet, then head. "And not a private number worth knowing that isn't in here or here."

He was that transparent.

"Even the ones I fucked over take my call. Know why?"

He shook his head.

"E.G.O. In their heads they're all artists, all part of the illusion. That's their most creative work, convincing themselves they're only

77

doing it for the art. Delusion. Every artist craves massive recognition all the fucking time. The Hooks got it right. Ego is not a dirty word, it's the engine that drives the whole machinery."

Maybe he'd overestimated Annie. There must be a way for him to channel into her artistic ego, find a door from there into her heart or at least her desire. "And we provide the sustainable pipeline of ego fuel."

Delaney stretched back, smiling, hands behind his head. "Yeah, just throw them scraps that feed their soul. Soul is their substitute word for ego." He scooped a glass bowl from his bottom drawer, plonking it on the desk. "Of course, for a little insurance, throw them some treasure. White gold dust and shiny pills. Their brains spark just looking at this stuff."

He stared at the shiny, packeted substances. When it came to sex, drugs, and rock 'n' roll, he'd avoided the middle bit. Wild, in-the-moment sex? His gift. Rock 'n' roll? In his blood. Drugs were a line he never stepped over or took. Nothing puritan, the scene just made him uneasy.

"Cost of business," said Delaney.

"We cover this under entertainment expenses?"

Delaney winked. "Here's another from my top forty. If you don't like a song, tell 'em it's got potential. Every song's got potential—you can rewrite the whole fucker if you have to."

He pushed Annie to the back of his head and typed.

"Here's another one. You're a unique talent. They'll lick your palms for more. Everyone's talent is unique right? Some are just shit."

Grinned. Nodded. Typed.

Delaney hit a button on his own tablet. Music filtered around the amazing speaker system in the office, some kind of RnB hip-hop thing. A generic female voice joined the generic sounds and beat.

"What do you reckon, Rockin' Robbie?"

Is this a test? The answer was so obvious it worried him. Was this one of his shit starlets or was Delaney expecting some clever insight? He decided honesty was safest.

"Nothing special about the music, not even a hook. Voice is vanilla on beige. No contrast, no emotional—"

Delaney's hands flung from the back of his head to the desk, landing with a thud. He stood. Robbie's memory flung back to primary school and Mr Stubbs--the nicest grade six teacher ever but grew like the hulk if you tested him.

"Stephanie is a unique talent and she's my new... girlfriend. Her track has to be in the top ten of the contest this week. Follow me." Delaney headed to the door.

The war zone in Robbie's mind battled against the need to avoid challenging his boss. His invaluable guru on one flank and the ferocity of Cat and Annie on the other, if he'd agree to manipulate the contest for Delaney's latest wannabe.

Delaney opened his door a fraction, smiled, then pulled him in to see the view.

Stephanie flowed like sexual silk to whatever she was listening to through her earbuds and the phone in her hand. Any nightclub door bouncer would let her jump the queue.

Delaney closed the door, one eyebrow raised under a double-barrel shotgun glare.

"She's got potential," said Robbie.

"When poverty is obliterated around the world, after peace in the Middle East, North Korea are a democracy, Australia accepts all refugees, and we have an Aboriginal prime minister," said CAT. No way was Robbie going to bump off a legitimate song entry for one of Delaney's desperate-teen-starlets-of-the-month.

"As Delaney's now official puppet, surely you can see if we let this happen once, he'll expect it again and again," said Annie.

"I promise that won't happen," said Robbie.

"You don't have the power to make that promise."

"I have to pull rank this time, sorry."

Cat flopped her hands and arms like a puppet. "I can see the puppet strings, Robbie. Social media will crucify us and the contest."

"Next week you can—"

Annie's mobile buzzed, and they all stared at it. She picked up. "Yes, this is Annie. Now? Ummm... sure, thirty minutes." She threw the phone in her knapsack. "Gotta go. School. Gotta go." Annie scurried out.

"I'll sacrifice one of my picks for this week," Robbie said to Cat's desk, not daring to face her.

She watched Annie disappear, barely remembering the cause of her anger at Robbie. Hadn't the poor woman had enough life junk thrown at her these last couple of weeks?

"And next week you can have an extra track," offered Robbie.

She shrugged and gave a half-nod. A song contest was nothing compared to anything that might have happened to Lachie.

Poor Annie.

"Graffiti?"

Wilma nodded, lowering her grey eyes.

ANNIE's eyes darted around the principal's office. Wisdom filled the bookshelves, a glaring, intimidating reminder she was way out of her depth. The first time she'd been invited in by Wilma created a warm buzz of a shock. Her Lachie had been recommended for the accelerated learning programme. She didn't even know the school had one. No warmth or buzz this time.

"Can't be Lachie. What about the other—"

"He confessed. Insisted he wasn't coerced." Wilma seemed more embarrassed at being the messenger than she was about Lachie's divergent behaviour.

Wasn't coerced. That's a Lachie kind of Google word of the day. She slumped into the fabric chair, a hand spread across her chest, but it gave no warmth or comfort from the ice cubes pouring into her gut.

Wilma pushed a tablet to her side of the desk.

She edged forward. Photo. The inner wall in the toilets with two lines: *"If you follow all of their rules, there's nothing left for you to choose."*

Wilma swiped the page to another photo.

"Sometimes the world is a liar." Just inside the door. All hand-painted. Maybe a thick art brush. Black.

"He said it was all from a song."

Her song.

"forget the rules." *How did he find my old demo CDs? Monaro's bloody face threw poor Lachie in a spin and now he's throwing my own lyrics in my face. Lyrics from a song she wrote when that douche bag Monaro was her manager for a micro-moment.*

"How was he able to steal the art brush and paint? The school should have tighter security in—"

"Annie, let's not get caught up in the how or even the what. Let's try to understand the why."

The ice cubes inside her shattered into icy gravel.

"Has anything major happened in Lachie's life recently?"

"No." Hyper-quick, falsetto "no". False "*no*". Icy gravel scratched and grated and numbed.

Wilma's eyes lingered, warm but steady, searching for something more. "Okay, if there hasn't been a major trauma, have the two of you fought over something? He's a bit young to rebel like this, but gifted children continue to surprise us."

She shook her head, temporarily not trusting her voice.

"We'll monitor his behaviour and performance. He may not even know why he did it." Wilma stood.

Annie picked up her knapsack and clutched it to her chest. "That's it? No punishment? I can take him home now?"

Wilma stepped close, her skirt, blouse and casual, short blazer gave a kind of conservative Camberwell feel with a scarf that was all cheeky Fitzroy vibe. Hard not to like the woman.

"He had to clean the wall and already served a detention at lunchtime. You've done a brilliant job with Lachie, I'm sure this is just an aberration." Wilma held her arm with both hands as they drifted to the door. "Do you think Lachie might benefit from a male influence he respects? Is there someone who—"

"He absolutely does not need a male influence." Fire roared from her head through every fibre, melting the icy gravel. She stormed out of the office.

ANNIE gripped the edge of the kitchen bench.

"Agh!" Her left arm cramped up. She stumbled away from the bench and massaged the taut, painful muscle that hadn't cramped since her teenage obsession with the piano. The pounding drums from the music room were dulled by the soundproofing yet still gnawed at her head. Lachie had dumped his schoolbag and dived straight into the music room, his usual *"I'm so starving I could eat a giraffe"* snack— Nutella sandwich and huge mug of Milo—sitting on the kitchen bench, untouched.

She opened the fridge to get the remaining stubby of cider, glanced at the two empty bottles next to the rubbish bin, and put the stubby back in the fridge. Getting smashed wasn't going to win her Mum of the Year awards. Hell, she must be on minus-a-million points. Inaugural winner of the "Mother of the Youngest Student to Ever Graffiti at his School" award.

Bloody Monaro. Life wasn't perfect with Lachie, but it was damn close the last couple of years. They had a routine, enough money, each other. Functional with an emphasis on the "fun" part. Then Monaro sneaks in, sticks out that size-eleven boot, and trips Lachie's whole world. *Fuck him.* He didn't deserve Lachie, and Lachie sure as hell deserved more. She had to get her son back on track.

Music. They had always bonded through the magic of music. She shook her hands and arms to loosen them up, straightened, and worked through a few repetitions of her breathing exercise. *Connect through music… get him talking… he's super-smart, we'll spin through this.*

Lachie smashed the drums so hard ANNIE didn't know what would break first, the skins or sticks. She couldn't even make out the underlying tune, if there was one. Rock-rage evidence lay scattered on the floor. She stepped over half a broken stick, picked up the bongo, and did her best to match his furious beats.

Lachie stopped cold.

She stopped.

Lachie launched again, more manic.

She tried again with the bongo.

Lachie stopped dead, eyes on the skin of the drum.

Lungs tightened a noose around her body. Heart burned from the lacerations of his silent whip. She wanted to pick him up, drop him in the corner, take over the kit, and attack it until she made the skins bleed, steel bend, and her hands blistered with agony.

She put the bongo down and shuffled out.

Drums and symbols blasted her through the door.

Crunch. Cat cracked another walnut. "Pathetic. In this moment in feminism, a principal tells you Lachie needs a male role model."

ANNIE reached for the steel nutcracker and picked up two walnuts from the bowl on the couch between them. Cat had insisted on coming over as soon as Annie began venting on the phone and turned up with a bag of organic walnuts. Annie had been craving salt and vinegar chips, but there was something therapeutic about the tactile crunching of the nuts.

"And she's a woman!" Cat's tone could have cracked a walnut.

"Can't believe it. Not from Wilma," said Annie.

"Blister sister."

She raised an eye before cracking a nut.

"Works so hard to get into a position of power, then goes all soft on the patriarchy, becomes a pain on feminism."

Blister sister. She grinned at another Cat classic as she picked at the nut fragments and munched.

"Let's make a list of all the important things he can learn from a male role model. How to interrupt a woman, how to treat a woman as an object." Cat cracked a nut.

"How to ignore a woman's opinion." Annie cracked a nut.

"Never understand or communicate your feelings."

"Make sure you have the most important ego in the room."

"Use your anger to justify physically hurting a woman."

She cracked a nut and it splintered over her lap, couch, and floor. Cat's sarcasm drove them up a depressing lane. Her period was peaking just when she needed it least. Typical. She needed to lie down with the old wheat heat pack Cat had bought for her from Vic Market. Her head pounded with waves of pain at the thought of facing Lachie in the morning.

"I'll crash on the couch, help get the dude to school in the morning."

Bless Cat's soul.

ANNIE pulled the doona back to uncover Lachie's angelic sleeping face. A sweet sigh soothed her soul. This was the Lachie she knew. The drumsticks protruding from under his pillow made her smile. He was still dedicated. And he chose to release his anger and confusion on the drums. That was healthy. Safe. She gently pulled the sticks out and a piece of paper slipped out.

A print of a magazine photo of her with Monaro.

Nine years ago. Seeded with Lachie, but tummy not showing.

Annie had to prop herself on the wall. Her own confusion swirled with a guttural ache for her son. This wasn't just about her and her... selfishness. The poor kid had a natural craving to meet his dad. Know his dad. Love...

Cat had shared so many horrible stories, nightmares, about children on this planet having to survive without a parent. Many without any parents. What right did she have to deny Lachie access to his father? Maybe wise Wilma had nailed it. No matter how much her inner conflict fought it, it was time to gently, slowly facilitate Lachie's time with a male influence.

TRACK 12

DING-DONG.

Disaster. ANNIE let go of the frying pan, straightened, stuck. The green numbers on the digital clock in her microwave glowed neon-like. Seven-zero-zero. Seven already? This was going to be a disaster. Should've listened to her gut.

Ding-dong.

The doorbell had somehow amplified to AC/DC decibels.

"Lachie, he's here. Right on time. Get your little butt out of your room."

Who comes right on time? She might be rusty on dinner etiquette, but she remembered that one. It was polite to be late. She quickly checked her hair in the oven glass. Best place to check hair—it never looked bad in the dark oven glass. But why was she checking her hair? This wasn't about her, it was for Lachie, who'd disappeared as soon as he heard who she'd invited to dinner.

"Lachie, *now.*" She took a couple of deep breaths, flipped off her apron and flung it onto the hook next to the fridge, then strode to the front door and opened it.

He looked different, maybe because he was out of the familiar context. Safe context.

"Buenas tardes, Mother of Lachie," said Diaz, a smile arced across the bottle of red and flowers in his arms held out.

Better Mother of Lachie than seven-syllable Annie, feminist sisters be damned. "Hey, Diaz, come in."

Lachie didn't come out of his room because he wasn't in his room. He'd smuggled into Annie's room and snuggled up in her bed, in his pyjamas, reading. Hadn't done that since he was five and his message couldn't be any clearer. Wasn't worth the battle. Plus, Lachie's intentions—planned or accidental—provided the safety valve in case she needed one from Diaz. Because the non-date dinner with Diaz had become exactly what she'd tried to avoid... a dinner date with only Diaz.

Not a total disaster.

She'd kept it casual by setting up on the kitchen bench with stools at right angles. The kitchen table seemed too crammed, intimate, and no way would she do dinner with Diaz on the couch. A few times the banter edged towards the fun zone, tripping her into laughter, but she was always catching herself, conscious of Lachie's nearness. She enjoyed the verbal sparring with an interesting adult, and by dessert, the wine and Diaz had combined forces to release her inner brake. Following one of his travel anecdotes about Columbia, they laughed loud. In harmony. Laughed in harmony then stared in silence.

Intense silence. Diaz not grinning or smiling, some otherworld contentment oozing out of his dark, chocolate eyes, body hovering over her corner of the bench. Silence that clanged inner alarm bells and clawed at bits of her body. Her "chill" selection had shuffled into EKKAH's "Last Chance to Dance", torturing the silence.

She found herself leaning towards Diaz—

"Mum, we forgot to pack for the excursion tomorrow." Lachie stood in the doorway, schoolbag in one hand, book in the other.

Her brain tried to scurry back from wherever she'd left it, scrambling for words.

"What are you reading?" asked Diaz.

"Book."

"Do you read a lot?"

"Lately."

"We can get snacks for your excursion on the way to school tomorrow. Set your alarm for thirty minutes earlier." She'd found a response, but her tone pitched high and raspy.

Lachie rolled his eyes at her, swivelled, then trundled back down the hallway.

"Who'll set your alarm?" *Slam*. At least it was *his* bedroom door.

She'd wasted a night on an idea that was always doomed to fail. Inviting Diaz was Lachie's idea, but she'd been clinging to delusion because Lachie's original suggestion for her to find "a number two" had been gazumped by seeing his dad Monaro. She stared at the wall clock to prepare her excuses for ending the... the dinner.

"Too much allegria." A dental poster smile under *that* hair. "We should do it again. Next time, my place."

In another lifetime, maybe. Her brain was slamming down shutters, but her body was opening for a festival. *No. No way.*

"I'm sorry about Lachie's behaviour, and this wasn't a date."

"Perfect. We can still look forward to the anticipation of our first date." Diaz's smile amplified.

She swung off her stool and realised the bad strategy of sitting on the end of the bench. Handy being close to the sink and oven. But Diaz stood between her and the front door. She kept her gaze between the hallway and the floor.

He spun around, loped to the front door, and stepped aside to let her open it.

She squeezed around, brushing both shoulders against the wall. Any contact with him now would be too much contact. Too many signals to misread.

"I'm sorry, Diaz, but I don't want a relationship." She said it to the door, then opened it.

"Then I look forward to you floating into school with Lachie. Buenas noches, Annie."

Seven-syllable Annie.

He skipped down the steps, placed one of those dark arms on the metal gate, and jumped over. Jumped over like an elite athlete without straining the fragile hinges. Strong, smooth, sizzle.

Disaster.

CAT didn't understand how her screen became so blurry. It was new and fine a few minutes ago. Hunched forward on her desk, head sculpted onto her hands, she read the words again. The blurring didn't slow her as she'd infused the words into her heart.

Why Have Me At All.

Title and hook line of Santi's new track. He'd emailed the lyric under the subject line: *Top Secret – Only for Secret-Ho Security Clearance.* All the message had: *track not dun yet.* The humour came to a crashing halt from the first line, each word stabbing her heart and slapping her soul. Lines so personal, so emotional, you couldn't turn away. Addictive agony. Musical masochism.

A cry—no—a tortured scream to his parents. If the music and melody were half as good, it would become a classic.

"Too dark. We can't include that in the lyricist and muso part of the comp."

Robbie. Why was…

"What the hell are you doing spying on my private email?" She closed the screen and swivelled in her seat.

Robbie backed up to his desk. "I… I… wasn't spying. I asked what had you so mesmerised and you just nodded."

"Rubbish. I didn't hear you and therefore I definitely did not nod."

"Sorry, I didn't mean to make you cry."

She raised a hand to her face, felt the dampness. No wonder the screen was blurry.

"And what's with the Top Secret Ho stuff?"

Cat sprang out of her seat. "Fuck you, Robbie fucking Marketing Boy. Fuck you." She stomped out.

Just as Annie slipped in. "What bullshit have you pulled to make her cry?"

She heard Robbie spluttering some rubbish in a guilty, high pitch as she headed down the hall.

Fuck him.

"You've got a volunteer CV that makes Melinda Gates look like a rookie Girl Scout," said Annie.

CAT swirled her ginger and lemongrass tea, blowing on it. She sensed Annie was skirting around some point. "That's the nicest thing anyone's said to me this year."

Annie dunked her choc-mint biscuit into her hot chocolate.

If anyone else on the planet did that across the table, she'd drown them in their hot chocolate. But Annie wasn't teasing, wasn't showing off. She loved her sweets, and sugar seemed to have a special relationship with her.

"But even Melinda doesn't put all her foundation's eggs into one charity omelette."

"Working with Santi is the most rewarding thing I've ever done. To see his talent, his confidence slowly evolve..." She took in a long, deep breath. "Not just the way he connects with music, he's reconnecting with himself."

"I just don't want you to... to run out of eggs."

She could never understand. Annie's parents were always there when she'd needed them even though Annie rebelled like a demon. Annie didn't know Santi the way she did. Something inside her was shifting, like he was helping her find her long-term direction. Not sure where, but for the first time in her life, she was thinking about more than the next three months. Her parents' conservatism drove her crazy, but in hindsight, they had laid out an easy life for her. Why did she deserve that? Why did kids like Santi or the thousands across Africa not deserve that? Which reminded her, Annie had a bigger issue closer to home.

"Have you thought about letting Lachie meet Monaro?"

Annie put a half-eaten choc-mint biscuit on the saucer, leant back into her chair and glared like Pink would glare at Harvey Weinstein if he'd *accidentally* walked into her changeroom.

"Okay, sorry." Where did that Monaro line come from? Was she even being defensive with Annie now? Or did Santi's lyric trigger something deep in her inner world?

"Bathroom." Annie shuffled out of the kitchen.

The silence tapped away at her conscience. *Why was I so cruel? Why —*

Bzzzzz, bzzzzz. Bzzzzz, bzzzzz...

Annie's phone rattled on the table. She jerked upright on the edge of her seat. The caller ID, *'Drum Teacher'*, flashed with the vibrating.

Bzzzzz, bzzzzz. Bzzzzz, bzzzzz...

She should stay out of it. Hadn't she stepped over enough lines today?

Silence. Good, he could leave a voicemail and Annie could deal with it. But Annie wouldn't deal with it, she'd ignore him, put herself and her body last again.

Bzzzzz, bzzzzz. Bzzzzz, bzzzzz...

She grabbed the phone. "Hello, Annie's phone."

"Oh, hola, Diaz. Annie's washing her lunch stuff at the sink. Hang on." She took the phone away from her mouth and projected towards the other side of the empty room. "It's Diaz." Back to the phone. "Sorry, says she's got to clean up and rush to a meeting. Oh, wait." Phone away. "Bachata? Tonight? Right." Back to the phone. "She'd be happy to see you at her Bachata class tonight. Playa Cafeteria, seven. Yes, the old church. Gotta run, adios." She placed the phone back on the table. It lay there quiet and innocent. She was smug and buzzing. Helping people was her thing. Annie would thank her for this one day. Maybe not today.

Annie swayed in. "Chocolate makes the world go round, Cat." She picked up her half-eaten choc-mint biscuit and finished it, squeezing her shoulder.

No grudges, instant forgiveness, the friendship moved on. Bless her sweet tooth.

"I'm really sorry, Cat. I genuinely thought you agreed to let me read your screen," said Robbie, hovering inside the doorway.

"Robbie, I'm sorry. I misunderstood what happened in there," said Annie.

The saccharine sweetness was making her ill.

"Oh, that's okay. Um... are you going to your Bachata class tonight?" said Robbie.

Annie shot eye spears at her, then back at him. "How did you know about my Bachata class?"

Robbie stumbled a half-step backwards. "It was just a fluke. I'd been wanting to take up some sort of Latin dancing and I tried the one at Player Cafe."

"Playa Cafeteria. But how did—"

"Talking to the instructor, Romney."

"Romina."

"Yeah, Romina. Told her where I worked and she mentioned you were a regular there."

Cat winced for Robbie, who was obviously lying, and for her own indiscretion with Diaz a few minutes ago. Annie was going to have two male stalkers there tonight and she was responsible for fifty percent of the problem.

"I won't go back. I don't want to spoil your privacy." Robbie backed away, head bowed like a rejected golden retriever.

"It's okay. I don't own the class. Let's see what moves you've got." Annie stepped close to him.

The pup looked terrified.

"Here's a free lesson. Don't ever lie to me again. I'll deal with Manny later. See you on the floor, Mr Marketing."

Robbie nodded, or maybe he was shaking, terror branding his face. He turned and disappeared down the hall.

Annie shook her head. "Can you believe the gall on that boy? As if he could hide the truth from me."

She grabbed the plate of mint-chocolate biscuits, waving them in front of Annie. "You better sit down, something I've gotta tell you."

TRACK 13

ANNIE HAD ALMOST CANCELLED THE WHOLE THING.

Bachata classes were her sanctuary. The one place she could lose herself in sensual music and movement without the nagging pressure to perform, no creative chisel chipping away in her head. Flirting a little was fun too, but male interaction was always safe as dancers had to move onto other partners, and Romina kept a tight dance floor when it came to unwanted advances from testosterone terrorists.

Cat's deviousness killed her mood but not her rhythm. Her temporary trust but not their friendship. The perfect forgiveness gift was obvious—Cat had to join the class to watch her sanctuary being turned into a circus. Perfect, because Cat suffered from dance floor phobia. Couldn't dance to save a starving child.

Cat's face as she stumbled and bumbled her way around the room almost made up for her inviting Diaz.

Almost.

Watching Cat stumble and bumble when she was partnered with Robbie did make up for her inviting Diaz. Determination to master the choreography cemented her face as each male partner survived Cat's wooden movement then somehow reached another level of intensity whenever it was Robbie's go. They turned Romina's simple but sexy

Bachata moves into a slapstick farce. The harder Cat tried, the more frustrated she became.

Served her right for her major wrong.

Forgiving Robbie for his stalking became easy because of his fun spirit. Smiling and laughing at himself at every mistaken turn, stumbling spin, and awkward shimmy. It was almost endearing.

Almost.

At the end of the lesson, Romina turned up the music and encouraged everyone to freestyle – use the moves they'd been taught but forget routines. All the other women twirled hair and fluttered extended eyebrows towards Diaz, the undoubted male star of the class. The three times they'd been paired up during the lesson, their bodies flew way past flirting. She was a natural and enjoyed Bachata, but Diaz was a Bachata beast. Argentine men must learn rhythm in the womb and the art of dance floor seduction by the time they finished kindergarten.

She couldn't stop her body sparking as Diaz strutted his hair, tight jeans, and loose shirt towards her, then her lateral vision caught Robbie running from the other side of the room.

Running.

From the other side of the room.

All eyes focused on him, even Diaz stopped to see what the hell Robbie was up to. About ten metres away, Robbie dropped to both knees and for a moment slid towards her... but his trendy jeans were cut in the trendy places. Shiny kneecaps stuck to the shiny floor and whiplashed him forward, his face completing the sudden braking manoeuvre.

Ecstatic laughter shattered through her, violently shaking out the tension wound up inside. Her cruelty triggered a domino effect around the room.

Robbie pushed himself up groggily into a sitting position. Despite the bloody nose, possible broken cheekbones, potential concussion, and a roomful of people laughing at him, he raised both arms and rock saluted her. She dropped to her knees and rock saluted back. The more she laughed, the bigger his smile.

Almost endearing.

ANNIE came out of the toilets composed, no guilt. Whatever Robbie had got himself into, *he* got himself into. Cat peeled off latex gloves and packed up the first-aid box as Robbie slumped on the velvet couch, holding ice in a towel to his forehead. His nose had two bandages stuck across, leaving his mouth open for breathing. Diaz lingered at the opposite corner near the exit with three female students hovering like seagulls. Romina clicked away at a laptop on a table beside the door.

Annie headed for the temporary emergency ward and plonked on the couch at a right angle to Nurse Cat and her patient. "Lucky Cat learned some skills on her international projects."

"Lucky his head is tougher than the floor." Cat took the ice from a grinning Robbie. "Any longer and you'll freeze the few brain cells remaining."

"That was some show," said Annie.

"Classy as a clown at a funeral," said Cat.

"Glad you liked it," Robbie said in a nasally strain.

"I could like you, Robbie, but… you probably don't know that track by Jake James," she said.

Robbie nodded gingerly. *"She just wants to be friends, I hate that line, I hate the way it ends.* But I probably won't remember this conversation, I think I have concussion."

"I could write it on your forehead with ice," said Cat, reaching for the ice.

He grabbed Cat's wrist. "Okay, I get it."

He seemed to hang onto her wrist a little, and she didn't resist. Something in Cat's eyes. Sympathy?

Cat jumped up. "Leave your car here. Take an Uber or I'll finish the job on behalf of the floor."

"My Uber can drop you off too, as a thank you for this." Robbie waved a hand around his face.

"Thanks, but I've got a better ride. See you two Latinos tomorrow." Cat strode over to Romina, who stood to greet her, taking Cat's hand and guiding her to photos of her performance dancing hanging on the wall. As Romina pointed at photos, she let go of Cat's hand and slid it around Cat's waist.

"She's got layers," said Robbie.

She nodded. Cat certainly had layers, but she sometimes wondered how many were organic and how many were just plastered on. The seagulls had given up on Diaz, but he lingered near the exit. Sizzling lingering.

"Guess he wins," said Robbie.

"Actually, I'm going to talk to him about a song."

"A Jake James song?"

She nodded.

Grin. Smile. Glow. You could cut a man out of the competition, but you couldn't cut the competitor out of the man.

ANNIE tightened the scarf around her neck. Melbourne winters were moderate except when the wind chill blew through. Short leather jackets weren't made for defending against wind chill. Damn fashion. Damn her occasional weakness for fashion. Damn Diaz, who didn't even have a jacket, his loose shirt fluttering like a flag, hair floating in waves. Still, it was better to clear the air outside, just thirty steps from the tram stop. *Ding, ding, ding.* The bossy tram bell sounded some distance behind her, probably at the traffic lights.

"It's really simple, Diaz. I don't want a relationship." The truth, but it was also a no-way-out for the guy. If he didn't want a relationship, he was admitting he just wanted flesh. If he wanted a relationship, he dug the hole bigger.

"I don't want anything you don't want." Not a hint of mischief in his voice or eyes.

Her mouth stayed wide open. She'd been ready to throw out one of her prepared lines but not prepared for his *"I don't want anything you don't want"* line.

"You want to sing, I'm happy to pay," he said, indicating a circle with his finger pointed at her face.

She snapped her mouth shut. Waved to Cat as she waited for Romina to lock the big doors.

"No, I don't want to sing." *Yes. You. Do.* Screamed her soul.

"Good, because I don't want to sing either." Mischief sprinkled from his eyes, slinking into her lungs and belly. "I like our silent harmonies."

Ding, ding, ding. She turned to see a car edging out of the tram's way while doing a cheeky U-turn, just fifteen metres away. She turned back to Diaz.

"That's my tram." She scooted the thirty steps to the stop just in time to catch it, needing to get her thoughts back on straight rails.

ANNIE glided down her street, which she usually did after Bachata class, yet this time the eleven-minute walk from High Street seemed to take only three or four strides. Noisy teenagers and the stop-starting of the tram ride didn't dilute the memory of Diaz's mischievous smile. Not one bit. It was warmer too; the wind must have died down. Melbourne! She'd thought about taking her jacket off on the walk home, but couldn't be bothered carrying it. Reaching for the gate latch, she had no doubt at a different time she might open the gates for Diaz but—

"Ciao, my Bella Stellina."

Only one breed of human called her that.

Italian in a baritone Aussie accent.

Her back extended to its full height and an inner wind chill froze her vertebrae, set her jaw, her hand arranging the house key as a weapon between her fisted fingers.

TRACK 14

ANNIE LET GO OF HER FRONT GATE AND TURNED LIKE A ROBOT.

Must be International Stalk Annie Day. First Robbie and Diaz crash my Bachata oasis, and now Monaro, outside my home.

The Diaz flirting buzz fizzled, and all the tension that had been danced off during the class returned with a vengeance.

Monaro stood between his open door and the car. Light from inside washed over him like a soft spotlight. Professional photographers would have been proud of the accidental effect. Helped him look twenty years younger, and for a moment, she was thrown back to their first meeting. A white, open neck shirt, black leather jacket, tight black jeans, loose smile, and those shiny pinch-or-kiss cheeks. She lowered her gaze to the front grille of the car, desperate to drop the memory. Dotted LED lights and sporty bonnet suggested the perfect ego-mobile.

"Ciao, my Bella Stellina?"

She was no one's beautiful starlet anymore. Never was. Maybe the bastard had already been inside. She whipped her head to the lounge window, but Lachie wasn't peeking through the curtains.

"Don't worry, I'm not stupid."

She let his last word swirl around the silent street. Monaro closed the door and walked to the pavement, stopping a couple of metres away.

"I'll get a restraining order if you don't leave now."

"It's me, Annie. I'm not here to hurt you or steal Lachie."

"Then go."

"I want to prove to you I can be a good dad. I want to share his life now."

"You ran away from that right a long time ago."

"They were wild days, but they're a part of our past."

"There's no *our* past."

He glanced at the house to remind her of the eight-year-old elephant inside stomping all over her delusion.

"I'm calling the police." She fumbled for her phone.

"Okay, okay. But I'm going to do whatever it takes to show you Lachie is the biggest deal in my life now."

"How convenient. Mr Sperm Donor is ready to step up after—"

"Annie—"

She began dialling.

Monaro shuffled back, hands raised in the air, palms out. Annie spun and flicked the gate latch. *Ouch!* A knuckle on her right finger jagged on the steel mesh. Monaro's car purred to life behind her. She dumped her knapsack over and fumbled with both hands.

"I don't want to do this through the courts, but I do want time with Lachie." Monaro leaned awkwardly across the passenger seat, window wound down.

She focused back on the latch. It opened, she bounded up the steps, and was greeted by Aoham.

"I have triple-zero ready," said the babysitter, poised to click on her phone.

"Close the door and don't watch through the curtains," she said, handing over her knapsack. She reached inside the entrance, grabbed the brand-new baseball bat, then stalked towards Monaro.

"Can't we just talk? Twenty minutes, just—"

She wielded the bat over her right shoulder without breaking stride. Felt good. Damned good.

"Jesus, Annie." Monaro flicked the ego-machine into drive and squealed the tyres down the street.

ANNIE made sure Aoham was safe in her Uber before closing the front door. She winked at the shiny bat in the corner. Who needed an intervention order on a douchebag when you had a baseball bat with attitude? Adrenalin poured through her veins, pounding her heart. She placed a hand on her stomach and steadied her breathing. A stab of pain from the injured knuckle broke through the adrenalin rush. She sucked at the trickle of blood, headed to the bathroom for a Band-Aid, but stopped when she saw a note taped to Lachie's door. He often left a funny or cute message when she was out late. Her inner buzzometer redlined again, this time without a burning edge.

That's my boy, back on track.

She tip-toed over, staying close to the wall, not wanting to wake him with creaky floorboards, then read the black printed note on white paper.

"Adults Only – Mothers Don't Qualify."

"A shit song isn't like manure, Robbie. Nothing good's going to grow from this track," said CAT.

"You're gang-voting me," said Robbie.

"We're just focused on the best outcome and if you use an inappropriate line like that again, I'll solo yank you through the high court of sexual harassment," said Cat. She looked to Annie for support, but couldn't attract her gaze, let alone a nod. Something was roasting inside Annie. She'd picked around the edges earlier, but couldn't get any meat.

"Okay, I'm sorry, but you've been smashing me like I killed Prince," said Robbie.

She caught the fireball in her throat before she spat it at him. Robbie was right. She had been overly aggressive, projecting her anger on a personal issue in a business meeting. Disappointment dripped on her pride.

Romina. Sultry, sexxxy Romina. Her flesh was still tingling in the morning and she'd anticipated another Latin-passion session before breakfast, but Romina had dressed and escaped by three-thirty, evasive about seeing her again. Wouldn't even give her mobile number, saying it was best to contact her at her dance studio. The flat, stiff business card with sharp corners the opposite to her curvy, swaying exit. Wasn't the first one-night stand in her life and she didn't lower herself to the social tags like *walk of shame. Stride with pride* was her philosophy, yet something jagged in her belly that morning.

"What's wrong with it?" asked Robbie.

She stirred out of her muddy thoughts. "Huh?"

"What's wrong with the song?"

Stubborn with a capital STUB-for-a-brain.

"It's trying to be an urban hip-hop rap track with a country melody for a hook, but it's like someone's dragging a thick white rope through my ears and pulling on the beat."

"Agree," said one-word-this-morning Annie.

Manny stuck his head in the door. "Good news. I'm personally on hold for the top ten that was due five pm *yes-ter-day*. FIVE PM YESTERDAY."

They were behind on last week's entries, arguing about the top ten that were supposed to be published online in an hour.

"Bad news. My team's all been diverted to the launch of the *Amazing Merger Music Collection* and I won't get this week's songs to you till Friday night."

Manny copped the triple cannon.

"Can't work another weekend," said Robbie.

"How can we do justice to eighteen hundred tracks in a couple of working days?" asked Cat.

"That's fucked." At least Annie had progressed to two words.

Manny pointed up in the direction of Delaney's office, shrugged his shoulders, and loped down the hall.

"Right. Your diluted Keith Urban/Eminem derivative shit is off. Annie gets the extra pick with that pop-ballad, Trust."

"I'm not comfortable with that and only accept under—"

Delooney blitzed into the room, waving his tablet high. "Social media hits are dragging. Stagnation is the enemy of progress, fertility for failure, don't ever forget that. You need to listen to more of Robbie's ideas."

"And you need to stop sabotaging us. This contest will eventually make a ton of money in new writers and material. That dust-collection album that all the team is working on will sell like a Christmas song at Easter."

Robbie didn't back her up; he backed up to the wall with his chair, probably afraid of the verbal shrapnel about to explode out of Delooney. Cat sensed Annie staring at her, but she glared at Delooney.

Who glared right back.

The printer in the corner whirred, the fan on her computer hummed loudly, music filtered through down the stairs from reception. Foreign sounds swimming in the silence.

Delooney grinned. "I do love a bit of Tabasco in the morning." He waved his tablet in her direction while glancing at Robbie and Annie. "Guts and creativity… can't beat it. Bring it back into this contest and you won't see me down here again." He strode out.

Annie followed him out, knapsack over her shoulder, and without turning around, mumbled, "Personal thing."

ANNIE stared at the thick document, the rectangle of paper with a bull clip sitting uncomfortably on the asymmetric, chunky, carved coffee table. She edged back into the plush armchair, arms wrapped around her chest. "Why did he send it to you?"

"Only lawyer he knows that's represented you," said Jordana.

"Against him."

Jordana nodded. "Unsuccessfully."

"You were just trying to fix my mess." And Jordana had done it pro-bono. Fought Monaro and his lawyers like it was her own management contract she needed to rescind all those years ago.

"He's trying to intimidate you, that's his soundtrack. But it is serious. The papers were lodged with the Family Court and this copy arrived about ten this morning." Jordana tried to pep her up with her straight white teeth that layered perfectly with her straight black hair and brown eyes. Jordana represented some of Australia's elite artists and bands. Unfortunately, Annie hadn't found her until it was too late back then. She'd lusted and trusted Monaro, signing his *"This is the standard term"* ten-year contract without blinking.

"This is surreal… and déjà vu-ish."

"His nine-year absence swings heavily in your favour. However, he did send substantial financial support and you kept burning the cheques. By the way, that took a ton of guts and integrity."

And stupidity. She could have done with all his money to fight him. Now he was steamrolling for fifty-fifty access, as if Lachie was a robot who could reboot his whole life to fit in with Monaro's latest whim.

"You know I'd love to help, Annie, but family law isn't my kind of music." She pushed a business card across. "Call Jenny, she's a sharp tiger. Beware though, the Family Court process can be lengthy and expensive."

She picked up the card, the Bourke Street address smelling of top-end fees. Fees she couldn't afford. Her shoulders tightened for a fight, and she sat up with a steel vertebrae. Whatever it took. Whatever she had to do to beat the bastard.

"I've got dirt on him. Stuff the Family Court couldn't sweep under the rug."

Jordana's eyes narrowed from sparkly wise to spiky wary. "That's dangerous territory. First, it's hard to package up as neat evidence. More importantly, does he have dirt on you?"

Dirt. Mud. All kinds of shit. He'd introduced her to most of it. She didn't want Lachie to hear about that phase of her history, not at his age anyway, and she would never play the victim. Ever. Her mistakes, her wild, desirous ride.

Jordana leant forward, elbows on knees hands clasped, almost in prayer. "My advice as a friend—talk to him. Do everything you can to avoid dragging Lachie through the court."

Dragging Lachie through the court. Her shoulders and back melted, body moulding back into the chair.

Dragging Lachie through the court.

"No," said Delaney.

"No to a loan, or no to the advance on my salary?" said ANNIE.

"No and no."

She'd met with Jenny Sharp-Tiger-Lawyer and was super impressed. Jenny backed her feeling that temporary pain for Lachie would be better than long-term brain messing by his father from Mars. She'd done her sums, just needed the retainer fee to let Jenny off the leash. She'd pick up part-time jobs to pay the rest of the cost, however long it took. Even teach singing.

"You brought the bastard back into my life, you owe me." Her gut tangled up tight as soon as she blurted the words.

Delaney picked up his thick Mont Blanc, wrapped it in his fist, and stabbed the writing pad in a slow, torturous tempo. "One way or another, you fucked each other without any help from me. I had no problem lending you the money for Lachie's teeth. Or the money for his drum kit... which has turned into a gift." He let that sink in, then beat a faster tempo with the pen. "But I will not help keep a child from his father. Not when the father isn't a junkie or violent. My ex-wife-rhymes-with-knife"—he stabbed his pen harder—"cost me seven precious years with my daughter. You insist on keeping Lachie from his dad, you're on your own." He dropped the pen onto the pad and pushed the pad away.

She marvelled at the strength of the Mont Blanc pen cap. Could she take a beating like that? Over Lachie?

"Friday feast to feed a beast." ANNIE placed the tray on the coffee table.

Lachie glanced at the bowl of ham and cheese nachos, three hot dogs plus mustard and ketchup, then swung his unimpressed face back at the TV. Normally, he'd dive for the nachos before the tray landed.

"I'll get the drinks. Prince Lachie can relax where he is, just turn that thing off."

She returned with the bottle of Coke and glasses and squished her way onto the couch. "Come on, it's Friday night. No tech or TV." A three-year ritual that Lachie loved and she cherished—homemade fun-food, soft drinks, and silly hijinks, which more often than not ended up in the music room.

"It's not a law," he said, eyes on the screen.

"It is in this house."

"Can't force me." He grabbed a paper plate and a sticky bunch of nachos. Cheese strings fell onto the table, but he ignored the mess.

She reached for the remote; he grabbed it and dropped it on the other side of the couch. Anger and fear swelled into a ball in her throat. No point giving Lachie more fuel for his Monaro fire. She should let it be, release the tension and chill.

"It's only fun if we both agree. I won't force you, but I am asking you nicely because these little traditions are special. Please turn off the TV."

"Bet my father would let me."

She dumped her plate, hot dog rolling off, smearing mustard and ketchup on the table over Lachie's sticky cheese strings. "You don't know a thing about your invisible father. But lately you've been just as selfish as him."

Lachie threw his plate at the TV and stormed into his room.

Bang.

ANNIE rolled the once white, now greyish bed sheet gently off the upright piano, then folded it carefully to minimise the dust fall-out. Pulled the timber and leather stool back, running her finger over the engraving on the side. *"For my darling Rianne, who makes music for my heart. Love, your Ommy."* Her mum's inscription and gift, part inspiration, part anchor. She'd dropped the "Ri" from her name first year at

VCA High School to cut the maternal chord and avoid comparisons with superstar Rihanna.

She hadn't told her mum about Monaro's reappearance yet, determined not to spoil her parents' Malta holiday because her mum would rush back on the next available flight. Maybe she'd sneak in a Skype call while Lachie was at school. No. No more loans. No more *I told you so* bashings. Her mum detested Monaro as her choice of manager, never trusted him, while her dad spat at the whole rock scene. He could never reconcile his diamond daughter with the rough rock rebel she'd become. They regretted every cent spent on her piano and singing lessons. Lessons her mother wrecked the car on. Their inner rage externalised when she fell pregnant.

Her mum and dad had developed a balancing method of doting over Lachie while treating her like a family insurgent. They'd softened over the last few years, once her commitment and consistency with Lachie was clear, but she always sensed an IED around the corner. An improvised emotional device that would blow up the common ground created by grandparenting. The piano was a direct link to her parents' angst and her creative outlet. Hence, the heavy sheet to help keep her away. Like an AA mentor. No songwriting till that Monaro contract was done. But she'd hit a wall with Lachie, and didn't want anyone's advice or consolation. She needed to reconnect with her true self and was drawn to her piano, the extension of her soul.

She shook her hands, took a deep breath, and let her fingers find the chords. A couple of the keys needed tuning on the Yamaha, but the old girl sounded okay. Muscle memory was a miracle of human physiology. A half-decent original chord progression flowed out of her hands and onto the keys. A melody poured into her heart and she was humming it before she realised. Played her way into a gravity vacuum, floating on a cloud of elation, blown by the wind of pent-up creativity.

"I'm sorry, Lachie, I'm so sorry. You should throw me in a dusty quarry. I'm so stupid, oh, so stupid. Sometimes my brain is convoluted." She sang the words to the sweet melody, larynx straining after a nine-year slumber. She'd left the door open and heavy curtain pulled back. Maybe he'd hear her, if he wasn't buried under headphones.

She repeated the silly ditty, each time adding vocal texture and piano riffs.

Lachie sat beside her. She stopped singing but kept playing. He picked up the melody. "You're not so stupid but your lyrics are, you're not so stupid but your lyrics are."

She added harmonies and a couple of scats.

Lachie flowed with it. "I'm so sorry, I'm sorry too. You should pack me up, throw me in the zoo."

Her smile reflected in his sparkling eyes. She'd missed his sparkling eyes in the last couple of weeks more than she'd missed performing in the last nine years. She stopped playing and he wrapped his arms around her. She wrapped right back.

"I just want to know what he's like."

"I know."

"You'll always be my number one-est."

Her tears dripped onto his shoulder. "I'll talk to him."

"I love you, Mum."

His arms tightened, squeezing more air out of her lungs. "I love you too, Lachie. More than anything, ever."

TRACK 15

"LACHIE, CAT'S HERE!" YELLED ANNIE. SHE HELD THE FRONT DOOR AS Cat breezed down the hall.

Lachie bounced out of his room. "Hey, Cat, I've been playing online so you better be ready to get smashed today." Hearing his energy and humour again re-tuned the natural song of their home.

"You go set it up and we'll mix the pieces together." Cat handed the box of Mahjong tiles to him and he scooted off to the lounge room. Cat had learned Mahjong from some Malaysian guy on some international charity project. Annie liked it, not because she was any good at it—she was hopeless—but because it was a tactile kind of game that kept Lachie away from a screen. Good habits she was determined to establish before screen addiction could become an issue, the number-one fear amongst most parents she knew.

"Bye, Lachie." She picked up her shoulder bag.

"Bye, Mum!" he boomed from the lounge room. No hug or silly face, but the tone was sweet.

Cat walked with her to the front gate, placed two strong hands on each shoulder, diva focus intense. "You're doing this for Lachie."

"I'm doing this for Lachie."

"You're not going to take any shit because you are the best mum ever."

"I'm not taking any shit because I'm the best mum ever."

Cat squeezed her shoulders, then waved at a newish red Corolla edging down the street. Cat had insisted on paying for an Uber rather than letting her take public transport to the meeting with Monaro, mumbling something about being dropped off at the front like a diva. She eased into the back seat, which felt weird, usually being a front-seat-friendly passenger, but for this shortish trip she needed a gig-like preparation.

I'm doing this for Lachie, I'm doing this for Lachie, I'm doing this for Lachie...

ANNIE didn't care what her hair looked like from the gusty wind, she needed to get out of the Uber a hundred metres before the hotel and fill her lungs with fresh air, loosening limbs and tension. The judges that voted Melbourne the World's Most Liveable City seven years straight had obviously never strolled through one of the city's wind tunnel streets in late winter. Her leather jacket didn't cope despite being zipped tight, but she didn't want a heavy coat that she'd need to remove in the hotel. The jacket was staying zipped up, as she had no intention of impressing or distracting Monaro. This was all about the best for Lachie.

That's why she'd chosen a Saturday afternoon and the shiny lounge area of a chrome and marble five-star pretentious city hotel rather than a cosy Collingwood cafe or funky Fitzroy bar. Bars and cafes that had shared half their history. No mixed signals. No mixed cocktails. No mixed agendas.

I'm doing this for Lachie.

Monaro. Early. The pin-up poster for being *fashionably late* was early. He looked at home—even though he hated these places—at a table next to the floor-to-ceiling window, sitting in one of the two armchairs.

Whatever the fresh, short walk achieved, her shoulders tightened and her hands clenched inside her jacket pockets as she anchored inside the entrance. The bastard would take great pride in matching the colour of his leather jacket, an identical darkish brown to hers, his a longer trench coat style rather than her cropped trend. Just a fluke, it meant nothing. She strode over and slid into the chair opposite.

For Lachie.

"Hey, Annie."

"Hey, Tone." *Fuck. Hey, Tone? Fuck emotional muscle memory and other psychological relationship quirks.*

A twinkle in Tony Monaro's eye and perhaps the tiniest curve of a grin, but he didn't ram home her slip into their prehistoric comfort zone. "I'm glad we're rocking with this as friends. All the child psychology books I've read stress how important it is to not use the children as weapons. They all say we need to be friendly for... for his sake. They—"

"They aren't Lachie's mother."

"But I am his father."

"Only a technicality."

When anger took over Monaro, like it often had, he became outwardly calmer in the first phase, stiller, eyes sweeping slowly like spotlights, not darting, not narrowing. He'd be difficult to read in business meetings, yet she'd seen through his cover from their first hiccup.

A waiter saw silence rather than tension and took it as an opportunity. "Can I get you a drink, madam?"

"No, thanks, I'll stick to water." She pointed to the jug on the round table and he filled her glass.

"Another mineral water, sir, with fresh lime?"

She'd guessed vodka lime and soda. A non-alcoholic drink had to be part of his carefully orchestrated show.

"I stopped drinking three years ago."

He must've seen the surprise on her Wikileaks face.

"Doctor's orders?"

"Yes, but not what your spiky tone suggests. I started getting pancreatitis after we... Anyway, it's horrible pain that rips around your stomach and lower back in waves. Put me in hospital on a drip and morphine three times. It can be triggered by gallstones or excessive alcohol."

"I would have put my money on your liver collapsing or blood pressure exploding your heart." His smile framed by a burnt orange T-shirt with red Japanese characters and the brown jacket stirred sympathy and opportunity. "Pancreatic cancer is lethal. Does this mean you're a high candidate?"

She waited for the smile to clamp and the other signs of rage, but he just ramped up the wattage. "Opposite. Thanks to the whole pancreatitis thing, we're monitoring my pancreas regularly. No booze, better diet, actually feel better than ten years ago."

He did look good for forty-two, and she'd had to show ID at clubs until she was twenty-five. She wondered if Lachie would be that lucky with youthful genes. The warm thought turned to a tinge of anger for acknowledging Monaro had any role in Lachie's make-up or future.

"Parenting isn't something you can delegate... float in and out when it suits you."

"I moved into a house near Lachie's school so I can help out with drop-offs and pick-ups."

Marrow in her backbone turned to ice. "You're stalking us now?"

"No. I'm on the city side."

Of course. The more expensive city side. The bastard was assuming he'd steamroll his way into Lachie's life.

"A three-month lease? Before your next discovery needs you on another international adventure."

He took a sip of his drink, condensation from the tall glass dropping onto his T-shirt.

"No more rock adventures. Bought the place." He peered at her over his glass as he sipped. "And I've delegated stuff in my business so I don't need to travel or be at gigs.

"Maybe Lachie will take the house one day."

"You don't know a thing about Lachie."

"I hear he's a talented drummer."

Bloody Delaney. Probably brought it up so he could brag about the drum kit he'd bought for him.

"He feels the beat and has a natural touch. But he's too smart to be a muso and too honest to be a manager."

"I'll always feel a failed manager because the best talent I've ever worked with stopped singing."

"You stopped working with that talent. You gave up on her."

"I believed in you more than you did."

"Which explains why you ran to Tokyo."

"I didn't run, Annie. I signed you to a ten-year contract and three months later you're pregnant and talking about schools."

"So getting pregnant was my fault."

"It wasn't part of our plan. My business was taking off, it wasn't time for me to settle."

"Settle?"

"I didn't mean settle for you, I meant settle down."

"In Japan with your green-haired version of Yoko Ono. You hypocrite."

"You weren't exactly Mum-of-the-Year material back then."

"Fuck off, Monaro."

Typical. His first instinct was to look around and see who was in hearing range. Image, image, image.

She made it easier by red-lining the decibels so anyone could hear her on the roof-top pool, fifty-two floors up. "Fuck off with your lawyers and bullying and all your bullshit short-term-champion-father shit. Lachie's a great kid and he's a great kid because you weren't around to mess up his life. If you really cared about him, you'd just fuck off and leave us alone." She flew out of her seat and stood over Monaro. "Again." She spun and stormed out through the sliding doors held open by a switched-on doorman who gave her the slightest bow.

ANNIE didn't slow her pace until she reached the park fifteen minutes from home, over ninety minutes from the city hotel. Walking was the underrated magic of the world, her go-to meditation in the absence of music. Late on a grey, windy afternoon, the park was deserted apart from a man walking a dog in the distant corner. Someone was always walking a dog in some corner of Melbourne. She stopped in front of the giant elm tree, its leaves thrashing and waving, some falling loose and flipping about in the wind.

She was envious of the leaves. A yearning to flit about in the air, free-falling and landing on new ground safely until the next gust of wind picked her up again and sent her on the next mystery tour.

Ping-ping. Ping-ping.

The phone message alert grounded her. She unzipped her jacket and removed the phone from her pocket. Three missed calls and one voicemail message, all Monaro. Hadn't heard them due to traffic and her walking trance. She highlighted the message and hovered her thumb over *Delete* but hit *Play* and put the phone on loudspeaker, not wanting Monaro's voice anywhere near her flesh.

"Annie, you're not thinking straight. In ten or fifteen years, you'll lose Lachie when he learns how you kept him away from me. Please, Annie, I'll tear up your contract so you're free to follow your music. Just give Lachie the chance to decide."

She deleted the message and the missed calls. Typical Monaro, bribery and manipulation. If he was genuine, he'd have torn up their contract years ago. She headed off, putting the phone in her pocket just as it started ringing. Monaro. She answered it.

"Now you are stalking and I have the proof on my phone and I'm walking to the police." She'd deleted the proof, but the bastard didn't know.

"Sure. You explain that to Lachie."

More Monaro manipulation. She hung up and shoved her phone into her pocket as deep as it would go.

Ring-a-ling, ring-a-ling.

"I'm filing for an intervention order, you harassing bastard, and I'll make sure Lachie knows exactly what kind of junkie bully you are. Now fuck off and choke on your ego."

"Annie?"

Seven-syllable Annie. Diaz. Shit.

"I'm sorry, I didn't think I was harassing. Lo siento, lo siento."

"Diaz, I thought it was someone else."

"You need help, Annie. I come now."

"I'm okay, just…"

"If this isn't a good time…"

She stared at the loose elm leaves spinning in the wind.

"Perfect time. Text me your address."

Diaz opened the front door of his terrace house looking the plainest and sexiest ANNIE had seen him in a white woolly jumper, blue jeans, bare feet. She nearly came at the huge bare feet.

"Welcome to mi casa."

She pushed Diaz back into the hall, unzipped and dumped her jacket on the floor, back-heeled the door closed. His eyes held hers for way too long, then he gazed over her nipples bursting through her bra and T-shirt, down her waist and jeaned legs, then slowly back up. She stepped forward, latched her hands around his neck and wrapped her legs around his waist.

"Take me to your room. Now."

"My palacio del paraíso is your—"

"And shut up." She kissed him, hard.

TRACK 16

CAT'S YEAR NINE PE TEACHER HAD BRANDED HER RUNNING STYLE *"LIKE A rabbit riding a rodeo horse. Arms, legs, ears, and head flailing all over the place. You're never sure what's going to land where."* The laughter in the gym, including from her so-called friends, had lacerated deep into her bones. She could've reported him for bullying, but made a deal instead. She wouldn't attend any more PE classes and he wouldn't mark her as absent. She had moved on and achieved whatever she'd achieved in life always in a hurry but never in need of running. Until tonight.

Sally-Anne from the centre had called. Usually a model of velvet calm, the tension in her voice was unmistakable. Santi was missing and had left an envelope on the recording desk for Cat. His twin brother, convinced something bad had happened, had whooshed in frantic, manic, and whooshed out. She didn't even know Santi had a twin brother. And what was in the envelope? Lachie's babysitter didn't answer her call. Neither did Ellen. Desperate to get to the centre, she called Robbie and roped him in to look after Lachie.

The tail end of evening peak hour traffic was a nightmare due to a car accident. The tram trundled so slowly it may as well as have been going backwards. She jumped from the tram three stops early and ran like a rabbit on a rodeo horse until she burst into the centre.

Sally-Anne put her hand over the phone and yelled through the glass partition, "I'm calling other centres and contacts. Envelope's in the studio!"

She dumped her satchel on the floor and stared at the envelope sitting on the edge of the mixing desk. Handwritten scrawl: *For Cat only.* Volunteer work had forced her to face starving children with bloated stomachs, the eyes of young girls who'd been raped, mothers wailing for teenage sons forced to fight a war they didn't understand. That familiar, horrific queasiness seeped through her as she stared at the envelope. She grabbed the office chair, caught her breathing, desperate to slow it down, then straddled the chair backwards, the black fabric backing offering a shield from the contents of the envelope. As her eyes adjusted, she noticed the envelope wasn't flat, felt the hard small item inside, opened it and took out the USB drive with a note: *"Why Have Me At All. I'm done."*

Not a suicide note. His song. Done.

Warm air gushed deep into her lungs, slowing into her normal rhythm. Couldn't help smiling. He'd probably gone underground because he was nervous about her reaction. He'd finished his first song and she helped him get there. She spun around in the chair giggling with relief, giddy with pride. Spun and giggled, holding the back of the chair like a rabbit riding a rodeo horse.

Boys. They were just boys.

ANNIE's head stopped throbbing as she unclenched the sheet in her left hand and the corner of the pillow in her right, resting it on top of her breasts, heart thumping like a heavy metal bass drum. The young guys she'd pulled in for her sexual needs over the last five or so years were just boys. Vehicles for release versus a worshipper of Venus —Diaz. Argentine Diaz. He floated her body through the Parana River, dragged her through the Valdivian forest, flew to the top of Aconcagua, and then blasted her out of the Iguazu waterfalls.

Sure, there'd been men who'd gone down on her before—and it was mostly fantastic—but Diaz had gone down on her a second time… after a tornado of fucking in a million positions… and this second time was just for her. Dehydrated and exhausted, he insisted on spoiling her one more time. Her legs slid down from the angled reverse V position, feet collapsing sideways. The dictionary needed another word for orgasm, one that covered this intense other dimension she was coming down from.

"That grin looks like the pussy who got a dozen canaries," said Diaz.

She covered her mouth with the sheet. Even Diaz the Venus Worshipper had to have his ego stroked. Why couldn't he enjoy the magic of lingering, wallow in the glorious silence of post-paradise paradise?

"Do you want bacon or smoked salmon with your scrambled eggs in the morning?"

Men and food. Eating was a universe away from her mind. Linger. That's all she wanted. Didn't need anything else going into or coming out of her body for a year, maybe a decade. She twisted her head.

Propped on an elbow, his hair looked as ridiculously good as ever, framing a grin and sparkly, proud eyes.

"I'm not staying."

"Who's going to dig you out?"

She smiled. Her body did feel moulded deep into the pillow-top mattress.

"I'll cook bacon and you can make a choice in the—"

"Have to get home before Lachie wakes."

"His instincts were good."

Her face must have scrunched up in a question.

He waved a hand between them. "He was keen for us to… to date."

"This wasn't a date." Not now, not in the foreseeable future would this become a dating thing. "And this"—she mimicked his hand gesture between their sweaty bodies—"would never have been on Lachie's mind." Plus, Diaz had no idea about Lachie's dad tripping onto the scene and she didn't feel like explaining. She spun her legs off the bed and stood, then plonked down again, her head spinning. Gasping, she did some quick, deep breaths. Her head steadied.

"I'll get some water," he said and scurried out of the room.

"Okay." She dressed quickly before he returned. One strange thing about Diaz—and she was sure more strange things would show themselves over time, they always did—no clock in the bedroom. She fished her phone out of her jeans and didn't have time to be shocked by the time—three fifty-three am—because the messages from Cat pulsed at her like beacons. She listened to the most recent one.

Anger and concern lashed through her head and veins. *What could possibly be so important that Cat had to leave Lachie with Robbie? Robbie!*

"Here." He passed her a small bottle of still water.

"Thanks." She grabbed the bottle and raced out the bedroom, down the hall.

"Did I say something wrong? Annie?"

She flew out the front door and slammed it behind her. No excuse. Absolutely no excuse for Cat to do this. Entrusting Lachie with *ROBBIE*. First she'd save Lachie, and then sort out that self-centred-borderline-ex-best-friend.

CAT spun in the office chair faster and faster and faster. She caught the image of Sally-Anne in the studio doorway and let the chair slow down.

"He finished his song. His first song."

Sally-Anne slouched on the door frame, head drooping.

She stopped the chair spinning with her bare feet on the carpet.

Sally-Anne raised her head, her long honey curls parted like a curtain across her face, revealing tears flooding down her cheeks.

"What's wrong?"

TRACK 17

Scrunched up on the floor, back to the wall, Cat starred at Santi on the chair, hunching over the recording gear. She could feel his gliding movement, smell his roll-up tobacco. He was there just the other day and he'd be back. Had to be back. She'd guided him to explore his natural music talent, helped him get his first part-time job, accidently shared her secret part-time job, *"Secret-ho biz."* She'd helped him rediscover his sense of humour, too. The world was finally shifting to fit Santi in, his baggage locked away in a deep vault, freeing him to be the full Santi. To live his life. Sally-Anne was wrong. The police were hopeless.

Not suicide.

Not Santi.

Not now.

The door flung open and Santi bustled into the room. She knew it, they were all wrong. She sprung to her feet to hug him, then froze. Santi was different, couldn't keep still, pacing around the studio one second, bouncing between his feet the next. Same clothes, same backwards cap, eyes frenetic.

Sally-Anne came in. "This is Gio, Santi's brother."

"This all on your head," he said, his eyes stilled for a moment, pupils like thin tiny slits slaying her, then back to his frantic pacing. "You gave him hope. Hope is the killer drug. Don't take much to overdose on hope."

Sally-Anne stepped close to her. "Gio, Cat respected Santi and his—"

"Respect? Respect." He spat out the words. "How can someone from your pretty palace life respect us? You know shit. Givin' up on the world is our zone, how we survive. You pimped Santi with hope… fancy words like mindfulness and goals and… dude couldn't handle the mountain of hope… jumped the bridge."

Her knees crumpled, but Sally-Anne wrapped a strong arm around her waist. *Jumped the bridge.* Reality diluted every molecule of her body into jelly, flooding her stomach with acid. *Santi jumped the bridge. Dead. Her fault.*

"I'm sorr—"

"Shove your pity up your hope pipe, bitch." Gio scurried out.

Sally-Anne eased her back to the spinning floor. Everything was spinning. Cat tried to close her eyes, but the flooding tears wouldn't let her.

"Your phone," said Sally-Anne.

She caught her ringtone, tried to say forget it, but only wails escaped her mouth, loud and deep, like from another person. Seemed like hours till she settled. Her stomach and throat hurt, eyes stung. Sally-Anne still hugged her tightly. Drenched in silence, her body barely able to fight gravity, she needed to curl up in a ball in the dark.

Twang, twang-twang. The rock riff of her guitar ringtone shook her bones.

"I'll get it." Sally-Anne scrambled to her satchel on all fours, took out her phone, looked to her. "Annie."

Annie. Lachie. Probably angry about leaving him with Robbie. Her head screened horrible visions on her raw soul, with a rap soundtrack screaming, *Jumped the bridge, you pimped him dead, bitch. Jumped the bridge, you pimped him dead, bitch.* She reached for the phone. An angry Annie would be a relief.

ANNIE stroked Cat's hair. She always joked that Cat could curl asleep on a coin, but tonight Cat shrivelled into a full stop on her couch, heavy head on her lap, eyes staring past the two empty vodka bottles. This wasn't the time for *I told you so.* Probably never would be a time. Cat had her causes. We all have our skins, shields that protect our self-image and lead the way we touch the world. According to an article she'd skimmed, humans renewed their skin every month yet underneath, the essence of who were are remained the same, barely changing from decade to decade, if ever. Cat cared, always would, no matter the cost, but this time the cost skidded beyond comprehension.

Slouched on the armchair, Robbie stared at the same two bottles. Bottles that hadn't poured any logic on the horror nor provided even a minor diversion. Annie had found him asleep on the chair and Lachie on the couch, the Mahjong tiles not packed away, then called Cat as soon as she'd trudged Lachie off to bed, anger deep-frying until Cat blurted out her horror news.

At least Cat had time to tidy her kitchen before she left, although she didn't realise it had been untidy until Cat had done her thing. "Thanks for sparkling up my kitchen."

"That's okay," said Robbie.

Robbie tidied my kitchen?

Slight head movement from Cat as the surprise penetrated her fog of pain, then back to the bottles.

Fire began to creep up her throat. This guy shouldn't have been anywhere near her house, let alone touching her daily domestic bits and pieces. He hadn't earned the intimacy, the trust. Then reality swamped her anger. More important stuff needed her attention, like Cat's guilt-loaded agony.

She twirled Cat's short blue strands around her finger. "You're staying here tonight." No response from Cat meant acceptance. She turned to Robbie. "You can't drive."

"I'll Uber. Pick up the car in the morning. Can take you to—"

"We're not going to work tomorrow. Cat needs—"

"I'm not an invalid," said Cat, lying on her couch like an invalid. "Too many songs in the contest for two."

"Let's decide in the morning."

Robbie rose.

"You should crash here, must be after four," said Cat, rousing upright, wrapping her hands around her shins.

That was effectively twice Cat had invited Robbie without checking with her.

Robbie checked his phone. "Three forty-five." Glanced at her, head tilted down.

He looked exhausted. They were all beat, even before the draining torture of the night.

"You take my bed, I'll stay here with—"

"No one is stealing your bed, Annie. Robbie can choose the chair or beanbag. I don't need babying or protecting."

Welcome back, Cat. Any Cat spark was a positive Cat spark in the scheme of things.

"Thanks. I'll get some blankets." She headed into the hall shaking her head. That was Cat. You felt you needed to thank her just for sleeping in your own bed.

ROBBIE was drifting to sleep when Cat started crying. He straightened, rubbed his eyes, and focused. Sobbing into the doona covering her mouth, Cat's soft, needy gaze triggered an ache to support her. But how? A pat on the shoulder? Briefest of hugs? Some words from the safety of distance? They were less than two metres apart. Too weird to ignore her—borderline cruel—but he could still feel the icy blood dripping off Annie's warning before she'd crashed in her room. *Touch her, I kill you.* He should get Annie, or a box of tiss—

Cat pulled back the doona and patted the couch.

Touch her, I kill you.

The warning haunted him even though he had absolutely no intention of touching her, other than the minimal gesture of a professional colleague in basic supportive mode. He shrugged off his blanket and rolled off the bean bag, covering the distance in a half crawl, then straightened on his knees when he got close to Cat.

Shit. His usual morning monument of pride prodded inside his jeans directly at Cat's eye level. Cat's open eyes level.

Erection.

Embarrassing.

Erotic.

Cat's lips moved but his inner mortification drowned out her words. He bent forward, twisting to hear better, relieved he could partially hide his navel. Cat wrapped a hand around the back of his neck, dragged him close, and kissed him. A passionate lips and tongue kiss. Like her life depended on it kiss. And he couldn't resist. A blood moon orbital kiss, so intense it knocked him senseless.

Cat released him and he heaved air while his twin self stared down on them confused, stunned. Cat unbuttoned her checked flannelette shirt.

Touch her, I kill you.

Cat's hand on the back of his head, pushing him into her cleavage. "Stay, please."

He fought every instinct his testosterone had trained him for, needing a moment of clarity, sanity.

This is wrong. She's drunk, depressed, I've got to—

Cat snored.

Her hand dropped from his head and he eased back. Cat snored like a horn section paid by the decibels, the sweetest sound he'd ever heard. He braced against the couch, head on the edge of the fabric to help suppress his laughter. He could record Cat's cacophony and get someone to turn it into a dance track.

Then he drifted back to the crazy kiss.

What the fuck just happened?

TRACK 18

ROBBIE SAT BACK ON HIS HEELS, MORNING LIGHT STREAKING ACROSS THE duvet protecting Cat from her waist down. Magic light that made her look vulnerable and kind of cute, in a Cat-cute kind of way, which was definitely not his kind of cute. Nuh-ah. He could even stare at her exposed breasts without... without... He reached for the duvet, needing to cover her up before Annie woke and got the wrong idea.

Cat farted. Loud and deep, like a donkey with an amplifier and a street-rapper's sub-woofer.

Robbie dropped the blanket, shocked at the intensity. Would've won the comp in a soccer change room. Laughter gurgled low in his belly, building for a release. He stifled sniggers with one hand over his mouth and fell forward, forehead bouncing on the old velvet couch.

"You sleazy bastard."

Robbie whipped up and around at Annie who stood over him Hulk-like.

"What, huh? What?" Cat sat up, oblivious to her open shirt.

"This sleazy bastard was—"

"I was just pulling the duvet up to cover her when she..." Cat half asleep, magic light, vulnerable. "When she started snoring and I nearly burst out laughing and—"

"I don't snore," said Cat, sitting straighter.

"Did he undo your..." Annie waved at Cat's chest. "While you were sleeping?"

Cat looked down, went grey, and drew the doona up to her chin.

"Did he touch you?"

Each syllable was a guillotine slicing through him. His head nearly snapped as it whisked back at Cat.

Cat stared at him. For eons.

Could've run to Mars and hidden. Couldn't move.

"Nup. I woke feeling... feeling claustrophobic and had to undo my shirt. He didn't touch me."

Robbie mouthed a silent *thank you*. Breathed. Smiled.

"But the bastard's lying about the snoring."

He turned to Annie. "Does Cat snore?"

"Like a pig with the flu snorting in mud." Annie shot her laser-gaze between him and Cat, then slumbered into the kitchen muttering. "Coffee."

"You took advantage of me," Cat said in a barely audible whisper, but her bloodshot eyes raged with suspicion. "I was drunk and depressed and you..."

"You dragged my head and pushed it onto your chest like it was a sponge bath."

"Bullshit."

"I went straight back to the armchair as soon as you fell asleep."

"Bull... I fell asleep? With your head on my..."

He nodded.

Cat stared at the toes of her right foot sticking out under the duvet. Then at him. "I don't believe you, but I'm not sure... but I'm sure as hell sure that you forced me to kiss you," she whisper-yelled.

Robbie winced and checked that Annie was still in the kitchen.

"How do you have it, Robbie?" Annie yelled.

"Two sugars, black, thanks." He turned back to Cat, quiet as he could muster. "I swear on all my vinyl collection I did not force myself on you." Even put his hand on his heart.

Silence. Silence from Cat meant acquiescence, usually. Her eyes weren't so forgiving.

He turned away. Cat's glare always made him turn away. Except when she was crying earlier, which started this whole madness.

ROBBIE hid in the Merger kitchen. That's what his world had come to, procrastinating in the kitchen, clinging to a few desperate minutes before wading back into the jungle of the contest office with Annie, Cat, and three hundred elephants. Times like this, an empty kitchen was a good kitchen. He shuffled over to the coffee machine like a zombie drawn to flesh.

Earlier, he'd bee-lined to Manny's cave.

"One minute she's pleading for my body, next I'm a rapist." Robbie summed up his frustration about Cat.

"Pleading?" Manny's eyebrows arched like the Sydney Harbour Bridge.

"I'm not going into the details out of respect, but her actions screamed way beyond any pleading."

"You made her scream?"

"NO. Not on any level. It was just..." Manny's grin stalled him. He'd fallen for the bastard's warped humour again.

Manny turned serious. "Emotional trauma sneaks up on all of us in different disguises. She wanted comfort sex. Some women go shopping, some hit the gym, others eat chocolate."

"Comfort sex..."

"Remember the poor thing is in shock, then there's anger percolating. Knowing Cat, probably a ton of guilt too."

"Guilt... I'd never thought about that. The kid was her pet project, wasn't he?"

Manny nodded. "Just comfort sex. It means nothing."

Robbie bobbed his head slowly, staring at the wall behind Manny. "And nothing really happened anyway."

"Nothing happening seems to be happening a lot lately."

He ignored the dig.

"Unless, of course, she sparked a little magic heat in your..." Manny waved a hand at his groin.

"What? No, of course not. No." He stood and stumbled backwards to the door, gripped the frame, then straightened. "You arsehole. Not everything has a funny side. I'm sharing stuff here and you're turning it into a circus. Sick bastard."

That's why he was hiding in the kitchen. Would have been easy to brush off the drunken-Cat-couch-thing with someone he could avoid for a while, but every time he snuck a peek at her in the office, Cat's fiery glare singed. He'd flick his eyes away and Annie's brown spotlights lit him up with guilt. He'd diverted to Manny, hoping for some clarity, and instead the idiot had tried to drag him into depravity.

He spooned a second sugar into his coffee, but only half made it into the cup. *Bugger*. Three hours sleep on an armchair was no problem. He could go five or six days with three hours sleep a night. This emotional confusion from Cat stuffed up his whole inner compass. She seemed to have skipped denial and projected all her anger at him.

"Ouch. Shit." Coffee splashed onto his hand as he stirred. Putting it down, he stepped over to the sink and ran cold water over his skin.

He sensed someone watching, flicked off the tap, grabbed a towel, and turned.

Annie in the doorway, arms crossed, eyes rocket-straight. Straight at him.

Maybe she'd come to explain Cat's anger, to comfort him. That would be a good sign for any future romance because surely, if there were sparks in the contest triangle, they flickered between him and Annie. How could Manny get it so stupidly wrong about him and Cat? He straightened up with an instant decision to bounce out of his inner wallowing, threw the towel onto the dish drying tray, and propped one leg up on a kitchen chair.

Annie pointed at the spilt coffee on the bench. "Bit shaky, are we." Not a question. Not comforting. Not good.

He picked up a damp cloth and stepped over to the renegade caffeine. Annie moved close, put her hand over his, stopping him from wiping up. The closest and most intimate they'd ever been. She never wore perfume, but he drew a deep inhale of her shampoo or soap. Some fruity scent.

"What did you do to Cat?"

"Nothing." Air gushed out of his lungs along with any hope of a future fling.

She stepped back, the chasm chilling the whole room. "What happened, Robbie?"

"Cat doesn't like chocolate." He slipped around Annie and scooted out of the kitchen minus his coffee.

TRACK 19

ANNIE SWIPED LEFT ON THE CONTEST APP. A RUBBISH SONG FROM THE first chord, and she had to stop it halfway through the stupid chorus. So many writers didn't get it. Shouting doesn't make it a hook, it just makes a lousy melody louder. Yet, she was grateful for the shitty songs because the mounting pressure from the growing contest entries had forced them to focus on their jobs. Cat and her earbuds swiped right and left with fervour, mostly left. Possibly some unlucky talents had their entry with the wrong preliminary judge at the worst possible time. Robbie, under his huge headphones, swiped a decent pace too.

A blue light email message indicator flashed on her phone. She ignored it, but the damned light wouldn't ignore her. She took off her headphones and tapped on the phone to see it was from her new family lawyer, Jenny. Her shoulders tightened around her neck. Despite Jenny's brilliance and genuine empathy, her first experience with litigation ten years ago had left deep scars, but the subject was Lachie, so she had to open the message.

Sorry Annie,
Tony's managed to fast-track the process and there's an informal meeting with Family Court Registrar 9.30am next Wednesday. He's pushing for

interim shared access and there's always a possibility he'll get it. We need to
meet in the next couple of days to prepare. Let me know what time works.
  Regards,
  Jenny

She put her phone down. Bastard. Bastard's bulldozing his way
through with money.

And where was Jenny looking while Tony's lawyer had slipped this
through? Damn lawyers. Time to prepare. Time for the "informal meeting" next week, as if time conveniently rolled out the red carpet for her
whenever she clicked her fingers. She had a job and Lach—

Robbie's phone blasted a new, guitar-lick ringtone. Royal Blood,
but she couldn't remember the track. He looked around embarrassed.
The deal was no ringing or audible notifications while they were
storming through song entries. He owes us a beer. Could do with
one now.

"Mum? You okay?" Robbie whispered. "Can you hear me now?"
He spoke just under a yell.

Cat heard him and removed her earbuds. If glares could burn, he
was roasted Robbie.

Robbie's eyes closed as he gave a long sigh. "Okay, Mum, I'll find
him. Yep, leaving now." He faced Annie as he grabbed his leather
jacket from the back of the chair. "I have to—"

She waved him off, didn't need the details. Her capacity for caring
was redlining with her stuff and Cat's. Robbie could deal with his own
shit.

Cat's phone wailed Adele.

Two beers for me now.

Cat answered it. The longer she listened, the lower she slumped in
her ergonomic chair. She dropped the phone like it had turned into a
giant redback spider and pushed away from the desk, tears streaming
down her cheeks. "Santi's brother."

The ungrateful fool had chosen Cat for his emotional punching bag.
Classic anger projection. Poor Cat.

Robbie hovered at the door, staring at Cat. Is that sympathy for Cat
oozing from his drooping head?

"Magic happens, clubbers, magic happens." Delaney squeezed past Robbie into the office holding up a small USB drive like an Olympic torch. "Not only do I bring you a track that automatically makes this week's top ten." He slowly turned to face each of us. "This boppy number could win the contest."

"This boppy number isn't in the contest." Annie tapped the iPhone.

"It is now. And you'll all thank me for discovering—"

"Discovering or disrobing?" said Annie.

"Please show a little respect to my new discovery. Pina's a seven-teen-year-old musical genius."

Silence of a ticking time bomb... Three, two, one.

"You're not respecting this contest and you're abusing your author-ity," she said.

"How did you ever make it this far when you haven't got the balls to date women your own age?" Cat screamed.

Delaney turned to Robbie for support. And he'd probably get it from the ambitious marketing yes-boy.

"I'm not supporting any more shit songs no matter how unique her blowjob is." Robbie stormed off.

Cat might've been grinning, her wincing face looked similar. "Fuck this." Her chair hit the wall as she slung her knapsack over a shoulder and bombed out too.

Delaney fiddled with his USB stick, silence reverberating like after-shocks. "It's good to see the kids growing up, isn't it? Why bite the hand feeding you when you can shred the whole arm to pieces." He placed the USB drive on her desk and tapped it. "Listen to it. If you still feel it's shit, dump it, but don't punish a potential superstar because of my harem of fuck-ups." Delaney spun with an agility that surprised her and waltzed out.

Annie stared at the purple USB drive. Purple. Lots of good omens —Deep Purple, Purple Haze, Purple Rain... she loved that album.

Fuck it. If a song can tickle something in me when the world is bashing my soul, who cares where it came from? Show me a pure, angelic rock star and I'll show you a liar.

She slotted the USB into her computer, waited for it to pop up on her screen, then hit Play.

Atmosphere.

From the first piano chord, the track oozed atmosphere, the elusive and rare gift of a classic hit. Pina's voice and the verse melody sparked through her spine, anticipation for the chorus stilled her lungs. So often the most promising tracks dissolved into disappointment, but as this song launched into the hook, her heart ballooned, every part of her body tingled. She'd kill to write a track like this. Bloody Delaney, he's finally fucked the real thing.

CAT stared at the gear and clothes in the "Camping & Tramping" window display, but all she saw was her shadowy reflection. Normally, her mind would be mentally buying gear for her next overseas school building mission, except the dark outline of twenty-nine-year-old Cat Stephens wouldn't get out of the way. She'd intended letting off steam walking around Albert Park Lake, but halfway around got annoyed with the look-at-my-amazing-leisurewear joggers, headed inland and ended up in Prahran.

Even if the afternoon sun wasn't on her back, she'd struggle to see who this fuzzy version of herself truly was. She'd run from mission to project to mission to project and what good had it done? Despite his brother's cruelty, she knew she didn't contribute to Santi' death. Yet his death dropped a black mirror in front of her she couldn't shake.

What was the point of all this third-world work when she had to drag her soul through the gutter of phone sex to fund it?

What could a passionate schlep really do for a scarred soul like Santi?

Who was she? Her thirtieth birthday placed a dark, giant boulder on the horizon of this year while her core cracked and crumbled. She hadn't even experienced a proper loving adult relationship. Almost thirty and her romantic biography contained a series of super-short chapters titled 'Flirtations, Flings, and Flunks'.

Her featureless reflection felt like a third-world map outline— barren, poor, broken. Potential for growth in so many directions but unable to move forward without...

Snap out of it, Cat, before you become a world-class victim.

She hitched her little knapsack higher and hiked towards her favourite spot in Greville Street.

CAT admired the creative window display of album covers and vinyl discs outside Deceptive Bends, the record store named after a 10CC album in the seventies and one of her favourite escapes in Melbourne. The title, inspired by a road sign in southern England, could be a summary of her wasted life… or a warning for her future.

Seriously, Cat, snap out of it.

She stepped inside and inhaled the vinyl, the musky covers, the pure authenticity of musical love that the brother-sister owners had created within the paint-cracked walls and vintage, high ceilings.

As soon as Anthea noticed her, she swung around the counter, scooted over, and wrapped her in a warm and loving hug that would have made Anthea's yiayia proud. Anthea stroked her face gently with one hand while squeezing her shoulder with the other. Sally-Anne must've passed on the horrible news. She soaked up the kindness and compassion. It hit her how much Anthea and Theo's friendship meant to her. She'd spent more time here than she'd realised. They'd donated a few records to Santi and were always interested in his progress. A shiver up her spine caused her to shake. Anthea hugged her again.

When Anthea sashayed back to the counter, Cat flicked through the first rack of albums for the thousandth time. Tactile. Sensual. Carnal. She'd been as guilty as most of her generation in downloading invisible music until she was introduced to vinyl by an ex-lover, Julene. The love-at-first-touch with vinyl outlasted her lust for Julene.

She noticed her heel tapping to a disco beat swirling from the store's speakers. She couldn't dance but standing still, her heel could lock into a beat. Then the seductive piano chords rippled through her entire nervous system like she'd been plugged into the amplifier.

She worked her way to the counter to ask Theo or Athena who had written and performed the track, but stopped when she spotted Robbie dancing on the mini-dance floor at the back of the store.

What's he doing here? This is her music cave, her friends, the last thing she needs is—

A chubby guy danced in. He must've been behind the DJ desk. Something about his disjointed movement and the way the clothes didn't quite sit right softened her. She'd been around enough mentally disabled people to know this guy carried something not on the standard menu expected by society. The music definitely suited Robbie better than any Latin beat. He was lost in the sound, grooving his shoulders to the rhythm, then he broke out in a silly dance that made Chubby Dude laugh.

She laughed. A sugary high she hadn't expected to feel again. Ever.

Robbie looked across, hesitated for a couple of beats, then continued dancing as he waved her over to join them.

She waved both hands as a no way.

He put an arm around Chubby Dude's shoulder, who immediately reciprocated, then they did some silly Zorba-like move. One of them was in synch with the music but she couldn't tell who, disoriented by her laughter.

"Whoa." Anthea and Theo had grabbed an arm each and dragged her onto the dance floor, then flung an arm over her shoulders and joined in with Robbie and Chubby Dude, Zorba dancing to the up-tempo non-Zorba slinky disco track.

Music was mad and sometimes the melodic insanity popped up just when it was needed most.

TRACK 20

ROBBIE COULDN'T BELIEVE THAT: A, CAT TURNED UP; B, SHE GOT ROPED into group dancing with him and Johnny; and C, she seemed to really enjoy it. Like a normal person. Cat rattled along in some parallel universe, their paths only merging at Merger Music. Even then, it was barely a merging, more like two dodgem cars crashing because other cars bumped them. She was brilliant with Johnny too, dancing with him after their Greek-inspired silliness like she'd known him for eons. He could list on two fingers how many people Johnny had danced with before: him and his mum. On her good days, when she used to have good days.

Johnny sat on the inside of the booth next to him, brown and white foam on his lips from the huge hot chocolate. Listening to his portable CD player under the headphones, Johnny nodded to whatever beat he had on while sneaking occasional glances across the table at Cat.

"How long have you been tainting my second home here?" asked Cat, fiddling with her chai latte.

"Tainting... aren't you the one on the wrong side of the Yarra?"

"Deceptive Bends is on the wrong side of the Yarra."

"Johnny loves the place. Anthea and Theo look after him whenever Mum... when she forgets to..."

"Must be tough."

"Promises to never do it again, then about every three months she caves and heads out to the pub for lunch, which means pokies till broke. If I'm working, Johnny takes the tram straight here. It's almost door to door. Anthea and Theo are amazing." He'd never talked with anyone at work about his mum's stuff or Johnny. Strange, yet natural with Cat. Mega strange.

"That stuff you told Ellen about the organisations you volunteered for was true."

She didn't frame it like a question, but he nodded anyway.

Cat smiled at Johnny. "He's got taste, I'd never heard that track." She angled her face at him. "How come you've never mentioned Johnny?"

"Most people don't get it, or they feel sorry for him or me. I don't need to explain, and I don't need sympathy. I love him and we both love music. Music saves us." *Shut. Up. Robbie. You've got some kind of bonding thing going on here with a complicated work colleague, don't push it.*

Cat raised her glass cup. "To music."

He clinked his mug. "Music." He sipped his black coffee and took in the eclectic Windsor crowd building inside the warm cafe before turning back to Cat. "Is it a good track?"

Cat turned from staring out the window with vague eyes and scrunched up brow.

"Santi. His song." His curiosity about Santi's track could kill the positive bonding.

Cat glared at him like his curiosity had killed their truce, then she fiddled in her bag and took out her phone. Probably going to request an Uber and escape this clumsy never-going-to-bond mess.

"You tell me." She slid the phone across the table.

He stared at her phone. Never listened to a dead guy's song. Not a newly dead guy. Dead guy with one degree of separation. Now he'd dug his own grave, Cat could see through him like Superman. What if he didn't like the track?

"You sure?" *Withdraw the offer. Take back your phone. Run out of—*
She nodded.

It was the same model phone as his, so he slipped in his earbuds, connected them to her phone, hit *Play*, and closed his eyes. Three seconds into the track, he knew it was special. His internal organs stopped what they were doing to listen. So much emotion oozed out of the lyrics and melody he wouldn't be surprised if blood dripped out of the earbuds. When the track ended, his insides kept spinning, dizzy from the extreme emotional river the song dragged him through.

With eyes still shut, he said, "This is why I want to be a manager. I wish I could've been his manager." Robbie's eyes sprung open. He'd never shared his dream with anyone apart from Johnny, not even close friends. She was going to think he was delusional, ruin the whole moment. He should have just kept his dreams to himself. And Johnny.

"Me, too," Cat whispered, her eyes watery.

ROBBIE wasn't surprised when Cat wound up their unplanned bonding session. Neither of them knew where to take it after Santi's song unexpectedly uncovered their mutual secret ambition. Exhaustion suddenly swamped her face, and she barely slumped into her parka. The sleepless nights she'd grumbled about to Annie—which he couldn't help overhearing—plus her long walk and dance diversion must've hit her all at once. Dusk in Melbourne autumn dropped temperatures and daylight quickly, but the shop and streetlights highlighted the lines on her forehead and bloodshot eyes. He zipped up his leather jacket too. Johnny never felt cold despite the chilly breeze, comfortable in his 'Highway to Hell' T-shirt.

"We can give you a lift."

"Too far in the wrong direction." But Cat hovered.

"Not on a donkey or my back, like in a car with an engine and wheels."

"Thanks, but I'm not in a rush." She turned to Johnny. "That was a cool track. I'm going to check it out and buy some of her music."

"Natalie Jam. Move. Dellshow Music. 2009," said Johnny, staring at his big Converse boots.

Cat kissed Johnny on the cheek. Johnny shifted from foot to foot, grinning.

Robbie's heart swelled. His brother didn't get much female attention, let alone moments of female tenderness. Mum always struggled with basic maternal instincts like hugs, and these days she hated music in the house.

Cat waved at him, checked the traffic lights.

"You should enter Santi's song in the contest."

She stared at him, feet wide, chin up, eyes squinting.

"Delaney's set the precedent. Won't be like we're cheating. Once we put it on the top ten weekly list, it's up to the punters to vote. Plus, I haven't heard anything better than 'Why Have Me At All'. The track deserves it."

Her eyes glistened under the flashing *"Now Open"* lights from the nearby Thai restaurant. "But his brother…"

"He can have the prize money if it wins, or he can donate it to the centre where Santi created the track."

Cat wiped tears with the back of her hand. She stared at him. Soft, vulnerable, a smile. A sweet smile that stirred his inner sugar. She turned to Johnny, kissed him on the cheek again, spun and walked north down High Street.

"She likes me," said Johnny.

He wrapped an arm around Johnny's shoulders as they headed to the car. Seemed like a minor miracle because if it wasn't for Johnny and his musical taste, he wouldn't be thinking, let alone saying, "I think she likes *me*."

"Jesse McCartney. 2013."

"You're amazing, Johnny. Souvy or burger?"

"Souvy. No garlic sauce. Extra onions. Chilli sauce."

The Spanish sun is setting in your eyes and rising in my heart.

ANNIE's unfinished lyric popped into her head as Diaz emptied the jug of sangria into her glass. The inspiration had come from a friend ten years ago, who'd fallen in love in Seville but had to leave the guy behind when her visa ran out. She'd never finished the lyric, never attempted a melody. No idea why the words drifted into her consciousness. Sure, Diaz spoke Spanish, but he was Argentinian. Mostly he spoke silent erotica and that was why she'd asked to drop around again, her nerves and skin recognising every sultry syllable of that lingo.

As cosy as Diaz's music school was, his home studio oozed cosier. Too cosy. Red lamps radiated a sunset haze off the walls, a futon with red pillows and a tan blanket with crimson roses winked from one end, enough instruments for a Latin ensemble scattered around added texture and glitter, while an upright piano beckoned at the other end.

"A peso for your thoughts," he said, eyes sparking.

I want to slap Lachie, kill Monaro, rip off your clothes and destroy your bed. She nearly spurted sangria across the small table as the raw honesty crashed through her mind. Sangria always snuck up on her. Sweet. Fruity. Dangerous.

"I was just thinking—"

Acoustic guitar and drums blasted the room.

They both turned to her handbag on the floor near the door as the opening chords of the power ballad 'Move Over' did a couple of loops. Times like these you took strength anywhere you could get it and on the way here, she'd changed her phone's text alert to the motivational woman-on-a-mission track.

"Might be Lachie." She put her glass down, getting to her bag in a few steps, fished around for her phone, and checked the message. *Mum!* Trust her to interrupt. Her parents had extended their time in Malta because her nannu's cancer had come back, but the old bugger had fought the odds for four months. Suited her just fine. Tonight was their weekly Skype and apparently Mum's Prince Lachie wasn't online. She typed a quick response with a white lie, otherwise her mum would just keep sending texts or persisting with Skype till she roused Lachie, and she couldn't risk Lachie blurting out about the sudden appearance of his father. She sent an additional text to make sure her mum backed off for a couple of days, then dropped the phone back in her bag.

Diaz smirked and shook his head from the piano stool.

"Modern women. Instead of enjoying the company they're with, they have to be texting someone somewhere else."

"No choice, it was—"

"Lachie?"

She shook her head.

"Texting, tweeting, Instagramming, whatever that basura is called, it all takes you out of the momento." He clicked his fingers on the last syllable. "And the magic in this amazing world only happens when you're fully in the momento. When you look back on this crazy life one day as we bump our walkers around the old people's home, the only thing that will put a smile on your pretty but wrinkled face are memories of the special people in your life and the momentos with them."

Rip his clothes off now and make this little couch earn its place. No time for the bedroom.

"I know what you want."

Bastard. Sex-under-ridiculous-hair bastard. Come get me. Give me a momento. Hell, give me a dozen.

"You want to play."

Diaz swung around to face the upright piano and lifted the cover. He slid to one side and patted the small space on the stool.

You know every key on my piano. Do I want to stop? Hell, no. The fresh, raw lyrics burst out of her creative cave. She'd have to work on it... if she remembered it after tonight.

"Move over, Diaz, not enough room for me *and* your hair."

They do it in their cars. They do it in the streets. Cafes, clubs, and bars. No one's being discreet.

ANNIE sang in the moment like a born-again vocalist, pent-up creativity and passion pouring out of every pore.

It started with the 'net. The future forgets. The more toys we get. The less we connect.

Singing wasn't Diaz's forte, but he added harmony and colour and a kick-ass hook melody.

We're all giving more text than sex. We're all getting more text than sex. We're all giving more text than sex. We're all getting more text than sex. More text than sex. More text than sex.

The boppy pop power anthem had oozed out of them like it was patiently waiting around the corner till they finally sat together at the piano.

It's an emotional mess. Dating is too much stress. She won't feel his caress. Too busy sending an SM SM SMS.

We're all giving more text than sex. We're all getting more text than sex. We're all giving more text than sex. We're all getting more text than sex. More text than sex. More text than sex...

They repeated the title a few more times and ended with a shout – *MORE TEXT THAN SEX*. Perfect, because it wasn't a track for a fade out.

She shifted on the stool to face him, his grin matching her disbelief at their smooth, first-time impromptu collaboration and the track it inspired. Creative juices flowed in her veins, chasing after adrenalin and endorphins swishing through her heart, swirling in her brain. Never felt more alive than in these moments, when she'd created something from nothing. Gravity gave in and let her float in an ecstatic haze.

"That's a hit," said Diaz.

The cold industry term crashed her back down to the piano stool. "It's a fun song, maybe a good one, but it's not a hit because no one's ever going to hear it." She noticed the microphone on top of the upright piano and the computer screen with some kind of recording software on the desk at a right angle to the piano, behind Diaz. "When did you turn all that shit on?"

"You are amazing, Annie. Truly *asombroso* when you are in the *momento*. I had to record our last couple of takes."

"They weren't takes, we were just fooling around. Delete it."

"Delete it? *De ninguna manera.* The creative gods will strike me to dust if I delete such musical magic. This song is topical, it's catchy, it's perfect for the download generation and speaks to the older wisdoms too."

"Please, Diaz."

"I'll work on the demo then get you a copy so you can play it to Delaney."

"NO. *Di naguna manera* or whatever you said before."

"What's the point of working at Merger if you do not take advantage of it?"

"I'm not ready for this." She spun around and scooped up her handbag and jacket.

"Ready for this?" Diaz waved his hand between the computer and piano. "Or this?" He waved his hand between his chest and her.

She'd come for a diversion and a sexual release or two, nothing else. Especially this. Maybe he'd always seen her as a way into the biz. Wouldn't be the first bastard.

"Delete it. Understand?" Her diva voice couldn't have boomed around the room with more power.

"Okay, okay. I comprender."

Annie watched him hit *Delete* and close the computer, then she strode out.

TRACK 21

CAT HAD STRUGGLED TO HIT THE OFFICE ON TIME THE LAST FEW MONDAYS, but this morning all three of them warmed their chairs early, keen to see the results of the public vote for last week's top ten as soon as voting locked up at eight sharp. Only the top two moved through each week to the final round vote of the contest climax.

Robbie had a permanent grin, at least every time she'd glanced across, which was more this morning than in the whole seven weeks of the contest. She hated how the modern world needed to pigeonhole people and this fickle industry squeezed everyone's perceived essence tighter and forever. So ironic for what was supposed to be a creative biz. Yet, she'd fallen for the same pathetic habit. Maybe Robbie needed his marketing cowboy character to survive and fit in? Maybe the Robbie she'd discovered at Deceptive Bends was the real one. Caring brother, patient, loyal son, passionate music fan, and humanity giver as opposed to the ninety-five percent of the planet who were takers.

Annie's glazed eyes and heavy lines helped snap her out of her own dark spiral. Cat's grief for Santi would never totally leave her, but at least her ground zero was in the past. On the level of importance for her future, Annie's current baggage could fill an airport terminal. Diaz seemed perfect for her, yet he'd turned out to be using her, a taker.

Monaro, taker. Trying to take Annie's most precious gift, Lachie, after indirectly taking Annie's creative gift, her very essence.

Delooney waltzed in carrying three coffees. "Robbie, with a grin like that, maybe you're on something stronger than caffeine?" He handed out the correct coffees, which Louise, his PA, had obviously ordered. Then he pulled out three small envelopes from his back pocket and repeated the distribution triangle. "I know Lou sent out e-invites, but I wanted you to have something tangible. This way you have no excuse to miss the party of the century."

Delooney's sixtieth birthday party provided more intrigue than care factor. If anyone could replicate the legendary bashes of the seventies, it would have to be Delooney. This party might be her last chance to experience the screen madness of parties in Almost Famous or Vinyl or Empire.

"Is it time yet? My body clock works on rock 'n' roll hours, doesn't start ticking till midday."

"Any second now, boss," Robbie said in his marketing cowboy twang. Definitely character. Delooney straddled the corner of Robbie's desk, one foot on the floor, and Robbie swung his screen around so they could both watch.

Of course, Delooney honoured us with caffeine and hidden nerves because of his little... don't pigeonhole, Cat... his 'friend' Pina's song. Tension tightened her muscles too, unable to pretend her vested interest in this week's votes didn't mean something to her. She turned away from her screen. Annie's neutral haze could help her get into a Zen zone.

"Yes, yes, yes." Robbie banged his desk three times.

Delooney rose. "No apologies necessary. Two more weeks and we get to the bone of this thing." He waltzed out.

Robbie grinned.

She swung to her screen. Tension eased from every fibre. Air rushed back into her lungs. *Track 1: Trust by Pina. Track 2: Why Have Me At All by Santi.* Her screen went fuzzy; she'd have to call Manny. Tears dripped onto her hands. Wiping her eyes magically fixed the screen.

Delooney slung back into the doorway. "And for the record, Pina is fifteen and too smart to pop her cherry, let alone tarnish her sparkling reputation with this rusty lion. Her mum is a teaching colleague of my daughter. If she can sing as good live as she does on the demo, we'll probably end up signing her." He swooshed out, then swooshed back in again. "And, Cat, I'm glad you slipped in that track by Santi. Almost made me cry. You've got good instincts. Would've signed him too." He swooshed out one last time.

Tears poured down her cheeks without waves of pain or grief. Warm, salty tears that nourished her soul. Through her watery haze, she couldn't miss Robbie's stupid, wide grin. She nodded and silently mouthed the words, *"Thank you."*

Squeezed into one end of the Merger kitchen couch, CAT had one arm wrapped around her shins, the other holding her phone on the contest page featuring Santi's name and track. She'd rushed her murky feelings out of the office before Annie or Robbie noticed. Everyone dealt with grief differently, didn't they? Who really knew? For her, it was like wading through a dark bay without a horizon. Sometimes the sun rose bright, and she floated along. Sometimes little waves lapped at her with painful glimpses of Santi. Sometimes a ten-metre wave crashed on top, spinning her breathless and dizzy but still no horizon. Nowhere to aim for, nothing to cling to.

Searching for a horizon. Story of my life.

The public vote confirmed her instinct for Santi's talent. Sure her ego got a boost, and his song deserved to be recognised, but a post-humous recognition would be the hollowest of all. In a way, clinging to the track was clinging to Santi. Did that help work through the grief or did it just prolong the painful part? This should've been a sunny moment, but her mood dial was still off balance, swinging like a pendulum.

The weekend couldn't roll around quickly enough. She'd lost count of how many weeks she hadn't attended the ashram. Friday night, their Australian guru was in town and hosting a community sitting. Annie wasn't a fan of the foundation, but Cat couldn't fault it. Fault lines seemed to crack around her whenever she stayed away from the community or ignored her chosen mantras. Just thinking about Friday stopped her tears. She wiped her eyes and cheek with a sleeve, then looked around the kitchen for the tissue box to blot her runny nose.

Robbie passed the tissue box across the wide coffee table.

When did he sneak in?

Strange, because it didn't feel strange that it was Robbie, not sixth-sense Annie.

"Thanks." She grabbed the box, yanked two tissues out, folded them together, and blew hard. Three times.

"You could play trumpet for a beat-box crew," said Robbie, grinning, choc-top eyes shiny.

"Only horn note I can do is ship horn."

Robbie laughed, a squeaky blast that blew out of his lungs and inflated hers, the squeaky laughter a complete contrast to what she'd expected. Made him even more endearing.

Surely, their unexpected ice breaker the other night wasn't so deep? She'd never heard him laugh. Poor bugger had always been the butt of all their jokes since the contest kick-off.

"You should start a business."

Robbie roped in his laughter. "Business?"

"Rent-a-crowd for stand-up comedians."

The walking rent-a-crowd for stand-up comedians squeaked the decibels higher, his upper body bouncing like a puppet on coke.

She'd sometimes wondered what made her feel better, laughing or making people laugh. Right then, in this most unlikely of moments with the most unlikely of men, the latter was edging it. For a split second, she thought he might be putting it on for her sad benefit, then quickly dismissed her cynicism. No guy could pretend to look so silly while belching out a laugh like that.

When Robbie settled, he took a tissue and wiped his eyes.

"At least you're smiling."

Was she smiling? She didn't know if those muscles would ever work together again. Didn't sound like he was trying to take the credit, but you couldn't let a dude like Robbie get too cocky.

"You came in here to state what a one-megapixel camera can do?"

"Sorry, Cat, I didn't mean to... Coffee. I came for a coffee."

"Can you do a—"

"Skinny latte, no sugar? Coming right up."

He remembers my coffee? Maybe that was one of his moves, remembering women's coffees. Probably a killer move in this hyper-caffeinated town. *Moves? Why would he be making a move? On me?* She watched him pack the coffee, warm and swirl her skinny milk. A rhythm to his movement, something like R&B or up-tempo soul. He danced better with a machine than he could with a woman.

"What are you doing this Friday?" she yelled above the noisy coffee machine, not sure how the question percolated.

"Nothing. You?" he yelled, not taking his eyes off the coffee, moving from foot to foot like his brother but on some kind of beat.

"There's a thing on at my ashram. Thought you might be interested."

Robbie's rhythm died. He slowly placed the glass with her latte on a saucer, then slumped on the bench with both hands, staring at his caffeine creation. "Ashram?"

What in Bowie's name was she doing? She'd never invited anyone to the ashram apart from Annie. All her instincts and all her brain cells ran a quick workshop to analyse his tone and they all agreed on one thing—she was an idiot.

TRACK 22

"Left," said Johnny.

"Too soon." ROBBIE stopped Johnny's hand before he swiped left on the track. They were hunched together on his two-seater couch, listening to the week's contest songs, chips, Coke, and their feet on the coffee table. The musical intro hinted at something good. Surely, it would bounce out again in the hook. But Johnny had sensed it early, the track went nowhere.

"Left."

Johnny swiped left and they waited for the next track to kick in.

"Think I need to swipe left on this cult thing with Cat."

"Forum said not a cult, just boring music and mantaras." Somehow Johnny still found forums online rather than social media groups.

"Man-traars. So many of these so-called gurus are sneaky entrepreneurs. Before you know it, they have your password and bank details."

"I'll go. Cat likes me," said Johnny, grinning.

The next track started with a sound worse than a seagull harmonising with a squeaky door at three in the morning. Johnny swiped left within five seconds.

"Maybe you *should* go." Maybe she only put up with Robbie now because of Johnny. Some projected kindness thing.

Johnny placed his hands on his hips and flapped his arms.

Robbie stared at his brother with a question mark face.

"Me your wing-man."

"No way. Never needed a wing-man and definitely not relevant with Cat. I'm a diversion, a pet project, a classic rebound project. Or she's recruiting for the foundation. Happy that she's finally accepting me as a colleague… but if I cross the line now, it will destroy everything. I either go as a supporting colleague, borderline friend, or avoid the minefield."

"You wanted Annie."

"That was different." And it struck him how quickly she'd slipped into past tense. Had he given up? Was he so shallow that delayed gratification was too much a step? Or so shallow that it was a fleeting physical infatuation? Whatever the reason, Annie simply wasn't on his sexual or romantic radar anymore. No reason necessary. No tension, past tense. He picked up the bowl and stuck three barbeque chips into his mouth. The seductive beat of the next track cut through his chip crunching. They must've gone through a hundred tracks without a right swipe. The track had momentum, didn't dilute, dissolve, or disappoint. It actually evolved into a pop-dance party, then the hook blasted the track into a carnival.

Johnny swiped right.

"I'm definitely cancelling the Cat-mantra night. We don't need the complication. She'll be fine on her own. It's her tribe. They'll all be hovering to recruit me to their *God is everywhere world*. I'll start arguing with them, piss off Cat, and that will fuck up our little bonding thing and worse, it could jeopardise the whole contest. What do you think?"

Johnny picked up his Coke, studying the glass closely, which created a prism effect of his face from the lamp behind him. "You think." He took a long swig of the drink.

Fair enough. It's my problem. I've got to find my path through the messy maze. I need to —

"Too much."

I think too much. But this is important. It deserves —

Johnny burped. Belched again. And again.

The little brother-bugger was right again. Wise beyond his mental disability. Beyond—

"Fuck, Johnny, that stinks." He grabbed a pillow and waved hard to dilute the burp stench.

Johnny laughed. Burped again.

He hit Johnny with the pillow. Johnny grabbed the other one and bashed back, harder.

Live events, rule one: better to pack them into a small room than book a huge venue that ended up half empty. Even if there were more people in the bigger space, space killed atmosphere. And ROBBIE enjoyed the vibe despite the overkill on *omms and teachings*. The large community room within the heritage-listed council building bulged with believers. Clever lighting and a ton of candles added a golden glow to the warm energy.

He sensed Cat's glances through the session but focused on the little stage. He'd confess later how he tuned out during most of the ceremony stuff, but he did enjoy the entertainment. Live music always sparked his soul. Expectations were low when the *band* squeezed onto the stage, but the acoustic guitar, sitar, and flute melded with the three vocalists into sweet melodies. No preachy lyrics, lots of emotive sweet harmonies, and a touch of spiritual scatting.

At the end of the official stuff, he and Cat shuffled towards Guru Larriboori, only one woman and two couples in the queue ahead. The guru's presence radiated. He'd make a great manager the way he connected with everyone so quickly, instinctively knowing when to spread humour, when to share wisdom for followers to grasp. Guru Larriboori was a terrific stage name too.

"You don't have to meet him," said Cat.

"I'm cool with it." *Don't. Use. Cool. Ever.* While he appreciated the dude's energy and the energy in the room, he was more an observer, not swept up in any *ommazing* spiritual revelations. "So, I just bring my hands together and bow a little."

Cat nodded, showing him the tiny but respectful bow.

He held up the folded leaflet with the guru's name and photo. "Do I call him Guru or Guru Larriboori or Guru-Dude?"

She rolled her eyes.

He stood back while Cat squatted on a large cushion in front of the guru. He couldn't hear their conversation, but watching a hushed and humble Cat was worth experiencing.

Cat hushed and humbled. Wow.

When she moved to the side, glowing, there wasn't a barrier between him and the guru's energy. Power pulsated through the guru's eyes and smile. He'd met charismatic men before—the music biz was full of them—but this was on another level. Another five or six levels, like comparing the volume of an acoustic guitar against a Fender blaring through a Marshall amp at an outdoor festival.

Cat brought her hands together and bowed, urging him to move and reminding him how to approach the guru.

He dragged his cement feet forward. The closer he got, the more powerful the sweet buzz flowing through his veins, the more terrified he became. He performed the simple greeting ritual and stared at the guru.

"What is your birth name?"

"Robbie. Robbie Guest."

"We are related. I too am a guest." Guru waved a hand pointing around the room. "We are all guests on this planet, all relatives." Guru laughed like a river of honey gushing through rapids.

Robbie smiled and his anxiety washed away under the guru's sweet current. He felt a touch of guilt for allowing himself to slide down a negative lane of assumptions instead of appreciating the presence of a fun, interesting man.

"Join our mission?" encouraged the guru.

He jerked back a step, away from the dark vortex they were determined to drag him into. Guru's lips moved again, but he didn't hear the words. Cat stared, heat from a hundred other eyes burning the goosebumps on the back of his neck. He edged back further from the superstar salesman smile of the guru.

Join our mission? Zealots with a capital ZEAL.

He coughed, choking on the smoke of a million candles, then spun round and bustled through the worshippers to the door and fresh air.

CAT caught up with Robbie, then slowed and matched his pace. He must have been heading for his car. Glimpses under occasional neon shop lights suggested colour had returned to the poor dude's face, but she couldn't be sure. At least he didn't wave her away or start running. He stopped next to a bright blue sedan, pulled out his remote, and clicked to unlock the doors. She wasn't into cars, but the Ford XR6 Turbo seemed about right for a marketing guy that couldn't afford a real sports—

Enough with the pigeon-holing, Cat. Mindfulness was a half-step behind. Maybe three steps, but as Guru Larriboori once told her, post-mindfulness was better than no mindfulness.

Why did I ask him to come?

They weren't really friends. The ice had only just melted on a glacial working relationship. Why?

Robbie stared at the pavement as his tan boots shuffled from one foot to the other, more like his little brother than a marketing cowboy.

"You okay? You kinda went grey in there."

He peered at her from under his floppy hair, his head on a forty-five-degree angle to the pavement.

"You lasted longer than the last person I brought. She left thirty seconds after the first group mantra started."

"I've got no problem with what kind of music you groove to in your life, Cat, or with anyone else's." He waved a thumb in the direction of the council building. "Just don't force your playlist on me."

"No one's forc—"

"He asked me to join your mission. Your bloody mission." He straightened, flipped his hair clear, chin aimed at her chest.

"No, he didn't. I was right there, he said—"

"*Join our mission.* Like the answer was obvious I would jump into his spiritual pool and splash around with the rest of you."

"Enjoy our session? That's what Guru Larriboori said, 'Enjoy our session?'" Laughter bubbled out of her.

"You sure?"

Nodding her head, she added a couple of snorts to the laughter.

Robbie smiled. "Must've been the acoustics."

"The acoustics in your predetermined cavern of fear." She tapped his head. The second wave of laughter surprised her more than the first. She'd been nervous about his reaction before the event and then his running away wrapped the nerves tighter around her gut until the relief of his stupidity gushed through her lungs with laughter.

Robbie's squeaky guffaws echoed off the shops, bounced over other parked cars, and spiralled into the stars. He leant back on his precious toy, sparkly eyes meeting hers every few seconds.

Maybe he was relieved too, or embarrassed, or both. Didn't matter, natural drugs—endorphins—flushed the tension out of her body, needing the car to support her.

Robbie settled first. "You're halfway in, may as well give you a lift home."

She managed to compose herself and straightened. "Sure."

Between the spiritual syrup she'd infused from Guru Larriboori, the goodwill from everyone else in the room, and the silly hysterics with Robbie, CAT didn't want the night to end despite it having nowhere else to go. They hadn't talked during the twenty-minute drive. How could they top the high on High Street? A high she hadn't expected in her inner world ever again. Robbie eased the big car to a stop outside her shared home, put on the handbrake but didn't turn off the engine or lights.

"Tea or coffee?"

He looked at the house with his forehead wrinkled. "Nah. It's late, I better get going."

Of course, the poor bugger'd had a nightmare in this house with Ellen and she'd helped tattoo his mortification onto his memory the next morning.

"Why did they call you Mudderee?"

She eased her seatbelt into its waiting position and raised the little knapsack from the floor by her legs onto her lap, fiddling with the straps.

"Sorry, if it's some secret group thing…"

"Madhuri. M.A.D.H.U.R.I. You pronounced it right, *Muddaree*. Good ear. Once you're accepted, the guru gives you a name in Sanskrit."

"Does it have a special meaning?"

She wrapped the bag strap tight around her hand and stared through the windscreen at the street, darker than it should be because the flame trees covered most of the streetlights.

"Sweet one." She looked out the passenger window at her home. Didn't deserve the name, the gorgeous house, perfect housemate who happened to be her perfect landlord, the community centre work.

"Like lobster."

His weird words flicked her back inside the car. "Huh?"

"Prickly and dangerous on the outside, sweet and tender on the inside." That grin normally spiked her, yet his eyes oozed honesty and something else… empathy?

"Let's keep it between us. Even Annie doesn't use it. Not that she's judgemental. *'I met you as Cat and you'll always be Cat to me'*," she said in her hopeless impersonation of Annie.

"I'll respect your wishes, but Madhuri suits you."

Sweet was one thing, syrupy another. Only one way to test how authentic this friendly-nice-guy-Robbie was. "Next month there's a weekend thing down at the Portsea ashram. Why don't you come down?"

Robbie didn't blink. No cowboy grin. Nothing.

"In separate rooms, of course." Why did she spurt that?

Grin. Juicy cheeks either side.

Juicy cheeks? Seriously, Cat. "Separate dorms. You don't have to stay the two nights. If you get spooked again, just hit the road." *Why, oh, why was she emphasising separate rooms and dorms?*

"Some records had a better flip side than the A-track. Chuck Magione's 'Feels so Good' was on the B-side. Some radio DJ had flipped it and the song turned out to be Chuck's biggest hit. Even made it onto *The Simpsons*."

"You can just say no thanks. I don't need a Wikipedia blurb on tracks from the seventies."

"I'd like to give it another spin... Madhuri."

Cat watched someone ease across, kiss Robbie on the cheek, and leave the car. Someone who looked like her. She watched this Cat-double flit up the steps, flick a wave back at him, and float inside the house.

Leaning back on the inside of the front door, CAT tried to reconcile the two "Cats" in Robbie's car.

"Nice to see you smiling again. You should go there more regularly," said Ellen, wearing a long flannelette nightgown, scarf, and thick dressing gown, carrying her recycled rubber hot-water bottle.

There weren't two Cats in Robbie's car. In fact, she was more centred than she'd ever been. Didn't matter why, no need to analyse or explain. She lightly jabbed Ellen's upper arm and strode down the middle of the hall to her own room.

"Kettle's hot if you want to fill your hottie," said Ellen.

Hottie? Couldn't believe Ellen needed a hot-water bottle; she was boiling.

TRACK 23

ANNIE HUSTLED INTO THE MERGER FOYER AND ALMOST STUMBLED AS THE stuffy air hit her, the crazy contrasts of a Melbourne winter: freezing wind outside, overheated stillness inside. She flopped off her Russian-style hat and untangled her scarf as quickly as she could with the other hand, bent forward, shook her head and flicked up.

"Delaney wants you in the dungeon," Tracey said from behind the reception desk.

"Seriously? I'm only ten minutes late and he knows the hundreds of hours we're doing on this contest each week."

"Some kind of meeting, wants you straight in," said Pierre, popping his head up from the computer screen.

"What meeting? I didn't get any notice." Maybe she had. The contest had three weeks to go. Twenty-five million people in the country and it seemed like twenty million were wannabe songwriters. The momentum tested all their energy reserves and whatever time management skills she had. Momentum with Lachie had hit a mountain. Mount Monaro. She entertained seeing a child psychologist for guidance, but who was going to pay for that? And when were those hourly sessions squeezing in?

"Cat already there?" At least Cat could cover for her.

Talkative Tracey shook her head without looking up.

"Everyone else is there," said Pierre. Tracey shot him a look and he ducked behind his screen.

"Who's everyone?"

Tracey answered the reception phone, but Annie hadn't heard it buzz. Weird. She dumped her coat and stuff on a visitor's chair, fluffed her hair using a meeting room window as a mirror, and headed for the steps to the dungeon.

Delaney's laugh boomed through the large timber doors. ANNIE stopped before opening and smiled. *"A chirpy meeting is a good meeting"* was Delaney's mantra, so whatever this meeting was about would be quick and easy. Hell, she could use some adult diversion even if it was childish adult diversion after the adultish child shit Lachie had thrown at her lately.

She opened the door, breezed in, and stopped dead. Dead still. Still as the chilled hairs on her spine.

Delaney half spun in his chair at the head of the table. "Hey, Annie, you know everyone here. Make yourself comfy."

He said it like Monaro was not sitting on his left side.

Said it like Diaz wasn't sitting in the next chair.

Like this was a weekly meeting of friendly, productive professionals.

He patted the table in front of the empty chair on his right, next to Robbie. "You sneaky creative genius, welcome back to the real game," said Delaney.

Lacking any instruction from her, muscles and joints accepted the invitation to sit while her brain projector spooled in super slow motion, piecing together the meaning behind the fucked-up vision in front of her.

"Best track I've heard since our favourite TV soap star walked in with her demo. Robbie drafted a marketing plan last night that will create more downloads than an ATM at the casino." He twirled his hand at Robbie, encouraging him to share.

"The zeitgeist lyric creates so many angles, Annie. The title alone will drive a million downloads and streams. 'More Text Than Sex'. Brilliant." Robbie's enthusiastic smile.

Her brain rocketed out of slo-mo as a million bits of data attacked her at NASA supercomputer speeds.

Diaz pitched the song to Delaney. Delaney brought in Monaro to manage the production and release for the joint venture label and roped in Robbie to do his thing. Falling over each other to be involved, like a bunch of dumb dominos.

"Terrific collaboration and Diaz did a good job on the demo, too." Delaney patted a USB drive on the table. Red USB drive.

She lasered on Diaz. Thought he'd been a gentleman in not contacting her since that night. In fact, his silence had increased her respect for him. Her desire for him. But the bastard had stolen something from their moment. Stolen the song. Stolen her trust. She needed to rip his long hair out one full fist at a time… then start on the shorter hairs down low.

"I'm tearing up our old contract, Annie. This deserves a fresh start full of positive juices." Monaro pushed a document across the table. His pinch-or-kiss cheeks screamed for a baseball bat.

She stared at her hands, interlocked on the table, taking a moment to push down the anger brewing in her stomach.

"And we'll handle the publishing, of course. You'll be looked after by Cat." Chirpy Delaney.

Cat obviously had not been included because if she was in the room, Delaney would already have been thrown out the window, Diaz would be screaming and dripping blood from his scrotum, then she'd have grabbed one of the famous guitars hanging on the wall and gone all Pete Townshend on Monaro.

She didn't give Monaro's document the respect of the merest glance, aiming her hate-seeking missiles at each of the scum-sucking parasites in the room, slow and steady. Delaney beaming. Diaz hopeful. Monaro cockie. Robbie was the only one who flinched, eyes frantic between her and Delaney.

"How ironic. A track about the lack of communication in the modern world brings everyone to the table as friends and resolves a number of issues." Delaney relaxed back into the Darth Vader chair, hands behind his head. "Not only are you a creative genius, Annie, you've also subconsciously facilitated a professional and personal chart-topper."

You manipulative idiot. Not even good manipulation.

Still on the edge of the chair, she turned her body and velvet venom to Delaney. "You can tell your mate, I wouldn't use any contract he gave me to pick up dog poo because it would disrespect dogs. Then you can tell that South American hyena if he ever contacts me again, he'll need two bodyguards, one for each tiny little ball. You can also tell him my son will never go near his casa-de-fucking-crooks again. I'm resigning now and only for Cat's sake, I'll walk out of here the second the contest is over. With six month's pay or I'll sue you and Merger for attempted copyright theft and extortion." She stood, picked up the red USB drive and tapped it on the table in rhythm with every word. "If one word or note or chord of this track is ever played again anywhere, I'll rip your tongues out with my fingers so that no one has to hear your stupid, useless shit ever again." She turned to Diaz. "And you'll need to hide in some Argentinian jungle, underground, with all the other lizards and snakes." She threw the USB drive at Diaz. He cowered and it bounced back off his forearm onto the table, spinning.

Annie spun and flowed out of the room.

ANNIE flung open the top right drawer of Delaney's desk, pulled out the bastard's bowl of binge bait, plonked it on the desk, and snatched a sachet of coke. She headed for the door, then whipped back to the desk, shuffled through the little bags and tiny pill bottles till she'd found two more sachets, stuffed them in her pocket, and slammed the door on the way out.

Embryonic thoughts and half sentences flashed through Annie's mind at supersonic speed, but her sluggish brain couldn't process. Muffled sounds from the offices outside and blurred visions from the bathroom mirror clashed against her racing pulse and pounding heart.

She needed this fix to spin her mind into a dance tempo. To balance her world again. To breathe.

The sink edge was damp under her hands. She picked up the shiny little bag, turned her back on the nosy mirror, lungs constricting by the second. No time for lines.

Fuck this stupid zip-lock bullshit.

Fingers frantic, tips of fingers numb.

Acid burned her lungs.

Walls closed in.

About fucking time. The lips of the stubborn little bag opened. She licked her little finger, dug it into the sachet and rubbed the coke onto the gum above her teeth. She straightened and surrendered to the chemical music, the seductive intro rhythm, like an old-school DJ aligning the beat in her brain with the rest of her pulsating body. She needed more, needed a kick-ass beat. More super-powder to turn her brain into a super-power, so she could destroy the scum collected in the dungeon.

She pulled out a credit card from her purse, spun around, poured the rest of the sachet onto the bench, and cut up lines.

TRACK 24

CAT'S TUMMY RUMBLED.

She removed her headphones and placed them on her desk, shook her hair, and rubbed her temples. Churning through contest songs with such an intense focus, she hadn't registered she was still alone in the office. She rummaged through her bag, but there weren't any snacks, so she headed to the kitchen for a smoothie. Annie probably had Lachie stuff to deal with. He'd been a nightmare lately and no one could begrudge her a late start. Unusual for Robbie. Maybe she should text him?

Text him? Why him instead of Annie?

She banged her plastic smoothie bottle rhythmically into her palm, head shaking.

Delooney shuffled out of the Dungeon, then Monaro, then... *Diaz? What was he doing here?*

Bottle and hand froze while she continued towards the kitchen until she saw Robbie shuffle through the big doors. Was Annie in there too? A cold bolt zapped through her gut. Why would she be the only one left out? But why Diaz?

Something wasn't rhyming on that lyric. Robbie's cowboy swagger was missing. He had a hunched back, drooping shoulders.

Fear in his eyes before he dropped his head again. Four alpha apes stuck in a huddle, none of them bragging, no one posturing. Annie's coat and bag on the couch. Was she still in there? The alpha apes avoided her presence, but she caught Tracey's wave, who pointed outside. She dropped her bottle on top of Annie's stuff and bolted out.

CAT hunched on the upper bluestone step, their usual little cave in front of a disused double-door at the side of the building, watching Annie stomping around like she was determined to smooth the century-old cobblestone laneway into blue glass. Cat's hands pressed against her tummy, aching for Annie, raging at the alpha apes. At least fifty percent of the wrath aimed at Robbie. Just when she thought he had deeper, sweeter layers, the pathetic idiot threw a spotlight on his transparent ego. Soulless ambition ranked high, but without a doubt, ego owned the number-one slot on his pop chart. How else could he allow Annie to be dragged into an ambush and then not defend her when it must've been bloody obvious she didn't have a clue? Ego strangled empathy with one hand and threw a thick curtain over rational thinking with the other.

"Fuck it, Cat. If it wasn't for this damned contest, I'd be gone already."

The contest had been Cat's idea, but she knew Annie wasn't lashing on her. Annie's rage sparked all over the place like a cut industrial electrical cable in a typhoon.

"A wise woman told me, 'Leave when it suits you, not them'. Doesn't suit you now."

"The fuck it doesn't."

"Line up another job first, then skate out of here on Delooney's balls."

"Three more weeks. That's it."

"That's it if you didn't have Lachie."

Annie skimmed her Adidas sole across a cobblestone with a venom that would have jarred Cat for months. On a snow-high, you're invincible. Best Annie wore it off out here. Delooney wouldn't dare challenge them for being away from their desks.

"Fucking Lachie. The little advanced-learning-monster shits on me after everything I've done for him. As soon as my parents are back, they can have him."

Nothing wrong with a parent venting in private. The more honest, the better the release. She was sure other parents had a moment or two when they'd love to scream a bunch of expletives about their kids. Shouldn't feel shamed for it. But there was no way Annie would dump Lachie. Not a chance. It was just the powder pushing her mind beyond the dark edges.

"And I thought Diaz might be a good role model for him. He's just another Monaro in long hair."

No point trying to calm Annie, she'd just redirect the fire at her. "Annie, you can't go back in today. I'll get your stuff and you can go through the songs at home. I'll drop by lat—"

"I…"—she stabbed her upper chest—"do not need a fucking babysitter."

"Okay, call me if you want to talk." She got up and stepped towards Annie, who stopped a metre away, a scowl adding to her razor blade eyes. Cat brought her hands together, fingers brushing her lips, sucking in a deep breath. "Annie, I promise not to go all Mother Teresa on you, but I'm begging, truly begging, as your dearest friend. Please, please, please, tell me you don't have any more coke." *For Lachie's sake.* She'd never harm him, but snorting lines rarely led to good personal decisions, let alone good parenting actions, and it would destroy all the goodness in Lachie's heart if he saw his mum like she'd been in the old days. Annie was juggling enough stress without launching into a bender.

Annie focused on tapping a cobblestone with her toe a few times, then shook her head.

CAT stood in the middle of the office while Robbie pretended he was concentrating on his screen. Five seconds… four… three…

Robbie looked up. "Oh, hey, Cat. Good news. I've got two tickets to the Dolphin Street gig this Saturday, thought you might join me."

"Two or three things you could've said, Robbie, and that one wasn't on the empathy chart. It wasn't even on the planet."

His cowboy facade turned droopy cow face. "I thought Annie knew. I swear, the way they were all talking, it was a done deal and we were just—"

"Buuuullshit, cowboy."

"Cat, I wouldn't do that to her."

"Did you defend her once you saw her nailed on the cross? When Annie destroyed them, did you back her up? Point out how angry you were they treated Annie that way? Tell Delooney you'd resign if he ever did something like that again?"

He turned to his screen, down to his keyboard.

"Even if you didn't know before the meeting, you sure as hell witnessed the lynching *during* and had a chance to stand up *after*. Five or six ways you could have stepped up, but you did fuck-all-below-zero. Slinked off like the delusional, ambitious coward you are. Didn't you?"

At least Robbie had the guts to face her. His inner cowboy had run off the ranch, slumped shoulders, head barely hanging by the neck. A neck that barely mustered the energy for an imperceptible nod.

"That's why women get repeatedly abused and raped. So-called men don't stand up."

"That's not fair. I would never—"

"Exactly. It's not fair. Not doing anything about ugly behaviour is the same as supporting the ugly behaviour. Silence slices through humanity, slashes the hearts of women, slays the essence of life. You did nothing. Nothing isn't good enough anymore." Adrenalin raced through her veins. She could feel her pulse bouncing the air. Fire swirled high in her lungs. What a waste of a speech on one stupid alpha ape. "Working in a meeting room rest of the day, maybe the rest of the contest." She glided to her desk, collected her song contest stuff, slung headphones around her neck, and whisked out the door.

163

The ninety-minute walk took ROBBIE over three hours, two of them sitting on a bench as he shuffled through the endless stream of songs, all left swipe. After Cat's blistering blitzkrieg, those poor entrants didn't stand a chance during his zombie-left-swiping.

If only he could've swiped left on the morning meeting. He'd started the long walk to and then around Albert Park Lake in a warrior state, listening to Royal Thunder's "The Sinking Seat". Didn't feel the wind, see the lake, the swans. How dare she throw him into the scum of male abusers? Did every little male blunder have to be dragged into the *MeToo* mire? What distorted mirror had she discovered that made her so bloody perfect? If Cat's speech was in public, she could've started a cult and would've been swamped with followers. Easy to throw grenades when you weren't in the room. Was he supposed to blow up his whole career? Wasn't like Annie needed any help defending herself. She was Madonna, Beyonce, and Pink all rolled into one power-diva.

The sun broke through halfway around the lake, reflections surfing the ripples from the strong, southerly breeze. He flipped down his sunnies, zipped his leather jacket tight, buried hands deep into the pockets. Swans glided by in pairs, ducks bobbed up and down in the water like the joggers flitting past him on the track. By the time he returned to Merger, Royal Thunder had slowed down and some of the lyrics in "Burning Tree" ironically doused his inner fire. He'd decided on his next steps. Actually, three parallel steps.

Step one turned out surprisingly easy—stepping up to Delaney. The buzz after ROBBIE had finished with Delaney quickly buzzed off as he neared the meeting room for step two: Cat. He knocked on the door, opened it, slipped inside, and stood with his back to the closed door. Didn't want to chicken out, didn't want to spook Cat.

She glanced at him, then made an exaggerated left swipe over her phone. He stood his ground. The round table and four chairs didn't leave much room anyway.

She paused her tablet, took off her headphones, and glared.

"How's Annie?" he asked.

She tilted her head a touch.

Maybe he'd hit the right words, the right note. Nothing calculated, he really wanted to know if she was okay.

"You get that from the library across the street? Empathy one-O-one?"

"You were right about this morning. I should have stood up for her."

"Hallelujah, you picked two of the tracks on the empathy charts. Bit late, cowboy, those tracks need action, not words." Cat raised her headphones to indicate she had more work.

"I told Delaney if he pulls another stunt like that, I'm resigning too."

Cat straightened up. "And his reaction?"

"Pulled out the magic bowl from his desk and some stupid quote from his arse. I threw the bowl against the wall and walked out."

"That was the bang a few minutes ago? You threw his sacred bowl at the wall?"

Robbie nodded.

Cat nodded too. "That might have to jump to number six in the top ten empathy chart."

"Is Annie okay? How can I apologise to her?"

"Don't know and too soon." Cat had downed her weapons but hadn't lowered her wall.

"The offer to Saturday's gig is still open."

"Don't know, too soon."

"Don't know, too soon" was better than *"no, never"*. He decided to quit while he was ahead, opened the door, and escaped.

TRACK 25

ANNIE PEELED THE ZOO PROMOTIONAL MAGNET OFF THE FRIDGE AND used it to cut three lines of coke on the plastic cutting board. Best to stay high. Couldn't pick up Lachie while she was on a downer. None of the conservative cliques at the school would notice her happy. They'd be all over her if she stumbled in looking sick or hungover. Stay high. Last hit today. Rolled up the five-dollar note. Only note left in her purse. Secret emergency compartment. Forgot it was there. Could've used printer paper but plastic was better. Smoother. Powder zipped up plastic. Paper got wet. Clogged up. Five dollars for a rainy day and this morning it fucking poured. Purple-ish legal tender. Purple was good. She liked purple.

In her hands, the note tore into two pieces.

"Fuck. How does plastic money turn into fucking tissue paper?"

She dropped the smaller piece onto the floor and rolled the two-thirds of the five-dollar note. Tight, but she had the nostrils of a golden retriever, lungs of a diva. Bent down and inhaled the first line. Braced herself against the bench to ride the initial surge. Shook her head as if that would speed up the electricity sparking through her body.

Yeah, I sure diva'd them to dust today. Who needs Diaz? I want sex, I can get it. Five minutes. Bar, club. I get hit on the damn tram all the time.

Annie laughed.

Monaro. Thought he was back in. Now he knew who he was dealing with. This is a permanent solo gig. My entourage is me, myself, and I.

She closed her eyes and reached for the ceiling. Her body buzzed like a carnival, eyelids strobed to a techno beat pulsing through her veins. It wasn't till she opened her eyes that she noticed it was already dark outside. Checked the digital wall clock.

Five-fifteen. Two more lines. Nothing to me in the old days. Like salt on a steak. Hell, I pay enough for after-school care. In advance too, may as well use it. Not like he misses me these days. Little bugger needs more time with other kids. Remind him he's not a bloody adult yet.

She snorted two lines in quick succession, shook her head hard again, then bounded into the music room. Nothing like a few minutes of crazy arse drumming to kill some time, take the edge off the day. *Ten minutes, then I'll walk to the school. Easy.*

Coke and shredding tubs. Should be legally compulsory.

ANNIE dropped the drumsticks and zipped back into the kitchen, grabbed a large glass, filled it under the tap, then guzzled it all down in one go. Filled it again and took another long swig before clanging the glass on the bench. She pulled the tea towel off the oven handle and wiped the sweaty proof of her intense drumming session off her face and forehead.

Forget legally compulsory, that felt so good it should be in the Constitution. No Aussie citizenship if you've never shredded on coke. Run that past Cat.

She glanced at the clock.

Nine past six! Shit.

After school care wound up at six. And it was a twenty-minute walk.

Shit.

She ran to the door, bounded down the steps, swung the gate open, and jogged down the street. Had to make it in seconds. Had to. Wilma... Lachie... no more school scandals.

ANNIE jogged all the way to the school gym. Running had never been her thing, so jogging that far surprised her. No wonder she was huffing and puffing. The big clock on the foyer wall screamed six-seventeen. No childlike squeals or other noises from the basketball court, which also filled in as the school hall. No one on the outside basketball court or adjoining playground either. Luckily, she wasn't the only straggler. Another mum opened the door behind her. Annie stretched an arm out to stop the woman passing.

"Can't you see the queue?"

"Sorry, you were in the middle of the room just staring up at the wall, I—"

"Will wait your fucking turn."

Nerve of the woman. They threw on a CDS—corporate designer suit—then tried to dominate everywhere they went. Probably drove an Audi, which must be the German word for "arrogant".

She pounced towards the counter.

Bugger. She'd forgotten to grab her bag, which had her purse, which had all her ID stuff and her phone. The school aftercare system had changed earlier that year to a fancy digital process. Had to tap into a tablet the name of who you were picking up, the system sent an SMS to your mobile with a code you had to tap in and then it was okay to pick up your child. She stopped halfway, stepped aside, glared at CDS woman, and waved her to pass.

CDS woman hesitated, then made a wide arc around Annie.

Stupid woman. Stupid rules. Stupid government Nazis that didn't allow the carers to release children without the parent confirming ID electronically—no matter they were on a first name basis with the parent—dragging the parent through the same process every fucking pick up. How many times did a mother have to prove she was the mother in this world?

If it was Summer or Sophie, it would be okay. They'd share a wink and they'd tick off and she'd walk Lachie home. She couldn't see which carer was still there because CDS woman blocked her view, like her ego expanded her very stature to fill up all the space.

It wasn't Sophie or Summer behind the counter. Wasn't anyone she'd seen before.

Bugger.

She strode to the counter.

Carer smiled. Not like most Chinese girls with glasses, this one had a funky angle. Red glasses, matching streaks in her black hair, red and black scarf, matching tartan skirt over black tights, and badges all over her black denim jacket, which made it impossible to find her name tag.

"Hi, I'm Lachie's mother."

Carer checked the tablet. "Hi, Mrs Vuci." She pushed the tablet across the counter.

"Ms Vuci, not Mrs."

"Sorry."

"It's two thousand and eighteen, you've got an Aussie accent, you must've grown up here. Ask if you're not sure."

"Sorry, I will. Thank you for the advice." Carer stared at the tablet.

"You know Lachie is my boy, who the hell else would be picking him up?"

Carer stepped back from the counter and straightened up. Red, knee-length lace-up boots bounced the fluorescent ceiling light. "Yes, Ms Vuci, but you know the rules."

"Left my phone at home." She was over this bullshit.

Carer intertwined her fingers, raised them to her lips. "What about your licen—"

"No, all my fucking ID is at home. And *you're* not following rules. No name badge. So, I won't tell anyone if you don't."

Carer tapped her name badge, sitting high on the right side of her chest. "Yan Yan."

"This is ridiculous. Bring Lachie around and he can ID me." To hell with the rules. What could they do, charge her for abducting her own son? She stomped to the wide-open doors of the gym.

Empty. Not at his usual spot up on the stage doing whatever he did on his tablet or reading a book.

"Can someone bring your phone for you, or you can go, I'll wait. It's okay."

"It's not fucking okay. Taking him home now." She spun back at Yan Yan, who obviously had no yin to her yan. "Where is he?"

Yan Yan checked the security monitors on the wall above the counter. "Lachie's in the music room with his father."

"Ms Vuci, I need you to sit down," said the police officer.

ANNIE couldn't remember the officer's name and the ceiling light shined off her nametag. Nametags haunted her today. Constable Something-Hyphenated, too pretty to be a cop, except for the toned arms and steely grey eyes.

"I want to see Lachie now."

"He's safe, in there with the principal, Wilma Sligo." She pointed to the ticketing booth where Yan Yan had been standing.

Wilma.

The police officer was a stranger. Didn't matter, but Wilma… Wilma was in her world, in the middle of Lachie's world. Wilma dragged out of her home and back to the school.

What have I done? Something clamped her gut and squeezed air out of her lungs. The foyer spun, photos of past principals and student achievement boards swirled around her.

The officer grabbed each arm. "Quick, shallow breaths. In-out-in-out-in-out."

She could just make out her instructions, like someone shouting from a long way. Instinct heard, and her lungs followed. *In-out-in-out-in-out.* The reassuring grip filtered through from the policewoman's hands as she was eased onto a couch backed against the wall. *In-out-in-out-in-out.* As oxygen flooded in, the foyer stopped swirling and she straightened her back, centred on the police officer's grey eyes.

"Would you like some water?"

She shook her head, just wanting to take Lachie home and curl up on her bed.

"Ms Vuci, I need you to go through what happened." Her pen and pad were out.

With air back in her lungs, her short-term memory sparked up.

"Why are you talking to me? You should be reading the riot act to Monaro. He came in illegally, he abducted Lachie. He's the one you should be dragging to the police station."

"My partner is talking to him now." She pointed towards the music room down the short hall. "However, it's clear he made no attempt to abduct your son."

"He should never have been allowed anywhere near Lachie."

"The carer understands her mistake and is deeply remorseful. But she only allowed it when Lachie saw him. Your son pleaded with Yan Yan to let him have some time with his father. She watched them on the security monitor the whole time."

Annie wondered what lies Monaro was spinning to the other cop.

"Yan Yan also tried your mobile a couple of times, but you didn't answer or return the calls. Under the circumstances, Yan Yan acted responsibly." The officer's tone on the last sentence clanged the guilty bell. Yan Yan had acted responsibly, Annie hadn't.

She stared at the music room door, banged the couch. "I need to take Lachie home now." She glanced at the huge clock above the entrance. Six-forty. "He must be starving. Have to make him dinner."

"Wilma's sorted some snacks for him. Before you go, we need to hear in your words exactly what happened in there." She pointed to the music room.

The vice around her stomach closed in again. She placed a hand over it. Focused on longer breaths. "I walked in to get Lachie, and he tried to stop me."

"Monaro tried to stop you?"

"Yes."

"How did he try to stop you?"

"Lachie was in the far corner playing bongos on a stand. Halfway there, Monaro stepped in front of me."

"Did he say anything?"

"He shouted, 'Leave him, he's happy.'"

"Did that make you angry?"

"Of course, but I ignored him. Till he grabbed me, then I pushed him away and went to Lachie."

The officer scribbled on her pad, then stopped, grey eyes searching hers. "When we arrived, Lachie was still in there. Yan Yan was helping Mr Monaro with his bleeding head. You were here, sitting, bent over."

"Do you have children?"

"This isn't about me."

"It's not about me either. It's that bastard in there, he created all this." Her turn to point at the music room. "If you were a mother, you'd have locked him up by now."

"Where was Mr Monaro standing when—"

"I've told you what happened. It's in your little book. Now I'm getting my son and we're going home." Fire sizzled again in her belly, her veins. She bounced up.

The police officer bounced up, stood between her and the office. Close. Constable Tylor-Shore, her badge boasted. "We can do this quickly and friendly here, or we can all go to the station."

No way would she go to the station, she hadn't done anything wrong. This nightmare was enough horror for Lachie; dragging him through a police station would deepen the scars. Over her shoulder, Constable Tylor-Shore's partner came out of the music room.

Constable Tylor-Shore followed her gaze. "Please wait here."

She nodded.

Constable Tylor-Shore met her partner at the end of the hallway, and she talked through her notes. He talked through the rubbish in his notebook, Monaro's bullshit. They came over together.

"This is Sergeant Kels."

"Hello, Ms Vuci. I understand you'd like to head off. We all would, but we have a conflicting story."

"Of course. He's a born liar."

"Apparently you were extremely angry when you stormed into—"

"He's just—"

"Please, Ms Vuci." A stern, deep voice. What a stop sign would sound like. "Your anger was corroborated by two witnesses."

She shot a glance at the office but couldn't see Yan Yan. *Two witnesses?* Hand over her stomach again.

"Would you like a moment to rethink your statement?"

Statement. Witnesses. Police. The old principals looked down on her from the walls, a jury unimpressed. Fuck them all.

She pointed at Constable Tylor-Shore's notebook. "That's my statement."

"Had you been drinking before you came to pick up your son?" asked Sergeant Kels.

"No."

"Why were you late?"

"I was working from home. We're under a ton of pressure on this song contest. Check that with my boss. Lost track of time."

"Did you take any drugs?" Constable Tylor-Shore and her steely grey eyes.

"Just heavy-duty painkillers. I had a migraine." Similar effect on pupils. The things she'd learned in her embryonic years in the rock biz slithered right into place.

"Could the migraine have contributed to your rage?"

Sneaky bitch, dangling a word like rage to slip her up.

"I had no rage, no anger, apart from the natural instincts of a mother who saw her child with his absent, non-guardian, non-father, non-good-for-anything ghost." Defensive muscle memory tapped into her angelic voice. Wheel in a church organ and she'd make the room cry.

"Mr Monaro has the right to file an assault charge. That's a serious process," said Sergeant Kels.

She imagined picking up a church organ and dumping it on Monaro. Breathing deep, she reached for her inner angel again. "First, I did not assault him. Second, he was the criminal who barged in here to illegally spend time with Lachie."

"There isn't a restraining order and he never tried to take your son, so technically he hasn't done anything illegal."

Restraining order. Why hadn't she sorted that sooner? She needed to get Jenny onto it as soon as she got out of this mess.

"Would you be willing to take a substance test down at the station?" Constable Tylor-Shore. They were playing bad cop, mean cop.

"Sure." *Fucking no.*

"We understand Lachie's a smart kid. Because of his age we can't use him as a witness, but we can interview him in the presence of an independent adult like Wilma as part of our investigation." Constable Tylor-Shore tapped her notebook. "Would his account match yours?"

Breathe. I can't breathe. Oh, Lachie, what have I done? Jelly legs, cement lungs.

The police officers grabbed an arm each and eased her back onto the couch.

Defiance deflated, fear impregnating every nerve. She curled up into a ball, eyes open, seeing nothing.

TRACK 26

CURLED UP ON HER COUCH, ANNIE'S HEAD RESTED ON THE PILLOW ON CAT's lap. Stroking Annie's hair calmed both of them. The police had insisted Annie see a doctor immediately for her fainting. Annie had agreed but refused a lift from the police, and Lachie refused to walk home with his mum. Struggling with an almighty downer and shock, Annie had called Cat in desperation. Cat collected them in an Uber, placating both Lachie and the police.

"Poor Yan Yan, I destroyed her. I was so fucking furious," said Annie.

"It wasn't just the anger, was it?" She bit her lip, not the time for *I told you so*. The doctor had been kind and quick—as it was these days at bulk-billing clinics—and they'd gone straight home without picking up any of the medication because it had been prescribed based on Annie's false information. She just needed the doctor's certificate to satisfy the police.

Annie took in a long breath, kind of a reverse sigh. "I need to find her tomorrow and apologise. Buy her something."

"Too soon. When all this is sorted out, she'll understand."

"I fucked up and now I'll lose Lachie."

Last time Cat had checked on him, Lachie was tucked under his doona. When she'd picked them up, she didn't recognise the poor kid. No smile, zombie eyes, head drooping to shoulder level. Normally, he'd be animated with Cat, chatting and teasing in all sorts of fascinating tangents. Not one word. Not even a kid-grunt.

"Can't happen. Not unless you pulled a gun on Monaro."

No response on the feeble attempt at a gag. Too soon.

"All he said was, 'Hi, Annie.'"

"Lachie?"

"Monaro."

"Don't torture yourself on this now. I can help you get all your facts down tomorrow, before you head to the police station."

"I stepped across and barged him with my shoulder. The weak bastard stumbled back and tripped over one of those little prep desks."

"That's how he ended up bleeding?"

"I guess. I was already heading to Lachie. Didn't see it, just heard the crash."

"Could Lachie have seen it?"

Annie nodded without lifting her head off the pillow. "He screamed 'Dad' and ran right past me. Ran to him. Him. I screeched at Lachie. Must've sounded like a deranged witch."

She understood now. The singer in Annie needed to get it all out vocally, had to confess to someone, sing her sins to someone she could trust.

"Then Lachie screamed. Oh, Cat, it was the most terrifying, soul-destroying sound." Annie shivered, blew out air. "Froze me to my core. Sobered me."

Finally, she'd acknowledged she was high. Maybe something good would come out of tonight's horror. Had to.

"He kept screaming, 'Dad, Dad'... Then Yan Yan rushed in... she saw Lachie on his knees next to Monaro, looked at me and shouted, 'Stay right where you are.'"

Annie, Annie, Annie... the more details she gave, the more she sounded like a criminal. Any mum would've been furious, but the coke added an ugly edge, the barge and blood. Bless the spirits the bastard only got a concussion. He even had the nerve to text Annie after he was checked out in Emergency. *Lucky for you my noggin is steel. That just leaves assault.*

"I went to Lachie, screamed at him to get up, we were going home. The terror in his eyes. At me. He cowered behind Monaro, beside the blood on the floor from... I nearly kicked that paternal pretender so hard... Yan Yan yelled out she was calling an ambulance... I screamed louder at Lachie... he cried... his whole body shook. My boy... terrified of me. Me."

She squeezed Annie's shoulder. Somehow Annie rolled up tighter on the couch.

"Then Yan Yan yelled out, 'I'm calling the police now.' The rest is a blur. I think I was going to run home... but Lachie, I couldn't leave him... They found me on the couch in the foyer." Annie shivered again, longer this time.

Cars rolled by outside with a frequency suggesting the beginning of a new day. No sunlight peeked through the edges of the curtains, but it wouldn't be long. How long before Annie could peek around the curtain of last night's memories without shivering? Without regrets?

"I'm going to lose Lachie, aren't I?"

"No, Annie. Monaro can be a dick, but the system will have empathy for you. Jenny's a good lawyer. She'll make sure you keep Lachie."

Annie raised herself on an elbow, her eyes hollow with fear.

"You don't get it. Whatever else happens, I've lost a part of Lachie. Shattered his innocence. That's not a mum's job. I'm supposed to protect him from... from... He'll never look at me the same. Ever." Annie's sniffling gurgled into a stream of sobs.

She stroked Annie's hair, reflecting on her own tenuous maternal relationship. Somehow, they'd survived her teenage years and come out with a mutual respect on top of their love, but in that case, she'd been the rebel. Her mother might've lost it a couple of times, but always under the stress and attacks she'd instigated. This was reverse rebelling. A mother momentarily off the rails was one thing, crashing in front of her eight-year-old son, another. Monaro's presence and blood added all sorts of messy layers.

But she wasn't there as an analyst or counsellor. Or to judge.

"Annie Vuci, there was only one Mother Theresa and even she had her critics. If I ever decide to be a mother, I'd want to connect with my kid like you have with Lachie. One bad song doesn't destroy the special life album you guys have created. You'll get through this one track at a time."

CAT sensed a shadow over her screen and turned to see Manny the Maori mountain towering beside her desk.

"Kia ora."

"Kia ora."

"I've just downloaded the last bunch of songs into your respective apps."

She indicated to Robbie's empty desk with her chin, stared at Annie's empty chair. "Thanks. I'll just do a thirty-six-hour, non-stop shift and we'll be done." Robbie's absence this morning of all mornings triggered an old, passive-aggressive habit. But seriously, unless his brother Johnny had some hospital emergency, the cowboy needed to be here working his butt off.

Manny stepped over and patted the back of Annie's chair. "She okay?"

She nodded, shrugged.

"The shit on Annie's list has already been culled. Only a hundred and three for her to check out."

About thirty-three percent. No question, music was subjective, like any art or entertainment, but the really bad stuff was obvious. Still, she wasn't sure if Manny was the right person to be culling the tracks on their behalf.

"Don't look at me like I killed Freddie, it was your new pal." Manny pointed to Robbie's desk. "He was here till three this morning just to do that for Annie. Probably drowning himself in caffeine to get in and start on his own bunch."

New pal? Had Robbie been exaggerating their friendship?

Nice gesture, though. Whether he still carried some guilt about the meeting that triggered Annie's bender or not, he did a good deed and good deeds in this biz were rarer than good songs.

"Nice to see you smiling again." Manny's grin cancelled out his own shadow, then the cheeky Maori mountain lumbered around and out the door.

Damn Manny. Digital or real world, the dude logged into gossip like Delooney attracted pop starlets.

CAT watched Robbie from the Merger kitchen door, thanks to Stacey tipping her off when he'd arrived. He had three short blacks lined up from the coffee machine and poured them into his large, reusable cup. She knocked and moved towards him.

"You want water with that caffeine?"

His half smile managed to crack some light through the baggy black eyes and unshaven face.

"You know you can just have a large, long black from that thing." She leant back onto the bench about a metre from his production line.

"Then there's more water per caffeine. This way, I definitely get three shots."

"You earned them. Nice thing you did for Annie."

Robbie finished pouring the last of the small cups, then turned to her at a right angle, face scrunched up into a question.

"Manny."

Robbie nodded, shrugged his shoulders.

It amused her how many huge egos she'd meet that constantly sought attention yet found it difficult to accept compliments. Fascinating paradox. But this time, Robbie seemed genuinely humble, probably still kicking around the can of guilt as an accessory to Annie's bender.

"Robbie, let it go. Annie will understand why you were in the meeting once the shit settles. And no one but Annie is responsible for her reaction after that."

He nodded to his cup. "Invitation to that gig is still open. Let me know any time before they hit the stage."

"Okay."

"Okay, you'll let me know?"

"Okay, I'll be there."

Bloodshot eyes focused on her with an intensity he had no right to have. Must have been the caffeine fumes.

"Strictly as two professionals. For professional reasons only," she added quickly.

A half-moon smile washed away the tiredness on his face.

Maybe she'd turned a simple SMS into a giant rock poster, but he had to know the boundaries. Give a dude like Robbie a single track and he'd download a whole back catalogue in his sleazy imagination.

"Friendly professionals?" His bloodshot lines turned to glowing neons promoting the Cheeky Bastard Show.

She stretched her arm for a handshake. "Friendly professionals."

His hand buzzed heat through her arm and zapped around her tummy.

Must be the caffeine fumes.

ANNIE blessed the Rock Goddesses that Lachie emerged for school on time, fully dressed. Any battle would have become another war and she was too brittle for a battle, let alone a war with Lachie. Her spirit was still buried in the trenches of last night's nightmare, under the bones of her self-respect. A stranger in her own kitchen, she hadn't been so self-conscious since her first public performance, walking on eggshells on top of broken glass on emotionally blistered feet. She'd resorted to instant coffees, two heaped spoons of it, plus three sugars. Overkill even for her demanding sweet tooth. Sipped at it with one eye on her phone as she scrolled through morning news, one on him.

Him, the too-mature-eight-year-old, so far pretending last night didn't happen. Maybe that was the mature way forward for them. Instant forgiveness and move on. *Can you carry a grudge when you're eight? Don't they just move on in a myopic bliss we lose as adults?*

"I did some research last night," he said before shovelling another spoon of cereal into his mouth.

Research? A school project I can help him with? Good sign, he opened a safe door. She scoured her memory. The science thing was last term. Some backyard agricultural experiment was coming up next term. She remembered reading about that in some notice. At least he was talking. Talking about a subject that wasn't last night. Talking like she was still his mum. She floated in his cereal crunching, the sweet rhythm crackling through her veins. She put her phone on silent, placed it upside down on the bench, and faced him. His gorgeous cheeks magnified behind the glass of Milo he gulped. Putting the glass down, a moustache of chocolate milk lined his upper lip, throwing her back to his kindergarten days, sweetness and fun. Innocence.

"What kind of research?"

"Apparently you can't divorce your parents till you're eighteen."

The kitchen bench separating them wasn't high enough to stop his words tearing through her heart. She gripped the bench hard. *He hadn't researched it. Just a throwaway line. Something he'd cut-and-pasted from social media. Teasing.*

"Only costs two hundred and fifty dollars in fees, but legal costs can be as high as one thousand." Lachie swung out of the chair, picked up his glass and bowl, bounced past her, and placed them in the dishwasher. "Think I might become a lawyer. They get paid heaps for doing stuff you can Google." He disappeared into the bathroom.

The buzzing of his electric toothbrush sawed her in half.

ANNIE sat on the bench under the sliver of sun streaking between two trees. She needed another lap around the huge park to find some structure in her thoughts, but she'd promised to be at the police station by nine, so six or seven minutes on the bench was all she had.

A quick chat to clarify a couple of things, Constable Tylor-Shore said on the phone just before she'd dropped off Lachie at before-school care, the scene of the crime.

Lachie.

No matter her pace, that morning he'd dragged a couple of steps behind all the way to school, her ultimate walk of shame. They weren't supposed to be like that until they were teenagers. The memory of treating her mum like a stranger on the way to the last year of primary school and early years of high school sent a shiver up her spine. Did all awful phases have to be repeated by generations? When she turned into the school street, she stopped and spread her arms up, begging him to stop. He stopped, head bowed, headphones tormenting her like bull horns. She waited till he looked up, his eyes centring between her shoulder and ear.

"I'm sorry," she said. The least she could do was apologise for scaring him last night. For screaming. A bit of mea culpa on the dangers of acting out your anger. Be the adult.

"Sorry for hurting him, or sorry for not letting me know my father?"

Her heart cringed under a ton of empathy. What decent boy wouldn't want to know his father? Simultaneously, clarity cleansed her mind with a scary soberness. What mother would deprive him of that?

"Why do you get to decide? I want to spend time with him, make up my own mind."

She nodded.

It wasn't a smile, but light flickered back into his eyes and held her gaze for the first time since last night's horror. "Is that a yes nod, or a hopeless horse imitation?"

"Yes, it's a yes," she said.

He headed for the school with Annie a half-step behind him till he stepped through the school gate and waved an arm up a few degrees without turning around.

Despite the growing nerves of her imminent visit to a police station, her thoughts were consumed by Lachie, her stupidity, and the future. No way around it, she'd have to call Monaro. Apologise for last night—whether he apologised for being there unannounced and unauthorised or not—and arrange time for him to spend with Lachie. She took out her phone, hesitated, sucked in deep and blew out hard, flapping her lips with the air. Then the police could close the file on the incident. The school wouldn't let it happen again, so Monaro couldn't sneak time with Lachie and confuse the kid. Scrolled down to his number. Yes, this way she'd maintain control.

Any sign of Lachie being unhappy and she'd block Monaro out for good.

Pressed *Call*. Kept ringing to his voicemail. *Damn*. She hung up, unprepared for a message. Another deep breath, more flapping lips. Hit *Call*. All the way to voicemail again.

"Hey... it's me. I'm sorry about last night. We have to put Lachie first. Call me and we'll make a time so the two of you can catch up... properly." She'd meant *properly* as in spending good time with Lachie, but voicemails were dangerous. Even she'd made tonal mistakes and maybe *properly* had an accusatory edge... like he didn't do it properly last night and therefore created all the mess.

She hit *Call*. Much safer talking than any message. Hung up when it flipped to his voicemail. Was he still asleep with the phone on silent? Or not answering on purpose? Nothing she could do now. At least she could face the police and tell them she'd apologised. They could all move on to more important stuff.

Constable Tylor-Shore led ANNIE into a room, similar to the small meeting room at Merger but grey, with boring police-lecture posters on the walls. Constable Tylor-Shore sat on a metal chair with vinyl upholstery and indicated she do the same on the opposite side of the small table. She expected the manila file and pad the constable plonked on the desk but not the large digital recorder already sitting there. Constable Tylor-Shore pressed a button on the recorder and a tiny red light switched on.

Her bottom barely balanced on the edge of the chair, eyes transfixed on the recorder, every sinew tighter than an over-tuned guitar. Last time she'd been recorded by Diaz led to this whole abomination.

Constable Tylor-Shore got her to confirm her name, date of birth, and address.

Something wasn't right. "You said this was just to clarify a couple of things, is that really necessary?" She pointed at the recorder.

Constable Tylor-Shore nodded. "I have to advise you that Tony Monaro has filed charges based on the alleged assault last night. You have the right to refer to a lawyer if you choose. You are not under arrest at this stage and can therefore leave this interview at any time. The preliminary investigation may take three to four months to decide whether there is a legitimate case against you. As part of the procedure, we would like to interview your son Lachie in the presence of an adult whom you are comfortable with, like a relative or his school principal. His statement cannot be used as evidence in court; however, it will help us decide if official charges should be processed. If you are charged with basic assault and found guilty, the judge will either fine you a substantial amount or commit you to three months in jail. If, as Mr Monaro claims, you are found to have assaulted him with intention to cause serious injury, the punishment is a maximum of twenty years in prison."

TRACK 27

THE ROOM STARTED SPINNING SOMEWHERE AROUND "YOU CAN REFER TO A *lawyer*". ANNIE had seen TV crime shows where police laid out a suspect's rights, but having charges dumped on her by police in a police station drained her soul. From then she heard the constable in third person, looking down on a shell, a ghost who looked like her, with white, not olive skin, and transparent eyes.

"Please confirm you understand," said Constable Tylor-Shore.

Annie's ghost nodded.

"I need to hear you say you understand the charges against you."

"I understand the charges against me." Guilt replaced the blood in her veins. She couldn't help feeling like a dirty criminal.

"You should know we'll also be officially interviewing two adult witnesses."

"Two?" she whispered.

"The after-school carer and another parent who claims you were high on drugs."

Something snapped the real Annie back. "That's ridiculous. She's just a grumpy excuse for—"

"She happens to be a doctor. A neurosurgeon."

She slouched back into the hard plastic chair.

"Annie, our own notes confirm her view. I'll ask you again, what drugs had you taken before the alleged assault?"

Alleged assault.

Two razor blade words rolled up in barbed wire scraped around her mouth, squeezed down her throat, and scarred her gut. She wiped her hands on her jeans, then covered her stomach. Shook her head.

"You understand if this case proceeds, you'll eventually have to answer that question in court under oath."

The tiny red recording light had ballooned to half a tennis ball.

"Annie?"

"Lawyer. Need my lawyer."

Constable Tylor-Shore opened the folder and placed a document on the table. "This is for the assault charges." She pulled out two other documents. "And this is the intervention order application." The constable pushed the document towards her.

A beacon in her hell-fog. "Yes, I'd like to file an intervention order to keep that bastard—"

"Too late, he's already filed this application. And based on his injuries, the magistrate will probably grant Mr Monaro his request for an interim order."

"How can the system be biased against men when the bastard gets away with this?" ANNIE prowled in the small space between the visiting chairs and wall in Jenny's office. The small cabinet and book-shelves crammed her pacing, a stark reminder of her potential lack of freedom if she gave in to the ridiculous charges and the ridiculous system that allowed the charges.

"He hasn't got away with anything yet. Although, based on what you've told me and these"—Jenny tapped the three documents spread across her desk—"he'll probably get the interim intervention order."

"We have to fight it. Not letting that monster win anything."

"Annie, please sit down and let's not strain that magical singing voice."

Fair enough. Jenny was on her side, no point yelling. She'd left the police station in a stupor and stumbled through the streets and park until anger and adrenaline flooded her veins. She was still too wired to sit.

"The interim intervention order is the least of your problems."

"But we have to fight it, right?

"If you have the time and endless financial resources, I'd say let's rip into him early and keep shredding hard until he crawls away. But this isn't about destroying Monaro, it's about the best thing for Lachie."

Annie stalled mid-step, then slumped into a visitor chair.

"My advice is to forget the interim order for custody." Jenny pushed that document aside, then pointed at Monaro's application for an intervention order. "You have to fight this because it can impact the assault charges and, more importantly, the longer-term Family Court process for Lachie, which is already in motion."

In her fury, she'd forgotten about the Family Court thing. She slumped back in the chair. "But he's the one who turned up where he wasn't supposed to be. How can he possibly get an intervention order against me?"

"The school has acknowledged their error, will review their procedures, and make adjustments to ensure something like that never happens again. Wilma also said she'd apologise to you in writing and in person."

"But he still gets an intervention order against me."

Jenny shook her head. "Worst case scenario, we get a mutual intervention order. Plenty of precedents and enough justification for that. Outside chance of getting his application squashed all together, but we'll need a barrister to make sure you get the best outcome."

"How much?"

Jenny scribbled a figure on her pad and spun it around for her. "That's a minimum."

Two week's salary. Of a salary that already had every cent accounted for plus some. "Only consolation is he'll be spending the same, I guess."

More head shaking from Jenny. "Because he's applying and it

involves physical injury, the police represent his case. Same with the assault charges if they proceed to court."

"How is that fair? He's got all the money and the police represent him? That's bullshit."

"Agree, but that's how it works. If the assault charges go to court, you need to add a zero on the end of that figure."

Jenny had already kindly agreed to waive the cost of her time for the Family Court stuff. There was no way she could expect her to do this for nothing, let alone a decent barrister. She was going to lose Lachie and every cent she had, and dive deeper into debt.

"You don't want to hear this and I'm not judging, but you need to do everything you can to avoid these charges going to court. This incident, no matter whose fault and what the outcome, have put all the cards in Monaro's hands. You have to find a way to talk this through with him. To work out a solution that's best for Lachie." Jenny got up, moved around her desk, and sat on the edge of the other visitor chair. "And the best for Lachie might be difficult for you, especially now, but that's what you need to focus on."

Groundhog Day. First Cat, now Jenny. Best for Lachie... Focus on Lachie... Lachie, Lachie, Lachie.

"This *is* all about Lachie. The last nine years have been aaaall about Lachie." Maybe it came out more metal than pop. Maybe laced with some acid rock for the guilt at her tinge of resentment towards Lachie.

Jenny didn't blink, just nodded and gently rested her hands on Annie's. "We need your feisty fox, not your vixen."

"That bastard brings out the worst in me."

"Aretha would turn in her grave if she heard one of her singing sisters hide behind victimhood."

Goddess Aretha Franklin. Only church she worshipped.

"If this is all about Lachie, you need to bury that coke habit forever. You need to commit to a rehab—"

"I don't need rehab, it was my first time since I found out I was pregnant."

"Right. Then find a counsellor or therapist and see them weekly until the Family Court process is over."

"Therapist?"

"Maybe I need to ask as a friend, only you know the answer to that. But I absolutely have to recommend it as your lawyer. People will accept the Monaro school incident as a severe trigger if you can show acceptance and self-imposed therapy. Acceptance of what made you so angry turns the spotlight back on Monaro as the person who behaved in an inappropriate manner to create that level of anger. Am I making sense?"

Post-mindfulness is better than no mindfulness--the mantra Cat had mumbled incessantly for a few months. In this case, the perception of post-mindfulness was her ally. She nodded.

"Good, because denial dings the danger bells." Jenny squeezed her hands, rose, scooted around the desk, and tapped her laptop. "Do you need any recommendations?"

She shook her head. "Cat knows a few."

TRACK 28

HELPING OTHERS SPUN CAT INTO A HIGH. IT WAS HER DNA. HELPING Annie buzzed her just below euphoric. Scrolling down the list of therapists she'd compiled in her tablet, she skipped past Reiki healers and relationship counsellors to the sub-heading of "solution-focused brief therapy".

"Perfect. I'll add three more links for you," she said.

Annie peered over her shoulder to get a closer look at the email of referrals Cat had typed up. "You've listed enough for a soccer team. I haven't got the time to check them all out. Two or three is plenty."

"I'll put them in recommended order. Check out as many as you need." She cut and pasted the three solution-based brief therapists to the top and fiddled with the order of a couple of the others, then hit *Send*. She turned to Annie and squeezed her arm gently. "I'm proud of you, Annie. Good things are going to come out of this. Sometimes you have to be dragged through the desert of life to find your personal oasis."

Annie squeezed her hand. "Well, that desert sand is getting stuck in my toes and bum crack."

She laughed. Annie making any joke was a good sign.

Annie slid behind her own desk, shifted the mouse, and reached for her earbuds. They still had a chunk of songs to get through this week.

"I'm going to a gig with Robbie tomorrow night."

Annie stopped in motion, holding the buds either side of her cheeks.

No idea why the confession spilled out then, or why it felt like a confession, so she added, "Do you want to come?" Even as the words dribbled out, she knew the timing was all wrong.

"Which gig?"

Now she was stuck. She couldn't explain why they were going to see this emerging band without giving away Robbie's secret ambition. *Weird. I'm hiding something from Annie about Robbie... but it felt right.*

"Dolphin Street. Robbie reckons they've got something. My soul hasn't lapped up any live music for ages and with everything else going crazy, I thought, 'What the heck?' It's a professional curiosity thing, too. With a band playing I don't even have to talk to Robbie to enjoy the night." *Toooo muuuuch blabbering infor-bloody-mation.*

Annie smiled. "Count me out of your soul-lapping. I've got a ton of head-scratching and heart-mending to get through."

CAT had to concede, live music came a close second to helping people. She'd survived a couple of clubbing nights and a few raves, but the raw connection with a real-time, interactive act turned her blood into gushing rivers of micro bubbles. It had been at least six months, which explained why she was already buzzing as she approached the Espy.

Robbie was early, in his black leather jacket and tight white jeans, one foot on the pavement, the other propped two concrete steps up. He sure was a master at cowboy contortion poses.

"Hey!" she yelled from a couple of metres, above the thrum of traffic on the Esplanade and the parallel Jacka Boulevard a little further down the slope.

"Hey." Robbie straightened up on the pavement, arms by his side, slightly forward, like he might come in for a hug.

She scampered up the steps and whirled through the entrance.

Being there for the support act meant you didn't have to battle the cattle to get a good vantage point. Usually. Standing on the raised area near the rear bar, CAT took in the eclectic crowd jamming into the Gershwin Room. Uni students from all corners of the planet (as Melbourne now as coffee and trams); suburban beer boys; young, former private school women with a variety of little bottled drinks and superbly torn jeans with various combinations of Kardashian lips and Beyonce hips; plus the veterans, the Espy super-fans who'd fought to keep the Espy as the iconic live music venue in Melbourne when big money was determined to turn the vintage building into high-rise modern apartments.

The refurbished venue had lost none of its magic. Jazz ghosts from the twenties, rock gods from the sixties, even the disco blimp in the seventies, all added layers to an aura so thick you could caress it. She'd raged with raunchy, emerging bands and rock royalty in every inch of the building. A couple of the vets she'd met lifted their beers to her. They'd led the fight to save the iconic pub for the punters. She dipped her head and raised her Corona in respect.

Robbie bopped beside her, almost in synch to Dolphin Street's beat. Both the male and female lead vocalists pulsated raw sensuality, the woman wielding her lead guitar like a mystical axe. Rhythm and energy and melody blasted out of the speakers. Five members, four musicians, three vocalists, one amazing sound.

Robbie moved closer, pointing to the front where most of the younger punters danced. "They know the lyrics. They're not just reacting to a tribal beat and alcohol, they know the bloody words."

She understood his enthusiasm. This band had already built a following from hard gigging and clever social media, but mainly good old-fashioned gigging. Too many young acts thought social media or YouTube could give them a shortcut. In this biz, there was no such thing. A band needed three things for longevity: songwriting talent, work ethic, and the ability to get on. A rare trifecta.

Robbie nudged her arm and yelled, "Gotta get closer!" He took off.

She found herself instinctively following him as he somehow wound his way through bouncing bodies and swaying glasses and bottles. A tap on the shoulder here, cheesy smile there, and the path opened up for him. On her own, she would've stepped on toes, copped elbows in the head, and knocked precious alcohol out of glasses.

A few metres from the stage, he stopped and grooved with the band again. No cowboy posturing here, just the goofy guy she'd seen from a distance dancing with his brother at Deceptive Bends, oblivious to everything but the music.

She closed her eyes and let the music own her. All of her. Traces of the smoke machine blended with alcohol fumes and sweat drifted through her greedy nostrils. She surrendered her body to the beat, her blank canvas mind to the words painted by passionate singing. The band in their zone, and she in theirs. The magic of the moment of live music.

Someone bumped her hard, knocking her into a freefall.

"Woops, sorry," said a solid young woman in a long, loose black dress and friendly smile.

Cat flailed for balance, then found herself wrapped in Robbie's arms. Strong arms.

Solid Woman winked at her, then bounced to the music again.

Robbie smiled and held on a few seconds. Awkward seconds. She extricated herself, no room in the pit to step away too far. Robbie kept a hand on her back. Maybe he wanted to make sure she'd recovered her balance, maybe protect her from another hit. A lot of heat from one hand, like a spotlight focused on her spine.

Should've worn that flannelette blouse over the singlet top. But she'd dumped it on her bed at the last second before leaving. She didn't want to appear ungrateful for him saving her from being trampled on the dance floor, but didn't want the awkward moment to make stuff more awkward.

His gaze lingered, stage lights flashing off his eyes, yet there was something new in the look. Something intimate, which she felt as much as saw.

The music stopped, giving her an obvious out as they both turned to the stage to applaud, arms high, Robbie's whistles piercing the crazed crowds'.

"Good find, Robbie. Cool name too, Dolphin Street." CAT liked the sound of it.

They were both on such a high with the potential of the band, as soon as Dolphin Street finished their set, they'd slipped out and sauntered from the Espy to under the clock tower across the road. The stone tower muffled the trams, revellers, and cars rolling past slowly behind them. On the Esplanade at the bottom of the steep grassy hill ahead, cars zipped by. Leaning on the old concrete balustrade with elbows and forearms, she found the boats bobbing on the bay under the pier's tall lamps mesmerising. She loved this little spot, an almost private mecca in the middle of a busy hub, overlooking Port Phillip Bay from high up. She could've been on a giant ocean liner, channelling her inner Kate Winslet.

Except Robbie was no Leo.

"We could do this together, Cat."

She spun her glare onto him. *We? Together?*

"I've been looking out for a potential business partner for ages. This biz can shred you to pieces, but if we can navigate the mess at Merger and the stress of this contest, we can handle anything."

She turned back to the bay, following the lights of an oil tanker or container ship heading out. The powerful, huge ship couldn't make it through the Rip—the notoriously dangerous tight entrance and exit to the bay—on its own, it needed the experienced guidance of a tug boat captain. She didn't see herself as a tugboat, nor an experienced sea captain. Neither was Robbie, so where did that preposterous idea come from?

"I don't want to come across as a groupie, so I have to make an official approach soonish, before someone else discovers them," he said, resting on his forearms.

Soonish... Her dream of managing music artists was only recently acknowledged and barely comfortable as an idea. Soonish sounded way too real, too soon. She didn't know if she was tough enough to be a manager in this fucked-up biz. She could be tough for an underdog cause, but the shady music waters attracted all kinds of sharks.

"Are they tough enough to survive? Can Dolphin Street be Shark Road when they need to?"

Robbie stared at her.

Her skin flicked back to the dance floor, his hand on her back. Heat she could still feel. Ridiculous. Probably the three beers they'd had.

Robbie turned and pointed at the bay. "Dolphin Street is a perfect omen. Dolphins won't attack sharks but if a shark attacks them, the dolphin will swim away, then swing back and hit the shark in the stomach with its nose. If the shark buggers off, that's it, but if a shark is stupid, the dolphin will keep banging it until the shark goes away... or dies."

"I underestimated those cute creatures. Here's to dolphins." She raised her fist in a jab position.

Robbie fist bumped her knuckles lightly.

She focused on the tiny waves tickling the beach to their left. The tranquil bay provided safe waters, glimmering under the stars and half-moon, but the Rip created a treacherous entry point. For any new business, the early days and years could be stormy. From what she'd seen in the music biz, it started with madness then got crazier. Could she be a dolphin? Why was she even thinking about such a major change now? And why with Robbie?

"I couldn't do this on my own, Cat, but there's something about the idea of working together that feels right."

Is he just saying what I want to hear? Is he that perceptive?

"Feels more crazy than right."

"Seriously, we have enough similar tastes in music and enough contrasts for the creative elements to work. We've proven that with the contest and tonight."

"Takes a lot more than that." She straightened up, patting down her black jeans.

"I have the marketing instincts and you're a natural nurturer. I enjoy negotiating contracts and you're a champion at fighting for an underdog. And let's face it, every new act is a huge underdog these days." He leant sideways on the balustrade. "To be honest, since I started thinking about partnering with you, I can't stop thinking about... about launching our own management company. I know you hated me and Delaney for bringing me into the contest, but maybe it's a bit of destiny."

"Accidental destiny."

"That's it!" Robbie shot up and did a tight loop, like a dog searching for the exact spot to wee, then stopped and beamed his smile. "You've got more marketing nous than you give yourself credit for."

"Maybe more than you give me credit for, but what's *it*?"

"The name of our company, Accidental Destiny. Looooooove it. You're a genius."

Accidental Destiny… or Accident Waiting to Happen.

Why did Robbie just goof around in front of her like a fun human instead of the marketing cowboy she had him pinned for? Looking at her like he'd known her forever? Maybe they'd had more than three beers.

"I like your smile, Cat. Sure beats that fire-breathing thing you aimed at me in the early days."

And why, oh why, was she smiling?

TRACK 29

ROBBIE WAVED THE TRAM ON AND SAT ON THE BACK OF THE BENCH SEAT. As the big beast rolled out of his way, he stared again across the street, at the dark second-floor office windows above Deceptive Bends. He visualised working through one window behind a desk and Cat at the other, phones to their ears, flashing computer screens, Johnny fiddling with his CDs on his private couch in the far corner, and a rolling soundtrack from their acts adding to the atmosphere.

He'd already flagged the idea of renting the spare rooms from Theo as a joke, but his subconscious must've been racing way ahead because Accidental Destiny was going to happen. He could feel it in his musical veins. Theo and Anthea would love it when they found out he was partnering with Cat.

Cat. What a crazy curiosity she was.

After a bunch of missteps and miscalculations in the early days, everything added up to them as business partners. They even hung out at the same record store without knowing it, and because no one ever talked work there, Theo and Anthea didn't have a clue about their Merger Music connection until she turned up the same afternoon he was mucking around with Johnny. He could see the sign on the door, only visible to those who looked for it. Accidental Destiny. Perfect location surrounded with edgy bars and cafes and eclectic shops. They'd set up the second room as a cruisy meeting room, no hint of corporate crap.

Partnering with Cat. Cat, so many angles and layers and tangents. They'd do it professionally with proper partnership agreements. He might have to dip in more of the working capital, but they'd still be absolutely fifty-fifty, and it would be worth it because they'd achieve far more together and quicker than anything he could do on his own.

Cat. That was a fun night. Even though they'd bounced words across pavement for hours, crossed roads safely without looking, and shook hands on their deal, she'd insisted on making her own way home.

"Robbie, this is a strictly professional relationship."

She must've said it six times through the night. As if it could be anything else. His inner studio buzzed because of their commitment to Accidental Destiny, not any romantic or sexual thing. Sure, he liked her now, and yes, she zapped some electricity when excited about something—talking with her hands so much they could create enough wind for sustainable energy—and yes, those deep green oval eyes had a sparkle, but this was strictly professional. Had to be.

ANNIE stalled a couple of metres from Delaney's office door. The morning police interrogation still gripped her shoulders and neck. She stretched her torso and followed her trusty pre-performance breathing exercise, possibly the most valuable trick she'd ever picked up from any singing lesson. She'd tip-toed around Lachie, who was still in divorce-my-evil-mother mode, then tripped through a preliminary meeting with Jenny and the barrister, Travis, in preparation of the intervention order defence.

Two things blared through that soundtrack—one, she had to get Monaro to talk, to drop the assault charges and negotiate an arrangement for Lachie time; two, she couldn't afford the alternative, couldn't afford defending the intervention order. Couldn't think about the endless pile of cash she needed to fight the assault charges. Jenny would be lenient with her fees and no question about Travis's ability as a barrister, but he didn't do cheap.

She was all out of fight. Lachie came first, not her recent version of putting Lachie first. Anger had eloped with denial, and she was left to bargain with Monaro, except now he was the one avoiding all contact. For both obstacles, cash and Monaro communication, she could only think of one potential solution—Delaney. Another set of breathing exercises, roll of the neck, wiggle of shoulders, then she knocked on his door and entered.

"I've been calling and texting all morning, thought you were ghosting me," said Delaney.

ANNIE shook her head. "Had my phone off all morning. Had a bit to deal with… and I'm not sure if ghosting is the appropriate term."

"Sit, sit." Delaney waved a hand at the plush visitors' chairs.

She relaxed into a chair.

"I've got something special for you." Delaney opened his infamous drawer.

Her stretching and breathing outside had been a useless waste of time. Shoulder and neck tension recruited a huge knot in her stomach and together they contorted her body into a thick industrial spring. *If he pulls out any stuff, I'll shove it all down his throat.*

His hand came up holding a large yellow envelope.

"What's that?"

"Your freedom and Lachie's future." Delaney patted the envelope, looking like a bunch of paper money had collected at the bottom rather than drugs.

"I don't want another handout. This time we draft up a proper loan agreement."

Delaney ripped the envelope open and poured the contents onto the desk. Torn up pieces of paper, some with typing, others white. He tapped his desk near the pieces. "Monaro has torn up your contract. That's your freedom. You can now do what you were born to do, gifted to do, and you can't use him as an excuse not to do."

She scanned the bits of paper without touching them. Glimpses of her anti-life puzzle... *Monaro's name... Term: Ten (10) years from the sign-... half her signature in blue.*

"This is the original?"

Delaney nodded.

"He's got copies." She slapped the desk. "This means nothing."

The bugger smiled, took out a smaller envelope and flicked it over like a playing card, scattering some of the contract pieces. "He thought you'd trip up there, so he got his lawyer to draft an official rescinding document. That's the signed original. By now your lawyer should've received a scanned version by email."

She stared at the white envelope but didn't know what to do with it, how to feel. Like someone had returned her soul as a vinyl record but she'd lost her turntable, nothing to play it on, buried deep in an inner storage chamber, key thrown in the rubbish years ago. Nine years ago.

"I was expecting more of a major key reaction, more Kylie than Sia."

"What's he expecting?"

"An apology."

"APOLOGY! He created the whole fucking mess by being where he wasn't supposed to be." She flittered a hand at the envelope and torn paper. "And this mess."

"He was desperate to spend time with his son and you slammed all the other doors."

"All the power is still in his hands. The sneaky... He has me under all kinds of ugly legal shit."

"You hurt him physically, but you did it in front of Lachie and that's what really hurt."

"Typical. All about his ego."

"This is all about Lachie. Think about that scene for one bloody second from the kid's point of view. You barged in there on a fucking bender. His mother was a madwoman, wild eyes, shrieking obsceni-ties. You pushed his father so hard the guy fell backwards and split his head, blood spurting everywhere. Monaro was wrong to be there, but you're wrong... you..." Delaney sat back, hands fidgeting until he intertwined fingers with both pointing fingers together aimed at her. *"You need* to apologise to Monaro in front of Lachie. Show Lachie the adult way to behave… then his scars might have a chance of healing."

She slumped back in the chair, hands gripping her thighs. Delaney was often the *"Delooney"* Cat loved to call him, but she couldn't fault his raw description or any of his sentiment.

Delaney got up, collected a box of tissues from a cabinet, sat in the other visitors' chair, and offered her the box.

She dabbed her eyes with the back of her hand to confirm tears, then pulled out some tissues and wiped them.

"But all this other stuff…" She didn't have the energy to spell it out, let alone fight it.

"He'll drop it all. Immediately. As soon as the two of you agree on a fair plan for Lachie going forward."

"He won't return my calls."

"He will now. Annie, I had to verbally slap him a little to tear up the contract, but dropping all the other legal stuff was easy because he didn't want more conflict. Deep down, all he wants is a decent chance at redemption with Lachie. He knows vanishing was stupid, but we all do stupid some time in our life. Hell, I lived most of my twenties and thirties way south of stupid. I invented more stupid than the Beatles had hit records. I haven't taken sides, but if he fucks up or does anything that messes with Lachie's head, I'll personally buy the one-way ticket and put him on a plane out of Australia. I swear on my record collection."

That bit of recalcitrant hair dropped over her right eye, and she shifted her head on an angle and eyeballed him. Magazine articles had been written about his record collection. His mansion was reportedly half home, half endless shelves of records. LPs, EPs, and singles. Mega hits and rare gems. Every genre from almost every language.

He reached over his desk, grabbed his mobile and scrolled down, then showed her the screen, eyes arched in a question.

Monaro's number and mugshot.

Lachie's father.

Ex-manager.

Ex.

She peered at the white envelope and torn up contract on the desk. Closed her eyes and breathed. In, in, in, out... In, in, in, out... In, in, in, out. As tension slipped out, relief oozed in. No more legal battles, no intervention orders and Family Court drama. Visions of her on a stage flooded in, singing under a solo spotlight, teasing the mic. Torturing the audience with her words, her phrasing, her tone...

"There's the million-dollar smile I missed."

She opened her eyes and felt heat on her cheeks. Not at the compliment but guilt that her first emotions visualising the end of the Monaro conflict were about her on stage, not Lachie. Too bad. She might have dragged Lachie into her super-stupid moment but in time, probably not that long, he'd balance out the nine-plus years she was there for him. Solo.

Delaney waved his phone with Monaro's headshot on the screen.

She nodded.

Delaney hit the *Call* button.

TRACK 30

SAME CLINICAL FIVE-STAR CITY HOTEL, SAME WINDOW TABLE, ONLY THIS time ANNIE arrived thirty minutes before Monaro was due. Instead of her rushing in late, she watched people scurrying for cover outside when a sun-shower caught non-Melburnians and delusional Melburnians without umbrellas or waterproof jackets. The heavy but short shower left the city centre glistening. Outdoor cafe tables quickly filled up again. She'd rather be down there, or in one of her favourite laneway cafes where the bustle of local and foreign tourists was so thick, it guaranteed invisibility. She could be one musical note amongst the symphony of organic Melbourne.

She finished her tonic water with fresh lime.

The waitress breezed over. "I can tell you enjoyed that. Can I get you another one?"

"Thanks. I'm surprised it tastes exactly like a gin and tonic."

"That's just the gin not talking." The waitress winked and spun towards the bar.

She laughed. Until she saw Monaro float through the revolving doors. She put her empty glass on the low table, sat back and took out two laminated index cards. When he got close, she stood and stretched out her arm for a handshake.

"Hello, Annie."

"Tony."

She sat down and Monaro did the same on the other side of the table. She didn't recognise the look. Not quite his business game face, not his Travolta-charmer with the sparkly-eyed grin, none of the other Monaro masks she'd shoved deep down in her memory. She placed a laminated index card upside down in front of each of them.

"These are the six non-negotiable rules that will guide us today and through all our dealings about Lachie. If we can't agree on this"—she tapped a card—"we can't move forward. If one of us breaks any of these rules, they forfeit all rights with him."

Monaro had been nodding gently but raised his eyebrows at the final point. "I respect your objective here, but I can't agree to anything till I see them. It can't all be from your perspective."

She'd been guided by the "solution-focused" therapist from Cat's recommendations. It was a simple session because Annie had wanted her to focus purely on this meeting and the best outcome for Lachie.

"I've had some professional guidance and as you'll see, most of it is common sense. We don't have to agree on everything today. Getting this right and fair is more important than rushing anything with Lachie." She flipped both cards.

Monaro picked one up and sat back to read.

She studied hers:

1: We don't have to be friends, but we must always be friendly—even when Lachie isn't present.

She'd read in a novel recently, *Three Women in November*, that when it came to divorce or a situation like theirs, *"The kids are okay if the parents are okay"*. They hadn't been okay, especially recently, but now was the time to draw that line.

2: We are his parents, not his friends, and therefore will not become PSPs (Point Scoring Parents). We will not use Lachie as punishment or a weapon against each other.

3: Until Lachie turns sixteen, we always have the final say. We make an effort to respect his views, but we are the parents.

4: In the next nine months, Annie reserves the final say in major decisions about Lachie—such as education, medical, mobile phone and other technology. After nine months—if Tony is still consistently spending time with Lachie— no major decision will be made without both parents agreeing.

Despite a large slice of her soul relishing the relief, the release from carrying all of the responsibility for Lachie, it took all of the therapist's expertise and patience to get her to agree to this. The therapist had suggested six months, but in the end, she enjoyed making a not so subtle statement by making it nine months.

5: We do not micro-manage or interfere when Lachie is with the other parent. And we honour the schedule as agreed. We are never unreasonably late picking up or dropping off without fair justification.

6: Neither parent will criticise the other in any manner in front of Lachie.

Guilty as tried. The therapist pointed out a simple piece of child psychology: when she'd criticised or negatively labelled Monaro, Lachie subconsciously felt *"Well, I'm half him, therefore I must be like that too"*. This mortifying spear cut deep because she'd been truly pathetic since Monaro showed up recently. Pathetic wasn't a good base for parenting.

Monaro flicked the card with his thumb a few times, then placed it on the coffee table. "You're right, it is common sense… and fair." He turned his gaze outside.

Something wasn't right. She didn't know this look, but there seemed a big *but* coming. Typical Monaro negotiating, manipulating, or bullying. She straightened, feeling the diva goddesses lining up behind her. If he was going to argue about such basic principles, then they had no hope of positive joint parenting. The war would continue, with Lachie the major casualty.

Monaro turned back. "What if I fuck up? What if he hates me?" It came out in a croaky whisper.

Monaro scared and vulnerable. No wonder she hadn't recognised the look, it was a brand new one—Monaro scared and vulnerable. *Wow, the power of children... of Lachie.*

Wow.

The diva goddesses massaged her shoulders and neck and she relaxed into the chair.

"All parents fuck up. I've been terrified of fucking up every hour of every day for nine years. In the end, all you can do is make sure your love and positive stuff buries the mistakes."

"I might need to call you a bit in the early days."

Maybe he was growing up, his biological child pushing out the inner child.

"As long as it's about Lachie, no problem."

He nodded and tapped on the card. "Want me to sign this in an agreement?"

Monaro deferring to her about an agreement. She liked this new angle to the master of angles. She shook her head.

"This is about Lachie. Either we make it work or you fuck off. Don't need a contract for that."

His Travolta sparkle grin shined. "I always believed you were strong enough to survive in this crazy biz." He pulled out his phone and took a couple of photos of the laminated card. "I'll refer to this anytime I'm stuck." Slid his phone back into one inner breast pocket of his jacket and the card in the other, then patted it. He stood and held out a hand to shake. She rose, shook his hand, wary of any attempt at a hug or kiss from Monaro, but he just smiled and strode off.

She slumped into the armchair and closed her eyes, seeing the hotel lounge and her body in third person. Walls rolled back, ceiling drifted away, windows melted. Her spirit turned into a hot-air balloon, guilt-free air raising her soul through the window, floating across studios with engineers and producers, then stages with her band behind and a massive audience below, the surge of adrenalin and endorphins so powerful, she sprung open her eyes and gripped the chair. Her life was changing, and it wasn't about Lachie or

Monaro or Merger Music or Cat. It was all about her and her creative dreams.

"Nice smile. That non-gin gin and tonic is really working for you," said the waitress, grinning. "Another?"

She nodded, sensing the *"nice smile"* stretching her cheeks further. Not an iota of guilt at her spirited balloon trip with her entourage of me-myself-and-I. "Make it a double lime."

CAT hit *Call* again, waited till the dial tone bounced to Annie's voicemail, and hung up. Tried the doorbell one more time. Nothing. Annie was in there somewhere. Normally, she wouldn't worry, but the house looked like it was hiding under a blanket, windows shut despite being an unusually warm spring afternoon, curtains drawn, no foot-steps or creaking floorboards, no music. No Lachie. She stepped over to the flowerpot with a dying yellow rose, her birthday present—Annie had many talents, but gardening wasn't one of them—dropped down and pretended to do her shoelaces, checked for any peering eyes in the street or nosy neighbours in windows, then lifted the pot and claimed the spare key.

Annie didn't blink when Cat entered the music room. Hunched on the floor next to her piano, back to the wall and arms wrapped around her shins, with Lachie's headphones over her ears, Annie wasn't tapping a toe or nodding to a beat, just staring at Lachie's drum kit. She slid down the wall next to Annie, her head close to a headphone but no music filtered through. No sound at all. She tapped her finger-nail on the headphone.

Annie got the hint and removed the device, laid it on the floor, then wrapped herself tight again. "I thought I was okay, flying into my dreams, but it hurts, Cat, hurts in agonising bursts. Like a kick-drum pounding here." Annie placed her hands around the bottom of her lungs at the top of her tummy.

It was obvious that Lachie's first afternoon with Monaro was going to be difficult. Obvious to everyone except Annie.

"Of course, it hurts. You're grieving. Grieving the end of your precious solo time with Lachie, grieving the end of a big stage of your life."

"What if he doesn't want to..." She flicked her chin at the drum kit. "To be here anymore?"

"Won't happen. Lachie loves you and will always want to be part of your life... have you in his life."

"Monaro's got money and charm. He might turn him against me."

She slapped Annie's knee. "Snap out of it, Annie. Monaro seems committed, but he couldn't handle Lachie on his own." She waved a hand at the drums. "You know every beat of that kid. His rhythm started in your tummy and continues in both hearts forever. No one can drown out that collaboration. No one."

A slow nod from Annie, then she picked up Lachie's headphones and hugged them to her chest.

Cat imagined every mother must face some kind of separation anxiety throughout the parenting journey. First time out with a babysitter, first day back at work, first day-care or kinder. Early days of school, first sleepovers at friends, first teen nights out, first time driving, leaving home. Each stage must wrench the emotional umbilical cord. Did that cord ever really get cut for a mother? Plus, those key stages usually provide time for pre-grieving, preparing heart and soul for the natural evolution of a child and the relationship with her child. Annie's complication with the unexpected return of Lachie's father dumped a sudden separation, one Annie couldn't have prepared for.

Annie fiddled with Lachie's headphones. "He'll change... growing so fast... he'll change."

"He'll still have the same heart and brain. And it's time for your change. Time for you. Nothing wrong with grieving. Honour the feelings no matter how painful, and don't dump them on Lachie."

Annie hugged the headphones tight, sliding her head onto Cat's shoulder.

"Life isn't all boppy melodies. Any time you need to scream or cry, call me. Save all the syrupy pop songs in you for Lachie, go heavy metal on me."

Annie placed the headphones on her lap and wrapped up Cat's arm tightly, squeezing in closer.

ANNIE breathed *in, in, in, out. In, in, in, out.* Heard the iron gate creak open, then closed. She couldn't make out Lachie's footsteps outside. Damn those sneakers. She strangled the front doorknob. The breathing exercise couldn't uncoil the afternoon's grief and negative projecting. Cat's welcome but ever so temporary diversion faded as soon as she'd disappeared. Disappeared so Annie could *"enjoy the moment with Lachie"* on his return from his first outing with Monaro.

Enjoy. Cat had actually used the word.

No chance of enjoying the moment, but she'd promised herself she'd be normal-to-neutral. Give Lachie the space to process his own feelings and instincts about Monaro. Let him lead the conversation.

The security door squeaked, and she flung the front door open so hard, it was a miracle the solid chunk of wood didn't end up flying through the house.

Lachie's finger hovered over the doorbell. "Hey, Mum."

"Hey, welcome home." *Welcome home? What happened to normal-to-neutral? Vocal cords betrayed me when I needed them most. Welcome home, like a dog marking its territory. You live here. With me.*

Lachie opened the security door, and turned towards Monaro's Audi.

Monaro's cheesy grin beamed through the open passenger window. "See ya next week, Lachie."

Next week. They had agreed to three weekly sessions because the first time would be awkward, tense. Second time they might move on beyond the basic form-filling questions and plugging gaps. Years of gaps. Third time, they would have a chance to edge to the beginning of a potential father-son normality. Then they'd review it and work out a mid-term arrangement. It was a fair plan, but somewhere deep down, a part of her must've been hoping for no "next times". Hoping for a torturous four hours for Lachie with no connection, no fun, and no desire to see Monaro again. The subconscious was selfish, transparent terrain. Consciously, she'd ridden the elation at her born-again musical future, then rolled down the low valleys of keeping Lachie to herself with a job that helped support him, and back up again, where she could see blue sky with musical clouds that floated her through her future.

Lachie gave Monaro a waist-high half-wave, spun, and cruised down the hall.

She closed the front door and pushed back her nosy curiosity. *How'd it go? Where did he take you? Have fun? What do you think of him? Are you hungry? What did he say? Do you still want to go through with the other two meetings?*

But he just trundled into his room, backpack shielding him from her stare. She slumped back onto the front door and closed her eyes. *Give him a break. Poor kid must have a million of his own questions stuck in a web of confusion created by his dysfunctional parents.* She wondered when he'd greet her with sparkly eyes and a baby-bear hug again. Yes, it was her stumbles that had closed Lachie down, but that didn't mean she didn't miss it. Creaking floorboards made her open her eyes.

Lachie had emerged from his room without his backpack and stood in the hallway. "Thanks for organising that, Mum." Hands in his pockets, he studied the polished floorboards.

The most positive words he'd uttered in a few weeks lit a beacon in her heart. She ached to run to him and wrap him tight. "You okay?"

He nodded, flicked her a fleeting glance, then slid back into his room.

ANNIE squirted a line of barbeque sauce on top of the mustard on her sausage, then sat back into the couch with her plate. She hadn't prepared their favourite Friday TV dinner on a Saturday night to impress Lachie, who munched on his roll and sausage propped up with cushions. It was a strategic decision. This way they could face the TV. At the kitchen table they'd be facing a mountain of tension and potential messy questions following his Monaro time that afternoon.

"Muh uuh," Lachie imitated a fail buzzer, picked up the TV remote, and fast forwarded through *Vocal Choice*.

That was the only way they could enjoy it. All the week's shows were recorded, and they watched every performance in full, plus the judging, until a melodramatic moment or fake syrupy praise poured out, then it would be super fast-forward to the next performance. All the artificial, often manipulative fluff flashed past on the screen, but the singing, that was real. A singer either had what it took to nail a track live or they didn't. They either improved through the show as competition intensified or they wilted. You could not hide in a live performance. That way, a week's worth of shows took them under two hours.

Lachie had the frustrating knack of knowing exactly when to hit *Play*, despite the fast-forward speed. Then he'd hit *Pause* before the beginning of the next act.

"It was weird," he said, staring at the frozen frame on the TV.

Typical boy--they communicated best while focused on an activity or watching something else. Even Lachie. Say what you like about being equals, but men had this avoid-eye-contact communication thing in the DNA of their DNA.

"Of course, it was. It's weird for him too." She bit deep into her roll. Better to spill sauce and mustard than all the other thoughts and questions bursting to spill out.

"I guess."

"He loves music. That's one thing you have in common."

He nodded at the TV. "We all do."

A chill spiked through her spine. Was that a cry for a *happy family*? It was natural for kids to hope their parents reunited—she'd read that in a book the therapist had lent her—but surely that was pertinent to parents who were once together with their children, not this situation. Did Lachie miss it more than she'd imagined? Had she let his smarts cover up his heart?

"If it wasn't for music, you'd never have met, and I wouldn't be here." He tapped the remote on his palm. "If you didn't have me, you wouldn't have to talk to him again. You could've been bigger than Pink."

She put her plate on the coffee table, spun to Lachie, put his plate next to hers, took the remote, dumped it on the couch, and held his hands. "Don't you ever think such rubbish again. Whatever happened with your dad, whatever else happens going forward, I have never regretted giving birth to you. Never regretted being your mother. You are the biggest hit in my life, Lachie, and nothing, especially not any career junk, will ever top it. If I do nothing else right in my life, I will always be proud of making you." She let the tears trickle down her cheek. Wouldn't let go of his hands for anything.

"That's the first time you called him my dad."

"Oh, Lachie, I'm sorry. I've been a selfish witch. He loves you and you deserve a loving dad."

"Still weird. Doesn't feel like my dad. Don't know how I'm supposed to feel."

"Give it time. This isn't a single track you can download; it's a collection of albums you both need to listen to together."

He removed his hands but held her eyes. She wasn't sure who was teaching whom right then, and it didn't matter because he'd helped her break out of her defensive selfishness. Lachie did have a dad and he deserved a loving dad. All she had to do was get out of the way. A little.

"Can't imagine ever feeling the same way about him as I do with you, Mum." He wrapped her up in a hug.

She was the luckiest, most powerful woman alive. No one and nothing would ever break the special bond she had with her boy. No one and nothing could stop her achieving anything. A lyric percolated from that mysterious pond.

Move over, I'm coming out to get it.

Move over, there's a vision in my mind.

Move over, I can see it, I can touch it.

It's a vision and it's mine, mine, mine.

She'd need to get it down on paper as soon as Lachie hit his bed.

TRACK 31

ROBBIE FLICKED THROUGH THE RECORD ALBUMS, BACHARACH TO BOWIE. He picked up *Reality* and scanned the cover despite owning all the Bowie collection, thanks initially to his dad and more recently, his own obsession. *Let's Dance* was his favourite musically, but he loved the record covers of *Reality* and *Scary Monsters*. His genius was obvious in history, but imagine discovering a unique act like Bowie today. Would it be easier to break an artist like him with YouTube and social media or would—

"You said you had all his discs," said Cat, the poster girl for the inner northeast and northwest. The non-chic of North Melbourne/Brunswick to Fitzroy/Collingwood, all layers and colours working with her chunky red boots. A lot more vibey than the first time they'd met here at Deceptive Bends.

He liked Cat's vibes. Crazy how two professional opposites could gel into a joint business venture.

"True story. I can't explain it, but there's some kind of magic in discovering them again and again in record bins like these."

A gentle nod, and the sun through the window bounced off her blue hair. Definitely vibey. Maybe it was nearing the end of the contest, or some distance from the Santi catastrophe.

"You gonna explain the sudden need to meet here or stand and grin all day?"

"Follow me."

ROBBIE reached the second level of Deceptive Bends and led Cat to the second office door on the right, opened it, then indicated for her to enter first. She'd love his plan. She loved Athena and Theo, loved Deceptive Bends. His surprise was such an obviously good idea, it was ridiculous.

She walked in a few steps. "Why are we here?"

"Your boots are planted on the polished timber floor of the first office of our management company, Accidental Destiny."

Cat took a slower appraisal of the space. The second-hand blue velvet couch he'd discovered at a bar closing down in Brunswick, the old club leather lounge at right angles, the two second-hand desks at the other end placed at angles from the two windows, which created a nice triangular space between their future workspaces. Workspaces he'd planned with Anthea for the feng shui that meant so much to Cat. Plus, the oversized leather armchair with attached side table he'd bought brand new.

He rounded her and opened the door into the smaller adjoining space, empty apart from the sunlight streaming in from the large French window. "And this will be our green room for meetings with potential and signed acts. You'll have a ball creating the vibe in here."

Cat hadn't moved, feet anchored wide, hands gripping knapsack straps, eyes flaring.

"We can reverse it if you think it will work better, make the smaller space our office and turn this into the creative hub."

He'd never seen Cat statuesque. Movement suited her as if energy hustled after her, trying to catch up. Vibey-Cat had left the building and volcano-Cat looked like she was holding back a megaton of energy aimed at him. He didn't know why, and he sure didn't like being thrown back to their early days.

"I thought this was perfect for us, that's why I negotiated a preliminary arrangement with Anthea and Theo."

"You thought… *You* thought choosing our office and doing the deal without any involvement or knowledge from me was okay? This was actually the end result of your thinking process? Obviously, I've been projecting a level of maturity onto you that you just don't have." Cat turned like a soldier and stomped towards the door.

"I was excited about our joint venture and—"

"JOINT venture. Not, *I'll find a joint for our venture without referring to my business partner because it's such a big first decision, but it doesn't matter what she thinks kind of venture.*"

"I'm sorry. I get it. I'm sorry."

Cat stopped in the doorway and faced him. "Hells Bells, Robbie, we've got a million things to sort out before we even think about an office. You're a cowboy when it comes to marketing and I mean that as a compliment these days. I'm big enough to admit my harsh judgment early on. But you can't stampede into a business, guns blazing, especially not when we're supposed to be partners. And you absolutely cannot assume you know what I'll like until we've galloped through a few hundred business decisions together."

Robbie plonked onto the leather couch. *What an idiot.*

"You've even assumed that's your spot and I'd go for the blue velvet couch, haven't you? Because I've got blue hair? Tomorrow my hair might be green and red. Do we go and get another couch, or reupholster?"

He shook his head. At least she hadn't stormed off and shut the whole project down. He'd been consumed by their venture every morning, waking with ideas buzzing, and every night before sleep overpowered him. It felt right and it felt right now. He didn't want to delay it any more than the song contest required.

"And who's the giant black armchair for?"

"Johnny. He loves black."

Cat's battle eyes softened and lingered on him. "That's important to you, isn't it? Having Johnny around?"

He nodded. "Won't get in the way, may even be useful. He's really good at—"

She raised two hands as stop signs, then shuffled over and sat on the edge of the blue couch with half a butt cheek. "Robbie, I get your love for Johnny. It's sweet, really sweet. And I like his musical instincts."

Fibres in the back of his neck unknotted. He didn't realise how important it was to him having a business where he could keep an eye on Johnny until he'd fitted out the office. Could've been a deal breaker. Yes, Cat had liked Johnny the first time, but having him lounging around every day in their work environment was a different level. Subconsciously, he must have known Cat would be okay with it. Maybe that was part of the unexpected, unplanned, unique connection they had that would help make Accidental Destiny a winner.

"We have to delay the whole thing."

"I guarantee you, Cat, this will not happen again."

Cat nodded. "I don't have my half of the working capital we calculated. It will take me a few more months, maybe a year."

"I'll lend you your share."

Spears flared from her eyes.

"With a proper loan agreement so that—"

"*I* will not borrow my half from my prospective partner. If we don't dive into this balanced, we'll never be balanced."

He slumped forward, face in hands, elbows on thighs.

Her right boot lifted then lowered to the timber floor, trampling all over his dream.

CAT took the longer, clockwise route around Albert Park Lake. From there she would scoot down Clarendon/Spencer and crawl up to her place in North Melbourne. Probably ninety minutes all up. Maybe seventy-five the way blood raged through her veins. Second time she'd skirted around the lake after seeing Robbie at Deceptive Bends in Prahran. During the original journey, something had opened up inside her. Certainly her perception about Robbie had taken a positive nudge. This walk slammed doors shut, the reverberations echoing out of her head and rippling across the lake.

Why?

Why did she overreact to Robbie's initiative? Heck, she loved that place and couldn't think of a better location to launch their business. *Their business…* Was she afraid? She'd already set a personal commitment to donating twenty-five percent of her profits, so it wasn't the sudden commercial path she'd tripped onto. Her inner entrepreneur had its own pent-up spirit. Building Accidental Destiny with Robbie was all-consuming despite the contest competing for her constant concentration.

If it wasn't the "business" maybe it was the "their". She trusted Robbie—how crazy was that after the fiery beginning?—and she had faith in his talent and work ethic. Effectively, he would be her first signing in the new biz, and she'd be his. So why smash his generous loan gesture out of the building? All it did was allow her to dive into the biz sooner rather than wait three more months till she paid off her credit card plus another six months, maybe nine, of scrimping and squalor to save her share. Nine to twelve more months at Merger and her "secret ho business".

Realising the extended time she'd need to commit to her soulless part-time gig stilled her. The city lights shimmered off the dark water. Santi's eyes would never shimmer again. Dark water still banked up behind her eyes when she thought of him, but her heart didn't sink to her stomach anymore. If she were advising Santi about this business situation with Robbie, what would she say?

RUN!

The silly joke untangled her insides, cleared her head. She stretched her arms and bent her neck back to take in the stars. She'd tell Santi to clarify exactly where they both wanted to take the business. Agree on a preliminary plan. Agree to review the plan monthly in the early days, then bi-annual reviews. Document everything. Business was business and memory wasn't. Memory got loosened up with emotions and greed and ego. But most importantly, she'd tell Santi to "go for it". Work as hard and smart as you can in the first year and give it everything you've got.

She launched into the sandy walking track again. What was the worst that could happen by borrowing her share from Robbie? Why not? Why not launch their biz now, or at least as soon as the contest was done. Contest. Still had over a hundred songs to get through before the morning meeting. The last selection meeting before the sixth and final weekly public vote before the successful twelve songs went up for the ultimate public vote. She'd do her share of the contest work over the next three weeks and allocate five meditation sessions focused on the biz with Robbie. Make a decision, and stick with it.

She pulled out her phone and typed a quick message to Robbie: *Give me two weeks to think about your suggestions.* She checked the time, then zipped into a fast walk, almost trot.

TRACK 32

ROBBIE STARED AT THE SONGS LISTED ON THE LARGE WHITEBOARD. SEVEN tracks in the column headed with three ticks--they were locked in for the final weekly public vote. That left five tracks circled in red that he and Annie had both selected, three different tracks that Annie and Cat chose circled in blue, and two songs he and Cat had picked circled in green. Ten tracks they had to whittle down to three. Red circle, blue circle, green circle. They'd been going round in circles fighting for tracks, arguing against tracks.

"I don't even remember why I picked those tracks anymore. Don't care. Just go with the two you guys chose and pull one of the ones I picked out of a hat," Annie said as she pushed herself away from her desk and spun around in her chair.

"We've all worked too hard to disrespect the writers. We owe it to them to be as rigorous with the process as we were first week."

Annie stopped spinning, stretched out her legs, and rested her head on the chair back. "Rigorous? My brain's in rigour mortis."

Manny waltzed into the middle of the room, brow furrowed with valleys and hills you could ski on.

He and Cat yelled, "Go away, Manny, you're not helping."

"Don't give a shit if we never talk again. I need those final tracks. We're being crucified on social media."

Robbie checked the clock on his computer for the three hundredth time in the last hour. "We're only ninety minutes late. Eleven weeks we hit the deadline. They can wait this time, builds the tension."

"*They* reckon you are rigging the contest for a preferred outcome."

"Fuck off." Cat banged her desk.

"You wanna shoot the messenger, I'll give you the rifle. Just do it *after* you give me the final tracks." Manny didn't budge.

"Two more hours. Max," he said.

Manny eyed Annie, Cat, then him. "You got sixty minutes. I'm getting dinner." He pounded out of the room.

"Let's forget the songs for half an hour. Do some final prep on the Live Contest Show, then come back to the tracks fresh."

"Good idea," said Cat.

"I got double rigour mortis just thinking about the show. How did we rope ourselves into running a massive live event?" said Annie.

"It's designed to give the writers the glory. Perfect finale," said Cat.

"It's become bigger than a Pink tour." Annie glared at him.

He was starting to regret coming up with the concept, although his original idea was based around a simple live performance of the songs in an intimate venue, with maybe sixty friends or family of the winning writers, possibly streamed live on the Net. Delaney had raised the stakes because his mate Glen was relaunching an iconic seventies live venue, Bombay Tracks, and the timing slotted in perfectly to run the contest event as a test night before the official opening. Cat reckoned the live event further strengthened the street cred for the contest and Merger Music, but the logistics of running a live show in a room licensed for three hundred created exponential migraines on top of the contest headaches.

They rolled their chairs over to the small, round meeting table.

"The three-camera internet shoot is now looking like a seven-camera live TV broadcast." He studied Annie.

Annie stared at the poster-size doc they'd handwritten, summing up the live event.

"That's brilliant, Robbie, what channel?" asked Cat. Was that pride in him beaming from her eyes, or pride in what they'd jointly achieved with the contest?

Why did it send a buzz through him? "V. They're also running with the song writing doco."

"That's great, Robbie, really is, but we don't have the capacity to manage all this." Annie waved a hand over the doc.

"Delaney's bringing in an event manager and a stage manag—"

Cat's complexion changed from glowing to fiery red. "Forget it. We can't let Delooney hijack this for his ego posse," said Cat. "This contest started for the writers, and it finishes for the writers."

"It will finish us, Cat. We'll end up in hospital on a drip," said Annie.

"Delaney made it clear everyone reports to us. This will not become a Delaney industry orgy, Cat. It's still about the writers, just bigger and with more crew," he said.

"I haven't got the energy for orgies these days. I might be fit for my age, but I'm still my age." Delaney plonked a large paper bag on the doc followed by a cardboard tray with three large coffees, then grabbed a metal fold-up chair from the corner and sat between him and Annie. "What's scratching your vinyl?" He smiled at Cat, handed her a coffee, then Annie and Robbie.

What's scratching your vinyl? How could he not love this guy? He'd have to write that one down and plagiarise it to death when he dealt with his acts down the track.

Annie tapped the doc. "This thing is becoming bigger than the Falls Festival." She unravelled the paper bag, removed a pineapple dough-nut, and bit off a chunk.

"Why are you backing it with more money and resources?" asked Cat, her scrunched up eyes looking for Delaney's angle.

"You and Annie nailed the impact of this song contest."

"Song *writing* contest," said Cat.

Delaney nodded. "It's already lifted our street cred and I have no doubt the dollars will follow. A live event gives it an extra rock edge."

Cat peeked into the paper bag, then pulled out a strawberry doughnut.

"Every name and wannabe is hitting me for an invite into the VIP area."

Cat threw her doughnut back and dumped the bag on the desk. "The writers are the VIPs. The VIP area is for the writers and four of their guests. That's settled."

"Talking some heavy A-listers."

She screwed the bag tight at the top and dropped it on the table in front of Delaney. "Your so-called A-listers, and we all know what the A stands for, can rub their over-priced designer T-shirts and torn jeans with the punters."

Sometimes Cat carried her intensity around on a hot metal rod, ready to brand you with an unforgettable sizzle. One day, Delaney would just sack her, which might not be a bad thing because then she'd need a job and she didn't want another job, so she may as well start the management biz with him. How could she be so clear about everything that mattered yet drag her military-style boots when it came to their joint venture?

Delaney passed the bag of doughnuts to him and turned over the poster page to its blank side. He grabbed one of the black markers and sketched out some kind of layout.

The doughnuts in his lap smelled good and his stomach roared with hunger, but he dared not open the bag while Cat was in war mode.

Delaney shaded in an area halfway on the side. "We can rope off this area around the smaller ground-floor bar for the Anal-Listers. It's raised so they can look down on the plebes." He tapped on a section at the rear. "Your writers and their special mates will keep the official VIP area on the upper level. They can look down on the Anal-Listers." He sat back and stretched his legs, hands behind his head.

Delaney might often end up at Smug Village, but he took Smile Street, Humour Lane, and Self Depreciating Road to get there. Robbie liked the route, the way it diffused heat, focused on the solution, not the conflict.

Cat took the bag off his lap and reclaimed the strawberry doughnut, pointed it at the official VIP area, held it up with a nod, and took a bite. No words yet a ton of acceptance, respect.

He scavenged a chocolate doughnut and devoured half in one bite.

"I'll make a bet," said Delaney. "All the writers and probably their mates will want to be down with the Anal-Listers before the winner's announced. The VIP area will be empty." Smug Village lit up in his neon smile.

"You're on." Cat stretched out her arm. "Writers aren't like that."

Annie took her hand and shook before Delaney. "I'm with him. Writers are exactly like that, they just hide it behind other insecurities."

Delaney clamped his hand over the two. "Count me in. Loser buys beers for the big after-after-party, or officially for my mates at corporate accounting, the debrief meeting."

Robbie swung his chair closer to Cat and supported her hand from underneath. "I'm with Cat on this one."

"We're just wasting time." She removed her hand, collapsing the four-way shake, removed the paper bag, and dumped it on Delaney's lap. "Now scoot, we've got real work to do."

Annie grabbed the bag, pulled out a chocolate doughnut and offered the bag to him.

He peeked in and took out the remaining strawberry doughnut.

Delaney put the fold-up chair away. "I'm outta here before Mount Manny gets back. Whatever he needs in…" He looked at his watch. "In forty-seven minutes, you better have it wrapped up." Delaney scooted out as the scrunched-up paper bag hit the back of his head.

"Nice shot, Cat," Delaney said without looking, then raised his hand with a thumbs-up as he walked out.

Annie jumped up and tapped on the whiteboard. "This one by Julene Sidique is special. I can feel the keys." Her hands played an imaginary piano. "And the hook is stalking me." She hummed the melody and then sang the chorus, "If nothing else happens, between me and you, thanks for passing through. Wherever your life takes you, whatever you do, thanks for passing through."

She sang it better than the studio-produced demo. Sweeter than anything he'd heard on the radio or download chart. Robbie turned to Cat as she turned to him with nirvana eyes—not the rock band Nirvana—serene, heaven-ish nirvana. Cat's awe-filled face, Annie's velvety vocals, his tingling spine, everything they'd been through for this marathon contest, it was all worth it for that single moment of Annie in her essence.

Annie stopped singing and tapped next to the two tracks listed in the green circle. "These are definitely the next best, your two picks plus 'Thanks for Passing Through'. We're done." She waltzed to her computer and shut it down, picked up her bag, and was half out the door. "Coming, Cat?"

Cat flickered from awed to exhausted, trudged to her computer, shut it down, grabbed her knapsack, and followed the magic as Annie sang "Thanks for Passing Through".

He turned back to the board. Annie had more musical talent and instincts on the tip of her little nose than he or Cat would ever learn between them in a dozen lifetimes. The three tracks she'd suggested glared with OBVIOUS written in capitals. He enjoyed Annie's voice as it faded down the hall. She'd wasted her talent for nearly ten years, but the world deserved her. She wouldn't listen to him, but he had to do whatever he could hustle to help her back onto the stage, into the studio, into millions of hearts.

TRACK 33

THE PILLOW FREAKED CAT OUT.

Seeing Annie at her front door in pyjamas under jungle hair on a Saturday night when they were supposed to go out was no biggie. They'd both had swipe-left-on-the-world moments and cocooned in Annie's lounge over a movie or binged on shows for a weekend. Annie in pyjamas under jungle hair hugging her bedroom pillow, that was a shaky combo she'd never expected.

She waved her phone. "You off the grid or am I off your grid?"

Annie turned and headed back to her bedroom, a million moons away from being ready to go to one of the biggest industry parties of the decade.

She'd texted and called about coming early, got no response, came early anyway. She was desperate to raise her Robbie business dilemma, since there'd been no chance to discuss it under the contest pressure and finale event prep. Tried working through the same process she used to help other people, yet somehow it wouldn't clarify anything. One moment jumping into the management biz with Robbie made perfect sense, next minute, none of the logic would stick. Meditation and mantras didn't clear her head, just threw her back to the Foundation session where she'd taken Robbie and his hilarious overreaction. Couldn't lose herself at Deceptive Bends because it now reminded her of bloody Robbie dancing with his brother, or showing off the office upstairs. Their office.

Why would she want to swim with the sharks, despite Robbie's cute dolphin metaphor? What value could she bring to a management business? Why her? Why wouldn't Robbie team up with someone with more relevant experience? She was destined to build schools in Gambela, Ethiopia. Maybe lead her own projects across less fortunate communities. Communities she refused to label third-world because they were first and foremost people. People suffering extraordinary injustice or bad luck. But was that her destiny? Destiny, three syllables, a million elusive thoughts. Annie would be an independent sounding board she could trust, a mirror she couldn't ignore.

She shut the front door but didn't lock it, then texted Robbie to let the Uber go when he arrived and come inside. He was due in thirty minutes and under normal circumstances, she'd be able to rouse Annie into her dazzling best in fifteen, another of those amazing-annoying things about Annie. Clutching her favourite big bedroom pillow wasn't normal circumstances. Her dilemma would have to wait. Annie needed her right now and she had no idea why.

"Don't think of it as Delaney's sixtieth party. This is your *move over I'm coming out to get it party.*" Cat loved the lyric when Annie had run it past her and couldn't think of a better way to spark Annie out of her funk. "The first industry gathering since your musical freedom. Your rebirth, your second coming."

"Your born-again-groupie thing is weird." Annie rested her chin on that pillow that she hugged tight along her shins, voice more dour than face.

She shifted on the edge of the bed, tucking a leg under the other. "At least your brain's ticking over. Talk to me, Annie. Why are you really avoiding this? Tell me before Robbie gets here."

"I don't want Robbie here. Not tonight."

"Share or he gets to see you like this."

"You wouldn't dare."

"Door's unlocked, ETA twenty-five minutes."

Annie lifted her head. "*Move over* is a lyric, Cat, not a rite of passage. This biz has changed so much... Nine years ago you could ride the crazy dragon, then jump off and hide before the dragon burned you. Touch a tiny sliver of normal, re-energise, then jump back on the dragon again, but now you're a fucking spotlight magnet every single second. Fans want to be connected all the time. Trolls used to hang at the bar or gutter where you could leave them behind. Now they scum into your computer and phone, and they clone into millions. They get into your digital skin, and you can't scratch them out."

"I know you, Annie, you can switch off. Heck, you're not even on any social media."

"But other people are, and they can't help bring that shit up. The world's gone click-lazy so they'll bring it up."

"You'll have a team, Annie. You'll be protected from all the rubbish."

"What team, Cat? I'd never work with Monaro again, but now I appreciate the way he protected me back then from the other fire-breathing bullshitters. I know I can't do this on my own, but I don't trust anyone in this biz. The only person in the whole damn industry with any decency is you. You're the only one I trust and you're probably jumping ship as fast as me after this contest."

What team? You're the only one I trust...

Her spine sprung straight, bags of doubt falling off her shoulders to the floor. A cocktail of energy stirred in her tummy, flowed through her heart, buzzed into her brain. Not euphoria that fades with time, a eureka lucidity that didn't so much clarify her path as shake the ground so hard only one road remained. Annie had answered her dilemma without Cat even bringing up the subject.

"This isn't funny, Cat. What's with the stupid grin face?"

"I know the perfect team for you."

"I know all the managers in the swamp. They're all Monaro with different clothes... except Correne. She's a gem and a genius but retired after her legacy with The Cat Empire."

Excitement bounced her off the bed and she stalked the room. "These management guys are new, and they *are* different. You can trust them, and you'll like them. They're perfect for you Annie. Perfect."

"No such thing."

She stilled, checked her phone, back to Annie.

"Okay, now you're weirding me out with the moon smile. Who the fuck are you talking about?"

"Me. Me and Robbie. We're setting up our own management company."

"You and Robbie?" Annie smiled. "I thought there was something going on with you two."

"Strictly business."

"Wow, Cat, you spat that out so fast, sounds like you might be—"

Ding-dong. Ding-dong.

"You said I had twenty-five minutes," said Annie.

She shrugged her shoulders. "I'll tell him to take a walk." Cat bounced up, grateful for Robbie's timing, because Annie had mapped out a dramatically different route for her journey with Robbie. Seriously, Robbie and her. How could Annie get it so wrong?

"No, let him in. If he's going to be a manager he needs to see this me."

She pounced into the hall and yelled, "It's unlocked!"

"Hey," Robbie said as he strutted in.

"Hey."

"You look amazing, Cat. Love that scarf-shawl thing and wow, the red ankle boots, never seen you in non-combat boots." His smile topped tight black jeans, white shirt with an embossed flowery pattern, and a stunning blue suit jacket featuring black and white flecks and a red kerchief in the breast pocket. Quite an upgrade on his beat-up leather thing.

"Never seen you in a real jacket." Okay, euphoria from her Annie-business-destiny-revelation bubbled.

"You guys writing a corny fashion blog or you coming in?" Annie asked from her bed.

"Get in here," she said to Robbie. "We've got business to discuss." She spun back into Annie's bedroom.

"Business?"

Annie had somehow settled her hair and the comfort pillow was doing its preordained job of supporting her back, legs crossed at the ankles exposed under her flannelette pyjama pants. Still, she oozed goddess.

"I've never seen you in ankle boots either. Are you having an early mid-life crisis or…" said Annie, her cheeky grin and raised eyebrows amplifying her curiosity.

She stared at her boots.

Robbie shuffled just inside the doorway.

"Cat tells me you're launching a management business together."

Robbie's face spiked from uncomfortable to uncertain, flicking between her and Annie.

"I haven't told him yet."

"Doesn't know you're starting a management business together, or doesn't know you offered to sign me?"

Robbie settled on her, uncertainty morphing into a grin.

"He knows about the business, even found our office. I was dragging my feet. Came here early to discuss my fears, but your speech inspired me, note-perfect Annie, as always. Note bloody perfect."

Was the light in Robbie's eyes excitement or anger that she'd made an offer to an artist without any consultation after all the indignation she'd spat at him about the office?

He turned to Annie. "Having you as our first client would be fucking brilliant. We both like you and believe in your talent more than you do. Some artists have a musical gift that deserves to be heard, you're a gift to music. Music deserves *you*."

Euphoria tingled Cat's skin and burst through pores. Couldn't be prouder of Robbie, or more at peace they'd found their mutual destiny. At least their imminent career destiny. She could still build schools in Uganda or wherever, later.

Annie checked them both out under her not-quite-jungle-but-still-crazy-sexy-hair. "If we're going to get into bed together for business, may as well sort out the basics right here." She shuffled across to the middle and patted the right side. "Don't be shy, Robbie. Cat, grab a pad and pen from the kitchen and jump on this side." Annie patted the left side.

"Keep those boots on, Robbie, this is strictly business."

Cat smiled in the kitchen at Annie's cheekiness.

"Have to wash the bedding tomorrow anyway. You know how to do that, Robbie? Housework isn't Cat's forte."

Cat strode in waving the pad. "Hey, I thought this was strictly business."

"Just looking out for my mate here. Full disclosure amongst close friends." Annie elbowed Robbie and winked.

"You really want *full* disclosure, Annie? We're gonna need a bigger pad."

Annie waved her onto the bed. "We've got a party to shake up. Let's just sign a basic commitment. You agree to manage me. I agree to it for five years. Three of us sign. The rest we can sort out later."

ROBBIE stepped into the foyer of Delaney's house behind his funky, fun business partner and the hottest new act in the country. Their act. Annie. Annie who had morphed from bedridden hobo to rock goddess in ten minutes. The party energy, hum of drunk conversation, and thumping soundtrack couldn't beat the music festival rocking through his mind. Taking a second look at the tiled mirror wall nearest to him, no wonder he was grinning. He and Cat were launching their own management company and Annie had chosen them, willing—no, wanting—to be their first client. Sure, Cat was probably eighty percent the reason. Maybe even ninety percent, but at least his ten percent involvement hadn't stopped Annie from entrusting them.

Gorgeous, musical genius, Annie.

The basic commitment Annie had signed was folded neatly and protected in his breast pocket. A million marketing ideas and media angles flooded his imagination, including unique social media hooks. Hell, she could be the next Sia of social media, never interacting on any social site except through her music and clips. Annie would love that. The media would lap it up. Fans would create their own Annie fan sites without any time or energy needed from them. Cat would love that. He took his phone out to note the Sia idea.

"Robbie Guest, how can you live up to your surname if you have the audacity to pull a phone out when there's so much wild life in mi casa?" said Delaney.

"Wildlife? Denigrating women at your age?" said Cat.

"No, no, don't insult the birthday boy." Delaney held up his left hand. "Wild." Right hand. "Life. Living wild, crazy adventures, or as the Frenchies like to say, vivre sauvagement."

"Happy birthday, boss. Wishing you many years of vivre sauvagement." He put up a hand and they shook with an LA-style high grip and shoulder to shoulder tap.

Annie kissed both cheeks. "Happy birthday, old fella. You look good for seventy."

Delaney winced, then glowed. "You're a genius, Annie. I'll start telling everyone it's my seventieth, not sixtieth, and they'll all be amazed at how good I look."

Annie smiled, hugging him tight. "Happy birthday whatever your unofficial age, and thanks for being so good to me."

Cat kissed each cheek. "Happy birthday and thanks for being so good to her."

"Enough with sentimental. The personality lubrication bars are that way, that way, and also beside the pool." Delaney pointed to the right of the foyer at what looked like a huge lounge room, then to the left at a huge space that could have been a ballroom. "Goodie bowls are scattered all over the place."

Annie raised her two pointing fingers in a cross.

"I respect your commitment to substance chastity." He raised his eyebrows. "Alcohol okay?"

"Hell, yeah."

"Good."

Robbie counted five security guards in matching black T-shirts and baggy black pants spread around the spaces he could see. "Hey, boss, what's with all the security? Are you expecting a few crazy ones tonight?"

"They're protecting the vinyl. Only house rule, no one touches the vinyl."

Of course, the legendary record collection. Squinting closer through the coloured lighting, slow spinning spotlights and smoky haze—part tobacco and pot, part smoke machine—shelving stacked with vinyl records covered the walls. Every few metres a display of covers facing the room gave an impression of stained glass in a cathedral of rock. He'd have to come back another time to worship them properly.

Delaney turned to Annie. "After you've had a couple of drinks we should talk about your future, now that Monaro has ripped up your contract."

He stepped closer to Delaney. "Actually, you'll need to—" Cat tapped his ankle with her boot, smiling, but her eyes nearly knocked him backwards. He spotted Delaney's latest starlet, Pina, approaching. "You'll need to focus on fun tonight, boss, and speaking of fun, hi, Pina."

Delaney spun around, arms wide. "Princess Pina, come and meet my favourite groovers at Merger. You know Robbie."

"Hi." Pina raised her glass towards him, more shyness than arrogance, despite the spectacular dress and white knee-high boots. Youngish for sure, but she owned her space.

"This is Cat, who definitely has nine lives, and I'm glad to be witnessing some of them."

"Hey, Pina, you are a gifted songwriter. If you can avoid joining this old dude at every party in town, you might have a chance in the crazy biz."

"Thanks, Cat. That's sweet of you to say."

"Except the old dude bit. That wasn't so sweet," said Delaney. "And you should know Pina doesn't follow me anywhere. She went to school with my daughter, so I've known her since she was shorter than those amazing boots."

"You didn't tell them before?" said Pina.

Delaney shook his head. "Wanted your talent to shine on its own. No family friend favours."

He nodded at Delaney with admiration and out of the corner of his eye, Robbie saw Annie give him a friendly salute too. They'd all assumed the ugly side of Delaney with Pina.

Pina jabbed Delaney gently on the arm.

Cat copied the gesture.

Pina put out a hand towards Annie. "You must be Annie. D gushes on about you all the time, reckons I should role model you, if you ever come out of recluse-ville."

He hadn't heard anyone call Delaney "D". Pina oozed a cruisy confidence, not brashness like so many younger people he came across in the biz.

"Pina, all you need for a role model is your creative clay and a mirror. We don't control the public final vote in the contest, but if it was my pick, your song is the stand-out. Your lyrics lasso around my heart and the melody is like a giant pair of wings. Can't wait to buy your track, tell everyone I was one of the first to hear it."

Pina's mouth opened wide, stayed wide, then she straightened another few centimetres and raised her flute to Annie. "You are one classy sister."

Annie held up an imaginary glass.

Delaney beamed like a proud dad.

Cat's eyes screened the same movie playing inside his head. They had to sign Pina, whatever her age.

.

TRACK 34

ROBBIE SURVEYED THE SCENERY IN DELANEY'S HUGE YET CRAMMED lounge room. Loud music clashed with louder shirts. Has-beens hanging onto their past, helped by the hangers-on hovering around them. Women of all generations almost wearing fabulous bits of cloth. Rock cowboys posing in posses, lassoing their own dicks with super-tight jeans. A couple of bemused, bona fide rock stars huddled in the far corner, protected by their mutual entourages.

Not long ago, he would have fluttered around the real stars like a seagull, desperate to swallow scraps of acceptance. Recently, he'd been anxious about the party, scrambling to understand his shifting inner world, as Cat would call it, but he couldn't pin it down. He wasn't uncomfortable, but he didn't really belong.

"I need a drink." Cat waved an arm at the room. "To wash this shit down."

"I'll get them," he said.

"Nah, I can skol half a beer at the bar. Coronas?"

"Perfect," said Annie.

He gave a thumbs-up and Cat disappeared into the crowd.

"You're better than this, Robbie." Annie flicked a dismissive wave around the room. "So much of this mob is consumed with consuming.

Drugs, alcohol, sex, gossip, praise, power, and more drugs. Focus on the music. Music drives the artists, music attracts the punters, music connects people with each other."

She nailed it. Nailed me. The typical imposter syndrome wasn't why he didn't feel a legitimate part of the crowd. Truthfully, he didn't like most of the crowd, didn't like the peripherals that obsessed the biz. Too often music was crushed into the back seat. Heck, he'd been part of it, squeezing everything through his marketing microscope. He did belong in this biz, just didn't have to do it like it had always been done.

"Trust me. I tried all the stupid stuff, it's not fun, not music," Annie said.

Love of music had seduced him into this biz and managing quality acts was the best way he could contribute to creating more musical magic for the world. It wasn't curing cancer or saving the planet from climate change, but it was the worthiest mission he could commit to within a career.

"When Cat gets stuck on stubborn island or anger mountain, don't fight her or run. Focus on kindness and understanding. Ask yourself why she is behaving this way. How can you react with kindness? Tell her you want to understand. *Really* understand. She's one in a million. You're lucky to have Cat as a partner and she's lucky to have you, as long as you don't start believing your self-marketing BS." Annie's mouth turned into a grin, but her eyes beamed *"Don't hurt her"*.

"Seems crazy now, but I like Cat."

Annie nodded. "I know, and she likes you more than she's admitting to herself. That's why you don't want to ruin a *blossoming friendship* fighting over business stuff." The way she emphasised "blossoming friendship", her grin, sparkly eyes, a ton of unsaid, plucked at feelings he'd resisted acknowledging. He *really liked* Cat.

At the bar, Cat took a long swig of her beer. Not crass, not classy, just Cat.

Annie jabbed his upper arm softly. "Here's the paradox—you get to Cat's heart by focusing on the biz. Not through sexy-cowboy shit, not clumsy-rushing-romantic. Focus on the work. Make your venture float, paddle with kindness and understanding. Cat will pull you into her boat."

"Hey, what are you two jabbering on about?" Cat held three beers in a triangle. Annie grabbed one, he took the other.

"Floating businesses and boats," said Annie.

"Boats?"

Robbie raised his beer between them. "To floating our business and welcoming all the talented boats into the creative harbour we build."

"Think you've stretched that metaphor a bit too much... let's stick to floating the biz." Cat clinked his bottle, then Annie's.

Annie clinked his and winked.

"Robbie! At last a friendly face!" shouted Stephanie, who broke through their little triangle and slopped a kiss on his cheek.

"Steph... aaa... Stephanie, hi."

"Don't look so surprised, I'm sure Delaney invited lots of his flings."

Surprised, yes, at her presence, at her friendliness. He'd barely met her once in Delaney's office months ago. In a plunging mini dress, perfect makeup, and acrylic stilettos, she looked mid-twenties. "These are my work colleagues, Cat and Annie."

"Hey." Stephanie gave them a half wave and spun back to him, close. "Work colleagues is good. Means I can show you around upstairs." She wiggled her shoulders, a dangerous manoeuvre with that navel-ending cleavage.

He glanced over Stephanie's bare shoulder. Couldn't read the fire in Cat's eyes. Jealousy? Disgust? Didn't dare look at Annie.

"Couple of people we have to meet. Why don't you hide in a closet and I'll find you."

"Oooh, I do love kinky. Haven't done a closet for months." Stephanie added a slow kiss to his other cheek. "Don't be too long, tiger." She headed for the foyer staircase.

Annie pinched his chin. "Back in a minute. I won't be too long, tiger." She headed in the same direction.

Cat's head angled with narrow eyes.

"I met her once in Delaney's office, never talked since."

"Don't think she's talking about talking."

Was that a glint within the fire? Was she teasing him? Cat grabbed a napkin from a nearby table, stepped close, and wiped his cheek. "You look good in smudged red lipstick." Cheeks, nose, eyes, a triangle of mischief.

Cat had red lipstick, how did he miss that? Did Stephanie incite a moral riot in Cat's head? Did our new business euphoria release raw lust?

Cat ran her fingers around his neck, pulled him down, rose on her toes, and kissed him. Her lips launched a million dance tunes beating through his veins, her tongue the DJ, spinning discs in his head. A century later, she eased down, her eyes kidnapping his full attention.

Lust, definitely. Lust that shattered Annie's advice. *Focus on the work... no sexy cowboy shit...*

Lust and shock, not at Cat's quantum leap, shock at his body's instant reaction, the powerful instinct to throw Cat over his shoulder and bound upstairs.

"Let's consummate our business upstairs," she said.

Scary synchronicity.

"Shit," said Cat, stepping back.

He followed her gaze to the entrance of the grand room across the foyer. Monaro and Diaz had attracted the eyes of most of the crowd— especially all the wannabe rock stars—plus Annie, who was marching towards them.

"Give me a minute. Text me which room you're in." She pushed him towards the stairs, then scampered after Annie.

Room. Cat. Lust. Disaster? Surely, it was okay if it was driven by Cat, not him? *It feels right.*

How long had that been hiding inside his head, his heart, and other parts? Had he pushed it down because of their business plans or because he never thought Cat would feel the same way? As he climbed the sweeping, half-circle staircase, Annie's advice whispered to him: *business first.* At least get the biz humming before jumping into bedroom harmonies with Cat.

They needed the quiet of a room to talk this through. Work out some sensible path. A one-path-at-a-time path.

At the top of the stairs to the right, a *"Do not enter"* sign must've been for Delaney's bedroom suite and famous spa and sauna set up, famous by Delaney's conquest stories. He strode the other way and shook his head at the hotel-type *"Do not disturb"* signs hanging off three doorknobs on the left side, one on the right. Music and echoes of sex—sensual and physical—created an acoustic orgy in the hallway. He opened the door with a *"Do not disturb"* sign facing inwards, peered around to make sure he wasn't interrupting, then stepped in.

ANNIE stopped in the foyer, needing a second to compose. Overheating wouldn't achieve anything. Doing a diva was one thing, hysterics another. She took a swig of her beer. How dare that bastard bring that bastard. Monaro knew how pissed off she was with Diaz. Hard to gauge what riled her more, Diaz having the nerve to come or Monaro bringing him. Did Delaney invite Diaz? She took another swig of her bottle and let the last dregs trickle down her throat.

"Gonna use that as a baton or grenade?" asked Cat, who'd sidled up to her right shoulder.

She grinned, checking out her bottle. "Waste of good glass."

"Want a reverse wing-chick?"

"Nah, this fun is all mine." She flicked her head towards the top of the staircase where Robbie was disappearing. "I see you don't need a wing-chick."

Cat followed her gaze and turned back a little flushed.

"Did he—"

"No. It's the twenty-first century and... this fun is all mine," said Cat.

"Are you sure?"

"Can't explain it, Annie. We went from opposing studios, to dancing through the same melody, and then a sudden key change right here." Cat patted her heart.

She felt a fool about what she'd told Robbie. Poor dude was heading for Confusion Alley, but this wasn't about her so she hugged Cat then grabbed Cat's beer. "Go, enjoy that key change, and keep the details to yourself."

Cat swirled and prowled up the staircase.

Who was she to give advice anyway? If there was anything she'd learnt about sex and love, it was the unpredictability. Hearts and pheromones had an eclectic playlist.

Diaz bee-lined for the bar, leaving Monaro, who quickly attracted a posse of young industry groupies. Damn, she was looking forward to hitting two ugly bears with one barrel. Monaro or Diaz? She finished Cat's beer, put both empty bottles on the tray of a passing waiter, and decided on a linear attack.

"Excuse me, folks." She grabbed Monaro by the arm and dragged him to the corner.

"I knew you'd come round," said Monaro, smile beaming, pinch-or-kiss cheeks glowing.

"If you brought that walking Argentine mop just to piss me off, you hit a bullseye."

"Didn't bring him, he was loitering outside, waiting for me. Underneath that dark mop he's a bit shyer than he makes out."

Delaney must've invited Diaz. She'd sort him out later.

"I know Italians confuse anger with passion and I know you're not so stupid to antagonise me when we still have a ton of Lachie stuff to work through, but you're mates with Diaz now?"

"Don't shoot him because of one mistake. We were all ambitious once."

His calmness should be aggravating, but the words threw an airbag in front of her anger. She was still ambitious. A renaissance ambition.

"His ambition lacked integrity." She punctured the airbag.

"Fair enough. One mistake." He held up a pointing finger.

"You're his manager now?"

"No, I just felt for the guy. It was a dumb move taking that track to Delaney behind your back, but he's genuinely remorseful."

Monaro showing empathy. For a man. He obviously didn't know Diaz had slept with her.

"You two would be good together, and I'd trust him with Lachie."

Another anger airbag. She actually stepped back to refocus on his eyes. "Did he tell you that—"

He nodded, raised his hands. "I don't need the lyric, the title was enough. When I came back from Japan, I wondered about you, about us.

You'll always have a sacred place on my turntable, Annie, and hopefully I'll have one on yours, but it's a digital world now. Lachie will drag us through a non-musical collaboration... and that's enough. We'll do the best we can for him, make some blunders, I'm sure, especially me, but we'll do our best. You've done an amazing job and I want to add a counter melody. Something different, but nothing that will reduce the core of the kid."

She would've stepped back further if it wasn't for a group behind her. Monaro had made a seismic shift with the opposite effect of an earthquake, closing gaps. Closing gaps in his personality, his behaviour, maybe the hazardous fissure between them. This joint parenting thing could work.

"I know Japan isn't on your Google Maps favourites, but I learnt something there that you might like."

Japan, where he ran to after dumping me? She didn't want to spoil the positive vibe so she changed the subject.

"You still picking him up tomorrow, or are your wing-man duties going to plaster you?"

Monaro checked his big, silver watch. "I'm heading home soon. Picking up Lachie tomorrow eleven sharp, from his mate Scott, right? Got it all in my phone."

She nodded. The guy always was better organised than her.

"Ikigai," he said.

"Ikiguy? As in yucky guy?"

"No, I.K.I.G.A.I. Ikigai. If you can find the thing you're good at and you love doing it and can make a living from it, that's your Ikigai. Writing and performing music is your Ikigai, Annie. You have to find a way past your fear."

Fear? Just when I thought he was closing gaps, he has to try and mansplain my own future and accuse me of fear. Has he already forgotten the nine years of being pregnant with and raising Lachie all on my own?

"Tony Monaro, are you harassing my favourite employee?" asked Delaney.

"Does she looked harassed?" countered Tony, focused on her.

"Never looks harassed."

"You invite Diaz?" she asked, grateful for the diversion.

"Now you look harassed. Don't feel so bad, I invited lots of people

I hate too." He pointed with his face towards a few people in the far corner. "Look at that twerp in the five-thousand-dollar black leather coat. Slimy accountant that represents the investment group. Thinks a coat like that makes him rock-n-roll. How many people in this biz can afford a five-thousand-dollar status cape? Maybe three. Dick."

"I was just leaving," she said.

"Not leaving here? Wait till you see who's playing live later. Maybe you can join them for a song or two."

"You'll have to talk to my new management company." Annie swirled away, but not before noting the surprise, maybe even jealousy in Monaro's eyes. Delaney looked at Monaro, who shrugged his shoulders. Fair enough. They'd both knocked each other a little off balance tonight.

ROBBIE stared at Cat's name above the text message he'd just typed: *2nd room on right*. Hit *Send* and there'd be no going back, a messy complication that might make their management business unmanageable. It wouldn't actually set him back because he'd never expected to be diving into to it so soon. But Cat's mutual desire to run a management biz changed everything and now he could taste it. Hell, they already had their first client and an office on hold. Tonight, Cat had added another mutual desire and he wasn't sure the two could run parallel.

Annie was right, focus on the work. Sex with Cat would be the ultimate delayed gratification. They could set a business target and when they achieved it, add romance and sex on the agenda. If they still felt the same way, with the business foundation strong, let their feelings and desire add to the balance sheet. Besides, was this the best time and location to consummate anything special? It was certainly the last place he'd ever expected Cat to suggest.

Yet... they weren't kids. Sex was nothing if it wasn't mutual, and their desire was absolutely mutual. Now that Cat had ripped it to the surface, there was no denying. No going back. There'd be tension in the business anyway if they didn't follow through on their feelings.

Curiosity would only pump up the urge. He shifted a little on the ottoman at the end of the huge bed. The bedside lamps had been turned on before he entered. Guess Delaney didn't want anyone tripping in the dark. Covered in thin shawls, the orange light added to the Indian feel of the room. Maybe each room had a different theme. A big industry bash in their boss's house wasn't the right time and place, but this room and bed were amazing, perfect for a first-time memory.

But first they'd talk it through, and this spot was as private as they'd find. He hit *Send*.

"Robbie, Robbie, Robbie, you're such a big tease."

Robbie jumped up, startled.

Stephanie stepped out of the closet. "Actually, I like a man with a bit of control. Suggests you're going to spoil me good." She stood with legs slightly apart, hands on hips, tongue exploring red lips. "Most men rush straight to dessert, but I like a good entree and looooong, main meal." Her hands moved behind her back and her dress dropped to the floor, lamplight washing over her tanned skin. All of her tanned skin. All her skin tanned.

He dropped his phone, clattering on the polished timber floor.

Bzzz, bzzz. Text message alert echoed off the floor.

"Shit." He scrambled on his knees for the phone.

Text from Cat. *"Heading up now. Warm the bed."*

"Fuck."

Frozen on his knees, Cat's message burned like dry ice in his hand.

"I hear your erotic urgency, Robbie. Okay, let's fuck." Stephanie kicked the dress out of the way and glided to him.

TRACK 35

CAT FLIPPED THE SIGN ON THE DOOR TO "DO NOT DISTURB". CALL HER A hypocrite after ridiculing the predictable debauchery at her boss's party, she was going to have wild sex with Robbie in a Delaney guest boudoir. She didn't feel like a hypocrite, just hypersensitive and hot, juices flowing and nerves tingling like they hadn't for months. Eons. As soon as she'd accepted her feelings for Robbie, consummation of their romantic connection triggered an uncontrollable urgency. She opened the door and stepped in, leaning back against the door to prolong the anticipation a few more sec—

What the fuck?

What the fuck was Robbie doing on his knees in front of her?

Naked.

Nineteen-year-old Stephanie, naked.

Hypersensitive sexual heat raged into a furnace of anger. She'd done the two-women-one-man combo a couple of times. In other circumstances, Stephanie's body would make a fascinating play-ground. On a purely erotic level she liked a two-woman, one man frolic. In truth, there wasn't a permutation or combination she hadn't played with. But she wasn't playing. Sex with Robbie was acceptance of her feelings for the guy, confirmation of their romantic connection.

Despite all the signs of being against type, this moment was meant to be a huge step to a mature, loving relationship. But he'd taken one tiny step to titillation with a… with a… Delaney groupie.

"Whatever you're thinking, you've got it wrong," said Robbie, still on his knees, that sparkly cloth of Stephanie's on the floor forming a triangle between them.

The pathetic plea of the pea-brain was right on type. Typecast gutter trash. Trash that didn't deserve any part of her, not even in business. She wanted to scream at him, machine gun the bastard to pieces with every bullet of ugly vocabulary she'd ever collected. But he wasn't worth it, so she straightened, opened the door and slid out.

"Cat, wait. Please."

She didn't even bother slamming the door. He wasn't worth it.

ANNIE watched Diaz posing centre stage with three women she didn't know. They obviously didn't know Diaz, who was just as desperate to feel part of the scene as they were. He looked like an exotic rock star, charmed like an exotic rock star, but he was just a rock, the kind you'd put under your car wheel when it's parked on a steep hill. Easy for Monaro to say it was just one mistake. Wasn't Monaro's song or trust Diaz had betrayed.

"Would you believe Pina's gone home already? Rattled off some excuse about school exams," said Delaney.

She turned to him, registering Pina might be closer to earth than most of the other talented starlets.

Delaney moved closer, eyes beady, movements sharp. Coke or speed. He tried to whisper but with the party decibels redlining and his senses screaming, he yelled, "Haven't spotted Stephanie, have you?"

"Try the playground or dollhouse."

He jabbed her arm.

"Oww." She rubbed her arm.

"Sorry just trying to—"

"There she is." She pointed behind his back across the room. "Just headed outside." She lied to the birthday boy, having a more important agenda than supporting his drug-fuelled, gravity defying friskiness. Delaney took off for the open French doors. Hopeful eyes, wandering hands, and sycophantic greetings couldn't distract the most powerful person in the room from his mission of sex with a nineteen-year-old.

Diaz's instant entourage had dwindled to two women. She hailed a waiter floating nearby, picked up two daiquiris, and took a couple of steps towards Diaz before Robbie ran in front of her.

"Seen Cat?" Robbie was breathless and flustered.

He stared like he wanted to ask something else or say something else, and it reminded her where Cat was heading last time she saw her.

"What have you done, Robbie?" Her protective instincts wrapped her tone in barbed wire.

"Nothing. Crazy story. Gotta find her." He hustled through the bustle, head whipping left and right.

Tonight, she wasn't in the mood for multi-tasking. First Diaz, then she'd check on Cat.

Diaz saw her coming and broke out that ridiculous smile, raking fingers through that ridiculous hair. He mumbled something to his audience of two and stepped towards her.

She stopped and held the daiquiris between them. "Would you like to share a drink or two?"

Smile upped in wattage, his head on a slight angle, hands pressed to his chest. "You have no idea what allegria that would bring me."

She emptied both strawberry daiquiris over him.

Even his hair couldn't cover his shock and embarrassment.

Diaz drenched in daiquiris. Delicious. She swirled, plonked the empty glasses on a table, and swayed out of the house.

I'm here for the contest, I'm here for the writers. I'm here for the contest, I'm here for the writers.

CAT would get through the last couple of event planning meetings, do what she had to do for the live contest gig, then goodbye, Merger; fuck off, Robbie. She'd ignored his constant texts and calls last night and throughout the morning. Ignored Annie's, too. Whatever she could have said to her, Annie's response would indirectly or directly have smelled of *"I told you so, I told you so, and I bloody told you so."* And she deserved it for letting that marketing cowboy sleaze his way into her heart.

Luckily it happened now before they kicked off any relationship, and before they tied the knot on their professional future with the management biz. What a complicated catastrophe that would have been. She deliberately sat at the project table at the furthest point from Robbie, Annie between them.

"What about a good cover band like Escape Goats? Top musos, a female and male lead vocalist. They'll pick up the songs quickly but are unknown so the writers would remain the stars," said Robbie.

"That's a terrific idea, Robbie. They'd be cheap too, and it leaves more budget for the live video shoot," said Annie.

"Ridiculous, cheapens the whole contest. Leave the musical decisions to us and you just focus on the venue and promotional stuff."

Robbie tried staring at her with those false eyes of confusion and hurt. The little weasel couldn't handle her laser glare so he turned quickly to Annie for support, just like he did in the very first meeting when Delaney dumped him on them.

Wimp.

Annie rolled her chair back from the table, checked out Robbie then her. "That's the third time you've slammed him this morning, Cat, and two of his ideas are really good. We have a ton of stuff to get through in the next couple of weeks and we haven't got a hope while that humongous elephant in the room is sitting on all of us, squashing the good out of everything this contest has achieved, out of everything we've achieved for the writers."

Achieved for the writers... That was the only thing that stopped her from lashing back. If Annie had any notion of Robbie's betrayal, she'd throw him out of the room, probably get Delaney's backing to throw him off the rest of the contest.

"I'm no expert, but I'd rather play counsellor than coroner." Annie spread her hands towards her and Robbie. "So, spill it."

"Robbie fucked Stephanie."

"I didn't fuck her."

"You... you were going to. I caught him on his knees in front of that five shades of grey wannabe, naked."

"You were both naked?" Annie asked Robbie.

"No just Stephanie. I was—"

"A disloyal douchebag of a sleazebag, pissing cowboy."

He slumped back in his chair, all puppy sad eyes. Annie was too smart to fall for that. This was good. Good to get it all out now. Ditch the bastard cold.

"Cat, I need to hear exactly what happened from the beginning."

"He—"

"From him. You get final response after we've heard all of his version. None of your nuclear glares."

So fired up that her butt took up a slither of the seat, she stood, pulled it in under her, and plonked down. She liked the idea of having a nuclear glare, except for the nuclear bit. Wind-powered or solar-stare didn't have the same kick. She'd have to work on something.

She nodded, closed her eyes, and listened for the bullshit.

CAT's rage had left the building.

A bit of anger hung around the echoing walls, and she didn't know whether to chase it out with forgiveness or laughter. Robbie's story, his tone, it all sounded true. A mockumentary or French farce, but true. She opened her eyes for the conclusive test.

No wimpy avoidance, Robbie's face soft as her favourite couch blanket, fluffy, warm, and covering her from chin to curling toes.

The heat of Annie's eyes tinged the side of her face, but she couldn't break away from Robbie. Words, thoughts, feelings flashed between them, bubbled in her tummy. Her heart.

"That's the best 'coming out the closet' story I've heard all year. Maybe ever," said Annie.

"I can corroborate his defence," said Delooney, arms reaching above the doorframe.

"Delooney, how long have you been spying?" asked Cat.

Annie and Robbie flicked their eyes on her, then back at Delooney. Whoops, first time she'd used his nickname to his face.

"Lost your knuckles, boss?" Annie tried to recover for her.

"Love the moniker, Cat. Not original, but you're the first to have the guts to say it in front of me. Respect." Delooney pointed a friendly finger at her. "Steph told me all about it later that night, or brunch next day." He grinned at Robbie. "You set her up nicely. Top wing-man work."

"That story stays a secret between us," she said. No need to embarrass Robbie or publicise their… their accidental meeting.

Delooney brought his hands together for an Indian bow. "My lips are sacred; however, Stephanie… well, let's just say her head might nod in one direction, but her social media fingers flutter all over the fucking place, as if keyboards are how she sources oxygen."

"You mean… everyone knows about…" Robbie waved a hand between her and him, pride in his voice, cowboy grin back.

Her tummy and heart bubbled again. She tried squashing her inner vibe, but it was like diving into a sea of coloured balls, the bubbling overpowering her.

"You need to Zenify this, don't hide it. Go with the flow. I'll throw a coming out party for your relationship."

"NO PARTIES!" she yelled simultaneously with Robbie and Annie.

"Nice harmonies. Even *your* voice sounded sweet, Cat." Delooney winked and smiled, more evil clown than funny and cute. He looked over the papers scattered on the table, the messy squiggles on the whiteboard. "That's how my head felt yesterday after the party. Of course, slinky Steph didn't help with her—"

Annie's writing pad hit Delooney in the chest, which was just as well, because she didn't want to throw her tablet at him.

Delooney raised his arms in surrender and backed out the door. "I need a final rundown of your plans for this gig tomorrow in the dungeon." He spun into the hall.

"You don't trust us, do you?"

Delooney spun back in a full one-eighty, pointing at the computer screen and tablets. "You might be eons ahead of me on these digital gadgets, but I've learnt a thing or two hundred about running live gigs, seen a million things go wrong, and know three hacks for each one." His grin filled the doorway. "Hacks—you like that lingo?"

As soon as Delooney took off, Robbie's eyes swung back to her. Sparkly eyes, holding back a smiling grin. Whatever clanked around his brain seemed to make him happy, which only warmed her inner bubbling. Thinking he'd cheated had created a clean escape and she'd latched on to it. Easier to blame him for a failed relationship before it even began. Smoke and mirrors. A hoax on her heart. It hurt seeing Robbie with that teen-ho. Anger was a dominatrix and she had been comfortable in the red zone. Now that she knew for sure how much he felt about her, there was no hiding. No running.

"I think this is where one of you is supposed to say, 'we need to talk'," said Annie.

She'd forgotten Annie was still there despite being within touching distance. Crazy.

"What she said." Robbie's sparkly eyes moved up and down. He must be nodding.

TRACK 36

ROBBIE HOVERED AT THE COBBLESTONE LANEWAY NEXT TO MERGER Music. He knew enough about himself to know he didn't know how any of this had happened. Him and Cat. Crazy. Setting up a management company together had already stretched his wisdom and imagination beyond capacity. Romance with Cat, liking her this much--crazy. How did her green eyes become part of his inner lighting, flicking on instantly whenever he thought of her? Her blue hair made all other hair colours on all people look abnormal. Her passion, which ran on a scale between zest and frenzy, electrified even when it was electrocuting him.

Lots of questions and potential obstacles clambered for his attention, but one dominated: was he just a novelty for her? Cat liked girls. Lots of girls. Sure, she'd always been kind of bi-ish, but according to Manny, her romantic and sexual history was more of a she-her story. Boys—and they usually were closer to boys than experienced men— provided a port here and there to explore, but her romantic cruise ship was full of girls.

A woman strode past in her corporate costume of tight black skirt, expensive blouse, and shiny stilettos. Still amazed him how women could walk with such composure on those things. It had been the kind of warm spring day Melburnians keep a secret—too good to share—and an urge for a gelato crept up on him. He caught himself in the moment. He'd observed the sexy, corporate woman and that was all, no lust or longing. Cat had tied him up in her web by stealth. He never saw it coming. He'd never known anyone so fierce yet so nurturing. Spiritual yet wild. Intense yet captivating.

Cat bounced down the bluestone steps from Merger's entrance and headed straight for him, smiling.

That dazzling warmth triggered his smile, having no control over it all. But how should he greet her now? Hug? Kiss on the cheek? Both? Kiss on her lips?

Cat jabbed him on his upper arm and kept walking. "Come on, cowboy. Let's do this mobile."

"How can I be sure I'm not just a novelty?" said Cat.

The question on the tip of ROBBIE's tongue. They'd spent all the walk down Kerferd Road avoiding the one subject on their agenda—them. Filled it swapping industry gossip, new tracks they'd heard outside the contest bubble, and drifting back to the Espy gig that unofficially, and unknowingly at the time, had become a first date. Then, as they meandered along the concrete walking path above the beach, Cat blurted that out. *How can I be sure I'm not just a novelty?*

He stopped.

She stopped, stared up at him, the sun hovering low on the bay behind her, the last few minutes before the huge orange ball would drop suddenly into the ocean.

"I was going to ask you the same thing."

Her eyes narrowed, then resumed their normal oval shape. She nodded. "I get that. Fair enough." She scooted off again.

He caught up with her. "I mean, is this your Freddie Mercury, George Michael moment in reverse?" Based on articles he'd read, both superstars had followed a hetero path, then thought they were bisexual, until they finally accepted they were gay.

"I don't know… definitely feels… different," Cat said while

checking for cars. The road cleared and she scooted across all six lanes without hesitating on the traffic island.

He jogged across to catch up.

"Different how?" Ego, curiosity, and fear teamed up to push the question out of his throat.

Cat shot him a glance without breaking her short but fast stride. "The other relationships kind of drifted in creeks or rivers, always moving, never settled, eventually hitting a rock or bank. This"—she waved her hand between them—"it's deeper… kind of a warm, safe lagoon."

Ego pushed away fear and curiosity, shoving a grin across his face, then an overwhelming joy flushed out of his heart and bubbled through veins, diluting even his ego to nothing. Joy. Underrated, underestimated joy.

Cat stepped onto Lagoon Pier. The timber structure seemed to have a calming effect as he'd never seen her meander. They weaved between Chinese tourists, a local couple pushing their retro bikes and the folks fishing who probably wished they had the pier to themselves. Cat led them to the first boat landing about halfway down the pier, stepped down the short steel ladder, plonked her bag on the timber deck, and sat down with her feet dangling over the edge, about half a metre above the dark green water.

He joined her, enjoying the teenage-ish simplicity. Must've been at least fifty people on the pier, but in that moment, it was just him and Cat. No, him *with* Cat. He had often been on a date or in a relationship where it was him and… him plus. Cat was different. He was really with her, even when they weren't physically together.

"Did you ever read that book, *Up Here*?" Cat said.

"No, but I saw the movie. An okay rom-com. Not my favourite genre, but it was okay."

"The end scene where the guy says, 'When I'm with you, I'm with me.' That's how I feel with you, about you. I've been in deep a couple of times—yes, women—but it's never felt like this."

"Wow, that's the second time today we've been thinking the same thing. Almost exact words."

Cat shrugged and nodded simultaneously.

He shrugged and nodded simultaneously. "To be honest, I don't remember the movie too much, but the title song was a catchy, pop-dance track and I think that line was the hook."

"We have to keep this organic."

"Organic?"

"Relationships are complex enough without artificial rules and barriers."

"That's for sure." He'd been with women who'd set up *tests* and all it did was make them both testy.

"We will stumble."

He kind of nodded.

Cat elbowed him. "We will stumble."

"Okay, yes, we'll stumble, but I'm not running, Cat."

"There's a good chance we might have a rigorous chat now and then."

"Feisty chats are better than simmering hate."

"I said rigorous."

"With you, rigorous would be utopia. I'll happily settle for rigorous."

Cat angled him a smile, then turned towards the beach on their right. The last of the kite surfers skimmed out of the water, jogged onto the sand in a fluid motion, and fought her kite to the ground.

"Cat, jealousy was an ugly issue with my last girlfriend. When you're confident and thriving, you'll attract people who are sexy or interesting or both, especially in this biz. And I want you confident and thriving. Always."

"You want me to be attracted to other people?"

"No, but it can happen. The key is to acknowledge it, then let go. As long as you don't act on it, you don't have to tell me about it."

"You're one big surprise, Robbie Guest. The more open we are in those moments, the more we share, the safer we'll be."

"Anything else we should cover now?"

"Enough projecting. Organic, okay?"

"Okay, organic."

An older couple stepped down to the wooden landing and faced the sun, the woman nestling back into the guy, his hands slid around her waist.

Cat turned forward. "Haven't been here before. I like this spot."

"Same. Now it's our spot."

Cat nudged him with her shoulder. "Didn't think you had corny in you."

"You're fertilising a giant inner cornfield I never knew I had."

"You're calling me shit?" Green eyes meshed with orange sunset.

"Organic. Organic life enhancer." He braced himself for an elbow or a dozen scathing comebacks.

Cat rested her head on his shoulder.

As if she'd done it a million times.

He slid an arm around her waist, as if he'd done it a million times.

Lights twinkled on city buildings to the right, Westgate Bridge lit on the left, Spirit of Tasmania ferry dead centre in the foreground, the distant sun linking the three with a half-dome of orange haze. Like his inner glow and balance, he hadn't realised he wasn't balanced until this moment with Cat. His heart, career, and purpose, all linked with Cat. *With Cat...* Still sounded crazy despite feeling so cruisy.

"I'll drop by our future office tomorrow and work out a deal to start the lease about four weeks from the contest gig."

Cat's head sprung so quickly he felt a breeze across his cheek and ear.

"Sorry, I remember. We should talk about the details, make a joint decision. I figured two weeks' notice and a couple of weeks R and R. What do you—"

"No." Her body went rigid. Too rigid.

"No? No on the timing? More notice? I guess Delaney deserves that."

The high lamp on the pier behind them put half her face in dark shadow. The one clearly visible eye shared none of the warm sunset haze.

"No business until I get my half of the cash together."

"Come on, Cat, we're a couple now. What's the big deal of me funding the starting capital?"

"We're not a *couple* couple. We've barely started to explore what this…" She waved a hand between them. "What this is."

"It is organic, right?"

"Don't shove my own words back at me, Robbie. Our business will be organic when I can fund my own share independently. Until then, we don't launch."

She had that glare on, the same warrior glare from the first contest meeting, minus the gnarling teeth. Still made him turn away. Damn sun had scampered for cover, too.

"But we made a commitment to Annie."

"Annie will wait. She wants to write a bunch of tracks before announcing anything anyway."

"How long?" He knew she didn't have any leave owing and was still in some level of debt from her Uganda volunteer thing, and now that he could taste it, he didn't want to wait six or twelve months to bite into their business. Couldn't wait that long.

"I've got a part-time thing. It's flexible and I'm ramping up my… my hours."

"I thought the community centre was voluntary."

She turned away, nodding.

Part-time thing. "So, what part-time thing?"

Her jawbone gnawed away inside her cheek.

Why is it so difficult to tell me? What could you be possibly be doing… short of selling your body? Nah, you would never sell your body. You're probably reluctant to admit working part-time for some global fast-food giant or—

Cat jumped up, scooped her bag, and turned for the steps up the pier.

He grabbed her arm. "It's okay, Cat. Whatever the part-time gig, I'd never judge you, no reason for you to keep it a secret."

She shook her arm free but stayed, a foreign look on her face, vulnerable, fragile.

The older couple sensed the tension, climbed up, and walked down the pier.

"I do phone sex."

Organic, cruisy and balanced held hands and jumped off the pier into the dark, cold water. With his heart. It wasn't his worst nightmare, but it wasn't far. It was cheating, wasn't it? He'd been looking forward to the kind of spicy phone sex you can only have with someone special, someone close... But Cat having phone sex with strangers... making them... making them... A shudder launched from the base of his spine and shook his head. He stepped back. Didn't mean to recoil from her. Didn't know how to take it, how to act. Felt like the slimy gunk clinging to the wooden pier in the water.

Cat winced, slid a half step towards him.

He raised his arms. "I need... I never would've... Time. I need time to process this."

He bound up the steps and scurried down the pier. Luckily the tourists, couples, and most of the fishers had gone or one or two of them may have accidentally been nudged into the sea.

With his heart.

TRACK 37

"HE'S A HYPOCRITE. SPINS SOME BULLSHIT PHILOSOPHY ABOUT JEALOUSY and how to handle it as adults, then dumps me on the pier like I'm a... a... Made me feel dirty," Cat said, then swigged more beer, then more, before plonking the pint glass on the bar. Luckily the bottle hit the thick cardboard coaster or she might've cracked the timber bar.

ANNIE sensed Cat didn't need any help from Robbie to feel dirty about her part-time gig, but this wasn't the moment for helping her self-awareness. She stumbled in that direction on her own. The some-times-volcanic Cat sounded more repentant than roaring.

"You look shocked too." Swig, plonk.

Shock? Over you doing phone sex? Doing it for so long and not telling me? Or telling Robbie first? Shock? Probably.

She flapped her hand and twisted her face to dismiss any concerns Cat had. "I'm surprised you're surprised about Robbie. Jealousy is based on ego and fear, and all men seem to hover on both spectrums, no matter how much they try and hide it." She sipped her beer.

"He doesn't understand how important it is for me to go into this as equals." Cat finished her beer and held up the empty glass towards the barman, who nodded.

"I'm sure he gets that." She picked out a couple of pretzels from the little bowl, then pushed the nuts and stuff closer to Cat.

Cat grabbed a handful, shoved them in her mouth, and crunched away.

Piercing horns and a funky guitar riff over the speakers made her straighten on her stool. "Respect" always did that. The Otis Redding song with a powerful twist from Aretha Franklin steeled the spine of every woman in the bar, chests bursting, heads nodding.

Every woman except Cat, who slumped lower, eyes barely seeing over the top of her glass. "I hate every second. Every millisecond. Sure, I convince the mirror I'm doing it for good causes, paying off debts that helped me help some helpless kids. You can trick the mirror into anything, like a lie detector test. Then the acid truth spills into my heart, burns through to the soul."

"Three things, Cat." She held up a thumb. "Secrets are cancer to a relationship, and you just cut out a big tumour between you and Robbie." Stuck out her pointing finger at right-angle to thumb. "Two, you *were* doing it for good reasons. Amazing reasons. If we all did one percent of the volunteer work you do, this world would be a utopia. Fucking utopia. Who cares how you paid for it as long as you didn't hurt anyone, and you didn't." She extended her middle finger. "He knows now your honesty is one hundred percent."

Cat stared at her refilled glass, half raised her hand in a rock salute, pointing finger and little finger extended.

Progress. If she got Cat to even fifty percent of her usual self-esteem, Robbie wouldn't stand a chance of resisting Cat's follow-up, whatever it may be.

"Great speech, Annie, but you've left out a few fingers." Cat held up a hand, matching her extended thumb and pointing finger then extended a third finger. "Deep in my soul, *I hate* what I'm doing. Lots of women and men do amazing volunteer work overseas and get into debt doing it, but they didn't do phone sex to pay for it." She skolled her beer with her other hand, then plonked the glass down. Extended a fourth finger. "And I continue to do it based on some self-justifying delusion." Added her little pinkie. "And none of them add up to more respect from Robbie." Cat closed her fist and rested it next to her empty glass. Her other hand clenched into a fist on her thigh.

She took both Cat's fists and held them. "If he's half the man you deserve, he'll get over this. If he doesn't recognise the special in you, that's only in you, he's not for you." She let go of Cat's fists and raised hers for a fist bump.

Cat stared, forced a smile, then bumped her fists.

ANNIE had no idea how it had evolved. Sometime around late primary school, she became the go-to girl for pouring your problems out. Not just friends, a circle wider than names she could remember, yet they all knew hers. A pseudo-counsellor when all she wanted to do was dance to Pseudo Echo and the other CDs in her mum's collection. Her mum said it was her eyes. People trusted big eyes. One friend said it was how she listened without dumping her own shit or pushing instant-easy-fix ideas, which only made them feel dumb.

Here she was nearly twenty years later, waiting for Robbie's latte to arrive before she dived into the unofficial almost-couple counselling session she'd somehow roped herself into. Only three other tables were taken up in the café, yet the steady takeaway trade for the afternoon caffeine hits kept the espresso machine swirling and gurgling—Melbourne's backing track—saving her or Robbie from needing to fill the air with words.

Robbie's chin-forward focus towards the window worked with his armour of black leather jacket over printed T-shirt, tight blue jeans, and tan boots. But it didn't cover his hunched posture or the way his right thumb flicked at his thigh like a gun-less cowboy. Contrasts and contradictions always stirred something in her imagination. Maybe that's why she'd become such good listener, observer of other people's issues. Her creative subconscious was selfishly mining for material.

"Here you go, chief, large latte with three sugars," the waiter said as he placed the mug in front of Robbie and spun back to the busy counter.

"Thanks," mumbled Robbie.

"Three sugars, a man with my kind of pancreas."

"Look, Annie, I'm here out of respect as a colleague. I'm sorry our management thing will never happen, not with me anyway, and we can't be friends because Cat is your BFF and that is one degree of separation too close. So, we stumble through the next couple of weeks at Merger, kick this contest gig over the line, then leave the building through different doors." He took a gulp of his coffee without leaving any on his lips. Bastard. She could never do that. He stared at her, unhunching a little, but his eyes flagged defeat not defiance.

"Don't be such a drama queen. You don't have an ounce of Freddie or George Michael in you to pull it off."

"Joke as much as you like, I'm leaving when I finish this." He gulped down more of the latte, glaring at the mug.

"Did she cheat on you?"

"May as well have. *And* she wants to keep on doing it."

"Fuck's sake, Robbie, it's harmless and discreet. Not like she's parading on the street under a red light, and she's definitely not disrespecting you. I've tasted every flavour of being fucked around, Robbie, and what Cat is doing isn't even on a menu."

"I don't like it."

"Well, grow some balls to go with your cowboy-rock star shit you're trying to pull off. Do you think she likes it? You reckon Cat's doing it for fun? It was killing her soul, even before she told you about it."

"Did you know?"

"No. Shows you how much Cat detests it, despises herself for doing it. But like I told her, she's not doing it to buy a fancy dress or shiny boots, she's genuinely helping kids in a fucked-up place, giving them the tiniest bit of hope to get out of their fucked-up life."

Robbie lifted his mug, swirled the contents. "You really didn't know?"

"That's how much you mean to her, Robbie. You're the only one she's ever told... and if it didn't blow up in her face, she may never have told me."

He lifted his mug, then put it back on the table without drinking.

"People would kill for that type of honesty and transparency. Cat's as raw and open as an Adele track. How many relationships get even close to that foundation?"

He shifted in his seat towards her, eyes mushy with vulnerability.

"Can you promise her that level of honesty?"

His head nodded above a shrug.

We all crave pure honesty in a relationship, but how many of us can truly live up to it? Most people—men or women—would be crushed by the burden of Cat's transparency.

"Let the stubborn woman do what she has to do. When she's raised her money her way, what's left to hurt you? Nothing. She dumps the guilty phone in the bin and walks away."

Robbie shakes his head. "No, she wouldn't."

"Oh, Robbie, how can her honesty break your trust? I don't get it."

"She wouldn't dump the phone in a bin, she'd recycle it. No land mass."

Humour was good, even if he wasn't smiling yet. Her throat muscles relaxed. The tension had crept up on her because you don't find many soul sisters like Cat. And Robbie had grown on her. She could see how Cat could stumble into a bunch of feelings for the guy. Plus, she'd invested in glimpses of her future with the two of them as her manager. The song contest was just the warm-up act for their true professional journey together.

"There's no baggage or danger from this, Robbie. Not like she has to work for an ex or do something illegal. It's just a gig for a purpose. Actually, now she has two purposes—pay off her international volunteer debt, and raise the capital to be your partner. Equal partner."

"She's got a good friend," he said to his mug, spinning it between his hands slowly on the table. He pushed the mug aside, placing elbows on the table, right fist tapping lightly on top of the left. "If this was just a business thing. About equal business partners. Just business... but it's not."

"That's why you need to work through this. There's something special between you two."

His fist-tapping rhythm stepped up in tempo. "She helps other men have orgasms, Annie. Does it fucking matter how or why?" Every syllable reduced in volume yet increasingly dripping with acid.

She recoiled, not at his vociferousness but the bluntness of his crude yet accurate summary. The intimacy Cat opened herself to despite not investing any feelings, no matter that it was on a phone rather than a bed. Hearing Robbie's point of view, feeling his pain, the tortured eyes, this issue was far more complex than she'd anticipated. She wasn't wise enough to help them find a solution, way out of her amateur counsellor zone.

"You know the worst of it? The horror that echoes around my head?"

She shook her head.

"She hears them come. Every single one of the sick bastards. She hears them." Robbie stood, rustled some money from his front pocket, left it on the table, and bustled out.

TRACK 38

"YOU'VE TICKED ALL THE BOXES, INCLUDING A FEW CONTINGENCIES I hadn't thought of, so power to all of you for that." Delooney unwound his fingers from the back of his head and spread them wide slowly. "So why does it feel like a funeral rather than"—he lifted two fingers on each hand as quotation marks—"a celebration of talented undiscovered songwriters?" His eyes focused on Annie, then Robbie, then her.

CAT flipped down to the two-page checklist they'd just worked through for the live gig finale. Aversion rather than revision. The bugger had used her line for emphasis, but damned if she was going to get defensive. Let Robbie answer him.

"You know I can see you all, right?"

The others must have been avoiding Delooney's gaze too.

"Fleetwood Mac, Pink Floyd, Ramones, Oasis… I could spit out another dozen. The band members all hated each other but still did their magic when it counted. Never let their fans down on stage."

"No one's letting anyone down. We're all exhausted, but we'll fire up on the day," said Annie.

"Last chance. Are you sure you don't want Carl G to take some pressure off? Best tour manager in Melbourne."

"Cat and Robbie have got this." Annie. Confident. Final.

She doodled over the rundown notes. A couple of weeks ago, she wouldn't have hesitated running the gig with Robbie. Now, nine days out, nerves were natural, but all sorts of red flags flapped around her brain. How could she and Robbie manage a live performance and a five-camera live TV broadcast on Channel V-Rock when they couldn't face each other? Couldn't speak without the words travelling via Annie. Couldn't fall back on a catalogue of successful events. This was their first. She didn't want to stuff up all their hard work and the special moment for the writers because of their dysfunctional relationship.

"We're primed for this, chief. Cat's run projects in third-world jungles. I've watched Carl in action a dozen times. He's good, but we don't need him. You guys can sit back and enjoy the gig as punters for a change." This from Robbie. Confident. Final.

Heat flashed up her spine and she couldn't tell if it was heading for the flammable anger tank. Was it because he spoke for her? Or that he dared to compare shadowing Carl at a rock gig in a modern rock venue in the friendliest live music town in the world, to the intricate complexities of running any of the projects she'd been a part of in dusty, desperate countries drowning in chaos? Didn't want to scare Delooney, but surely it was better to be honest now rather than embarrass him and the writers on the night. She could not work with Robbie, and it was time to make that clear. Let Carl and apprentice Robbie run the event.

Clean break now.

Far away from Merger.

Far away from the music biz.

The big door flung open, and Pierre burst through, puffing, crimson-faced, spooked.

"You need to…" He gushed in air a few times. "You need to come up now," Pierre said to Delooney.

"Pierre, you weren't built for running. Stroll back upstairs in your cute blue loafers and tell whoever it is I'll be there in five." Delaney turned to Robbie.

"NOW. You need to come up now." Pierre gulped air.

Everyone stared at Pierre, the gentlest, most effeminate guy you'd ever meet with the softest voice. She'd never heard him speak at a normal volume, let alone yell.

"Relax, son. I don't want you taking time off for a heart attack. Unless it's Sir Paul McCartney up there, whoever it is can wait five fucking minutes."

"It's Stephanie's dad. He's screaming at everyone that you fucked his daughter."

Delooney actually grinned, cheeks glowing. Ego before empathy. Sadly, fucking young women was behaviour that enhanced his reputation in this messy biz.

"She's a big girl. She can—"

"She's a big fifteen-year-old girl. Fifteen. That's what he's screaming. You raped his fifteen-year-old girl, and he wants to smash your head in before calling the police."

Delooney's glow turned to ghost.

CAT doodled, occasionally exchanging glances with Annie, totally ignoring Robbie on the other side of the boardroom table. After Delooney had established from Pierre that Stephanie's dad wasn't waving a gun or knife, just his phone with the local police number already tapped in, a quick Google and social media search established him as George Clayton, sixty-three, grey-haired pharmacist and current mayor of a leafy, inner eastern council. Delooney quickly morphed into the stress-beating rock warrior he once was and headed to reception. Consensual sex with young, sexy starlets might enhance his reputation in the music biz, even in the post "Me Too" days, but bedding an underage girl was a disaster. Apart from the criminal-jail ramifications, it would destroy his career with public company owned Merger Music. Destroy his career anywhere. Full stop.

Sympathy for super ambitious Stephanie wasn't at the high end of the spectrum. Maybe the scar from the Robbie bedroom thing at Delooney's party ran deeper than she realised. Besides, with her ridiculous physical maturity, none of them had recognised her as that young. Stephanie's worldliness, appearance, and height obviously came from her mother, an ex-model now running a retail fashion store in Hawthorn. But sitting in the dungeon was too much for her curiosity juices. She pulled the fancy speaker phone unit to her end of the table and dialled reception.

Someone answered and for a couple of seconds she heard Delooney trying to interrupt a very loud Clayton, but it was difficult making out the words.

"Tracey?"

"Cat, can't speak right now."

"You need to divert the phone to the answering service so no one from outside overhears. Got that?"

"Yep."

"And please put your headset mic on the counter as close to the action as possible. We need to hear this."

"Ummm…"

"Tracey, it's for Delooney's sake."

"Okay."

They heard a crackle and bump and then the argument was clearer but not quite loud enough.

"There's a volume button low on the right," said Robbie.

She avoided his eyes, found the dial, and wound it as loud as it got.

"But we met in a nightclub. I had to assume she was over eighteen," said Delooney, firm, calm.

"You assumed your dick, you sick bastard," said Clayton.

Hairs spiked up on the back of her neck.

"Mr Clayton, you can't get into clubs these days without showing ID. She must've—"

"You seduced her with drugs and your sleazy power bullshit. You played on her desperation to be a singer and you're going to pay for it."

"She looks older than some of the weather girls on TV."

"Fifteen. And she tells her mother everything. You have no morals. You're a fucking role model for juvenile delinquents. Men like you that give us all a bad name. Hooked on sex, ego, and the fumes of your own heavy breathing." Clayton breathed heavy. Exaggerated. Haunting. Ugly.

She hit the mute button and sprung out of her chair.

"What's a matter, Cat? You okay?" said Annie.

"I know… I know that voice."

"How do you know the…" Annie stopped her own sentence as she'd worked it out, then snapped her head towards Robbie.

She followed, unable to resist checking to see if he got it. Robbie held her eyes. Flames around a pupil of steel. Anger? Passion? Devastation at the reminder of her part-time job?

"Crucify the fucking hypocrite," said Robbie.

Annie nodded, slow, deliberate, deadly.

TRACK 39

CAT SLIPPED AT THE TOP OF THE STAIRS, REGAINED HER BALANCE AND steadied, taking in a few long breaths.

"Hitting *Send* now, then you." Clayton's guttural growl shot another icy shiver up her spine.

She zoomed around the corner and stalled. Clayton must've been well over two metres tall and almost a metre wide, with a thumb hovering over his phone, and Delooney backed up against the wall.

"Don't you fucking dare." Her diva-roar stunned her as much as it stunned Clayton and Delooney. Bless Annie's subliminal training.

"If you're the lawyer around here, you can deal with the police. I have a right to defend my daughter's dignity."

"George Clayton, *you're* my client."

Clayton lowered his phone, thumb still hovering over the *Send* button.

"You're not my lawyer. You're just a cheap diversion."

"Speaking of cheap, you lied about your real name, but you *are* my client."

Delooney's head followed the conversation back and forth like a tennis match, but she focused on Clayton as she edged closer.

"Stay out of this. I've never met you in my life."

"Said your name was Kenny. On the phone calls. The phone calls you made to me, Kenny." She mimicked his husky breathing. Exaggerated. Haunting. Ugly.

Clayton took a half-step away from her, phone arm dropped to his side under drooping shoulders. He glanced at his phone, then back to her.

How much had he got away with in this world from his size and bullying? Bullies were high on her top ten shit chart. She'd ridden the instinctive internal retching from hearing Kenny Clayton's voice, then fought her animal defensiveness at his hypocrisy. Control nudged her into a Zen zone. Something good was going to come out of this ugly incident. Not sure what, but her inner vibe flowed.

"Let's calm down and sort this out in the meeting room." She pointed at the meeting room beside her.

Delaney quickly stepped towards the room, but she raised her hand to stop him.

"You go to that one." She pointed at the meeting room on the other side of the foyer. "I need to speak to him solo first." She opened the door near her. "Come along, Mr Clayton."

Clayton hesitated, put the phone inside his blazer, and looked at the front door.

"Or do you prefer Kenny?"

He scurried past her into the meeting room, head lowered.

CAT had sprinted out of the dungeon and scampered up the stairs to face Clayton fuelled by fury, yet the longer she sat in the room with him, the more Zen flowed through her. Following the "less is more" principle, she luxuriated in silence as he squirmed and fidgeted. The whole building was eerily silent, as if everyone had heard about the confrontation and held their collective breath in anticipation of a fiery ending.

Let him break the silence.

It was a good strategy because she had no idea how to play this out. On a scale of one to ten, Clayton's phone-sex sin hovered closer to one than ten. His hypocrisy and bullying blasted way past ten, but she wasn't here to judge.

"I can't… my wife, she can't find out."

"Or your daughter."

Clayton bent his head, nodded.

"Or your fellow councillors."

Head lower, nodding imperceptible.

"Or the residents that voted for you."

Head hanging.

"Not to mention your clients."

He was at the end of a shaky pier with giant rocks tied to his feet, staring into the endless depths of Lake My-Life-Is-Fucked. He placed his elbows on the table, needing to support his head in his hands. Shook his head, eyes down.

Out of nowhere, empathy flooded her.

Not for Clayton, she didn't give a damn about him.

For Robbie.

Watching the humiliation Clayton was suffering, the complete crippling of the man he thought he was, portrayed he was, helped her understand how difficult it must be for Robbie to accept her phone-sex gig. It *wasn't* a normal gig, it was a sleazy way to earn money. Robbie had every right to be shocked, confused, repulsed.

The flood of empathy carved out a river of ideas, solutions to every immediate and short-term problem in front of her. She stepped forward and in as caring a voice as she could muster said, "I can fix this."

He looked at her, unconvinced, head still resting on his hands. "I can't pay you much."

"No money. From you. Ever again."

He straightened up. "Sorry. Please, I didn't mean to offend you. Anything, I'll listen to any idea, if we can just bury this here."

"Wait there." She got up slowly, pushed her chair back in, watched the broken man from the door. Whatever problems Clayton had, whatever shadows haunted his family, none of it was her problem. She didn't need to fix him, just spare him. She stepped out and closed the door.

"It's a deal, Cat. A win-win-bloody-win. May all the good karma in all the cosmos fall gently at your feet," Delooney said as he extended his arm to shake hands.

CAT ignored his hand but held up hers as a stop sign.

Delooney tilted back in the chair till his head touched the wall. He wasn't used to the cramped conditions of the smaller meeting room.

"First, I need to run this by him."

"But we just agreed—"

She doubled up stop signs with her other hand.

"Okay, okay, I trust you, Cat."

CAT slipped out of the small meeting room, strode across to the larger room, opened the door without knocking and stood in the doorway.

Clayton jerked his head up from his arms, which were resting on the table, face greyer than the manicured hair, eyes red, a possible smudge of tears on his cheeks. Maybe there was hope for self-redemption, but she didn't care. Not her shift.

"You might be lucky. I'll be back in ten minutes."

She shut the door and turned back into the reception area to see Annie and Robbie whispering with Tracey and Pierre. All four swung at her, curiosity shining across eight eyes.

"We couldn't hear anything down there. You okay?" said Annie.

She nodded, then pointed to Robbie. "We need to talk. Dungeon, now."

"You can't click your fingers and—"

"Please, Robbie, it's important and urgent." She headed to the stairs, turning to see Robbie shuffling behind. "Tracey, offer Mayor Clayton some water. No poison."

In the dungeon, Robbie took up his seat opposite where CAT had been sitting earlier, and plonked his elbows on the table, his chin between thumbs and fingers. She pulled out an adjacent chair and sat facing him, side-on to the table.

"You have every right to be confused, disappointed, even repulsed."

He turned his head to face her, but kept his chair and body towards the table.

"I've bounced around those hellish emotions more than anyone else could. Have you ever read *The Obstacle is the Way*?"

Robbie shook his head.

"The crazy thing is, Robbie Guest, that sleazy phone work, the big obstacle in *our* way, has floated a solution from the rock gods into our lap. A solution that ticks all the boxes for us moving our business forward."

"Great to see your inner entrepreneur bursting out, but this isn't about business for me. Not anymore." Cold eyes, icy low voice.

"Good. Me neither."

Robbie turned his chair towards her.

"I like you, Robbie. I don't fully understand it, but our time together is a parallel universe, like nothing can touch us, nothing else matters. We don't deserve to lose where that might take us because of one stupid part-time job I've had."

"Had? You quit?"

"I'm going to if... if you like what I'm about to lay down. Delooney has agreed for Merger to give us an advance that cashflows our management business beyond our projected needs. He also agreed for Merger to administer our independent publishing business." She studied his eyes for anger because they'd never discussed the publishing thing.

"That's smart, Cat. Publishing is the cash cow. If Merger does all the admin grunt, all we need to do is sign the talented writers. Which also means we're not relying on just managing performers. Two income streams, one ticking along with minimal effort from us."

He gets it. She let out the air burning her lungs.

"We put your money into an investment account as the security on

272

our business overdraft, which we should never need, thanks to Merger's cash injection. I'm comfortable with that, and as soon as we're stable enough, we replace your security with our business money."

"I know Delaney's desperate, but he doesn't own Merger anymore. There must be a catch."

"No catch. Just a first look deal, but we both know Merger and how limited they are on the kind of acts they'll invest in. Plus, after today, Delooney will owe me forever. If we really want to sign one of our acts with a direct competitor, he won't stop it."

"Delaney won't be there forever."

She hadn't thought that far.

Robbie's brow furrowed, eyes focused past her.

She'd been naive, this wasn't so simple. Adrenalin drained out of her and she felt her body slump back into the damn Darth Vader chair. She didn't have a grain of businesswoman in her, just faking and fumbling.

Robbie zoomed in on her again. "We'd need to limit the first-look deal to three years. That's fair on both parties. That way, Delaney isn't compromised and we don't ever want to use this moment again. Leave it all behind us today."

Simple. Clean. Brilliant. Robbie's inner Gudinski met her entrepreneurial avatar, and together they'd slashed a path out of the jungle. Business and personal. Teamwork and couple.

He put both hands out, palm up.

She stared at them, overcome with relief as warmth gushed through her. She took his hands, swallowed his eyes, drifted in their parallel universe.

Ring-ring, ring-ring.

The phone on the table startled her.

Robbie laughed, hitting the speaker button.

"Delaney doesn't do waiting. You lovebirds done yet?" asked Annie.

Robbie grinned. She'd missed that grin.

"Coming right up," she said.

Robbie hung up the phone. "Put them out of their misery. We've got a show to run, a business to launch."

CAT stood next to Robbie and Annie near the reception desk as Tracey and Pierre peered over.

Clayton had the strength to look Delaney in the eye.

"I'm sorry. It's Stephanie's sixteenth birthday next week and I'm all hyper-sensitive about her growing up so fast. I take back the... the silly words I yelled earlier." He turned to Tracey and Pierre. "Sorry about my behaviour. Hope I didn't scare or offend you."

Tracey and Pierre shook their heads.

"We're all good, Mr Clayton. They're used to seeing far worse around here from coked up musos. Apology accepted," Delooney said as he offered a hand.

Clayton shook it, eyes down, then slipped out of the building.

Delooney turned to them. "Don't you have a major event to prepare?" He clapped his hands as he headed for his office. "Guitar strings don't swing in the wind. Drums don't beat their own skin." He winked at her as he glided past.

"I don't care how you pulled that off, Cat, I want to be your first client," said Annie.

"You already are," said Robbie.

"I'll email you a typed M.O.U. tonight," she said.

"What does M.O.U. stand for again?" asked Annie.

"Music, Onwards and Upwards." Robbie grinned.

"Memorandum of Understanding," Cat said.

"I like Robbie's version. You guys draft it up, I'll sign."

She headed for the stairs. "Come on, you two, guitar strings don't swing in the wind. Drums don't beat their own skin," she mimicked Delooney.

"Microphones don't collect their own saliva," said Annie.

"Empty studios never record shit," said Robbie.

They laughed and hustled down the stairs.

ANNIE had been staring at the pink blossom on the large tree for so long it became a hazy, giant fairy floss. She shifted on the wooden bench, uncrossed her legs and stretched them out, then squeezed her eyes shut. Her thoughts weren't as pretty as the tree while she replayed the end of the planning meeting.

"There's no other way," Cat had said.

"It's perfect," said Robbie.

After Escape Goats covered the twelve final songs on behalf of the songwriters, they'd open it up to the public for the final voting. Manny insisted that sixty minutes was enough to handle the volume of texts and social media votes. But an hour was a long time for a live audience to hang around. They needed some filler entertainment. They weren't expecting a major reality TV-type voting surge. The contest had exceeded all their social media expectations, but it was still a niche event. The band would take up about ten minutes with a medley of the final songs, just to the first chorus of each. A thirty-minute break was good for the bar and toilet rush, but a fifty-minute hole was way too long, and they were determined to not throw in a DJ or music videos, which would obviously feature famous songs.

So, Cat had suggested Annie sing.

She'd argued the night was meant to be all about the songwriters of the ten final tracks. They quickly reminded her she was an unknown and any song had to be an original, not a familiar hit that might dilute the ten entries.

"But it will still be a fantastic way to do a soft relaunch of Annie Vuci," said Robbie.

Twelve minor piano frames scaled her spine in staccato. The part of her soul that had been bursting to perform got bruised with every chord.

"But the show's only two weeks away and I don't have an original song."

"You do and it's a killer track," said Cat.

Staccato switched to a forte of minor keys pounding slower, louder on her vertebrae, with sharp keys all over the place. She wiped the perspiration from her palms across her jeans. Turned for escape to Robbie... but he just nodded.

"You know how much I love that track. Killer with a capital KILL," said Robbie.

The minor keys reached a crescendo in her head.

More Text Than Sex.

They wanted her to sing "More Text Than Sex", the track she'd accidentally written with Diaz.

The cover band, Escape Goats, only had four more rehearsals for the ten contest songs. Now they had to squeeze in one more unfamiliar track. Escape route.

"It's not fair on Escape Goats. Not fair on me. Four rehearsals aren't enough."

"You don't need four." Robbie grinned.

"It's one song and you'll be amazing." Cat was channelling some kind of Delaney. "We won't push you, Annie, but we have no doubt you'll nail it."

So, she'd drifted through her favourite park to this bench, eyes and mind under the haze of a giant pink fairy floss. "More Text Than Sex." Diaz. She'd need a giant, real fairy floss, a truckload of sugar to sweeten the idea. To forget the way Diaz had tried to leverage their embryonic friendship behind her back. How could she perform the track they'd co-written? Processed sugar could fix anything and she needed a big bag of yummy before telling Cat and Robbie she wouldn't do it. She bounced up to head for the last remaining corner shop in her hood. Sat down again.

Who was she kidding?

Ikigai.

Ikigai, the simple philosophy Monaro had brought back from Japan, must've been gnawing away deep in the back of her head. The instant Monaro had spelled out the essence of Ikigai, it resonated, but she'd had to ignore the philosophy, because she'd had to ignore her own essence the past nine years. Plus, it had come from Monaro and her reflex was to resist anything from him. Writing and performing music was her Ikigai, what she was good at. It was her love and passion, and maybe, just maybe, if the world connected with her music —maybe downloads, maybe live, maybe both—it would become her profession. She'd buried her essence for two damn good causes, raising Lachie and running down Monaro's management contract. Now it was her time, or at least there was time for her. Her Ikigai.

She'd collaborated with others in her early days. Co-writing brought out the best in her and reduced the stress of creating by more than half. Something intangible and magical when it worked. Diaz was fun before he tried to take advantage of her connections. "More Text" was a half-decent pop track. You could fumble through dozens of co-writers before clicking creatively with someone the way she had with Diaz. Plus, Diaz wasn't dealing with a teenage Annie. She had a life foundation now, and a dynamic management team she trusted.

But they'd sexed up their pro relationship. Sexed it up so much, Diaz had raised the bar on sexing up.

She stood. Maybe she'd pass by the shop and grab some old-school raspberry frogs. You could solve the Middle East political nightmare with enough raspberry frogs.

TRACK 40

ANNIE HOVERED BETWEEN THE DOOR AND RECEPTION DESK, HANDS gripping her knapsack straps, feet anchored wide to help her resist swaying to the infectious Latin Jazz music filtering through the speakers.

Diaz swung out of a teaching room, body in perfect synch with the rhythm, one hand carrying a djembe drum. He saw her, halted, and raised his free hand like a stop sign.

"Not thirsty," he said.

"I'm unarmed." She spread her arms in a triangle from her body, palms open.

That hair framed a smile above twinkling eyes. He put the drum down and stepped forward, arms out for a hug.

She raised both hands in a double stop sign.

"Just stay there a beat." She glanced at the doors to the teaching rooms. "Everyone gone?"

He nodded, eyes like spotlights. Slipped his fingers into his light blue jeans pockets. She wasn't sure how they got in, the denim was surely painted on to his skin.

"This is purely a business visit."

Eyes dulled, smile backed off to a grin.

"Are you capable of conducting a business-only relationship with me? Song writing business."

"That question is a tango for two."

"I'm giving you a chance here, Diaz. No jokes."

He raised his hands chest high, palms up, and looked around. "Giving me a chance? You are in mi casa de los suenos."

"De los what?"

"Dreams. My house of dreams."

"Okay, I'm not picking on your school, I admire what you've created here. But do you want to write songs? Songs that have a chance to be listened to by... by more than family and friends?"

"Si."

"Everything we write would be split fifty-fifty for royalties. Everything we write, whether finished or not, I have first option on recording. If I don't record it within three years, we, or you, can pitch it to other singers."

"I can dance to that rhythm."

"No dancing. We only work during the day, no alcohol and no touching."

"Sounds like the Saudi School of Songwriting."

She shrugged.

"What if we write some magic, we're buzzing from the allegria, and in the momento I reach up for a high five?" He raised his hand and mimicked a high five. "Is that forbidden?"

"With a shower of rocks."

Grin and sparkle.

"This is the second best news I've heard all year."

"Second best?"

"You're coming out of the creative closet, Annie. That news is allegria for all the music lovers on this planet." He stepped closer and stretched out his hand. "We can't shake on this?"

She shook her head.

He dropped to his knees. "It's a deal, Annie. I'm honoured to be part of your musical Mecca." He raised both hands, then placed them on the floor either side of his face like Islamic prayers.

Annie rolled her eyes and shook her head. Laughter gurgled from her toes, rumbled through her tummy and chest, then exploded from her throat.

ANNIE clapped her hands high above her head on the one-three beat. The band behind her stopped playing and joined in, except the drummer who maintained the beat with stick on stick high in the air, standing behind his kit.

"We're all getting more text than sex. We're all giving more text than sex," sang the crowd. Loud. Passionate. Clapping on beat.

She could've jumped off the stage and moon-hopped across the venue above their heads, her heart and brain full of adrenalin, endorphins, and every other ecstatic element her body's chemistry created. The interactive breakdown of the song wasn't planned, just one of those magical moments that happened when a live performance connected with an amazing audience. The lighting crew caught on quickly and had blue and pink colours alternate on the stage to the one-three beats as well as turning on the house lights so the crowd was visible right to the back of the room.

Diaz must've been standing on the cross bar of a stool because he was at least fifteen centimetres taller than everyone else, clapping with the tribe, deliriously happy.

But no one beamed taller than Lachie, sitting on Monaro's shoulders in the dance pit a few metres from the stage. Pride oozed out of his eyes with a smile that stretched across his pinch-or-kiss cheeks as he clapped with arms high. Thankfully, he wasn't singing. He'd probably heard worse language, but not on her watch. At least she could share the blame this time with his dad. She noted the weirdness of the normalcy of that thought, but only fleetingly. The musical connection with the crowd was the sweetest, most intoxicating moment of her life. The drummer boomed in with the kick drum and the band launched into the chorus on cue with her as if they'd rehearsed this interactive break a hundred times, rather than zero.

She grabbed the mic stand. "We're all getting more text than sex, we're all giving more text than sex," she sang over the crowd. "We're all getting more text than sex, we're all giving more text than sex. We're all getting more text than sex, we're all giving more text than sex." She glanced at the drummer and keyboard player. "We're all getting more text than—"

Boom. From the kick drum, a fraction of a fraction of a second after the rest of the band cut their playing.

Perfect finish.

This wasn't meant to be her stage, but the audience embraced the song from the first time she sang the chorus. She and Diaz made the song, but the crowd made this magic. She waved, bowed, blew Lachie a kiss, bowed to the band, and floated off stage.

Into Cat's arms and her world-famous hug.

Otherwise, she'd have collapsed. Her Ikigai reincarnation. Amazing. Overwhelming. Warm tears spilled out of the pressure valve of her eyes. Tears of relief? Joy? She licked her upper lip, marinated in the salty taste of nine years of delayed gratification.

Cat stepped back, gripping her shoulders tightly, wiping her cheeks with the back of a finger. Probably smudged her show make-up. Who cared?

She wiped Cat's cheeks. Musical tears. Musical tears they cried in harmony.

"That was musilicious, Annie. Fucking musilicious," Robbie said before wrapping his arms around both of them and squeezing her into Cat again.

Safest place she'd been in years. No chance of falling. These two most unlikely of unlikely lovers, and Lachie—who'd come from the most transient of lovers—were her mother-tribe. They'd nurture and nourish each other like a micro village.

Robbie clapped and jumped on the spot a few times. "Got a show to finish. Let's move it, Cat." He adjusted the headset and little mic as he scurried along the closed stage curtain to the other side.

Cat gave her one more juicy hug, then bounced down the steps to the back passage, heading for the upper VIP area.

Delaney, sober and still, and no starlet on his arm.

"I couldn't be prouder if you were my own kid," said Delaney.

"Felt like I'd walked you down the aisle of your musical church and watched you marry your soul."

She stepped over to him, kissing his cheek. "You were my musical dad, keeping me sane and in touch with music when I didn't have a note to follow." Kissed his other cheek. "Now I'm leaving home."

"See you at the goodbye party. I mean after-party. I mean debrief meeting." He winked at Annie.

She gave him an exaggerated wink back.

CAT had worked her way around each of the top ten finalists—twelve songwriters in all as two tracks were collaborations—and congratulated them on their achievement at making it this far, as well as encouraging them to keep on working on the craft no matter what the outcome of tonight's public vote. They had a responsibility to share their gift with as many people on this planet as they could reach. Every song they created was worth something to someone somewhere, didn't matter if it was just the personal satisfaction of finishing a track, a reaction from someone they loved—their dog, family, and friends—or the number-one downloaded song on the charts. Creating original music from nothing was an achievement worth celebrating.

It was no earth-shattering sermon, but doing it one-on-one gave the nervous writers the warm eye contact they deserved. Soon, they'd be paraded on the stage then the top three would be announced in reverse order till they got to the winner.

All the songwriters and their guests had crammed away from the front of the VIP deck, avoiding the curious glances and stares from the crowd below. Except Pina, who stood tall with legs shoulder-wide, hands in front with fingers intertwined, like she was visualising her future on the stage in jeans, T-shirt and brown leather jacket, ankle boots, hair in simple shoulder-length waves that looked natural. Her mother joined her and even from behind, Pina's smile glowed as she wrapped her hands around her mum's arm. This speech would be a little different, but she didn't want to spoil the mother-daughter moment so she hovered a few metres to the side. Pina waved her across.

"How awesome was Annie? She rocked the house down," said Pina.

"Sure did."

"Mum, this is Cat. She's from Merger and runs this contest with a guy and Annie, who just sang. Cat." She pointed at her mum. "Rafaella."

Rafaella, as comfortable in her skin as Pina.

She held out her hand and Cat shook it.

"Hi. Your daughter is very talented but more importantly, she's polite, humble, and comes across as a pro. You should be super proud."

Rafaella didn't flutter as if the compliment was all about her; she turned and glowed at Pina.

"We are proud, no matter what happens now." She turned back to her. "And you should be proud of what you and your team have created with this contest. Hopefully, it won't be a one-off."

"Thank you. Annie, Robbie, and I are proud, but this is our last job for Merger so it may not happen again."

"Bummer," said Pina.

"I'm sure you'll all be snapped up quickly if there's any intelligence left in the industry," said Rafaella.

"Actually, we want to do the snapping up. Robbie and I are starting our own management and independent publishing business. Pina, we'd like you to be our second client."

If Pina's bone structure wasn't strong, her eyes would have expanded all the way to Mars.

"Wow, really? Me?" Pina looked at her mum. Not like a puppy-dog or entitled brat, simply seeking guidance. Her mum smiled back at her.

"Not expecting a decision tonight, just wanted you to know before heading out there, because the result doesn't matter tonight. We think you're a special talent and cool chick. We'd like to help you become a professional writer and performer."

"That's a wonderful offer, Cat. We'll need to talk about it at home," said Rafaella.

"Dad's in the audience, probably up the back, nervous as an upside down turtle."

She liked this kid.

"No rush, and we should probably meet properly and talk things through before you make any decision. I'll be in touch in a couple of weeks. Taking a break after this. See you at the after-party." Cat headed for the steps.

"Cat," said Rafaella.

Cat turned.

"You said second client. Who's your first?"

"Annie."

Pina's smile stretched as wide as her galaxy-wide eyes.

CAT's veins fizzed with euphoria. Sometime in the next few hours or days, she'd crash with exhaustion. But right now, on the cusp of the top ten being introduced onto the stage, before the announcement of third, second, and first, she held onto the wall rail backstage to stay grounded.

They'd done it.

From a crazy little contest idea with Annie all about honouring songwriters, to running a flawless live show, they'd come in just five minutes behind schedule. A minor blip on bloody perfection. Blood-sapping-but-worth-it perfection. She was where she was meant to be, doing what she was good at, and she had to admit that nothing, not even the most rewarding volunteer work, gave her this buzz. Not even close.

Was that shallow?

She had to stop the inner J-and-J—judge and jury. They had helped twelve writers break down their own J-and-J, given them a glimpse of the glitter they had inside. The entertainment biz was like a showcase pyramid. If you could step off the slippery sand and scramble onto the base level of the pyramid, people in the biz took a little notice. Hang in there, scratch and claw higher, you never know who might discover you, what opportunities would open up. This contest had lifted a bunch of writers onto that first level. Her mission with Robbie was to help as many talented people scale the pyramid. The rest depended on the talent's work ethic and dedication to honing their craft. And a little luck.

Annie nudged her with an elbow and pointed across the stage. Behind the curtain, Robbie, halfway across, was sprinting to her. What was the idiot doing? The curtain was going up in ten seconds and he had to be on the other side to guide half the finalists, while she corralled the other half.

Robbie slid the last five metres, stopping right in front of her. She wanted to yell at him to get back on the other side, but a smile cemented her face. Her lips wouldn't move. Until he bent down and kissed her. Then her lips went all rogue. He picked her up, spun around, lips and tongue connected the whole way. Eased her down and scampered back to the other side just as the curtain was opening. Whatever music her body was playing, she didn't want it to stop.

Leon, the MC, announced the first finalist, the crowd erupted and red-lined the decibels until all twelve songwriters were lined up. She didn't dare look Robbie's way until their final task was done, giving each contestant a touch or smile on their way on to the stage, to calm their nerves, if that was possible.

Annie joined her, and they wrapped an arm around each other, pride glowing at the flock of newly discovered talent. From their idea.

On the other side of the stage, Robbie threw his headset away, kneeled on one knee and blew her kisses, alternating his hands.

Fireworks exploded in her heart and lit up every single blood cell.

Forget the coloured smoke and shonky mirrors of social media. Music is still the most powerful form of spiritual connection, from the cathedrals of major stadiums, churches of pubs and intimate bars, to the pop-up altars of street buskers and festivals, music preaches to our soul. Its disciples aren't always traditional role models, but their diverse sermons help us hobble through this increasingly fractured life. Music never judges us, but it sometimes helps us question. We seek its comfort and revel in its inspiration. Through music we learn how similar we are, no matter our colour, beliefs, money, age, or gender. Whatever our internal tune, we're all part of a larger opus. Whether our taste is specific or eclectic, there is always someone with whom we can harmonise.

Like that bozo on the other side of the stage.

THE END

Writers sweat blood to get stories out into the world and reviews are our super-food. Every time you leave a kind review, you're doing a wonderful deed for all writers, all stories. Thanks, Jim.

Don't miss Jim's debut novel, Up Here

When you've had two dream marriages, choosing your eternal soulmate in heaven is one hell of a dilemma.

www.JimShomos.com/up-here

The most original romantic-comedy this century. Artisan Book Reviews, 5*

Up Here touched my soul, a beautiful romantic comedy about love, hope and courage. Alli, 5*

Jim Shomos must have written this with a twinkle in his eyes, as moving, as it is funny. Ella, 5*

Kissing Scars

Leads your heart to a festival of love. A romantic comedy novella inspired by a true story.

www.JimShomos.com/kissing-scars

Intoxicating, organic, and simply breathtaking. The Never Ending Bookshelf, 5*

Three Women in November

An incredible true love story.

www.JimShomos.com/three-women-in-november

I loved this book...despite the tears streaming down my face. Michele, 5*

Get VIP release news about Jim's coming books at:

www.JimShomos.com

ACKNOWLEDGMENTS

To the wonderful composers that I have had the joy to collaborate with as a lyricist: Russell Zimmer, Theo Marantis (my Elton John), Marcus Knight, Erica Scholz, Julene Siddique, Farah Whalen, Cameron & Paul Mitchell, and Debbie Bignell.

A bunch of people were generous with their time and wisdom when I ambitiously pursued a career as a songwriter and artist manager: Ron Leigh, Jim Keays, Daryl Cotton, Ashley Henderson, Glenn Wheatley, Phil Dwyer (my generous music lawyer), Paul O'Gorman, and Carl Gardiner. My one-and-only management client, Steve Wade – when I chose family and a day job, I'm delighted you went on to find terrific success as lead singer of Little River Band.

Louise Gough, at Film Victoria you approved development funding for this story as a TV series. Originally titled 'Tracks', I'm glad it's evolved and found life as a book.

My invaluable author friends Angela and Alli, contributed to elements of this book.

To my three amigos, who build or slam my ego as needed: Bruce, Chris, and Ted.

Carolyn, you are a wonderful editor. Helen, you designed the perfect cover when I had no idea what it should be. Michelle, for your amazing eye for detail. Leanne for your interior design magic.

More Text Than Sex song co-written by Theo Marantis, Marcus Knight & Jim Shomos

ABOUT THE AUTHOR

Jim's stories have skipped across film, TV, web, songs and novels.

He has collected nominations and awards in Cannes, Film Victoria and from the Australian Writers' Guild.

Rumors of an insatiable passion for Haigh's Chocolates, Arsenal, Melbourne Victory, cycling, and blueberry muffins. Sometimes cycling for blueberry muffins.

Jim's first novel, Up Here, began life as a screenplay and was short-listed in Top-5 of the Australian Writers' Guild 'Romantic comedy competition' alongside The Rosie Project.

www.JimShomos.com/up-here